Luz at Midnight

a novel by

Marisol Cortez

FLOWERSONG
PRESS

FlowerSong Press

McAllen, Texas 78501

Copyright © 2020 by Marisol Cortez

ISBN 978-1-953447-95-1

Library of Congress Control Number: 2020946866

Published by FlowerSong Press

in the United States of America.

www.flowersongpress.com

Set in Adobe Garamond Pro

Cover art by Davíd Zamora Casas

Typeset and design by Matthew Revert

www.matthewrevert.com

For all the women and queer folks who taught me. To mi querido San Antonio.

ACKNOWLEDGMENTS

Cover Art: "Question Everything" by Davíd Zamora Casas (2010).

"Sludge Ponds, Sacred Dances" appeared in *Voices de la Luna: A Quarterly Literature and Arts Magazine* (February 2020).

Portions of "Kansaztlan" first appeared in "Sioux Falls, South Dakota," included in *Runaway: An Anthology* (Madville Publishing, 2020).

"La Hora es Ahora" on pages 128-9 based on an original collaboration with Pájara Nohpalli Napoli.

Letter on pages 158-9 adapted from personal communications with Angelo G. Flores.

"OYE MI AMOR"
Words and Music by FHER OLVERA and ALEX GONZALEZ
Copyright 1994 BIG COJONES MUSIC and TULUM MUSIC
All Rights Administered by WC MUSIC CORP.
All Rights Reserved
Used By Permission of ALFRED MUSIC

"When I am with You" by Jalāl al-Dīn Rūmī. From *The Essential Rumi*, translated by Coleman Banks, with Reynold Nicholson, A. J. Arberry, and John Moyne. HarperCollins, 2010.

Table of Contents

It seemed to me, quite early on, that there's stability, there's inertia. So I tried, using statistical techniques, to document the inertia, to uncover the constants that make science possible. It is because there are constants that we can understand things. But I've also tried to explain why things are the way they are.

—Pierre Bourdieu, *Sociology is a Martial Art*

The public and the politicians want to blame a culprit for each blackout, because they imagine a Newtonian world of cause and effect, of crime and punishment. Occasionally, flagrantly guilty parties such as Enron deserve to sit in the dock. But without malicious intent or incompetence a blackout may still occur.

—David E. Nye, *When the Lights Went Out: A History of Blackouts in America*

I could hike faster and stronger while manic. On a hike, I remember looking from the top of a viewpoint over the city and freeway, thinking 'it's all magic.' That isn't too crazy of a realization, since we know from advances in physics that things really are glued together with a sort of magic at the deepest level.

—*Internet Blogger Jim G, "My First Manic Episode - 1999"*

PROLOGUE

Improbable

Improbable: everything was stacked against it, everything you could possibly imagine. The fact that I was married, with a two-year-old child. That I had been offered a job here in Kansas, two states away, and was poised to leave San Antonio again, lugging behind me in a moving truck entire geological eras of sedimentation. Hector, the high school friend I had married; la Nena, our daughter, just barely not a baby anymore; a degree, the calcified accumulation of years of schooling. The fact of Joel's eviction: from his apartment, but from something else too, something totalizing, an absolute eviction from everything. Something he knew, because he told me; something I knew, because I'd seen it. His illness or holiness or genius, or whatever it was. The fact of Joel's promotion as the *Volt* went digital, making it unlikely he'd follow us north. The fact of Luz's disappearance just before we left town, as mysteriously as she'd appeared.

Regardless. It was as though the difficulty, the seeming impossibility, made it all the more imperative that we continue to talk, to figure out what it meant. A love so powerful and terrible it could not be ignored. When I met Joel—really met him, met him all the way down—everything I'd assumed I wanted suddenly seemed wrong. So ill-fitting I had to divest myself. And once I had taken off the cicada shell of my previous life, I could not put it back on again. So not two weeks after Joel and I went to the coast together, I told Hector I wanted to divorce. Can you believe that crazy shit?

Actually, Hector asked me if we should, and I said yes, and we were both relieved. We had finally spoken aloud what we'd long feared was best, the knowledge we had most strenuously avoided, and we had survived its speaking. It was okay. It was better than okay—it was right, it was right at last. I try to explain this to others and it sounds impossible, but that's how it happened. A part of me had been absent from the beginning, and this absence had been a presence in our midst for a long time, both of us hoping that not talking about it could change its meaning. Neither of us wanted it to mean what it meant.

When I agreed to marry, after my surprise pregnancy and the birth of Nena, I thought, *Someday I will meet someone and fall in love, and then what will I do?* But I had immediately dismissed the thought because it *was* so reasonable: no sense worrying since it wasn't happening right then. And maybe it would never happen; or, if it did, maybe I could choose to ignore it, make it go away, rationalize desire as impractical or illusory—a delusion, to think a life together with someone could be grounded in anything other than the economic arrangement it would inevitably become. I had reasoned so in the past, when I—or Hector—had crushed on a classmate or work buddy, breaking up to chase after what we would come to conclude was mirage or fantasy, before getting back together.

And so I figured I had immunized myself against the improbability of love, having chosen to have a child and then very deliberately to marry for pragmatic reasons. We were wed in a courthouse ceremony in Califas when Nena was four months old; two years later, on arrival in Kansas, we would notarize our divorce papers in a UPS store, the notary and counter guy trying their hardest not to eye one another, then us, in disbelief as they watched us conversing and cracking jokes. The ways Hector and I married and unmarried each other says everything about the reasons we both stayed—and later left.

All of which makes those ten years sound like an offense, a drudgery or a disrespect. You could see it that way, and I wouldn't fault you. But those years were also friendly and companionate. We were cousins from the same provincial village who had clung to one another as we navigated strange new planets of alienated adulthood, who tried for ten years to change the meaning and course of our connection. Who had a child and married for not unreasonable reasons. Though it hadn't been right, who could say it had been wrong either, taking in the soft curve of Nena's full cheek, the liquid black of her watchful eyes, the miracle of her tiny hands and teeth?

But then I encountered the crazy brilliance of Joel, blue and beautiful amid the confusion swirling around the node mining, the petition drive, the intrigue of city scandal. And I realized that the situation I had discounted had arisen much sooner than anticipated, and that everything I had wanted, that had laid the foundation for the massive edifice of my life, was not in fact what I wanted, what brought me deepest joy—and sorrow. What it opened in me was a fullness, a capacity for both incredible gentleness and incredible ferocity that I had not known was there.

Something in me had broken open—like the hidden gas line beneath that old refinery, severed by hapless construction crew, tripping an explosion that spelled out the end of an era. It was about Joel and not about Joel at all, I knew that. Joel had only unstoppered it. Not that it could have been anyone. But for some reason I didn't understand, it was Joel who had that power, who awakened a longing so wide and deep it crashed to my surface like oil or water, creating a river unfordable, a shallow sea. It shot through me, the flaming tail of a meteorite, cracking my rib cage open like thoracic surgery. It drew a cry from so deep it split my skin like the fragile membrane of a ripe persimmon, its orangey flesh concealing juice rich and dark as iodine. But I knew it had always been there, an ancient, secret source in an underground cavern, searching for the right time, the right hand.

Each time Hector and I had broken up previously, sex had thrown us back together. And in continuing our physical relationship, we'd had to work backwards from there and figure out what the rest of our partnership meant. This time, after we decided on the divorce, when Hector inquired about the possibility of ex sex, I refused.

I have to tell you something, I said.

Oh. I don't want to hear. He shook his head, turning his face away.

No. It's not like that. At that point Joel and I had not even kissed. He had looked at me sideways and I had burst into flames, on a day we ran into each other at the street theater action outside City Hall. A few days later, we sat silently together in a makeshift lean-to on the Gulf Coast, craftily fashioned from an old sheet and some bamboo rods. Joel had cut slits into the sheet to fortify it against the wind, and we sat beneath eating slices of South Texas melon lightly salted with sand, Luz at Joel's feet sweeping her patient tail from side to side—watching us, presiding over something. We had sung songs together, sitting on the floor of Joel's apartment. When I sang for him I heard my truest voice appear in spite of myself, the voice that sang clear and strong, unselfconscious, as it did only when I was alone. That's how I knew.

What it is—I'm in love with Joel. As I said it, the three of us—Hector, Nena, and myself—were sitting together at the table eating a late pancake breakfast as though it were any other Sunday morning. The apartment was a wreck, moving boxes strewn everywhere as we prepared to leave San Antonio again, so soon after we'd arrived. I felt sick inside, a queasy, oily panic in my chest spilled atop the impassable gulf had I wrenched open between my life and my longing.

Hector had stopped chewing, looking at me. Is it...the kind of thing you feel at the start of any new relationship? The excitement, you know, when you first like someone? Or...is it something you've never experienced before?

Never before, I had whispered.

Oh. Now at my admission came a look of wonder from Hector—a respect, a deference to something that in its very improbability could not be controlled or reckoned with or understood. I'd had to respect it too, to lay down my will, to recognize that it was agency and not love that was delusional, my overschooled notions that one could direct life according to mental blueprints, steering clear of crisis of any kind. My life with Hector had been a level-headed one, without intensity or volatility, and I had needed that for a long time. But now it seemed I no longer did.

When Hector heard me, he saw it too, the finality of my knowledge. The knowingness of knowing. Even though it had not been two weeks since the beach trip. But when he heard it, he lay down his will next to mine, and we let each other go without bitterness.

I know it sounds crazy. But that's how it happened.

I. Form from Nothing

Three Months Earlier:
One Weekend in Early June
San Antonio, Texas

CHAPTER ONE
Black Sun

Friday, June 4, 12:14 P.M.

The smoke drifting over the highway, at the tipping point of spring into summer, reminds Citlali of birds. Like that one time she saw a swirl of starlings, as she stood on the edge of a cornfield somewhere—where?

Imagine this: the secret logic of a flock of birds in flight, swooping, swerving according to their own inner time signature. Somewhere, someone with the right knowledge must have traced its architecture, plotted it carefully, unwound its inner springs to reveal the mechanism, the rhythm, the organization. It couldn't be random, she had thought at the time, eyes trained to the aerial zigzagging of hundreds of starlings, a protoplasm of birds swelling and contracting in a single body like an ever-changing Rorschach blot, like pointillistic thumbprints smudging the sky. *A murmuration.* That was the name for it, mentioned in an NPR feature she heard years later about a massive cloud of birds that appeared before sunset in Denmark during spring, a seasonal skydance halfway across the world. Was there a leader or navigator, Lali had wondered, a conductor who indicated which direction to take? Or were they all followers, of one another or something else, attuned somehow to what each other individual was thinking and feeling? *Scale-free correlation*: the scientists on the radio said at first they'd thought murmurating starlings were like flying avalanches, with each bird a snow particle poised tippy-tippy-toes at criticality, capable of shifting speeds as a single body. But now the scientists, particle physicists, knew that starlings were more flying magnets than avalanches, simultaneously shifting not only speed but position. They were electrons, they said, pulled into synchronous orbits under the spell of magnetization. As one bird veered right it signaled seven of its neighbors to do the same, who signaled to seven more and seven more, a lightning game of telephone without static or degradation. *Low signal to noise ratio.* It was an anti-predator tactic sparked by the peripheral approach of a falcon or hawk, the starlings banding together to form a collective more powerful than any individual could be. But how did that first bird trigger the movement of the whole if each member of the flock was busy responding to every other member? Was there a first bird to speak of? How did it all shift all at once, how did it burst spontaneously into total transformation, as if from nowhere or nothing?

Somewhere, someone knew the principle of organization.

But not me: I don't have the language to say how it works. I can only watch and marvel.

That is what she thought then, watching starlings swoop and pulse as one body as she stood outside a gas station half a lifetime ago, on the edge of a field at the center of the continent.

***

Not the dazzle of synchronized starlings this time, just regular grackles headed North with an urgency, fleeing something. Lali is distracted, driving to the credit union on a lunch errand—trying to gun it so she can be back at the Centro office for a 1pm conference call with the youth climate funders—so it doesn't occur to her what they might be fleeing until she turns on the radio, NPR again. She hears the report like a premonition before she sees it for herself, uncanny, the heavy cloud of black smoke blowing over the highway from the southwest, from somewhere near the river.

An explosion at the old refinery, says the radio.

CHAPTER TWO
Luz is Born

Saturday, June 5, 12:42a.m.

Somewhere, someone had written that it is desire that powers the universe: and so the mother of Luz was none other than longing herself, the longing to be, a call into being. A yell down the well of nothingness to draw up response in a second, an other. An urge that exists first for itself, intransitive, and only then seeks satisfaction in a difference from self that creates the very condition for response. Beyond physicists and classicists, few know there is an erotics of creation too: that desire's etymology, "desidus" in Latin, means "away from a star." Everything began in an original spasm of longing, a great crying out that formed the molten stars and their empty interstices. Creating the liquid and the solid, the flow and the substance, the scalar and the vector and the tensor. That is where she came from, best it can be discerned.

To figure it out, everything complicated had to be reduced to something simple, everything mysterious likened to something already understood. That was the way the story had been pieced together, told and retold, written and erased and written over again, so that the books taught things out of order. They started with what they knew best and spiraled out to what was uncertain, and what was uncertain made them circle back again to the beginning, to revisit and revise what they thought they knew. The tidily serialized shape of the story, then—chapter one and chapter two and so forth—was not necessarily the shape of its writing. That shape was much closer to the unpredictable wildness the story longed to understand. That was why chapter one was motion, what happened without concern for what it was, or why; and only after that matter: what it was that moved. Or was moved, in the passive voice preferred by the story.

Because many tellers collaborated, there were many shades of meaning describing all the nuances of motion: how fast a thing moved or how quickly it changed speed; there were words for the force created by the resistance to change multiplied by how quickly a thing sped up or slowed down. There were ways to talk about what happened when one moving thing collided with another, rules which predicted that motion might change its form again and again, but never disappear. That was all there was, when you came down to it. Motion and resistance to motion, a tendency toward inertia and its disruption.

There were words for forces exerted over movement through space, and over movement through space and time together. There were words describing an ability to make something else happen. Energy was the currency of everything's unfolding, a flow and a cash, a neutral unit of exchange transforming one thing into another. A conversion into, an alchemy, a making happen.

Once you had motion down, you could talk about what moved and what that movement did. Small pieces. The smallest, indivisible. A conceptual model, really, since one could not see these pieces, only infer them by their actions. Not that there was no material basis for the inference. There was, in the powerful lines of force whose invisible fields bent action into costs and consequences. If you did that, then this. That went for history as much as for physics, the effects of force fields forevermore seared into the names of Jemez, Bikini, Hiroshima. There were conceptual models precisely because there were necessities and determinations. An idea of the smallest divined from the movement of the biggest, which had put the question into human minds to begin with: What made the sun move across the sky and the moon seem to follow you when you walked? Like the largest heavenly bodies, the smallest pieces moved because something made them seek one another. It wasn't quite the same thing as the force tethering moon to earth or earth to sun, but something like it, maybe. Guide wires pulling the smallest pieces together, catching them at their outermost orbits where tiny sparks buzzed and whirred like a cloud of bees. Too many sparks and the thing spun off kilter, inexorably sucked toward another with too few. Like the stickiness created by pieces of amber rubbing together, a charge was the buildup of intensity or presence. A demand for reception, a grab at equilibrium. It made the smallest pieces cling together in favorite combinations; it made bigger pieces fuse tightly and purr, or bounce around each other like lotto balls in a tumbler. Creating flows and differentials, hot spaces and cold. But everything rolled and crested and troughed and trembled and crashed and smashed: that remained the basic point. What it did was what it was, substance a kind of mechanics. The bright confusion of a living hive, vibrating at all frequencies at once.

There were formulae for it, but that didn't matter so much. Formulae were things to memorize without understanding why, or how, only to forget. Formulae were crudities men had devised to depict what they couldn't quite capture, men who stepped into rivers trying to quantify change. They had fractured wholes into increasingly smaller parts, only to piece them back together as the calculus of segments accumulating beneath a curve—approaching flow as their number approached infinity, but never quite making it there. Men who called each other geniuses for the units of measure they named for themselves, who pinned these names to the earth and its inhabitants, like the medals for naming they also named after themselves. In this way a leaf falling to forest floor could be described by its quantity in Newtons, as the product of its mass and pull to earth. As it landed, one could measure the impact on a passing ant in a number of Joules, the force of its weight times the distance it fell. Joules over time was power, counted in Watts: the name of a Scotsman entranced by engines, at the dawn of an industrial age whose new machines would transform finite seams of black pressure into work, into light and heat and smoke filling a finite terrarium.

No matter. Beyond the skeletal poems of formulae was phenomena herself, in her singular multiplicity—that was different. There were the stories and the names and the medals, and then there was she who dispersed energy away from a center and she who drew it back together. She who made things happen and other things not. She who repeated and who disrupted repetition. She was the very condition of longing that then took herself as object. From her original cry flowed Luz, and at the sound of her birth there began a great crying back, a harmonic quavering of joy and anguish at all frequencies, a flowing forth of equations and poetry alike.

***

Dark and profound, she did not have an idea of Luz before birthing her. Not even she knew why it happened, or why it happened where it did: la Brackenridge, near the river. Not far from where the springs began, their dry mouth tucked deep within the pocket of the nuns' campus; not far from the zoo, across from where the city people had long swept their stray animals into a pile for incineration, and where midnight cars subsequently stopped to dump their unwanted litters. Not far from where families barbecued on Easter Sunday, camping in their cars the night before so they could stake out a choice table. Why and where were the sketchy parts: neither she nor the equationists nor the poets could have explained that.

How, maybe: something about the way pieces of ice in a cloud became polarized during a storm, positive and negative energies pulling apart as particles collided. A cloud battery, in essence, searching for a circuit as the people of the city below rushed to their sagging porches and dusty driveways to witness a promise of the first rain in many months, to feel the wind tear wildly at their clothes and hair, to feel an ambient wildness answered by a presence within, part exhilaration and part terror. Something or someone searched for them, turning them out of doors to see for themselves despite warnings, shooing them back inside with a broom like children or kittens. What was going to happen?

She rolled into the city from the North, restlessly, searching for grounding, for a meeting with something or someone she didn't know yet. How would she know what she was looking for, then? It must be that whatever, wherever, whoever she met was what she was supposed to meet. Maybe it mattered but maybe not. She was furious, frantic with pent emotion, arms surging and summoning like a conductor. With all of her strength she forced apart the sticky, crackling energy of the ground itself. She pulled its buzzing sparks of amber upward through the air, sucking quicksand through a straw. As they rose along their luminous channel she stretched in descent, beckoning as she forked and branched, reaching for the ground with her many hands, for something growing there like claymation, reaching back.

Clasping branches a second later, the switch closed and amber flowed. As she flashed skyward she felt the massive belly of her power drain to earth at Brackenridge Park in a single catastrophic surge, narrowly missing the train tracks and its curtains of bamboo kindling. Seconds later, she swiped at the air again in another knife stroke. An avalanche of boulders tumbled through the sky in response, and she shred a utility pole in the process, which carried its own river of power west from a downtown substation. As the clouds cracked over one half of the city, the other half went dark.

Shaking with the cold of her newness, Luz crawled glistening through a gale of bamboo, tail low and fur matted and wet. She found the banks of the swelling river and traced them, finally stopping somewhere north of the water, to sleep and sleep until the storm had passed.

CHAPTER THREE
Joel Finds Luz

Sunday, June 6, early early

In San Antonio the Gulf wind blows on your face constant-ly, even 150 miles inland. If you've grown up here you may not realize it, but if you've lived anywhere else for a spell and then returned, it's noticeable enough to be striking. You feel it and then remember what it is: the nearness of bloodwarm water, the stink of surf and crude refining. The smell of an earth transformed into economy. Yet still the earth.

You can walk across the bridge with its humble rise that crests the train tracks, where at its apex you can turn your back to traffic and stand looking down at the cars crawling slowly past. If you've ever sat at a railroad crossing and wondered what they carry, now is the time to find out. They may be empty, save for a dusting of pea gravel at the bottom. The slatted ones pull automobiles, intermittently visible in slices like images in a zoetrope. The closed ones, most likely coal. Once, not so long ago, they'd pulled coal in open cars, but since the federal phase-out they'd hidden its transport, especially after the nationwide youth uprisings that blockaded rail shipments to coal plants. The cylindrical cars, of course, are conduits for chemicals, trafficking acids and complexly-chained hydrocarbons in their bomb-shaped vehicles. Coal, cars, and chemicals, the three Cs of the apocalypse. They were trying to change all that, carbon to post-carbon, but in the meantime—

From here you can see the scrap metal yard abutting the tracks, the rust-red soil around its mountains of shredded cars impossibly devastated. Billowing shreds of many-hued plastic bags are snatched in the barbed wire coils atop its keep-out fence, like items of clothing pinned to a wall in memorium.

You could walk underneath the bridge, where no cars would rattle you and the sidewalk would be spacious, but you don't because you never know at this time of night, and if something did happen there would be no one to assist. Once, walking down below, you stopped to inspect a busted computer monitor ingloriously wedged into an open manhole—and looked up, then back, with alarm to realize that someone you passed earlier was approaching at a fast clip, closing in on the distance between you. You tried to stay calm, but when they crossed to your side of the underpass, running diagonally for the tracks, you thought violence was surely the intent. Finally, last minute, they veered off to leap the tracks just seconds before a passing train roared by, cutting off your path and swallowing up the sound of your own heart thundering in your chest.

So now you don't take chances; you walk above, over the bridge, against traffic, on the half-width sidewalk like sidling along a ledge. Cars are not so bad, and if they see you in time, many will cross over into the other lane, polite or nervous. But if there are buses, you do your best not to look up, trusting that no passing protrusion will swipe at something loose on you—a belt loop, a necklace, the single string of faded red from the ashram so many years ago now—and catch you in its powerful wake, dragging you to your death. You look down or away as buses pass, so that the too-close swirl of hurricane exhaust won't scramble your already scrambled head.

You do not live in this neighborhood—that's why you come here, to avoid the possibility you could run into someone from the *Volt*—but on nights like this, when it feels like you're from nowhere, where nobody knows a you who is unknowable, it helps to walk there. You park your car at the edge of the city park, the oldest in this part of the country, which marks the place where springs used to flow, where springs birthed the city centuries before you moved here. From there, you amble over to a street named after another river, wishfully named for a climatic state unknown here. *Frio.* You pass the complex where the city tries to route its homeless, its—urban outdoorsmen. And women. You think with a secret smile, knowing there but for the grace. You pass the corner where day laborers keep their daytime watch before you pass the university annex, its architecture sensitive and modern compared to the careless, functional ugliness of the courthouse across the street. After that, the police department with its cache of cars continually swinging out of the parking lot at all hours, like solitary wasps emerging from a pulsing nest on mercenary runs, making you nervous. You know from the reading you did upon settling here that these two structures used to be manufacturing centers for computer parts. And before that, they were empty lots cleared by the removals of Urban Renewal. The appearance of a disappearance. Before that they were neighborhoods, poor but resilient. Now they are holding pens of state surveillance.

After these buildings is a sunnier prospect: the paletería, its rainbow array of frozen melón and limón, pecan and chile mango sleeping for the night, dreaming of children's hungry mouths. Then a Stonehenge shell of a vacant carwash, then the funeral home. Once you saw a flyer stapled to a telephone pole there, for a benefit barbecue to be held in the parking lot the following day. There were pictures of a child, name given in full, and below this two dates bookending a span of two years, nine months. For six dollars you could get a plate of sausage and chicken. It stayed with you for days, the terrible realization that the family lacked funds to bury such a small child.

A gate to the Westside, the bridge begins after the funeral home on the corner. You like to ascend to stand with your back to traffic, looking north to the place where tracks vanish into the horizon. Then you turn and walk back the way you came, back to the park and your car. Sometimes it takes six hours. Sometimes it takes all night. It depends on how long you stand when you get to the bridge, and how determined your thoughts are. You know the thoughts are essentially without referent— worn grooves in your brain that have become so well-tread it is hard not to fall in—but it's hard not to feel they point to something real and actionable. After years, you've discovered the trick is to accord them enough reality that you can allow them simply to rise and pass without reacting. You open both doors of the house, front and back; you bow as they enter, then step aside. They will rumble and rummage and break shit, but they'll pass through eventually. Still, it's important to hold fast to the knowledge that although their reference to reality may be oblique, the thoughts grasp for autonomy. It's when you forget this that they fill your head as though they had no other possible meaning, speaking inside you like voices from outside.

Voices would be bad—can't work when they come—so you have to respect the thoughts enough to leave them alone. It requires a certain humility, a certain discipline, not to identify.

So you turn out of doors as soon as they start, walk—sometimes run—a real path with feet and heart pounding, in the hope this will derail the train of your own mind, its slow determined crawl toward the certainty of damnation. It's not certain, it only feels that way. It's only a story, just thinking, let it be. You pray beneath your breath, lips moving, a long oratory meant to spring spontaneously from your heart, the way the church people taught you so many years ago. You pray with your feet, hoping your words will be met with the listening, loving presence you once experienced during your church days. Resisting the pull of the bomb-shaped cars of the three Cs, thinking of the time you rode to the top of the Tower of the Americas right after you moved here, to this city, and you saw what can only be angels—it doesn't make sense that it was anything else because it was specks floating on the air, like little flecks of golden dust in front of your eyes. It was the golden-winged filaments of the hummingbird heartbeat that wove the fundamental textile. It just doesn't make sense, anything else, anything.

Walking usually works but sometimes it takes all night, yeah.

At the end of walking you'll be back at your car. You'll drive home. If there's night left over, you'll take a pill to help you sleep. If not, you'll put on some fresh clothes and go in to work.

***

Tonight, this particular night after the storm and flash flood of the night before, you decide to risk Brackenridge, the park nearest your apartment. Its curfew makes it unlikely you'd run into anyone besides other interlopers, and anyway—you'd gotten into a rut walking always the same route, from the park of the minor springs to the shallow bridge and back. Maybe that groove was fortifying the ones inside your own head. Best to change it up.

You leave on foot, heading south on the wide, night-quiet thoroughfare, so straight you can see traffic lights swaying in the wind for several consecutive blocks as they cycle unevenly through red, green, yellow, red.

It is beautiful out but you notice only subconsciously, subcutaneously, a subtle bodily rush of delight or relief beneath the skin while above deck your mind whirs onward, in the practice of trying to stop itself from whirring. The air is clean and wet as dark earth, charged with something elemental from the storm that knocked out power in other parts of the city. More low-lying parts, while you live in the protective shade of choicer areas uphill, right on the brink: of old money, of poverty. It's like this: you yourself don't have Wi-Fi but your neighbor does, and you can catch the signal.

Not that these were conscious factors in your decision to settle here, when you arrived for the *Volt* job; but you do like the museum across the street, and the city gardens—the fact of these things, even if you don't go there regularly. You like the used bookstore, a minute or two on foot from your apartment, where you pass time on weekends browsing the shelves for things not to read in their entirety but to start and resell, in a practice of filling the agonizing, rudderless space between Friday and Monday. And best of all you like the access to green space—the long, narrow strip bifurcating your street, hardly a park at all save for the gravel jogging path that circles a few standing Spanish oak and mesquite. Beneath their spotty shade is a shallow, cattail-lined pond fed by a drainage ditch, what you've learned is a remnant of the city's first gravity-fed reservoir system. During high summer the pond will be dry, but now the early June storm has filled it, and in the weeks to come an invisible installation of peepers will sound from its reeds each evening. It's things like this you need, reminders. The bats crammed together in the cracks of parking structures. The beady-eyed, oily-colored grackles that flood the winter skies to cluster atop powerlines, ugly but indomitable.

You like the crumbling fountain behind the bus stop at the edge of the linear park, its sides and bottom painted blue to make the water look fresh, even when it isn't, where the homeless men will sometimes bathe. You've gotten to know a few of them, a couple by name. Once you let one of them stay with you for a few days—Antonio, dressed in tasseled moccasins and black Aztec calendar shirt, thinning hair braided into two long trensas—until the day psychosis hit him while you were at work. When you came home that afternoon, the kitchen had been trashed and Antonio was gone. He'd left a note written in tight, leaning all-caps, something about pot being grown in certain dumpsters of the city corresponding to the election of councilpersons in those districts. The content made no sense, but the fact of the note was clear-headed and thoughtful: you knew he was acknowledging he couldn't stay, because of things he knew he couldn't control. You could relate.

For a while after that you would see him occasionally at the bus stop—no hard feelings, despite the kitchen—before he disappeared altogether. But there are still others you recognize, who recognize you, who nod in greeting. Maybe they heard about the incident with you and Antonio.

***

She was a conscript, not into the labor of military service, though there was that; but more immediately into an elaborate staging, forced to play a role in a vision belonging to someone else. It would have been inoffensive in that it had little to do with who she was or what she did, except the other believed so strongly in the incontrovertible reality of this vision that it had become material, powerful. What was in essence a flight of fancy became, when earnestly acted out, a story that jailed, a part in a play performed at gunpoint, so that she was made to be other than what she was, do other than what she did. Anyway, it would not have been so important except there were many who believed, many who attracted more to make manifest their belief, in a story of absolute newness that bestowed rights of claim, a child's fantasy of possession without loss. It is there, so it can be mine. And if it is mine, it must always be so. The mistake of the travelers, and of the city people they became, was not that they had a story. It was that they did not know it was only a story.

She was older than newness and longer than stories, so long she knew there was nothing except loss, constantly—no longing or reaching or grasping that was not at the same time a dropping. And so it was she felt Joel coming, seeking her. She sensed his presence from where she clutched at the creature who had appeared the night before, after the lightning storm. She was waiting for Joel. The creature whose smallest particles had been assembled at random by lightning, invented by lightning, was a gift for him. But he had to come find it. He didn't know he was looking yet.

He would have to ford her waters and head north, walking waist deep for a time in a way she remembered from the time of the original people, at other times splashing easily where natural slopes formed tiny falls, or where mats of water lily clutched at her throat to form bottlenecks. He would have to move upstream, at times climbing out onto the banks to walk—past the bicycle bridge, past the zoo at night, past the outfalls where the city people had figured out how to keep her flowing even when the springs were dry, which was almost all the time now. They had tapped her mother source in so many places there was no longer enough pressure to keep her running. Instead they had threaded her through an ever more delicate meshwork of pipes that delivered her for drinking and fouling, before gathering her again into a single flow. This they strained through industrial sieves that deposited her back into the bed where she otherwise would have coursed directly. It worked well enough, but it kept them from seeing that their inhabitation was an endless regress of solutions to the unintended problems of previous solutions, when there were other ways.

Where he had entered she was shallow and slender, fifteen feet across, though higher than usual from the previous night's storm. Before the city people she had been ten times that and crystal clear, rocketing to the earth's surface to roll downhill for miles and miles, from one mother to another. She is army green now but not as dirty as you'd think from the outside. When sunlight hits her surface in just the right way she becomes a window of amber opening onto the ancient bottom. Sometimes a red-eared turtle or toad or snake would surprise you. Farther up would be fat white ducks and smaller mallards, preening or sleeping one-legged on the turrets of the bike bridge, heads tucked beneath a wing. And their babies, fuzzy and striped as honeybees. And the city people had left her banks alone as she ran through the park, letting loose her long-haired canopy of pecan and river cane, latticed with hanging veils of kudzu.

It's not so bad after all. Joel's thought breaks loose from the grooves like a sigh escaping into the largeness of sky, a tear trickling down to join a torrent.

He finally leaves her waters where she crosses the Hildebrand underpass, and wanders up through where the nuns built their tiny campus, toward the blue hole that birthed its sacred river. This park too cradles a springhead. He leaves her waters not because he climbs to the banks, but because the last of the city people's greywater has dried first to a stagnant green, and then to muck and then nothingness, clearing before him a dry trail of scalloped rock. Joel walks and walks, the river rocks hurting his feet even through the rubber bottoms of his tennis shoes, till he comes to a footbridge overhead marking a fork in the channel. It is dawn and he is exhausted, and that is good. An awareness of physical exhaustion means a return to his body and brain. Beneath the footbridge, he hoists himself onto the banks to slump over, panting, feeling consciousness slip away.

It was Sunday, no work to worry about later. He could sleep there for a while, where Ya Gna Wena waited for him, cradling the gift within the clutch of yellow-belled flowers called Esperanza at her banks. She had been waiting for him there all day, since the storm. She could wait a little longer until he woke.

***

It wasn't the light in his eyes that woke him, but the sensation of wet warmth on the inside of his forearm, the sound of snorted breath and the smell of its earthy heat. He was nudged awake by the butting head of someone drooling onto his arm. Quickly Joel sat up to find himself gazing into the quizzical face of a wrinkled, nearly hairless boxer—or boxer mix, judging by her wolfish muzzle and pricked ears. She was old, easily 15 years, her legs thin and knobby; when she yipped in greeting Joel could see she was missing teeth. But she was spry and muscular nonetheless, an intensity winking in her black eyes.

Where did you come from? Joel asked, pushing himself to his knees to examine her for collars or tags. He looked around but saw only one other person in plain sight, a sister in veil and jeans farther up the hill, striding intently past without looking at him. Her thoughts were elsewhere as she walked, head down, beneath a black parasol.

Joel put his arms around Luz. The name just came to him. Well, you're mine now, I guess, he murmured into the prickly fur at the back of her neck. Her buff coat smelled dusty and dry and sulfurous. He would have to sneak her past the apartment manager, or argue. But that wouldn't be too hard, he was convinced. He was good at making a case.

So from his knees, he collected her and rose—she was light and strong as riverbank bamboo—and began the walk back to his apartment. The whole time she lay in his arms, trusting as a baby. No suggestion at all that a few weeks later Joel would return to his apartment to find its back door swinging open and Luz gone for the first time. No suggestion of the eviction notice he would find taped to his front door after the third or fourth escape: *Lease says no dogs allowed. We warned you Mr. Champlain!*

CHAPTER FOUR
Lali Calls the Utility People

Monday, June 7

On Monday morning, when on the third day without power they wake to an apartment that won't be roused from a grey-black dawn and a fridge gone warm and silent, Lali calls City Power and Light a second time. Hector is already gone for the day. Normally she sleeps through his departure—he wakes at 4:45 to leave by 5:30 for his 6A.M. telemarketing shift—but this morning it is too hot to sleep without the fans running, Nena splayed on her back in her dipe with hair plastered to forehead. In the dark they had whispered about what they should do before Hector dressed without showering and hurried off for the day, grabbing a speckled, off-gassing banana on his way out the door.

Lali had cleaned her glasses absent-mindedly with her shirt as she thought, wiping their greasy lenses and tortoiseshell frames before shoving them back up the bridge of her nose. She'd call again, it was the only thing she could do at half past five in the morning. The utility people staffed their customer service centers 24/7, the vultures. Gotta make that money. Yesterday, the man on the phone sounded merely harried, but today he sounds harried and surprised and bored all at once. Who could blame him? It's probably the end of his graveyard shift, stuffed into a cubicle in a big airless, windowless room where it doesn't matter if it's night or day, like Hector at his job.

The utility staffer tells Lali the power should have been restored to her neighborhood by now, they are working on it as quickly as they can, sometimes it takes a while, it should be any time now. They are recommending that customers without power seek shelter during the hot hours of the day with friends or relatives, who might also share refrigerator space so customer perishables don't perish.

Too late for that. She thinks of the anaerobic pot of beans they fed to the compost the day before, the frozen geometries of vegetable medley melted into mush, the WIC cheese misshapen and sweating in its plastic wrap. They'd spent the hot parts of Saturday and Sunday moving around the city from swimming pool to library to mall, public places where they could linger without having to buy anything, not returning to the apartment until sundown. Each time hoping they would come home to lights and fans.

Now it is Monday, so at least they have other places to be, in other parts of the city. Glasses on, plain straight hair passably combed and tucked behind her ears, Lali rouses Nena early so she can drop her off at daycare before the sun is too high, squeezing a breast against her mouth before she has time to complain about interrupted sleep. Some mornings they fight and scuffle all morning like cats, breast to clothes to car to school, Nena lunging and Lali retreating and vice versa, but this morning Nena unlatches calm and wakeful. Sometimes, gazing down at her child, Lali still cannot believe Nena emerged, healthy and whole, from the salvaged wreck of her body. She bows inward thanks—to corporeal elasticity and the blessing of calm children and the Gulf wind that blows them uneventfully to the lab school on the community college campus, where ten little faces encircling a tiny table look up from their cereal bowls when they enter the toddler room together. Amazingly, Nena sits and eats without protest. She never just sits and eats.

From Nena's school it is just a few blocks to El Centro, slumping in its repurposed complex of offices, its outer walls colorfully muraled. When she first started working there, Victor had guided her through the maze of offices, papered with banners and posters, pointing out which rooms had been the offices of the first Black lawyer in the city, which had belonged to a dentist before that. And below was a barbershop where old men still congregated, and next door Centro had big plans for a magnificently falling-apart, boarded-up structure that once housed a plumbing supply company: stacked inside even still were pyramids of ceramic sewer mains. On Victor's heels, Lali had studied the posters and flyers thumbtacked to the walls. One poster she'd seen before depicted an open-mouthed big fish chasing a scared little fish, then a swarm of little fish in the shape of a bigger fish turning around to chase their would-be predator. *Organize!* it read. Other posters featured stormy-browed Che, a smiling Evo Morales. Those faces she recognized, but the captionless portraiture of long-faced men in military finery gave her pause. Were they Spanish? Wouldn't be, in that space. Mexican revolutionaries? But they were very clearly not 20th century faces. Mexican independence from Spain? Not Miguel Hidalgo—wasn't he a priest? Many months later, she still doesn't know who they are.

When she enters that morning, scooping up the newspapers piled outside the front door on her way in, Victor and Marcos and Papa and Dulce are crowded around Victor's computer, laughing at something. Lali hesitates for a moment as she passes through their space, raising her hand in greeting, unsure of whether or not to join in. When after a moment no one motions her in, Lali continues walking to the office she shares with Chela. It's dark; Chela isn't there. Listening to the laughter in the next room, Lali sits for a moment at her desk, looking at her hands. Then she rises and returns to the adjacent room, standing in the doorway.

They look up as she hesitates, adjusting her glasses; they wait for her to say something. Finally, she figures out what to ask. Is there a staff meeting this morning? They are supposed to have staff meetings every Monday, but everyone secretly hopes they won't. So mostly they don't, working separately on their various campaigns, and when they do there is such a backlog of things to discuss they go on all day, and they have to send someone on a run to the nearest taquería to get food for everyone. That was the good part.

We might have one, Victor says, depending. Be ready.

Guess not then, she thinks. And also: the gathering in Victor's office is more family business than work, meaning her omission is no misreading. Eh, she'll be out of there in a couple months anyway. And now she knows she is free to go about her day.

Lali had been hoping someone brought tacos that morning, actually. That sometimes happens, or sometimes if there has been a Saturday event there are leftovers in the fridge. But there is only coffee, brewing in Marcos's office. Marcos had bags of beans piled in a closet from a farmworker co-op in Oaxaca, and she had overheard him talking animatedly to Centro visitors about buying it to sell up north in support of peasants' land rights—but the mountain in the closet had not diminished perceptibly since she started working there, and it seemed they mostly drank it for themselves, cup after cup. It was good coffee. And in the yellow kitchen, just past the posters of the unknown most likely revolutionaries, there was day-old pan dulce, dry but tasty enough. She tosses a pink concha onto a plate, coffee into her cup, and carries both back to her desk to start in on the pile of newspapers.

It's not a bad habit, to open her day with an ear to the ground. Usually she'll start with the big daily for the official word, then she'll check the little weekly paper for its muck-raking counterword, flourishing above its thick understory of politely advertised blow jobs. Then the bilingual paper with its parallel columns, one in Spanish and another in English for any bolillos or pochos who might be reading. After that, if there is time, the endless churning and tweeting and blipping of online news feeds, scrolling like NASDAQ. Usually there wasn't time, though, save maybe for the Champ's blog. He covered the city's environmental beat, so she always read that.

Today she is looking for news of the refinery explosion she heard on the radio right before she saw it for herself, like a premonition—but the big paper says explanations are pending investigation, and even this is buried beneath exclamatory news about the storm, the storm. In a city that has sucked itself dry, the fact of rain makes front page. How many houses lost power in which neighborhoods, and how many car engines died when their drivers attempted to ford low water crossings, and a picture of some wiseacre vato in sunglasses tubing down the street in the rain with a can of beer in his hand. Thirty years after all those famous utility sit-ins organized by an alliance of inner city neighborhood associations led mostly by seniors—hence the name VAMOS, *Viejos Against More of the Same*—it was still the Westside whose streets flooded, the Westside that lost power. Then there is the press statement of the utility people about restoring power, so vague as to be void of content.

In *El Bilingüe* she reads a story—she covers the English copy with her hand to slog through the Spanish, for practice—it was as slow going and strenuous as hacking one's way through waist-high grass with a machete—about an elderly couple not far from Lali's apartment who had been found suffocating in their tiny shotgun house. Utility workers discovered them as they made their rounds through the burned out neighborhoods, fixing transmission towers and testing transformers. The woman who came to the door was 86, the sole caretaker of an 87-year-old husband with emphysema.

Are your lights back on? Fridge, air? the workers had gone from house to house asking, in Spanish or English or Spanglish as required.

The tiny stooped woman at the door in her housedress explained that yes, the lights, but they didn't have no air or heat. The wiring in the house made it dangerous to run the little window unit in the living room, and many years ago when they moved in, the utility people told them the gas leaked so bad they wouldn't turn on services for them—said it was a liability issue or something. So in the long summer of March till November, they set up a chain of box fans to cool the house, while in the winter they plugged a hotplate into the outlet next to their bed and used the electric coils to heat the room, like a space heater. The house, you could see it was small, so it worked well enough.

But when the power went out after the storm over the weekend, they lost not only the fans but also the oxygen equipment her husband needed to breathe. The workers found him gasping at the back of the house, reclining in a chair pushed against an open window. He stabilized at the hospital, but not before another case surfaced, this one on the Eastside, this one fatal. VAMOS had called an emergency meeting at the Westside Senior Center, *El Bilingüe* concludes. Todos están invitados.

She should go. Chela too. Where was she? This was exactly what VAMOS had said would happen if the city raised electric rates like they'd voted to do. And now it had happened, and the increase hadn't even kicked in yet. And now that Lali knows it has happened, her awareness bobs like a cork when she tries to submerge it and start her day, her week, the things she should be doing. At Centro there was never any stable set of tasks to complete; there was only the latest hemorrhagic crisis and the heave-ho scramble to apply pressure. Never any time to stop and think. She'll be gone in a couple months anyway, flown north to start a teaching position in a Kansas college town— back to the deliberate pacing of academic work rhythms, the systole and diastole of the semester, the luxury of feeling outside the immediacy of real-time events in some important sense. In academia one was committed only to the time it took to think through and finish something, however long that took. Five years or more, the eight years it had taken to finish her Ph.D. in political science, her dissertation on environmental conflicts. Water politics. That's why she thought this job would make sense, but—

But at El Centro the time frame was now now now. Demand statement drafted in time for the meeting. Email blast to your list a few days before an action or press conference. Press release by 5 the night before. Follow-up calls to media the next morning to make sure they were coming. Text blast to your peeps right before the action. Letter to the editor no later than a week after a major development. Blog entry after each action. Media hits in the binder for end-of-the-year reporting to funders. Constant blast of tweets and status updates as one did things, to close the gap ever more tightly between their happening and their documentation. She's getting better at it, the seduction dance of courting media response and the uplifting of organizational narrative frames. Branding, leveraging. That was what they called it on the weekly conference calls with the funders, a national coalition where El Centro is one of just a handful of grassroots groups within a sea of Big Greens. Still, once Victor had looked at a flyer she had worked on for an entire week, one side in Spanish and the other in English—a week was ridiculous, admittedly; you needed to be able to crank out a flyer in 30 minutes, that's why their rickety card table desks were covered with iPhones and Macbooks and their rickety building a fire hazard from all the power strips and outlet adapters—and his only response was, Where's our logo? The suspicion, the constant squinty eyes of not getting the credit, of getting too cozy with other groups, of disloyalty to the family. The logo as family brand, as coat of arms.

It helps if she starts each Monday by planning her priorities for the week, first the papers and then her priorities, but now this latest crisis had interjected itself. It propels her up from all plans and into Victor's office again, where again she hesitates, not sure what she means to ask. By now he's on a call, so she ducks back to her side of the wall, grabs a loose-lying sheet of paper, and scrawls her question. Poking her head back around to the other side, she flashes the paper: Where's your cuz?

Glancing up from his call, Victor mouths exaggeratedly, pointing in the direction of outside: In the garden!

She finds Chela outside, prepping a bed in her rubber boots and work gloves, sweaty hair held back by blue bandana. If it was hot when they woke at the buttcrack of dawn, now at five till nine it's even hotter, overcast and sticky.

Leaning on her shovel, Chela rights herself when she sees Lali coming, passing a gloved arm across her forehead and smiling. Hey mujer. What's going on?

With the men the conventional greeting Lali learned on her first visit to Centro was to take turns slapping hands down low then bumping fists. There was always a moment of panicked humiliation or hilarity in it for Lali, a scrambling to strike an authenticity she did not feel. It was supposed to look natural and cool but felt absurd, scripted. But with Chela it is good and right to hug and kiss each other on the cheek.

Look at this article I just read. She pushes the bilingual paper at Chela.

Chela scans it and looks up, eyes wide. What the—?

Yeah, Lali says, as Chela continues to read. The one on the Eastside is super close by. That boarding house a few streets down?

Chela closes her eyes, scanning a mental geography. Hiiiijo. That's right. Lowering the paper, she slaps at a mosquito on her arm. VAMOS called it, she murmurs. Damn, this stuff just keeps piling up. All the shit hitting *all* the fans. Like, did you hear about the explosion at that jankity old refinery on the river? The one they closed a couple years back that they're trying to turn into apartments now? So apparently a construction crew accidentally severed an old gas pipeline, and—

Hands blooming before her in illustration, she mimics the sound of combustion like a kid smashing toy trucks together.

Yeah, I actually saw the smoke on Friday when I was coming back from the bank. And then later that night was that crazy thunderstorm. Did you lose power over at your place?

The electricity, no. Loca, we live on the Northside, remember? Well, the north side of downtown. They laugh.

But we got hail the size of golf balls, Chela says, and one of the trees in the front had a limb crack off. Poor Ramona was going apeshit, scrambling from one room to the other and trying to dig up the floors. I had to bring her under the covers with me, chiflada!

When I left for work this morning, the power was still out at my place.

Fucking City Power and Light. They should change their name to Shitty Power and Light.

For real.

Chela pauses, reflecting. You know what, though—we complain when things start breaking down, but it's like a monster we've been feeding this whole time. We thought we had it chained, but suddenly—

Chela jumps at Lali with her hands curled into claws, knocking her glasses askew and making her laugh. Suddenly it's bustin out and chewing on your face! Chela roars.

There's supposed to be an emergency meeting tonight, at the Westside senior center. Lali taps at the bottom of the article.

We should go, right? Bring the youth?

Yeah. I was hoping you'd want to. Okay, maybe after I get Nena from daycare I can swing back over to pick you up.

Chela shakes her head, frowning. Don't worry about it. I can get a ride with Naima. I'm sure La Alianza will be going.

Naima? Really? Y'all are okay now?

We're okay. Better, I guess. I mean, we're still living together. And she's talking to me again. Chela shrugs. I don't know. Shit's still all fucked up, actually.

Yeah, I remember you said that, Lali says quietly. She doesn't want to pry.

But Chela keeps talking, tugging at the teal plugs in her earlobes, lifting a hand to the back of her head and scratching, agitated. She thinks I'm messing around. I mean, I know I get rowdy when I'm drinking, but—ehhhh! She exhales noisily.

So yeah, I *was* drinking the night of Angelica's exhibit opening—you know her, right, Angie Rosales, who painted that mural on the side of Alianza? Well, Naima was out of town, and when she came back, someone who saw me and Angie talking that night said some fuckin thing to Naima about it. Man, she cold-shouldered me for a solid week! No talking, kissing, hugging, *nothing*. But you know what, maybe I was flirting. Or letting myself be flirted with.

Chela glances away from Lali momentarily, gazing over the

top of her shovel toward downtown, the Tower of Americas enshrouded in haze.

But it's only because I'm never sure where we stand, you know? Like one part of her is still holding back, even after three years together. Sizing me up all side-eyed and suspicious like she's just waiting for me to fuck up. I mean, I know I'll never be as politically sophisticated as she is. But when she withdraws—I just feel like some stupid kid she found washing beer glasses down on the strip and took in off the street. Some loser who still skates down at the park with the high school boys. I seriously thought we were going to break up this time. I spent the whole week at my mom's, unable to get off the couch—remember how I missed all those days of work? It was cuz I wanted to die.

Chela's eyes fill. Lali lowers her own out of respect, listening.

I just, Chela starts. She pauses, fighting to regain composure. I just want her to love me back as hard as I love her. Shit, she says, wiping her eyes. I'd settle for her frickin *approval.* You know what's even worse, though? That whole week at home, I felt like Amá was relieved we were maybe breaking up. She didn't say it, but I could *feel* it. The whole thing played right into her church BS about my *homosexual lifestyle.* Naima thinks I should cut off contact with them like she did with her folks. She thinks I should quit Centro too, and come work with her at an organization run by queer women instead of crusty old vatos like Papa. But it's hard, you know? Papa is my tío; Victor, Marcos, Dulce, they're my primos—they're *family.* I mean, Amá brought me tacos when I couldn't get off the couch. She remembered my favorite kind, too, barbacoa on flour with onion and cilantro. Even though she knows I'm vegan now—well, sorta vegan, I guess. She probably got her fingers crossed that being gay works the same. Like, you try to go vegan but really you want the meat! Fuuuuck me, Naima would shit herself if she'd seen me eating cow's head. It'd be like one more reason to break up. Chela laughs ruefully, shaking her head.

Ay, Chela. I'm sorry.

No, *I'm* sorry, Chela sighs. I know it's probably TMI.

It's okay, says Lali. I don't mind. Just hoping you're okay now.

Better, says Chela. But her face is still sad.

Well—if for some reason Naima can't give you a ride, let me know. I'll be ready.

After she plans her week. If it is plannable. Because what if they—? Lali has started for the building, but the image of Chela's monster keeps slowing her down, fusing with a memory of dancing with Paloma at that first action, forming a chorus line across the street from the utility headquarters, high stepping and chanting: *We kick nodes! To the curb!* Because Chela was right—it wasn't just nodes now, it was everything, the mining and the utility increases and the explosions. How to connect it all? Something about it gathers energy about a center. There once was a monster who...no, there once was a little monster who lived in the ground. People found it and took it back to where they lived. At first it was happy and friendly as a child, keeping houses warm and streets lit.

And then what?

Well, then it got bigger and stronger and scarier, so they had to chain it up. They should have let it go, left it alone, but they were attached to their own desires and longings.

And then what?

The more they fed it, the bigger and hungrier it got, of course. And the hungrier it got, the more they fed it and the bigger it grew. And then one day...

Chela! Lali calls, turning back around. I have a great idea.

II. Force and Motion

Roughly One Year Earlier
San Antonio, TX

Research Notas 1:
This I Called San Antonio de Padua

*We marched five leagues
over a fine country with
broad plains,
the most beautiful
in New Spain.
We camped on the banks
of an arroyo. This I called
San Antonio de Padua
because we had reached it
on his day.
Signed
General Domingo
Teran de los Rios,
June 13,
1691*

These words, which
once bade supplicants,
agents of the crown, to
arrive on shallow shores of
what once
was inland sea

are now inscribed
on the bleached bone
steps leading up

to the entrance of
Development Services
—limestone steps
dug from the karst
of northern hills
I am sure. These words,

these steps
now form
the shallow shore
where newestcomers grasp
at El Dorado
of permits
to dig and infill
and extend or else bear
applications to waive
and abate
and incent
investment: these words

of welcome, powerful
and subtle
as lunar pull
on earthen tides.

CHAPTER ONE
Lali Comes Home

They called it a third industrial revolution. That's what the city was calling it, at least, in the report they had issued which made such a great splash: a great transition away from carbon, necessitated by the federal state of emergency on climate called just a few years prior. Fukushima had eventually arrived on the doorstep of San Francisco, so even though the city people were saving face by politely avoiding talk about their earlier push for nukes, nukes were effectively off the table; and when the licensing agreement for the plant on the coast expired, they hadn't renewed it. Across the nation, coal plants already pushed to the edge of closure by plummeting prices began shuttering en masse after the feds issued their mandate for carbon capture technology. And supposedly cleaner-burning natural gas had proved a bust, with fracking promising to suck up more water than was available amid crippling drought, not to mention the methane it flared and leaked into the skies at 84 times the heat-trapping potency of carbon dioxide. At first cities had tried to retrofit their plants to run on C-Free, the first synthetic, carbon-free fuel on the market, spun and spliced in the centrifuges of a Connecticut lab that had figured out a process for producing carbon-free fuel from the genetically-modified RNA of plentiful soil bacteria. This idea too they were forced to abandon when it proved too expensive to scale up quickly. And in the meantime, while they scrambled for alternatives, the city people had hit upon the idea of redeveloping all those shuttered coal and gas plants. That was the policy now: *Residential Repurposing of Carbon Infrastructure Assets.*

And so the energy descent the movement people had fought for, even before Al Gore made his famous PowerPoint presentation of a film, had arrived. There was nothing left to try but the sun and the wind, sucked up into industrial scale battery storage, if possible—and if cities could make the shift quickly enough while also keeping the lights on. Time was running out, time was up: since 2010, each summer had seen more triple-digit dog days than the one before it. And the winter before Lali's return to San Antonio was, bizarrely, the coldest on record—rolling blackouts blanketing the city during a winter storm that stalled over South Texas for several weeks, freezing the river hard enough to skate on for the first time in over 100 years. In what they called a polar vortex, the Arctic circle had been knocked off its perch at the top of the globe, a hat tipped by bullies off a kid's head to slip over the eyes, farther south than ever before. Deep in the Rio Grande Valley, the oranges and grapefruit had frozen on the trees and dropped to the earth from glassified limbs.

But now it is April and summer already. She is from here but she has forgotten how hot it is, even in April. Or maybe things had changed in her long absence, grown even hotter than what she remembered. All she knows is that in the gash of California's Central Valley, the high summer sun had seemed to stand feet from your face, getting up in your grill like a playground bully, but it had left the air alone. In California, the differential of shade and nightfall still held meaning.

Not so in San Antonio. Here, the air is thirsty for all the heat it can hold. This city is different that way, built to radiate outward from a center teetering at a nexus of the four directions: trees to the east, coast to the south, hills to the north, and to the west desert. Not that California didn't burn in its own way. In California there were heatwaves and flash fires, entire forests of ponderosas and sugar pines combusting spontaneously. Or once, when she was heavy with Nena, a heatwave had descended and lasted for four or five days. Come midnight, the cats still lay splay-legged on their backs in the middle of the kitchen floor, panting. She worried then that they would all die; and, scared for the baby forming inside her, she'd drawn a cold bath and lay there all night and through the next day. Living in Nor-Cal, they had no a/c; the house had been built without it. But when that heatwave had lifted, they'd asked their landlord for a window unit. And he had complied, grudgingly, but raised their rent.

It had been a running argument between Lali and Hector—which was hotter, Califas or Tejas? But the heatwaves, Hector would always protest. And yes, the heatwaves, and on top of those were earthquakes and budget crises and strikes, the upground rumblings of giant underground things, fault lines shifting and rubbing. California was the France of Aztlan, its borderline youngest sister who ran on a higher rev, hotter and crazier and out of control. The enlightened civility of its prohibitively tiny parking spaces and gas mileage standards and mandatory smog checks was belied by their necessity in the reality of furious traffic, furious activity, and furious competition. Everyone converged on California to get something and go.

Lali and Hector had been no exception. They had gone there so she could get a degree, her doctorate in poli sci—Hector had finally finished his B.A. too along the way, in graphic design—and they left when she was almost done, because Nena had come and Lali needed her family nearby if she was to finish. And more than ever she'd just needed to finish, to get out and get a real job. Hector was counting on her; Nena was counting on her. Lali was counting on it too. So they had gotten out of California right before the metaphorical house came crashing down, amid the onset of killing drought and wildfires and tuition spiking like fever, closely followed by student protests and occupations over slashed public programs. California was hot that way, a fever that came on suddenly with the power to kill you—but overlaid atop a seasonless backdrop of serene blue sky, the nighttime relief of the Delta breeze.

In San Antonio, though, the heat stays and stays, inert and unmoving as death. Its persistence is an immediacy that opens her body like stomata, to be absorbed into a landscape of home as soon as she is back, in the strange double take of memory. Realizing not simply what she has forgotten but how much she has not, realizing the impossibility of forgetting and also of being forgotten. The heat of April is a surprise, but the surprise itself is a greeting or welcoming back. The surprise is the shock not of the novel but of a forgotten familiar, an uncanniness: *unheimlich,* in German, had that double meaning that Freud loved, meaning something at once homely and strange. She remembered that from grad school, a class on social theory she'd had to petition to take for credit since it was outside her program. She'd been an outlier in a department full of quant-heads and policy wonks, in love with theory, compelled to explain not just *how* but *why* things happened. Probably she should have gone into soc or anthro or even philosophy, God forbid. But her program was the only one she'd applied to that took her, so she couldn't complain. And she'd finished with honors in record time, so neither could her program.

All that spring and summer until Lali's savings run out, Nena goes with family three days a week so Lali can finish her dissertation—*Flow,* it's called: *Water Movements in Political Life*—leaving the other days to be filled with errands and outings that take forever on the bus, in the heat. She has a car but Hector needs it to get to work. On their return he'd looked for something closer by and better suited for his degree, but finding nothing quickly, he'd settled for the telemarketing gig on the far Northside. Later he'd buy his own clunker off Craigslist for a couple thou, but those first hot seasons back Lali and Nena are carless. In California she'd toted Nena in a pouch strapped to her front or her back, but it is too hot to do that in South Texas, and Nena has grown too big and squirmy besides. Too hot, and there is no money to buffer it.

You learn ways to adapt. You carry water bottles filled with ice that melts by the time you get to where you're going, the free city pool or the public library. Enchilada red, that was how they described the color of its exterior. You remember when they built it; you skipped school once to go check it out. To sheckalo, in the tongue-in-cheek Spanglish of your extended family, your dad's side, anyway. Mom is white but she's been here so long she says it too, unselfconsciously. You remember a

Physics class from 10th grade—after you were uprooted from San Anto to rural areas north but before you ran away from home, the year you ran away from home—with a Mexicana student teacher who pronounced her *ch* as *sh*, and how relentlessly the Anglo kids in polos laughed at her, until one day she fled the room crying. And the way the coach in charge of the class laughed alongside these students, and called you too sensitive when you challenged him, his doughy face pouty. His festivity spoiled. It was because your own body bore the struggles over this hot land, Brown and white, that your heart had run after the teacher running out of the room, knowing you would never stand with those who laughed, even if your body passed for one who did. And because of this you never took another science class again if you didn't have to, though science had been your first intellectual passion as a kid, inhaling marine biology textbooks in a furious effort to understand enough about hydrology to save the oceans from oil spills and plastic waste. Hot landscape full of stories like this, a free association of lines drawn between places and bodies and stories and the bigger histories embedding them, back and back and on and on with no clear determining logic, no master referent. Just one thing reminding of another, and another. *And here was where I*, and *here I remember that*. This was coming home.

The pool or the public library, and when you got there the ice would be melted but the water would still be cold. Or, once, right after moving back, you rode the bus to a *paletería you remember visiting as a child, an igloo-shaped building with smooth walls painted such a bright shade of chicle blue you've wondered if your memory was actually a dream. But no: twenty-five years later, there it stood—and you could still get* a shaved ice in a foam cup with one strata of mango and another of lime, squeezed over the top with fresh lime requested in embarrassed Spanish. When they slid the little window to take your money or hand you a paper-wrapped cup, you could feel the window a/c from the interior, you could smell the cold—the smell of freezer, of freon. Here in this city you sat patiently outside at a crumb-dusted picnic table with your sticky nena, nursing melting raspas as you stared at a colorful map of botanas, its cartography of treats hung to neon green siding. Raspas you could get natural—finely shaved ice with the fruit and sugar blended in—or in the old style, coarsely ground ice with syrup, or even topped with ice cream. Frito pie. Hot Flaming Cheetos in a silver cellophane sack, smothered with the orange plastic of canned nacho cheese and topped with pickled jalapeños. Pickle juice popsicles! Fresh cups of fruit dusted with chile or smothered with chamoy sludge. Chicharrones or their swine-free counterpart, the fried-hard wheels of red wheat flour called durritos. You could do these things on the bus in April, but you could feel it coming, the sticky, tropical heat soon to roll off the Gulf. April was a window of time whose air felt blank white, a sheet of paper waiting for writing, a summoned story premonitory in its absence. Come May Day it would be impossible, inescapable—in your house, in your lungs, in the folds of your body filling with sweat thick as glue.

It is strange to think that just two months before, in February, the river had frozen and blackouts blanketed the city, extinguishing all light. Her parents had emailed pictures of the snow back when she and Hector were still in California, shoveling all their shit into boxes as they prepared to come home. The coldest winter on record, her mother had written. She was from Chicago; she would know a cold winter. Now, in April, there is no trace of it, as they sit at a green picnic table, trying to eat raspas faster than they can melt.

There Are No More Acts of God: Blackouts (Rolling and Otherwise) in a Time of Transition

Posted by Joel Champlain (jchamp@thevolt.com) on April 25

When the power cut off for 22 hours at José Hernandez's house this past February in the middle of a record freeze, he didn't know why. "I thought we had gotten disconnected," he says. The summer before, they had gotten the dreaded pink disconnection notices in the mail from CPL due to a $425 bill they couldn't pay. But Hernandez had arranged an installment plan and paid it off faithfully after seven months.

Regardless, he knew what to do. "With no power to run the space heaters, we had the kids sleep with all the dogs to keep warm," he laughs, remembering. "Like they do in the Arctic."

It's an anecdote that feels less quaint now that the Arctic circle is melting during summer, then dipping down during winter to encircle South Texas, with flooding and hurricanes and drought in between—all of which portend further power outages.

But what Hernandez learned only later was that this particular outage was, in fact, intentionally orchestrated by the city's public utility, in concert with a shadowy state regulatory body that oversees Texas's sizable corner of the grid.

"On the news the next day, they said they had planned it to save power. They were supposed to shut off the electric in different neighborhoods around the city for just 30 minutes each, taking turns, kinda spreading it out. So I don't know why, at our house, it took a whole day to come back on."

Welcome to the wonky world of the rolling blackout.

Acts of God

It seems a basic point that a world of difference lies between an unplanned power outage, like those accompanying electrical storms, and the planned outages of February's Arctic front. Not from the perspective of residents like Hernandez, for whom the end result is the same. But for utilities whose job it is to keep lights on during times of high demand, one is an "act of God" which absolves the utility of responsibility—and the other is "PR hell," in the words of a CPL administrator with knowledge of the situation, speaking on conditions of anonymity.

But the difference between unplanned and planned outages should also matter to those of us concerned about straining tensions between growing demand and finite supply in a world steadily running out of options for keepin' on keepin' on in our accustomed ways. Unplanned outages and their dramatic impacts tend to grab our attention. There's nothing flashier than a lightning storm or a freak blizzard that kicks distribution capacity in the teeth, or—as occurs occasionally—the chance rattlesnake or wild turkey that slithers or flaps its way into a substation and shorts it out for a few hours. For many of us, there is nothing more visibly disturbing than the "blackout scar" of elders found dead in stifling single room occupancy apartments, as has happened during heatwaves in Chicago and Seattle most recently. Poor old people, we say. What a tragedy of chance and nature.

But since Katrina struck in 2005, it's become increasingly difficult to put our faith in (or hide our collective responsibility behind) the idea of any purely "natural" disaster. The winter weather weirdness of late—and the planned energy rationing it triggers—may be highly visible in its effects. But both reveal the shape of a city we didn't know existed, a set of social calculations hidden in plain view.

Invisible Grids

For the past 25 years, University of Chicago sociologist Karen Farringer has studied cities' climate mitigation strategies. "I started out studying heatwaves," she says. "And heatwaves are interesting. Because unlike disasters like Sandy or Irma, where we can see how histories of inequality are at fault, with a heatwave there's just this sense you're dealing with something impersonal, something beyond human engineering or control. And I would argue the opposite."

According to Farringer, heatwaves and other natural disasters illuminate an order of ordinary suffering that is anything but random. "It's socially produced," Farringer states, "in numerous ways that escape ordinary perception." In San Antonio, for example, we might ask why it is the power fails disproportionately on certain sides of town, or how those already marginalized by economics or race then become more vulnerable to extreme weather conditions. Nature does what nature does, but it is patterns of human decision making that turn nature into disaster for some and recreational or leisure space for others.

Not to steer too far clear of my opening salvo: let us not be distracted by spectacular displays of nature's power, however disturbing—as three weeks of near-zero temperatures in South Texas certainly were. Instead, let's see in these highly visible markers of climate chaos the more subtle, but equally disturbing, human policy decisions dwelling beneath the threshold of ordinary perception. As global temperatures rise in this time of transition, it is the *planned* outages whose complicated meanings are all the more critical to parse and communicate. More than would-be acts of God, rolling blackouts reveal the shape of forces that lie beneath the visible, as well as the shape of things to come.

As explained by Max Ellis of the Electrical Regulatory Commission of Texas (ERCOT), the regulatory body overseeing the electrical grid for most of the state, planned or "rolling" blackouts are an "intentional pulling of the plug" that utilities undertake as a precaution against widespread electrical shortages when reserve power falls below a certain threshold—about 14% in Texas.

When ERCOT decides electrical rationing has become necessary, these temporary outages travel around the state in measured doses (hence "rolling") as the state attempts to spread out the goods (or bads?) in an equitable manner. Typically, ERCOT will call first on commercial users who have volunteered to shut off operations in exchange for lower utility rates; if this doesn't help, power will be cut as a last resort to residences either at random or in targeted areas, exempting high-need places like hospitals, fire stations, police departments, and nursing homes.

That's the theory, anyway. In practice, as most things are, it's more complicated. Says Jesus Maldonado, liaison between ERCOT and City Power and Light: "Usually, it's not only high demand that triggers emergency rationing. It's high demand when you weren't expecting it."

Most often, it is high demand plus unanticipated malfunctions which catch the grid with its p(l)ants down, as happened this past winter when an extended, late-season cold snap led to frozen pipes on power plants, killing 7,000 MW of generation capacity. With high demand for heating plus multiple plants offline, ERCOT called on utilities to shed 4,000 MW of power, roughly equivalent to 3 million homes, or 45-minute rolling outages affecting 330,000 customers—the first time Texas has seen rolling blackouts during the winter months. For some ratepayers, outages stretched to hours and even days when already-switched-on appliances tripped already-overloaded circuits as the utility attempted to restore power, as most likely happened in the case of José Hernandez.

These utility woes are only compounded by the Texas tradition of energy deregulation, a trend as critical to the discussion as it is eye-crossingly obtuse. As explained to me by Barbara Hanley, professor of political science and head of the Energy Research Institute at Texas A&M, deregulation means the privatization of energy production, so that power generation and distribution are governed by market forces. "So when there are shortages," Hanley says, "electricity becomes more valuable, and costs can spike to $3,000 per megawatt."

What this means for the utility ratepayer is plain: somebody somewhere is making moola when the grid fails. And for the most part, these scarcity-induced spikes in cost are passed on to ratepayers—with the poorest hit hardest of all. The lower your household income, the bigger the proportion of that income you spend on energy costs, not least because older housing stock in poor neighborhoods is less energy efficient. But it is also the poorest households that suffer most when a deregulated market fails to deliver reliable power.

Clean, Green, and...Cha-Ching Cha-Ching?
On the heels of this past winter's record lows, a raft of acronyms—from the TWC (Texas Water Commission) to the NWS (National Weather Service) and the NOAA (National Oceanic and Atmospheric Administration)—began predicting the hottest temperatures and worst drought we've seen since record keeping began in 1895. With it comes the threat of further rolling blackouts, and the inevitable question: Is Texas prepared? While the cities of Europe and of the American Midwest and Northeast are no stranger to heatwaves claiming dozens and in some cases hundreds of lives, Texans have tended to attribute this to a regional lack of preparation or constitutional inability. This hometown pride may in hindsight reveal itself to be mere hubris, as climate destabilization produces more heatwaves and cold snaps, more tornadoes and tsunamis, more drought and blackouts—in short, more "acts of God" of the sort that zapped us this past winter.

Undoubtedly, certain quarters of the city will respond with a cry for more baseload to meet the demands of growth and expansion without the threat of blackouts. With the deadline looming for cities to comply with the Federal Transition Act's required 50% cut in emissions, coal is a no-go, while Fukushima has slayed boosterish dreams of a nuclear renaissance, at least until the ever-briefer half-life of public memory passes. What's next, then, in the hunt for a post-carbon fuel stock without cost or limit? We'll find out for sure this summer, when the city rolls out its local transition plan in a series of public meetings. Whatever it is, histories of myopically technocentric solutions to environmental crises that are social at root suggest it can only be 100% safe, clean, and risk-free—not to mention totally profitable to boot!

We shall see, as they say, what we shall see.

CHAPTER TWO
Joel Takes a Node Tour

The idea for the story—a big one, he could feel it—snuck up on him one Sunday morning in early May as he read the city paper on his couch, lying on his back with his bare feet propped on the arm. Out of the blue, an announcement had appeared in the paper: following passage of the Federal Transition Act, the utility people had made the momentous decision not to build any new coal or gas plants, and to shutter their oldest and dirtiest within ten years rather than relicense them. It struck him as ironic. Those were the same plants that for decades City Power and Light was supposed to install with scrubbers. And they had dragged and dragged their feet on it, using it as a pawn—dangling deferred promises like a carrot before the noses of the white environmental organizations and the movement people alike, until everyone was at each other's throats—or as a bargaining chip for other things they wanted to do. Ultimately, CPL decided whatever they wanted to decide, announcing it in the papers or in info sessions they called public hearings, then wondered why people got upset when they were working so hard to pat themselves on the back. That was what got him. The movement people could fume all they wanted about being shut out of the process until the very end, the public part of that process as last minute as the appearance of Homo sapiens on the stage of evolutionary history—but real inclusion would never happen, not so long as private decision makers held the real reigns. The regular people those decisions impacted most would always be outside the meeting room, or the meeting to plan the meeting, or the conversation over lunch where the idea for the meeting before the meeting was first hatched. They would always be outside because it had already been decided, even before it was decided, right from the start. It was a windup toy set in motion long ago.

But now CPL had decided to shut the shit down. Already they had closed the gas plant on the river south of downtown and, in a model redevelopment project that had made Mayor Mike the darling of the U.S. Conference of Mayors, they had gutted and remediated it for conversion into a mixed-use development, with apartments up top and boutique retail and convention stable below. They had similar plans to upcycle the refinery further downriver. All of it right in time to meet the deadline for the radical cuts to carbon emissions required by the emergency transition plan the feds had passed after the last international climate gathering.

Well, good. Good for them all...except the folks who had been living nearest to those scrubberless plants for the past twenty years and would be for ten more. And the generations of people who had eaten the fish from the cooling reservoirs that had doubled as county recreational facility. And the mobile home community near the old gas plant, forcibly relocated as land values spiked like clockwork when they announced plans to redevelop the plant. *The Stacks.* That's what they were calling it.

The momentousness of these announcements was only underscored by their incidental reporting, a stifled yawn toward the back of the Metro section, in front of a rousing op-ed by the head of the Texas Secessionist Party. *Transition never, Texas forever!* And then, at the end of this lazy little article about ending coal and gas, where all the good stuff landed—Joel knew from his DIY, seat-of-his-pants journo training that you shoved the simple stuff up front and ended with extraneous detail—he read that the city had hung its hopes for a renewable future on something new, a mother lode of rare earth minerals discovered throughout South Texas, a concentration of potato-shaped nodules wedged into the seismic ridges of the coastal plains. The semi-arid hardscrabble between San Antonio and the Gulf Coast, exposed millions of years before by the recession of a shallow sea, had gotten a bad rap: entirely barren, entirely worthless, entirely ubiquitous.

But now modern science, backed by a revived rare earth mining industry, had uncovered a secret fertility, and San Antonio was its key. The mining of rare earth nodes had taken place on a small scale across other plays since the early 2000s, but a South Texas startup had found particular success along the coast, and now they were crowing that they had discovered the world's largest deposit beneath San Antonio. Seismar had already completed exploratory testing to identify the position and extent of deposits, already produced a preliminary economic analysis declaring these new methods of extraction to be not only feasible, but *profitable*. Node mining would be safe, green, carbon-free... lucrative! In a revolutionary step toward a regionally-integrated, "mining to magnets to megawatts" model of renewable energy production, the Seismar mine proposed for the northern edge of the city would extract and process rare earth oxides, selling them to magnet-manufacturing factories in Dallas. These sites would sell their turbines and solar panels to megafarms in West Texas which in turn would zap fossil-free electrons back to San Antonio. They had figured out *all* the things, they were calling it the *Texas Transition Trade Triangle*—and San Antonio would be its anchor and spearhead. All the city needed to do was lease its mineral rights to Seismar, part of the transition plan the city planned to shop around this summer.

Joel had read enough industry-drafted press releases to catch the scent of one passed off as news by lazy editors, but never one quite this fragrant. *The Texas Transition Trade Triangle?* You couldn't make shit like that up. It had set the wheels turning in Joel's mind in a way he had not experienced for some time. His down periods were less sadness than a gaping absence that was the inverse of excitement. A mortal inability to excite, a fatal flatness. Medication ironed out the emotional crests and troughs but could not fully shake a core sense of missing some foundational driving force or appetite. He suspected that was the neurological blank space the meds attempted to color in, but it felt ontological and beyond the reach of human intervention. And anyway, he had flushed the meds. They didn't work well enough to justify the cognitive dulling, nor the risk of the grotesque and involuntary facial spasms described in the pamphlets his pharmacy stapled to the little baggie containing his prescription (*discontinue immediately if you experience grimacing, tongue thrusting, lip smacking, repetitive chewing*). There was also the possibility of increased suicidal ideation, as if he needed more of that; or serotonin syndrome (including shivering, diarrhea, confusion, severe muscle tightness, fever, seizures—oh, and fucking death). So now a polar vortex of brain zaps had moved in to remind him of his decision to quit cold turkey, an intracranial doubling or echo when he moved his head, as in a fever, a bodily reminder that a connective prop once there had been removed. A synaptic stutter.

But the article fired something or made something flow. It shoehorned him off his greasy couch and into the library on a Sunday, of all days. Within a couple of weeks even his home computer desk—he did not take work home with him usually—was covered with clippings and papers and reports requested through open records law, and the wall above his desk rippled with yellow sticky notes. That was how he outlined a story that felt too big, a bronco threatening to throw him. Taking shape, though, he could see something taking shape. Something like a triptych, a single story in three acts that would follow the life cycle of the stuff from ground to refining to disposal. He'd kept an eye on the big paper since that original story and saw their coverage was going to be surface in that way, focused on the dollars, partial in its pretense to impartiality. But that was an aperture for him to jump through.

What it meant was that he would need to see the mining for himself. Seismar had its entrepreneurial eye on San Antonio, but they'd been quarrying the sealands south of the city for a couple years, and already the tales had drifted north, of so much equipment traveling by so many trucks there was not road enough to convey it all without crumbling to pieces. Nor was there enough housing or food in neighboring towns to provide for all the men pouring into the sealands from other parts of the state and country, even, looking for work. In fact,

Joel had gotten the idea to check things out for himself from the taco truck guy who usually parked across the street from the *Volt* office. For a week the guy was gone, and when he came back Joel was astounded to hear that he too had struck out for the sealands, following the men who had followed the trucks.

I made a mint out there, yessiree! he had exclaimed, leaning out of the little truck window to hand Joel two bean-and-cheese folded in hot foil. They don't even have grocery stores in somma them towns! It's like here and Corpus and nothing in between. They're puttin up Family Dollars fast as they can, but even those can't meet the demand. Every night the tortillas are gone from the shelves. And all the hotels are spilling over with guys. You got six to a room there, guys sleeping in bags in the bed of their Fords. You got RV towns poppin up next to the mines. And man…they are all starving for tacos caseros! You get tired of the Whataburger and Golden Chick and Donut Palace pretty fast. It's been great for me. Lunchtime, dinnertime, breakfast…I made more cash in one week than I do here in a month. Only reason I even came back here was because I ran out of meat. Here they want bean and cheese, Big Red, like you got. But there it's all meat and beer, fajitas and Tecate. I'm in town a few days on a run, then it's back to the sealands.

Crazy! Joel had mumbled through the goo of his tacos, seeing in his mind the wall above his computer desk at home with its hundred golden post-its, waving at him like undersea anemone, rippling like a dream. He saw them dance into view, combining and recombining, rhizomatic, elemental, nucleic. Taking shape, stepping out of inchoate nothingness to become something material.

***

Sure am glad you're working on this story, the Sister says, looking him over as she drives. She dresses like a nun, in plain slacks and button-down blouse and black orthopedic shoes, her short hair upswept; but she wears red lipstick and gold hoops that sparkle and dance against her brown skin. Traces of her former secular life as a married woman, a councilwoman.

I read everything you write, she continues. But I don't know anything about you. Are you from here?

Joel shakes his head, throwing back a handful of roasted almonds from the tin wedged between them on the console. Nope. I'm a transplant. Invasive species. He grins. I grew up in Philadelphia. Our family moved to Texas in my teens, to Waco.

Philly, huh? I did a fellowship at UPenn there for a year, in public policy. Oh, I loved it. It was a sabbatical after all my years inside the city. They had me teaching a class on minority politics, so I got a chance to sit down and really reflect on the history of my city. The students were so smart and serious, all these young men and women going into government because they wanted to help their communities. They weren't Chicanos like here; most of them were Black or Puertorriqueño, some Asian. But they all wanted to know the same thing, whenever we got a chance to talk one-on-one. Always the same thing. How can I be *part of* the system but not *of* it?

She looks over at him. What about you—you been at the *Volt* long?

A few years. Not for much longer, though.

Oh? Why's that?

Because I want to disappear. He squelches the thought, a violent intrusion, like an ant beneath his thumb.

Well—everyone says we're going to get bought out soon and converted to an all-digital format. It's where journalism is headed. And everyone's been under constant pressure lately to get clicks and web hits, to write shorter copy—blog posts, lists. Focus more on nightlife, eating and drinking and concerts, less on traditional news reporting or investigative work.

He grins again, but it's not funny, not really. Everyone walks around the office scared for their own necks.

What a shame, she says, shaking her head. So many people don't read the daily paper, but they do follow what you all put out every week. And you, you do such important work especially.

It's not just flattery: there is something so genuine and open about her that he can't help but soften. She had come to mind after he heard her on public radio, talking about the destructive effects of mining and refining rare earths in California and China, and the potential for similar impacts on the vast underground aquifer beneath San Antonio's Northside, which supplied the city's drinking water. But of course he had heard of her before that. The fights between her order and the Vatican and the media over her public office, her dissident council run with its string of no-means-no votes on rezoning decisions, and her traveling eco-ministry were much beloved among the movement people he rubbed elbows with on his beat. All he had to do was look for her on the website for the nuns' college, dial her department phone—she had an office but didn't use it, said the receptionist, worked mostly out of her car, but it'd be fine to pass on her cell number—and that weekend they were driving, the turning wheels in his mind becoming the wheels of the Sister's mobile office, spinning him out of the city to the in-between spaces of the sealands.

Sure, I'll take you, the Sister had said, just like that. No *well, I have to* or *let me check and get back to you.* How about tomorrow? she had asked. It was part of the work she did, the work that had chosen her. She'd been able to accomplish certain things during her time on city council, but she preferred to be mostly itinerant now, working mostly under the radar, and her order had given her free reign to do pretty much as she pleased. Talking to folks, gathering information, giving it to those who struggled to bring visibility to their suffering—that was what Sister Soledad Soliz had always enjoyed and felt called to do. For many years her work was about bringing public attention to the issues she fought for, about visibility and enunciation. Now she found she did her best work when no one suspected a thing.

Like this one time, she tells him, she was out giving a tour of the sealands to a woman who had come in from out of town to do a study. A white woman chemist who worked pro bono farther up the Gulf Coast, quietly teaching Black and Houma communities living in Cancer Alley how to sample air for themselves. Sister had wanted to know how the mild radioactivity of the mining tailings and the chemical leachate from the refining process was affecting the soil and air and water. So she had invited her chemist friend to come down, and together they had driven to the sealands on a Sunday, when the roads were less congested. At one point they stopped in front of the entry gates to one of the bigger mines to snap some phone photos. One of the diggers happened to be inside, a white man in a white truck, probably from one of the nearby hamlets—though, Lord knew people were coming in from all over the state. And Sister had smiled and waved without pretense, and he had opened the gate and walked over looking wary.

Help you? he had asked, eyeballing the two older women inside the car. One with a phone in her hand and the other with notepad and pen in her lap.

Well, hi there. I'm taking my friend on a Sunday drive to see the mines. She's here from out of town, and she is very, very interested in what's going on. She's heard all about it.

Oh yeah? the digger had said, a slight frown at the corners of his mouth.

Yes sir. Sure is incredible how much money is flowing through these parts.

At this the digger had relaxed. That's the truth! he'd exclaimed. And deciding they were no threat, he had turned to walk off, calling over his shoulder: Y'all ladies have a good day, now.

She cackles from the driver seat at the memory. And it was the truth! None of it a lie! All that money *is* incredible, she recollects with such irreverence that Joel does a double take at the tiny woman beside him.

Well, she had learned that while institutions limited what one could do, they made other things possible. Power inhibited and power enabled. The habit—meaning that symbolically of course, because she was a plain clothes nun—freed her from the encumbrance of being beholden politically to anyone or anything. People talked to a woman who looked like Abuelita. And people who wouldn't otherwise talk to a journalist or politician or researcher or activist from the city talked to a nun. Though probably they should, no one feared a nun, and a nun had no reason to fear anyone either. A nun was disinterested; a nun was accountable only to what was right. Everyone knew that.

So glad you're writing about this, she repeats to Joel, her words like a comforting pat on the knee. He can't help but smile, pulling pen and notepad from inside his breast pocket. Yes Sister. Sure thing.

***

She is from the city, but she has a small town woman's eagle eye for the anomalous, what's in and out of place. She drives with the NIOSH Pocket Guide to Chemical Hazards on her dash, pulling over to flip through its pages when she spots a truck sporting its multicolored diamond of identification numbers. 1267, she mutters, tossing the guide Joel's way. Look that up, will you? Pulling over to point out this or that mine for him to photograph, this or that open disposal pit where they store the wastewater. See, that one is lined, but this one isn't. Here, get a photo of that. They're supposed to be lined, she says with lips pursed, reaching for her phone to dial the state environmental office. Joel snaps pictures out the window as she wrangles with the operator.

They must know you there already, he teases.

This one sure didn't know anything, she huffs. It's a Sunday, so she's just an operating service.

She points out different kinds of camps—one a cluster of RVs in a graded-gravel rodeo site; another on the grounds of a prison, a barracks of conjoined, windowless boxcar efficiencies with a/c and kitchenette and bathroom, probably. Some companies provided housing for their workers and some workers were left to fend for themselves. She points out a pasture on St. John's Road cleared to make space for another RV park. Poor St. John, Sister says.

How'd you get into all of this anyway, Sister? Joel wants to know.

A small smile creeps over her face. Off the record now, she says.

Go for it, says Joel, laying down pen and pad.

My grandparents landed here, between San Antonio and Corpus, after coming north from Mexico during the Revolution. My grandfather had been a rancher, and he found work as a ranch hand outside George West, growing cotton and raising sheep and cattle on someone else's land. My father, he was the oldest, and he left the ranch and came north to San Antonio, where he met mama and found work on produce row. We lived west of there, in the corrales at first. Tenement housing, basically, a cubicle of cubicles open at one end like a corral—that's where they get the name. Courtyard in the middle with one water spigot and outhouse for 20 families. Later we were able to move into our own house, a little yellow-painted shotgun casita with indoor plumbing, but even then it was crowded, always crowded with the five of us kids plus Mama and Papa. Must be why I have such good memories of visiting my grandparents out here in brush country! All that clean air and water, all that space to run around.

By then, after years of landlessness, my grandparents had managed to buy a few acres from the rancher they worked for. And when they passed, they willed the land to the order of sisters I'm part of. The sisters don't do anything with it, but it was nice to have it stay in the family, so to speak. Then, a couple of years ago, when Seismar was about to open its first mine, our order was contacted by a broker wanting to lease the land. When we asked if he was interested in the mineral rights, he told us nah, there's nothing under there but caliche and clay. Well, not a year later the mining started, and we found ourselves in a situation where we were forced to lease the mineral rights. That landman had lied to us.

Forced?

Yes. What happened was, all the landowners around us were leasing their mineral rights to Seismar if they weren't selling off their land altogether. We were the only ones holding out, and it wasn't much acreage to begin with. And under current state regulations, if a certain percentage of a pool of landowners leases out their mineral rights, the rest are forced to lease too. The way the laws are written, we were not free to refuse.

So the order is getting mining royalties from Seismar, Joel says slowly.

That's right.

There is a moment of silence between them as Joel contemplates how directly he dares ask. So what do you do with the money?

She smiles again. Let's just say we use it for good works.

***

Headed out of the coastward-sloping sealands and back up toward the city again, they stop at a Buc-ees nestled in the armpit of a highway on-ramp. While Sister Soli runs to the restroom, Joel stands in the middle of the store's long rectangular space, in a place where Sister can't possibly miss him, feeling lost with notebook and pen in hand. What a waste of space, he thinks at first, before realizing the architectural design is intentional, as all design must be: it is a space meant to be filled with people. People in camo, shorts, and flip flops; people in t-shirts with funny slogans—*Check Meowt*, reads one, below a cool cat in sunglasses. An Indian family pulled by a white poodle on a leash. Rural youth with Skrillex undercuts and trans flag patches on their backpacks, some of whom will leave for the city and some who will stay. People passing through and people who live there. People to fill a perimeter lined with foam coolers stacked beneath taxidermied deer heads arranged to look like they are fighting antler to antler; with bagged road snacks weighing many pounds; with peanut butter fudge and Dippin' Dots, kolaches and tacos, piles of smoked meat and sausage, belts and belt buckles, pyramid displays of pickled okra and quail eggs. Monster soda fountains with 20 selections and a rainbow of flavor additives. It is amazing—*incredible*, in the sly double sense Sister had captured in her comments about the flows of money moving through the sealands of South Texas. Would I miss this at all? he wonders, imagining the collapse of civilization he has always assumed was imminent and inevitable.

Back in the car once more, he feels exhausted from hard listening and careful response, from shooting photos and taking notes. Beside him Sister chats on, but Joel's attention drifts. Out the window, lightning flickers within a gathering of thunderheads miles away, off in the distance some place where it may rain. He thinks of an interview he read not long before, with a clean tech capitalist interested in harnessing lightning power: a "lightning farmer," he called himself. A T. Boone Pickens kind of cat, a self-made West Texas entrepreneur interested more in opportunities to be taken, markets to be cornered, than in ecology as permanent economy. Anyway, who wanted permanent economy when you could have volatility, when you knew how to surf the booms and busts of the Pecos desert with the best of 'em? Heaven's Plenty: that was the name of his start up. This guy was a born-again too.

Apparently, previous attempts to harvest lightning had all proved ill-conceived. Apparently, thunderstorms were as powerful as atomic bombs, and strokes of lightning so hot they could melt sand into hollow glass channels where they struck the ground. Apparently, the intense heat, light, and voltage of a single stroke of lightning was so powerful it could—at least theoretically—re-engineer matter at the atomic level, scrambling electrons so as to instantaneously form and reform reality. A carrot into a unicycle: poof! Heat and light into electricity and possibly into dollars, just maybe, plz?

But all that heat and light had proved difficult to capture. Earlier schemes had attempted the obvious, constructing towers, industrial lightning rods essentially, which shunted energy away to a storage device. Yet the ax of Tlaloc had proved too wily and unpredictable to be channeled efficiently. Not only that, but by the time lightning struck ground there was little usable energy to be captured. You'd have to construct dozens of towers to power a few lightbulbs for a year.

What this guy was doing with his vast oil and gas wealth, then, was piloting a method for harvesting power in the clouds, before lightning touched ground. Cashing out his big coal for big renewables. He had engineered a special balloon for it, a drone you could launch during thunderstorms. He was also working with the UT Permian Basin Department of Meteorology to devise a program that could predict the formation of rare, especially powerful kinds of lightning, like the elusive positive lightning which seemed to strike out of the blue, forming not from the bottom of a thunderhead but from its positively-charged cloud top, traveling horizontally for long distances before striking the ground. Because this bolt traveled so far before flashing, it accumulated huge amounts of voltage. The trick was to collect not upon striking but right before. It wasn't guesswork, it was science. All it required for success was enough time and money.

Joel likes the eccentric ones. This guy, and the scientist from Japan everyone had been talking about a few years back, who had experimented with water and demonstrated that emotions could shape the fate of water molecules. Love and gratitude caused it to freeze in perfect formation. Anger and heavy metal music created distorted, asymmetrical flakes. There was the guy who had mailed him a letter at the *Volt* office the other week, about a device he'd invented that converted atmospheric pressure directly into electricity—no fuel at all! He'd taped that one above his desk at work. *I KNOW for a fact my machine does NOT violate any of the laws of physics and I Can prove that in Court !*

And then there was this node business. Moving tons of earth to uncover ancient moon rocks and distill their metals chemically, to process pure ores into the promise of carbon-free electrons. The dream of all work and no waste. Tlaloc's fertile rains without his killing floods.

Yeah, you couldn't make shit like that up. As Sister drives on still pointing and talking, he gathers it all in his head like a snowball, rolling and patting it into shape, into story.

Great Neodymium! Mining South Texas for the Strongest Magnet in the World

Posted by Joel Champlain (jchamp@thevolt.com) on June 3

The Texas boom economy is happening—again.

"It happened once already, last century, with Spindletop," says magnet magnate John Gelder, CEO of mining company Seismar. It's taken some journalistic finagling and a couple weeks of phone tag, but I'm finally inside the only operating rare earth mine in the United States. We're standing at the lip of an immense quarry scratched out of the sandy soil, peering down the sharp grade of its terraced walls.

"And then it happened again more recently with the fracking," Gelder continues. "Who'd have thought it could happen here a third time? Especially after all the complaints about fracking causing earthquakes. But it was because of the seismic faults exposed by those underground explosions that we found the nodes."

In what is becoming a major discovery for both science and industry, the nodes in question are terrestrial versions of the same metallic nuggets sought for decades by would-be plunderers of the open sea, chock full of concentrated rare earth metals, in particular neodymium. According to Steven Foster, chair of the Economic Geology department at UT Austin and head of the research team that broke news of the nodes back in 2013, these potato-shaped formations are leftovers from an earlier geologic era, deposited in striated bands as the inland ocean known as the Western Interior Seaway receded from what is now the South Texas coastal plains 65 million years ago, at the end of the Cretaceous period. "Many terrestrial heavy earth mines in fact began as hot springs or hydrothermal vents," states Foster from his UT lab. "That's true here too."

Just a couple years prior, Gelder was working as a foreman for a struggling natural gas production company, trying to cash in on the death rattles of the fracking boom. A rock collector with a BA in Earth Science, he kept noticing the volcanic-black eggs that occasionally shot up the wellhead along with the briny wastewater, particularly after they'd been blasting near an active fault line.

"I took it to a geologist friend in Austin, and he discovered it was 15% neodymium, 5% dysprosium, 5% a bunch of other stuff. We're talking about the raw materials for the strongest magnets in the world. The stuff that's going to get us off fossil fuels once and for all."

One month later, Gelder had divested himself of the hunt for natural gas and formed Seismar, a start up mining company. He applied to the Texas Railroad Commission for a permit to open the first domestic rare earth mine since the one in Flatlake, Nevada, which closed in 2010 after a devastating leak of radioactive wastewater. And while he waited for his permit, he began quietly buying acreage all over South Texas, anticipating that once the node news hit, a wave of exploration, prospecting, and permit applications would crash over the region like a new interior seaway made of money.

He has not been mistaken.

But Gelder and Seismar have the advantage of having gotten there first. Modeling itself after other large-scale mining operators in China and Brazil, Seismar is vertically integrating mining, processing, and refining at its first site outside George West, halfway between San Antonio and Corpus Christi. They plan a similar operation for the Mud Creek site on San Antonio's far Northside, right inside city limits. There, the city owns land once used as an open-pit limestone quarry, and which according to UT's Foster also contains "the single largest deposit of rare earth nodules in the Western Hemisphere."

With the land already zoned for mining and the mining permit secured from the Texas Railroad Commission, the only hurdle remaining is to persuade City Council to lease its mineral rights to Seismar at the Mud Creek site. And from where the city sits, that prospect looks pretty tasty: in exchange for the leasing agreement—the city would maintain ownership of the land and all surface rights—Seismar is promising to direct 25% of revenues from its Mud Creek operation to the city's transition budget.

"Look, we started out a local company, and even though this thing is about to blow up in a global way, we want to give back to the community," Gelder tells me, eyes wide and earnest as an anime schoolgirl. "It's very important our strategy be local and regional first. Already the industry is seeing a tremendous level of regional cooperation and integration with the opening of the VientoSol megafarm west of San Antonio. Pretty soon one of those farms'll be outside every major metropolitan area. And then Dallas won that factory to make the magnets and turbines and panels and batteries that'll supply the farms. And to make *that* stuff, they're going to need a supply of metals that is low-cost, plentiful, and ideally local—right? Right. So where are they gonna get them?"

It sure ain't China or Brazil, says the grin on his face.

Heavy Metal

Nestled together toward the bottom of the periodic table, the rare earths are a family of 15 moderately heavy elements known as "the lanthanides," with scandium and yttrium thrown in for good measure. Contrary to their name, rare earth metals are not uncommon—in fact, they're about as common as copper. But ever the cosmic trickster, God and his crew of rainbow unicorns pranced about the earth's surface sprinkling them like glitter and binding them with other ores and sediments instead of concentrating them in pure veins for our convenience. Necessary for the strong, tiny magnets of our hard drives and headphones, rare earths are ubiquitous in consumer electronics. Such characteristics have made them both lustrously attractive and notoriously uneconomic to mine.

Five rare earth metals in particular—dysprosium, terbium, europium, yttrium, and neodymium—are crucial to the renewable energy technologies that will make or break transition. These elements strengthen the permanent magnets used in wind turbines, produce the chemical cocktails that fill energy efficient lightbulbs, and make possible the battery storage necessary to make electric vehicles and solar panels viable. Any industrial scaling up of renewable infrastructure will require a scaling up of rare earth mining too, on the order of hundreds of times the current rates of production, according to estimates provided by the Transition Technology Working Group.

Until the recent availability of federal loan guarantees for domestic sources of rare earths, only one mine has operated in the United States, in the Great Basin Desert town of Flatlake, Nevada. The main source of rare earths domestically and globally from the 1940s until the 1990s, the Flatlake mine closed in 2010 due to a massive leakage of radioactive wastewater from its tailing ponds onto the desert floor, not far from where the Carson, Walker, and Truckee feed into the Humboldt River.

The case of Flatlake calls attention to the if-it's-too-good-to-be-true dimensions of rare earth mining. As with other extractive industries, fracking for natural gas most recently, rare earth mining risks contamination of water, soil, and air both in the extraction and refining phases, largely from the naturally occurring radioactive residue (usually thorium) excavated alongside desirable metals, and from the toxic acids required to separate specific elements from surrounding ore. According to the Industrial Ecology Research Institute at the University of California Los Angeles, every ton of refined rare earths—that's five megawatts of electricity, or 1,000 homes at industrial-sized power demand—creates a one-ton doppelgänger of radioactive tailings and a swimming pool full of acidic wastewater.

Oh, and did I mention that the Mud Creek site lies over the most sensitive recharge zone of the aquifer that supplies San Antonio's drinking water?

The United Rare Earth Association website is far more sanguine about such prospects. Radioactivity can be diluted with lime, which can be baked into seawalls; thorium can also be recovered to burn in the transition tech nukes of the future. It's all about knowing how to turn externality into opportunity.

Potato Power

Before South Texas burst onto the neodymium scene, the political and economic scarcity of rare earths (if not their actual scarcity) meant the industry was beginning to set its sights on syfy woowoo like the mining of asteroid belts and moon rocks. Slightly more probably, mining companies had begun reviving abandoned plans to harvest metals from deep sea hydrothermal vents; or, more likely, to trawl the seabed for potato-shaped nodules of manganese and other metals ("polymetallic concretions," as scientists have described these geologic spuds). Searching for alternatives to Chinese exports, Japanese researchers back in 2005 discovered vast deposits of polymetallic nodes on the seafloor of the Pacific with such high concentrations of rare earth metals that half a square mile of deposits could meet a fifth of the world's demand.

Contractors from around the world rushed the International Seabed Authority, global regulator of seabed mining, for permits to trawl remotely operated vehicles—sea drones—across the bottom of the ocean, sampling for mineral content. Anxious for flat screens and defense tech as much as for wind turbines, the world prepared for another round of sea vacuums, as well as another round of global debates over the long-term impacts on ocean life of sucking up large swaths of the sea floor and spitting them back out again as sediment. As reported in the *New Zealand Herald*, where debates over the effects of seabed mining for ironsand have been ongoing for several years, "it is accepted by all sides that seabed mining destroys every living thing in its immediate path."

A Harvest of Lightning

So we end where I began—standing outside the Seismar mine, but this time with Sister Soledad Soliz, San Antonio's famous eco-nun. Before I received clearance to tour the inside of the mine, Sister took me to the Sealands to linger outside the metal cattle gates of the Seismar property as she schooled me on thermodynamics.

"You heard of the *perpetuum mobile*?" she wants to know. It's Latin, I know that much, so it must be a Catholic thing? Or something to hang over a baby's crib to encourage contemplation on the imponderable mysteries of the eternal?

But no, she laughs. "It means 'perpetual motion.' Since antiquity, humans have dreamed of inventing a machine that runs forever—a device that creates more energy than it uses, or that runs on problem-free energy inputs in infinite supply."

Ah, okay. Well, I was close.

If you Google it you'll see a long list of attempts: from Bhaskara's wheel in 12th century India to the Crookes Radiometer—the famous diamond-shaped metal vanes that whirl like magic inside the vacuum of a glass bulb when exposed to light—to the free-energy devices of today, which purport to produce rotary motion by "unwinding the curl" of electromagnetic fields. Yet for those who quested after a free, unlimited source of energy for producing frictionless motion, in the end "only their confidence was unlimited," in the words of one would-be inventor.

As Sister reminds me, Rudolph Clausius's second law of thermodynamics means that work, the conversion of energy into force and motion, can never be 100% efficient; in other words, the usable energy of a system tends toward zero over time. As energy becomes work, as a system transforms fuel into the movement of electrons, the inevitable result is waste—heat, ash, emissions—until nothing useable remains to convert into work. Our air conditioning units, for instance, make the insides of our homes cooler, but their operation increases the overall waste heat of the system. What entropy means is that ours is a universe in which tightly organized systems tend toward disorganization—in which there is no free *lonche*.

None of that stopped the architects of the industrial revolution from trying to wrest human economic production from Clausius's gloomy predictions. If only we could discover a limitless energy source or invent an efficient-enough machine, we might realize our dreams of an escape from entropy at last. But as our late industrial society now careens into full-on collision with ecological limits, you'd think we'd be making our peace with Clausius, instead of chasing the dream of overriding these limits for a few decades longer—by plucking lightning out of the clouds, or making a carbon-free gasoline out of engineered microbes, or using thorium to create a nuclear fire hot enough to consume its own radioactivity.

Or, maybe, mining for potatoes of magnetic ore in the brush country of South Texas, to power the wind turbines and solar batteries of an all-renewable future?

"Do they really think this will last?" Sister asks, gesticulating at the mine behind us. "Do they think this will still be here in 20 or even 15 years? Sooner or later, supply will tap out and it'll become uneconomical to mine. I'll tell you what'll still be here, though—a bunch of toxic rocks and poisoned aquifers and unemployed miners."

Later I pose Sister's same questions to Gelder. What about low-level radioactivity? What about Flatlake, what about the porosity of the aquifer geology at the Mud Creek site outside San Antonio, where his company wants to expand?

"I'm sure we'll have something figured out by then," Gelder tells me, squinting out across his quarry, its terraces stairstepping down thousands of feet through ancient clays, looking for all the world like an inverted Pyramid of the Sun.

CHAPTER THREE
A Visit, an Interlude 1

Sometimes, in the middle of it, their eyes will roll open, not intentionally but it just happens that way. Back when it was newer and scarier, they would sometimes pause and sit up, legs wrapped around one another, and simply hug and hug. Or sit facing one another, not moving, looking into each other's eyes. Completely awake, completely present. Sometimes she will blanket his body like one soldier taking a bullet for another, the sacrificial gesture of a best friend, rocking gently against him. Her hair falls like a veil of golden filament around his face, like a rain of shooting stars, dusting the pillow beneath him.

Sometimes he will cover her eyes with one hand, reading the shape of her lips. He can tell when she is studious, when she is working, when she feels pleasure. Sometimes they will both spread arms and interlace fingers, pressing mouth to mouth without kissing, passing the same breath back and forth. Once they stood at the edge together for minutes and minutes, clasped tight without moving at all, summoning an energy that built and built between them like an emergency but still they didn't fall. When it could not get any bigger it became a golden ball of light suspended between them, which they held first with their minds and then with breathing careful and focused as long distance running, until finally they could venture to pass it between them at the waist, exchanging it slowly back and forth across a single field. On her laptop next to the bed she'd loaded some relaxation videos on YouTube—she liked to fall asleep to one hour loops of rainfall or Amazonian birds—and when the rain video ended and the next one began, it was the uterine, otherworldly shrieks of Baleen whales that enveloped them as the orb of golden light passed between their bodies.

Sometimes that summer, in the grey of earliest Monday before he drives back to the city in time for his first committee or constituent meeting of the week, when she stands peering out the trailer's tiny window holding shirt to breasts as though she had to worry about being seen out there in the sealands, sometimes he will approach from behind to sweep her hair aside and kiss the raw exposure of her neck. With the other hand he will cup the slope of her belly, pulling her backwards against him. Her head rolling aside to receive him, he will feel the hummingbird flutter of her pulse beneath his lips. Later that afternoon they will sit together on the trailer's asthmatic wooden stoop, gazing out across the chalky scrubland, past the fenced warnings enclosing the mine. He'll take her hand in his. He could pick her hands out of a lineup, he thinks. The shape and feel of them. He presses one to his lips when they stand, both reluctant for him to drive back to the city. Next Friday, though?

Next Friday.

CHAPTER FOUR
Lali Takes the Job

Many months later, on the car ride back to where Lali left her bike after the first time hanging out at Joel's apartment—a desperate unspoken something clinging to the space between them, in the interstices between dialogue balloons—*don't go don't go don't go*—Joel would remind Lali they had met the night of the Extractivism Film Festival. Had they? She wouldn't remember until then, with something bordering on incredulity, because at that point he'd been just a friendly someone standing conveniently nearby when she wanted to know whether the coffee was free or cost money. She didn't have any, that was why she had asked. But she had wanted coffee, the bitter cinnamon of whatever fair trade bean they brewed at La Alianza, cut with fatty milk and sugar brown like honey.

I think it's by donation, said the man standing smiling near the concessions counter where the coffee dripped and sizzled like bacon popping in a pan.

That September was the time of no money and no job, after she had finished her dissertation and graduated but before she knew what would come next, and before the state of Texas approved their application for food stamps. Throughout that first-summer-back there had been intermittent power outages, too, which had startled and unsettled them. It was the time of no money and no job and nothing anyone wanted to eat in the house, and when the city people and Seismar began to shop

Mud Creek around town, Lali barely noticed. She was too busy trying to scrape together bus fare so she and Nena could at least get out of the house during the day, Nena clinging to her neck in the heat and wailing *ma-ma-ma!* on the bus as she thrust her hands down the front of Lali's shirt and rooted around for a treat. Lali ducking her head to avoid eyes cutting sideways in disapproval at the sight of a two-year-old child demanding pecho. Nena, shhh. When we get home, okay?

It was a time when they could only wait, limbs slingshot cocked like starting-line runners, for what would come next. She thought she'd thought of everything before they left California, but she had overestimated her ability to anticipate and predict. The plan had been to squirrel away enough to carry them through the fall push of the academic job search. She'd know by the following spring if she'd gotten anything; if not, she'd get a local job and play again next year. Two years was all she'd give it. If she crapped out at least she'd be home. But it was only September and already the money was gone.

One afternoon in late September, in the enchilada-red library where she would go to draft job letter after job letter, sixty tailored versions of the same template by the time she was done, sixty applications and a thousand tiny edits—like milking mice, her father once commented as she stood at the kitchen counter shelling pecans with a toothpick to fill the empty time between meals, starving but refusing to eat—one September afternoon in the library, she saw a flyer for a film festival tacked to the community bulletin board. Beside it was a job ad. *EXTRACTIVIST CINEMA!* said the flyer on the left. *TRANSITION JUSTICE ORGANIZER NEEDED*, said the flyer on the right. *Here in San Antonio we have been in the belly of the dirty energy beast. Now we are promised a transition away from dirty energy—but at what cost for our communities? Who benefits, who loses, and who decides??*

Looking around to see if anyone was watching, Lali untacked the job ad from the corkboard, folding it up to slide into her back pocket. Then, thinking twice, she untacked the other flyer and took it too.

***

The day of the film festival at La Alianza—a flat, gray Saturday in early October, Hector at work—Lali had taken Nena to the little park nearest their duplex to play. Neither hot nor cold, the changing season was like a holding of breath, an uncertainty or ambivalence. She had tagged behind Nena as the toddler wove her way through picnic tables, collecting pecans shaken free from the trees overhead, until a stray dog came bounding through the park, running straight at them. Scooping up Nena, Lali had scrambled for higher ground, panting as she ran with child squirming in her arms. Stray animals running loose were nothing unusual, but watching this one from the empty basketball court above the park gave Lali a strange feeling. She watched its loping stride, alternately uncoordinated and then intent, focused, heatseeking. The dog would circle lazily around the trashcans, running nowhere in particular, before barreling its way toward a group of kids skateboarding on the tennis courts or a family decorating a picnic table for a birthday party.

Something not right about it, something off or dangerous. Back at home, she had deliberated on whether or not she should call the city's animal control line. All around town when she came back home were billboards of an abuelita clutching a Chihuahua beneath one arm, with the other shaking a finger at gente for their loose dog-running ways and their unspayed, spraying cats. *Estás loco si no spay/neuter!* she scolded. The city had started the campaign at the urging of the animal welfare people, who had just succeeded in shutting down the city's catch-and-kill policy, and with it the crematory in Brackenridge Park. But in all likelihood the dog would be put down if she called. On the other hand, judging from its erratic behavior, the dog's days were numbered even if she didn't call. Even so, the way it had charged them—a child could get mauled, as they nearly had. Phone in hand, she stood on the porch of their upstairs duplex for a few minutes longer, gazing out over the vacant lot across the street. Sky still that flat and indeterminate October grey. On either side of the lot were once-dilapidated wood frame houses in a metamorphosis of restoration by young architects and lawyers; house by house the wave advanced down their street, headed for the homes of those who had long lived there. A block in transition before their eyes. Finally she turned away to dial the city, then went inside to microwave a bowl of instant oatmeal. She thought about what they should do with the rest of their afternoon, and remembered the flyers still folded in the pocket of her yet-to-be-washed pants.

***

What made her take the flyers—it wasn't only that she needed a job fast, but also that she'd felt a political restlessness stir. Just before California, she'd quit a part-time gig collecting signatures for a big green lobbying group to volunteer full time for a grassroots campaign to halt a sprawling fuel tank farm, proposed for an East Austin neighborhood on the banks of the Colorado. And there, collecting signatures again but in such a different way—door-to-door, intimate, real—she'd felt something shift and awaken in her, some new understanding about the complex political interweaving of oil and water and money and color, some new rootedness in place or rightness, like falling in love or coming home. But by then it was too late; she and Hector were on their way out the door. Academia had allowed her to chase after that nascent understanding by reading and writing about the politics of water, but it had also interrupted something, making its lived enactment impossible.

Now it was back, her urgency not simply to understand and explain but to act, like a feeling she'd been cooped up inside the house for too long. For a while she'd hung out with some anarchist kids who gathered Sundays at a slanting, paint-peeling house to pick through dumpster scores, chopping and cooking what was salvageable and hauling it in wagons to the park to give away. She had gone to a house show benefit with Nena: bring canned vegetarian food to donate, get in free to see the Ill Eaglez. Hector couldn't go because his shift started so early in the morning, but Lali dressed Nena in a white t-shirt and black pants, que punkera.

That was the night she met Chela, working the door in black T and knee-length cutoffs held up with rainbow suspenders, her long dark hair spilling over her shoulders. Lopsided smile and crowded front teeth. Hey, thanks, she had beamed when Lali handed over her plastic bag filled with evaporated milk—the only thing extra they had to give away. WIC always gave you too much milk. Later Chela had strolled over to where Lali sat on the grass in the front yard watching Nena, arms clasped around knees, and she'd stretched out her hand for Lali to shake, beer in her other hand.

Hey, thanks for bringing some cans. She hauled Lali to standing. These boys, she sneered, surveying the lawn, tipping the bottle to her mouth to swallow. Most of them didn't even bring any canned food to donate, just came to get trashed and mosh. It's called *Food* Not Bombs, assholes.

Right? she said, grinning when Lali laughed.

She was glad Lali donated, glad Lali came, glad she had come back to town. Together they could figure out a way to make Food Not Bombs political again, instead of about getting shitfaced! She was little bit drunk herself but she was happy. She had a round face, a young face, with black almond eyes—younger than Lali by a decade, looking just out of her teens. She was braless beneath her black sleeveless shirt, with fuzzy pits and fuzzy legs above skater shoes. Rainbow striping tattooed on her forearm and plug earrings in each lobe. After a moment her girlfriend joined them, a slender woman around Lali's age with skin the color of milky coffee. She wore a men's embroidered guayabera and circular wire rims atop a hawk nose; a fall of loose dark curls swept to one side of her face, revealing the shaved underside of her head and a curly-cue rat tail at the nape of her neck.

There they were again at the film festival, Chela and Naima: Lali can't make out any faces in the dark of Alianza's upstairs performance space, but when the lights come up at the conclusion of the final film—about the Kichwa's decades-long fight against ConocoPhillips, a case study she'd come across in her dissertation research—everyone grabs a chair and intuitively scoots it into a circle, and there across its diameter sit two familiar faces. Lali waves, they wave back.

Lali remembers meetings like that from her time in Austin, before she and Hector left Tejas for California—back when she was Chela's age, fresh-faced and frisky and unencumbered by the anxieties of grad school and parenthood. Strategy meetings to plan council visits or public actions, meetings in that same shape of chairs in a circle. But this is the first time she has tried to participate in any kind of public sphere and respond to Nena simultaneously, dismayed by how difficult the task, how precious the privilege of unbroken attention. Sitting outside the large circle of chairs, she half listens as Nena squirms off her lap and runs away, running back to slap her hand on Lali's chest, impatient. *Mamis? Mamis!* she demands, eliciting laughter from those sitting nearby. Someone kindhearted but clueless brings Nena paper and markers, not understanding that she is just too little to focus on anything except what she wants moment to moment. What she wants is to push the buttons to make the elevator door open. She wants to walk toward the open flight of cement stairs which promise to twist an eager young child's neck upon descent.

And between distractions, like glimpsing a suggestion of something solid behind a slatted fence as one passes—brain filling in the blanks where the eyes can't see straight on—in between, Lali hears the circle talking about the difficult position the potatoes put them in. Transition was necessary, but *how* it happened mattered as much as *whether* it happened, and the potatoes were definitely shady. Wait—what? Not really potatoes—though potatoes would be amazing right now, she thinks, fried with onion and jalapeño and seasoned salt—she has only the microwaved instant oatmeal in her stomach, oatmeal and coffee. But no, they meant minerals and metals discovered beneath the city, concentrated inside rocks that *looked* like potatoes. It was a new project the city was about to roll out as part of their transition plan, on the far Northside of the city. They were holding public meetings about it, and then there would be a vote. Soon. Soonish. A vote on whether the city should mine? No, on mineral rights, whether the city should lease them to some mining company. Sizemart? Seismar. The company had approached the city people saying they'd already identified the location and extent of the mineral deposits, and the city had commissioned an economic feasibility study and now was holding hearings—but not to ask the people if they should proceed. As always, the hearings were more to tell the people that they'd already decided to proceed; in fact, they'd already signed a preliminary agreement with Seismar.

But history showed there would be problems. Of course—it was like any of the cases she'd read about, the long-running legal battle between the Kichwa and ConocoPhillips over contamination of the Amazon, or the cancerous legacy of uranium mining in the Navajo nation, or an abandoned gold mine in Colorado that poured three million gallons of contaminated wastewater into the Animas River. That must have been what the speeches on the radio were about, then. A few months and twenty degrees hotter ago, she had flipped to NPR right before pulling into their driveway, and she'd overheard a snippet from a live public forum—that's what it sounded like from the hollow acoustics, live and local, recorded in a school cafeteria or church hall—in which a woman inveighed with voice high and quavering against the love of money as the root of all evil. It had sounded important, but at the time Lali lacked capacity to pay much attention: her head was back in the crowded, unhappy office of the Texas Health and Human Services, where she'd spent all morning and afternoon fighting with the state over denied food stamp benefits. Now she realizes what those hearings were about, now she knows. As someone stands at the back of the room filming the meeting, the circle buzzes with talk about who will write an op-ed and who will speak before the city people, who will make the signs and what should be on them. They talk about the rallies that will be required before the vote. *We need to pack council chambers*, someone cries, vehement. *It's the only way they're gonna listen.* She remembers that energy, that voice of conviction from an earlier time, before the qualifications of grad school or the ambiguities of parenthood. That urgent tone, stirring something abandoned or interrupted in her, so different from the caution and hesitation of academic speech, trying to account in advance for all complexity and anticipate all counterargument. There are Chela and Naima, listening and nodding; there is the man from the coffee machine, sitting to the left of Alianza's director. Something he says, something about the way he says it. When he speaks, his words seem to carry weight. Has he written something, or studied it? People ask him questions like he knows something.

When the meeting finally ends, they dismember the circle and stack the chairs, then stand around chatting in clusters. Chela spots Lali and walks over with Naima and Alianza's director, regally wrapped in her bright rebozo—Victoria was her name, Mama Vee. First unabashed Brown lesbian feminist in the San Antonio public eye. They've never met, but Mama Vee takes both of Lali's hands in hers and says: So glad to hear you've come back to San Anto. Too many of us leave for California and never come back. And when Lali mentions her application to the organizer position at El Centro and their tentative offer, Chela grabs her in an enormous hug and swings her around.

No shit! she whoops. That's where I work! They said you'd applied, and I was hoping you would get it.

Back on her feet, Lali grins back dizzily—but in the same moment sees, peripherally, Naima exchange glances with Mama Vee like they know something. Skeptical or suspicious. What did it mean?

Research Notas 2:
San Antonio is a Colonial City

I know I opened this series of notes with a poem—it rolled out of me the day we attended the Seismar hearing at Development Services, inspired (if that's the right word) by the epigraph engraved on the front steps of the building—but it seemed a fitting way to break in a fresh notebook. What I really want to do, though, is sketch out a preliminary understanding of San Antonio's political ecology, the political ecology of home, synthesizing fragments of analysis from various sources to refract the present moment through the light of the past. Six theses on San Antonio de Padua: a unifying theory, to the best of my ability. If we're ever going to move from reaction to real action, we first need an argument about how it all works, an analysis that ties everything together. If we can get the analysis right, surely we can figure out which switch to throw to make the thing jump tracks—creating some new possibility, some outcome other than what's come before. That's my hope, anyway.

***

Some of the best early political analysis of the city can be found in an anthology called, simply, *The Politics of San Antonio* (1983). In this volume, Brischetto, Cotrell, and Stevens point out the central contradiction of San Antonio's political life: that although it has "long been a Mexican city … Anglo political and economic domination has been a settled fact since 1847."[1] But the origins

---

[1] Robert Brischetto, Charles L. Cottrell, and R. Michael Stevens, "Conflict and Change

of this entrenched reality are far older, and lie in the city's colonial history, with its complex and often violent encuentros
between Native, Spanish, Mexican, Tejano, Black, and Anglo
communities.

A Spanish colonial outpost established in 1718 as bulwark
against French imperial claims to the East, San Antonio began as a string of five missions built along the San Antonio
River—Espada, San Juan, San José, Concepción, and San
Antonio de Valero, aka the Alamo—with the forced labor of
local Indigenous communities. By the time General Domingo
Terán de los Rios wrote the 1691 diary entry memorialized on
the steps of Development Services, the San Antonio River valley had been a site of human settlement since for over 11,000
years, according to carbon dating of flint projectiles and debris
mounds unearthed along the riverbanks. As environmental his-
torian Char Miller writes, Native peoples "migrated between
semi-permanent settlements situated along the spring line," as
James F. Petersen calls the group of artesian springs exposed
along the 200-mile length of the Balcones Escarpment, an up-
shearing of limestone formed millions of years ago in a seismic
event and which now stairsteps down from the lower part of
the Great Plains to Texas's Coastal Plain.[2]

The river basin's two major springs in particular—one at its

---

in the Political Culture of San Antonio in the 1970s," in *The Politics of San Antonio,* ed.
David R. Johnson, John A. Booth, and Richard J. Harris (Lincoln: University of Nebraska
Press, 1983), 75.

[2] Char Miller, "Urban Nature: An Introduction," in *On the Border: An Environmental History of San Antonio,* ed. Char Miller (San Antonio: Trinity University Press, 2005), 4. In the
same collection see also James F. Petersen, "San Antonio: An Environmental Crossroads
on the Texas Spring Line."

headwaters on what is now the University of Incarnate Word campus, the other at what is now San Pedro Park—were hubs of ceremony for many of the hundreds of Native bands, clans, and nations that originally inhabited South Texas and Northern Mexico on either side of the Rio Grande. Mary Ann Noonan Guerra notes that "as recently as 1924," the Ponca "stopped at this site en route from Oklahoma to northern Mexico to gather peyote used in religious rites."[3] Members of the Miakan/Garza band similarly maintain that these two springs constitute sacred sites along a ceremonial route that for millennia have traversed the four fountain springs of Central/South Texas on the way to the Paxe (peyote) medicine gardens of South Texas.[4] According to Fray Damián Massanet, a Franciscan priest on a dual missionary-military expedition with General Terán, the original name of the San Antonio River was "Yanaguana," as given to him in the language of a people camping there who called themselves "Payaya."[5] But as pointed out by Juan Mancias, Tribal Chairman of the Carrizo/Comecrudo Tribe of Texas, the name recorded in Massanet's expedition diary and handed down over five centuries was linguistically inaccurate. What the Spanish heard as "Yanaguana" was "Ya Gna Wena," pronounced "yah gah nah wena" and meaning "place where I rest." And what they heard as "Payaya" was "payau'p," meaning wolf or wild—a word that, in Mancias's native dialect Hokom,

---

[3] Mary Ann Noonan Guerra, The San Antonio River (San Antonio: The Alamo Press), 40.

[4] Indigenous Cultures Institute, "Sacred Sites," last accessed August 25, 2020, https://www.indigenouscultures.org/sacred-sites_

[5] Guerra, 8. "I named this place San Antonio de Padua because it was his day," Fray Massanet wrote on June 13, 1691. "In the language of the Indians it is called Yanaguana."

named the river (*Ahamatau Payau'p*) as well as the people who rested there seasonally and ceremonially.[6] The Tap Pilam Coahuiltecan Nation—descendants of the autonomous bands and clans of South Texas/Northern Mexico—similarly identify "Yanaguana" as a Pajalat name meaning "land of spirit waters," referring not to the river itself but to a more generalized region or spirit of place.[7] Though the city has appropriated the name to mean the river narrowly—as in Yanaguana Cruises, Inc.—the original usage seems to carry a much wider meaning, suggesting a water- or land-based sense of place that grounds culture, identity, lifeways, and knowledge.

Just as it was for its original peoples, the San Antonio River soon became a frequent place of rest for the Spanish *entradas* as they sought to cement claims on Tejas, turning San Antonio into a "stronghold of Spanish occupation."[8] And as they colonized the region, the Spanish would erase many of the linguistic and cultural differences distinguishing the over 200 Native bands they encountered there, lumping them into a homogeneous grouping they called "Coahuiltecos," after a regional lingua franca that developed post-contact.[9] Though

---

[6] Juan Mancias (Carrizo/Comecrudo Tribe of Texas), personal communication, 2020. See also Marissa Muñoz's interview with Mancias in "River as Lifeblood, River as Border: The Irreconcilable Discrepancies of Colonial Occupation from/with/on/of the Frontera," in *Indigenous and Decolonizing Studies in Education: Mapping the Long View*, ed. Linda Tuhwai Smith, Eve Tuck, and K. Wayne Yang (New York: Routledge, 2018).

[7] Karla Aguilar (Tap Pilam Coahuiltecan Nation), personal communication to Greg Harman, 2019.

[8] Guerra, 57.

[9] Alston V. Thoms, "Reassessing Cultural Extinction: Change and Survival at Mission San Juan Capistrano, Texas," ed. Alston V. Thoms (College Station: Texas A&M University, 2001), 22. As Thoms writes, "With the coming of the Europeans and the onset of the

contemporary descendants of South Texas's original bands and kinship networks have come to adopt "Coahuiltecan" as a term of self-identification, the name refers not to a single tribe or language group but a "geographically defined designation widely used for linguistically and ethnically diverse bands of hunter-gatherers who inhabited Coahuila and other states in northeast Mexico as well as south Texas."[10]

Missionization would further invisibilize Native presence in South Texas. Decimated by European disease and squeezed off traditional hunting and gathering grounds by Spanish incursions and Apache migration—the latter themselves displaced by southward-moving Comanches—remnants of the Payaya, Pajalat, Xarame, Paguame, Pakawan, Hierbipiame, Tilijae, Borrado, and others entered the missions for their own survival.[11] There the colonial project mashed and masticated them up with peoples displaced from all over Coahuila, Chihuahua, and Tejas, producing the "indio" as generic category and

---

Spanish Colonial era ... Coahuilteco appears to have become a lingua franca for the region. In other words, the fact that many people spoke Coahuilteco dialects in the seventeenth and eighteenth centuries probably tells us more about Spanish Colonial history and the missionization process than it does about pre-Columbian ethnic and cultural affiliation."

[10] Thoms, xv.

[11] It is important to point out, however, that many Texas Native people did not enter the missions, and those who did routinely fled, chased by runaway patrols and requiring continuous recruitment to maintain a pool of Native labor at the missions (Thoms, 35). Mancias likewise recalls tribal stories passed down about "indios patas rajadas," Indians with cut feet, suggesting the violence inflicted by Spanish missionaries on runaways. According to Mancias, North Texas cave paintings give visual evidence of these stories, displaying a tall figure with cross emblazoned on the chest and sword in hand standing over smaller figures with bleeding feet.

subjugated caste. And as "los indios" took on the Catholic faith and Spanish surnames of their padres and patrones, they became in the process "Mexican" and, later, "Hispanic" or "Latino."[12]

Following Mexican independence from Spain, a second colonial process would occur as an influx of Anglo settlers arrived from the East, shoehorning the newly formed and largely Indigenous-descended nation to the South from its foothold in the region. As with Spain, as with México, these settlers would set themselves up to govern, looking to expand the reach of agricultural economies based on African slave labor against a Mexican government which had recently barred it. And being a sparsely populated outpost of far-northern Mexico, San Antonio found itself precariously positioned. Distrito Federal with its eagle and snake could hold it only loosely in its talons. I can't get into the Alamo and all that, which cultural anthropologist Richard R. Flores calls the "master symbol" of the modern racial order emerging in the late 19th century—not to mention the site of slave auctions. Can't get into the mythic tale of the victory of Santa Ana, which for generations became the internalized shame of school children the color of the land: those valiant but helpless scrappy freedom-seeking Texians slaughtered as they slept by Mexicans too cowardly to wait until they woke. Can't get into the Treaty of Guadalupe Hidalgo that ceded half of Mexico's northern territories to the U.S., whose violation displaced Mexican families from lands either granted or ancestral, leaving a bleeding gash at the Rio

---

[12] John P. Schmal, "Indigenous Coahuila de Zaragoza," last updated October 17, 2017, http://www.somosprimos.com/schmal/indigrootsmex.htm

Bravo instead of the Rio Nueces. *Una herida abierta*, Gloria Anzaldúa has called it, an open wound.[13] "Multiply-occupied space of the trans-Nueces," Cherokee scholar Kirby Brown has called it, referring to the many layers of colonial rule layered over Indigenous land—Spanish, Mexican, Anglo.[14] Mission City; Military City, USA; River City; Alamo City, we call it today. San Antonio is a city of "master symbols" that reproduce a mythic retelling of the city's deep colonial history more than they illuminate its complicated encuentros.[15] And perhaps that's all that needs mention for now, except:

On the river trails in Brackenridge Park, named for the banker philanthropist who first harnessed the spring-fed head-waters of the San Antonio River for municipal waterworks, the Junior League has sponsored an informational sign depicting brown-skinned Indians frolicking on the river. The sign reads, in part: *Native Americans camped here near the headwaters of the San Antonio River for thousands of years before Spaniards established a permanent settlement here. The area's abundant water sustained a rich array of vegetation and wildlife and provided a cool retreat.*

It's an acknowledgment, of sorts. Still, it is difficult to access stories of what it was like here 500 years ago that have not also internalized the master symbols, or which present pre-colonial history from the perspective of its survivors, as something more

---

[13] Gloría E. Anzaldúa. *Borderlands/La Frontera: The New Mestiza* (San Francisco: Aunt Lute Books, 1987), 25.

[14] Kirby Brown, "Historical Recovery, Colonial Mimicry, and Thoughts on Disappearing Indians in Elena Zamora O'Shea's *El Mesquite*," *Nakum* 1, no. 1 (December 2010): 31.

[15] Richard R. Flores, "The Alamo: Myth, Public History, and the Politics of Inclusion," *Radical History Review* 77 (Spring 2000): 101.

variegated than that static and monolithic "thousands of years." They exist, these stories, they survive, some in their original languages—but they have been submerged, swallowed up within larger stories that remain the first and last word to this day.

It's often been pointed out that the city's patron saint is the saint of lost things. But perhaps these lost things are simply hidden in plain view—our very names and faces and tongues.

CHAPTER FIVE
A Visit, an Interlude 2

All these plays were pretty much the same. It was like getting stationed, Magdalena imagined, for the men living in boxcar housing and for the wave of women who washed up behind them. Like a war zone that way. Landing on the shores of these arid coastal plains like landing on the moon, working women followed the men who followed the trucks like support services—but then, so too were the bodies of the men. Whether male or female or some other gender, their bodies were instruments of service, like the cranes and backhoes and earthmovers employed in their exploratory scrape, interpreting layers of rock into the abstraction of data, maps of topography and lithography and keystrokes telegraphing a tally of projected economic impact. It was some kind of mania turning the turbines, driving the inflation and dysfunction of markets as much as love. A priapic dream of eternal expansion, up and up and up forever, that had you chasing mirages of water in the desert. Desert in the water. This time it would be different. This time it would last forever. That's not to say she was above chasing the crumbs dropped along the way, a forest trail spelling out the recipe for survival. Obviously.

All plays were like that. Still, she had more mobility than the men. She had figured out a way to come and go with the tides, working for a few months at a time and moving on when the work evaporated, living off her savings. Magdalena had planned it so that she had to work only eight months out of the year. The men, they were stuck in place once they arrived—in the camps or in towns abandoned once mania swung into depression and the companies pulled out after getting their rocks off, sometimes overnight. Stuck in job sites, stuck in motel rooms or encampments or RV trailers, with nowhere to work but the local DQ, which paid only $8 an hour again instead of $15. Nobody wanted them after the companies left.

You did have to be careful. Not saying you didn't. One of her first times working, not here but in the mines of central Oklahoma, a hard-hatted digger had straight up propositioned her one evening outside a local grocery, where she stood reorganizing her bags so that she could carry them back to her car in a single trip. Help you with those? he'd asked—not even because he knew how she made her living either, though maybe he sensed it. Definitely not because she approached him. This was just because he could, because he was used to an easygoing universe where the scarcity of familiar faces meant why not. With a friendly smile he had commented on the weather, the break in the heat they'd enjoyed for the past few days, and then he'd drawled: Wanna kick it with me in my trailer? So confident it wasn't even alarming—almost.

It had made her smile—almost. He wasn't bad looking. But Magdalena had to decline.

You sure? he had the nerve to ask.

Oh, I have a partner, she said, looking up into his face. It wasn't that so much as she wasn't interested. But it was convenient, and it was true.

A partner, huh? Man or woman?

Man, she said reluctantly. She hated how men felt at liberty to ask women who were otherwise strangers such pointedly personal questions. On buses or at gas stations or wherever. *What's your name? How old are you? Are you married? Are you Italian, Greek, Latin, an Indian?* Even more, she hated the social trap set for women in which she felt cornered into answering truthfully, not wanting to reveal her own fear or deal with the stress of being called an uppity bitch—*fuck off asshole, I don't have to answer any questions*—or simply because she was an honest person. An exploitation of her honesty because she was a woman.

Really? Well, he's one lucky man.

Oh...well, thanks, said Magdalena, to be polite. Here was the weird thing, though: she felt compelled to be polite, compelled—incredibly except it really happened—to touch him lightly on the shoulder as they parted even though she wasn't interested. Just to let him know she wasn't offended, that he had no advantage, that they were equals. Or to let him know she wasn't scared. Was she? That subtle, jumpy compulsion to feign bravado had been how she'd known the encounter hadn't evolved past some core threat of sexual violence, however equitable or nonchalant their interactions had seemed.

So she didn't shop at night anymore, and never at the 24-hour Walmart, after hearing stories of women followed from the aisles all the way back to their cars. Another woman—not someone she knew personally but someone whose name she knew, who worked out of a club as a dancer and dated on the side—had gotten arrested recently, the first arrest in the sealands play. It was big news in all the small town papers throughout South Texas. But those women were all dancers. They had more public visibility, so any dating they did put them at greater risk. She'd sworn off dancing some time ago, when she'd hit on the idea of traveling from town to town. It was more direct and less risky to work for herself, with no club elbowing in for a cut and no large base of faceless men who knew her face. She'd stay one town over, usually, then start her shift around 10 or 11 at night. Three nights on, two nights off. Hit the hotels first, then the camps. Sometimes, around 4 A.M., she would cross paths with missionaries from the local evangelical church trying to catch the men as they rose for their shifts, handing out flyers advertising services in the area. They even had little bibles specially made for the men, Giddeons of the play. Like her, trying to cash in on opportune loneliness. But they'd left her alone, aside from a flyer or two. She tried to stay out of their way as well.

By that autumn, she knew which camps flowed in that particular play and which were slow. She knew which doors to knock on and which trailers to try, and which to stay away from too—including one that sheltered the only other woman she'd seen in the play, aside from the townies and other working women like herself. Not that it mattered so much from a business standpoint. Money was money. But this one clearly had her own traveling visitor to the small circle of RVs clustered at the entrance of the dig. All that past summer, every Friday night through early Monday morning, when she drove the county road into town from her own motel room, she'd see a black Prius parked outside the small RV alongside the company woman's white company truck. That RV had to be the only one occupied of the four or five there, because some-times she would see them sitting together on its tiny stoop, their shirtlessness illuminated by the RV's weak yellow porch light. A stocky Brown man with the thick mustache and soft body of a professional—a lawyer or some such—and a tall, willowy Anglo woman, talking and smoking and drinking and laughing. Imagining themselves alone, Magdalena thought. Imagining themselves the first, the only: this time, it would be different.

CHAPTER SIX
Powerlines

The first time Lali meets Paloma is at city council, in October. Of course I remember you, corazón! You were at Alianza the night of the mining films with this darling baby, weren't you? Lowering herself slowly into the chamber's theater seating, Paloma reaches over to stroke Nena on one velvety cheek where she sucks contentedly away at Lali, who has been nursing the child preemptively since they arrived at the meeting. She's hoping that by the time they call her to speak, Nena will be calm and accommodating.

So. Did you get voluntold to come here by Alianza? the older woman laughs, winking one black eye.

Lali is about to explain that no, actually, she is there as an emissary of El Centro, which has taken her out for a series of test drives before they commit to any hiring paperwork. See how she does first and how she likes it. First is the Wednesday evening Citizens to be Heard—where she has prepared some thoughts on the follies of green modernity and a carbon fundamentalism unconcerned with questions of justice, surely that would convince them—followed by the Thursday demonstration in front of City Hall. Then Saturday is the People's Power Summit. A week of actions, all culminating in the city's mineral rights vote the following week. She is about to explain all this, but from the head of the chambers Mayor Mike is calling out the older woman's name: Paloma Villalobos...Trujillo? His intonation curls up at the end in the shape of a question, as if in disbelief.

That's me! says Paloma, heaving herself from her seat, a mariachi's vihuela tucked beneath one arm. Here, she says to Lali, thrusting a stack of flyers at her with verse on both sides, Spanish on one and English the other. Take one and pass em, she instructs, before approaching the dais to hand one to each council member in attendance. Then, having settled herself behind the podium, she pulls the little guitar to her breast and begins to strum and sing in a pleasant contralto, the council members looking up from phones and papers with eyebrows raised, not uninterested.

Desprenderse ya! La minería no!
La hora es ahora.
Desprenderse ya! La extracción no!
Está muriendo Pachamama.

Antes, había petróleo en su pecho
y querían la última gota.
Antes, había uranio en su pecho
y lo querían más, hasta Fukushima.
Antes, había el gas natural
en su pecho
y el fracking lo querían todo, hasta que
se convirtió en un fracaso

Pero la Edad de Piedra
no terminó por falta de piedra.
En la Edad de Piedra
no utilizaron la última piedra.

Wake up already! We say no mining!
The hour is now upon us.
Wake up already! We say no extraction--
Mother Earth is dying.

Before, petroleum lay in her breast
and they wanted the final drop.
Before, uranium lay in her breast
and they wanted more, until Fukushima.
Before, she had natural gas
in her breast
and with fracking they wanted it all, until
the whole thing became a disaster, a mess

But the Stone Age
did not end for lack of stone.
Even in the Stone Age,
they didn't use up the very last stone.

Ahorita estamos usando más buses y bicis	Now we're using more buses and bikes
Pero todavía hay muchos caballos	But still there are plenty of horses
Ahorita raramente usamos caballos y carros	Now we rarely drive horse-drawn wagons
Pero todavía hay muchos caballos.	But still there are plenty of horses
Si, hay minerales en la tierra	Yes, there are minerals deep in the earth
Por qué desea el último trozo?	but why do you want the last little piece?
Si, hay metales en su pecho,	Yes, there are metals in her breast,
Pachamama—	Mother Earth—
Por qué lo desea todo?	but why take it all?
Desprenderse, ya! La hora es ahora!	Wake up already! The hour is now!
Están matando Pachamama.	They're killing Mother Earth.
Desprenderse, ya! La minería no!	Wake up already! We say no mining!
La hora es ahora.	It's time, the hour's now upon us.

Following a shallow curtsy, Paloma glides serenely down the aisle to her seat, vihuela slung to her back like a quiver. As she passes, the few Wednesday night regulars in the chamber whistle and stomp their feet.

***

The second time Lali runs into Paloma, she is throwing fake dollar bills embossed with Mayor Mike's victory face at the utility people as they walk, heads down, toward city hall with a grim determination. They are headed for the mayor's office, after a closed door session with Seismar representatives, but first they must pass through the the crowd on the curb, rippling with signs and banners.

Later, as the sun sinks behind City Hall—but before Chela urges them from sidewalk to streets to march unpermitted—Paloma and Lali tuck arms around each other's waists and sway hip to hip on the curb, kicking their legs in sync like chorus dancers, first to the left and then to the right. *We kick mines! To the curb!* There is another chant, a rousing call-and-response they invent on the spot, which goes: *Men-ti-ro-sos! Sin ver-güen-za! Liars, liars, shameless liars!* Lali standing when Paloma squats and squatting when Paloma stands, to the beat of the chant. The older woman feels soft beneath Lali's arm; she smells like anise or cardamom or cinnamon, something oily sweet and tropical spicy.

Wow, you're fun! Paloma pants when they are done, sweat glistening on her forehead. What's your name again, corazón? Did we even introduce ourselves?

When Lali tells her, laughing, Paloma's face lights up.

Citlali Sánchez-O'Connor! I love it! Qué musical, con Nahuatl y Español y qué, Irish? It's like a—a what do you call it. The rock samples the archaeologists do. Where you can see traces from each wave of inhabitants in all the different layers? And Sánchez like the mayor, ja!

Sánchez like the everyone in San Antonio, says Lali.

How different from Papa's response on her first visit to El Centro, looking her up and down when Lali introduced herself. Which side of town you live on? he had wanted to know. It was a coded inquiry all mixed people recognized, a sneaky version of the Mexican test, intended to suss out essences, quanta. How different, too, from the guy at the HEB checkout when she first came back to town, who had squinted from her face to the name on her driver's license and asked, point blank: Are you white? What are you? But no, Paloma loves it. She motions over a man in feathered fedora and bright red vest, which matches ruby red lips set beneath a twirly Dalí mustache. Rafa, have you met Citlali? She is a wonderful dancer!

Well no, I haven't! says Rafa, extending a hand like a king offering his ring. You never introduce me to anyone cool, he pouts playfully, poking Paloma in the shoulder. Mucho gusto, Ms. Citlali.

Mucho gusto, Lali murmurs. She feels shy, unaccustomed.

Can you believe she gets to do this full time now for El Centro? exclaims Paloma. They just hired her as their Just Transition organizer.

Well, it's about time we had a good dancer here, Rafa says, hands on hips. I'm getting *so fucking sick* of marching around angry all the time with these signs!

***

Lali encounters Paloma a third time at the People's Power Summit: the older woman is sitting in the front row at a panel presentation, outdated handicam wedged to eye socket, when Lali walks in late. Late because her stomach is full of an emptiness, an inexplicable anxiety that pulls at her to stay home. Late too because her neighbor—an older man who lives alone, one of the veteranos of their changing street, who wanders Nogalitos each morning collecting cans, who driveway-feeds unfixed feral cats indiscriminately, seemingly unconcerned as to whether their many offspring live or die—flagged her en route to her car with a question.

That power line there above their houses…why was it buzz-ing like that? Ever since the blackouts. Had Lali noticed? She hadn't. Couldn't she hear it? But it seemed quiet enough now, as they stood anxiously assessing the runners of wire crisscross-ing their street.

And late because she first went south on Zarzamora when she should have gone north, to the community center named after a local voting rights organizer, where in the evening they teach ESL and computer literacy classes. When she arrives at the center she has missed the opening blessing, but the scent of burning sage and copal still hangs thick in the air. The danza group is packing up to go already, barefoot in headdresses, anklets of nueces rattling with each step. The opening plenary is that way, one of the danzantes tells her, pointing around the corner to a large meeting hall. Don't worry, she smiles, it just started.

Before taking an open seat beside Paloma, Lali grabs a swift look around the hall at the crowd of maybe 75 gathered behind them. At the front of the room, a fine-boned older woman in a plain beige windbreaker draws diagrams on the white board. She leans knuckles on the tables set up for the summit's opening panel, golden hoop earrings sparkling as she gestures at the board behind her, dry erase marker in her hand like a conductor's baton. She must be the second speaker, judging by who sits and who stands; seated to her left is a smartly-dressed woman Lali recognizes from the foundation that gave the money that made it possible for El Centro to hire her—or hire someone, she is quick to add in her head, afraid of jinxing her-self. Texas is like ground zero, test site for the transition, Victor had explained during Lali's first visit to El Centro. Mad mad feria is available for organizing cuz of that node play and the power plant redevelopment stuff. Those fools are gonna fuck the whole thing up if we don't get in there with our own plan. We want a *just* transition, not *just* a transition, me entiendes?

Up at the board, the speaker tells a story about what she learned many years before from the aquifer protection coalition, who would visit her city council office when big zoning decisions were before her. When the growth to the North took off, the Council was continually making big decisions over land use, week after week after week. And one afternoon some folks had come to her office and taught her about the precious geological formation beneath the city—a limestone cistern up to 700 feet thick that contained more water than all the rivers and lakes in Texas. They brought maps showing the northeasterly sweep of the aquifer from the Mexican border up to Austin. There was the contributing zone to the north, where rain and runoff alike entered the earth, and the artesian zone to the south, where the springs flowed. And there in between was the recharge zone, a stripe of blue cutting across the northern part of the county, on a collision course with the new development council was zoning each week—and where they now wanted to site the Mud Creek mine. The aquifer protection people had brought a porous piece of limestone karst for her to hold. Forty years later, it sat on her desk still: a living membrane of stone, carved and hollowed by the underground movements of water over millenia. A hole-y rock to filter the rain that returned to earth. A holy rock whose scallops and chambers echoed the sculpture of hip, the spongey architecture of marrow. Once the city had been 36 miles square, its growth evenly spread to the four directions. Then deliberate decisions had been made by the rich and powerful to locate essential services and infrastructure far north of the central city, away from the people who needed them most, and at the expense of basic infrastructure like sidewalks and streetlamps in older parts of the city. And in the process they had slowly paved and built over the places where the earth opened its throat to the sky.

None of it was random: that was what they had to understand. What was happening now had happened before, again and again. There was a pattern, there were outcomes that skipped like a stuck phonograph—oh wait, did they still have records?—and behind those patterns was a decision-making body whose collective volition materialized its desires. It was something she had figured out during her mayoral run. When it became apparent she was neck and neck in the runoff with her opponent, a former developer lobbyist, the head of a major construction contractor had once scheduled a meeting to find out where she stood on some zoning case. Not with him, she told him at that meeting. In the week to come, several other important men had canceled pending meetings with her, and she began to see how they worked. Together, invisibly, dispatching their Spanish-surnamed lobbyists to the meetings but staying conveniently out of sight. Names and faces were not important. It was more the function they played, an agency seemingly without an actor. And therein lay the significance of their power: they directed things unseen, so effectively it was as if things happened because that's just how they happened. And this at the very moment when, more than ever before, those elected to council looked like the rest of the city. They were the children of the movement, those solemn little boys at the dais, the children who'd inherited the gains of their parents' and grandparents' struggles, but they were not from the movement. Sullen little boys dragged to marchas with their Raza Unida mamas. More importantly, they were not the ones who really moved things.

She had pieced this together only later, after she lost the election. She'd conferred with her campaign manager, and together they had created a list: who exactly had canceled that week, after she'd made it plain to just one of them that she was not for sale? They had counted seventeen that day, all of them men and all of them white, seventeen white men, but the number was more figurative than literal. It might have been 26 or 903. The point was: whoever decided what happened to the land decided the future. It was the same in any city. First and foremost were the landmen—the private equity firms, the financial institutions, the real estate companies, the developers. But the landmen didn't work alone. They needed others with more local concentrations of power. Lobbying and legal firms. Energy companies. Media and communication corporations. The municipal utilities. Then there were the construction companies and insurance agencies who hired thousands throughout the city, who had the technical expertise to authorize the plans and wishes of the landmen. All of that apparatus was in motion before the city people even came onto the scene. Those folks were cacahuates compared to the landmen and their technical facilitators. The city people were there to run plans by, not to make them. They were the traffic cops, the rubber stampers, the givers of gold stars. If they had reservations and regret in their hearts—well, look at who paid for their campaigns. Even Mayor Mike, Westside child, great Brown hope, took money from the biggest developer lobbyist in town. How could he not? That was the point.

No, anything they did had to start with the landmen, because they were the ones who established the parameters of thinkability for how the city should grow and where. Where they turned their invisible gaze, trees cleared themselves, hills cleft for roadways to pass, and soil smoothed itself of a hundred thousand rhizomatic synergies like a coverlet pulled tight across a bed. That was what they had to understand at the outset, if they were trying to do anything about anything. Who moved things, and who only appeared to.

***

As the second speaker takes her seat—*Sister Soledad*, Paloma whispers, turning one eye away from her camera when Lali asks: *What is her name?*—Chela rises, the third and final panelist. Sister had stood for her presentation, but Chela sits, conversational. I grew up on the Southwest side of the city, she begins, hands clasped before her on the table. Near the old airbase. All day and all night the planes would fly over our neighborhood on their way back to base, sounding like they were scraping the rooftops off of houses. My whole family is military. That's how we got a leg up, after my grandparents came north from México when my dad was in his teens. And all through middle and high school I thought that's what I'd do too. I'd see those planes and I'd think about flying, about becoming a pilot, a woman pilot. My dad and my brothers had been Army grunts. When the Air Force came to our high school to table they seemed special—smarter, more laid back. I heard if you were Air Force, you went on to become an engineer or medic or scientist. I wanted to follow my brothers but take it further, make my family proud. But a couple of things happened that bent my life along a path I never anticipated or even knew existed—

The first thing that happened was: when she bloomed, she became the first openly gay person in her extended family. At first, of course, it wasn't an open thing. Back in middle and high school, queerness was a nagging awareness unhappily simmering beneath the skin of the day-to-day, Chela wondering if she could keep it in or if it would go away, until the day she was outed in the middle of her junior year. That day, her ROTC instructor had discovered Chela with another girl from her squad, kissing behind the gym when they should have been drilling. He had sent a note home to both of their parents, and somehow the rest of the squad had found out too. Right away Lety had turned on Chela to save her own rep, joining in the subtle and not-so-subtle snubs that dogged her the rest of the year. By the time Chela began her senior year, she had ditched both ROTC and soccer team for the punk and goth kids who hung out at the end of hall in the art wing, the boys in Bauhaus shirts with black-painted fingernails and the girls who carved into their skin with razors.

Her parents loved her but didn't understand it. They were the kind of working class Mexicanos where it was totally fine to be queer, so long as you never talked about it, ever—like her older half-sister who had lived with another woman for 25 years, never calling herself gay or bringing her partner around. It was okay to be gay, so long as everyone understood that it really wasn't okay. They hurt her casually that way, without understanding they were doing it or why it would matter. They hurt her in the soft, open part of her where longing welled up, the blossom point where the divine entered her and unfurled in the most tender impulse to cradle the face of another in her hands. Instead it was voices from the other room, late at night, as she walked past. No one was "gay" where they came from. There wasn't even a word for "gay" in Spanish—they used *jota* or *homosexual,* slurs or the clinical language of pathology. Could jotería be an American thing, they wondered, caught from the gringos like ojo or brujería? Where else could it have come from? Not from them or who they were. In loving women she had become adulterated or polluted—less Mexican, less a part of them or what came from them. They loved her but; they accepted her because she was family—but it was a mute, awkward acceptance that told her they didn't know how to talk about that softest, most tender and giving part of her; they said nothing instead of saying, yes, it is good and right and beautiful. It was an effacement that hurt as much as the whispers of her ROTC mates.

She met Naima at La Alianza after graduating high school, as soon as she had flown her airbase neighborhood for the Nuestra Madre gayborhood strip at the living heart of the city. Naima was eleven years her elder, from a military family like Chela's, a mixed girl from the Rio Grande Valley with a Puerto Rican father and a white German mother he'd met overseas. Principled and whip-smart, Naima had been the first out and proud woman Chela had known in an intimate way, the first woman whose pain reached and touched her own, the woman who had politicized her around queerness and race and gender. They had transmuted each other, remediated each other, scorched earth into molten gold, discovering a secret fiery fertility amid the shit they'd been handed. Naima was born on base in San Antonio, but she had grown up in the backwaters of the world—from Fort Irwin, California to Leavenworth, Kansas to Alice, Texas once her father retired early, a tiny town that had somehow reminded her German mom of home. People thought kids from small-town high schools didn't turn out to be dykes or get a full ride to college for a degree in gender studies, with an emphasis in queer theory. What the fuck was that, even? What an embarrassment for her folks when friends or family asked what she was majoring in. They didn't know at that point what her older brother had done to her for so many years, before he'd eventually joined the Marines too and moved out. Even when she told her parents, they had nothing much to say except that she had to be remembering wrong or misunderstanding Berto's intentions. It hadn't really happened like she said it did. Whatever happened, he hadn't meant it. Certainly, enlisting had straightened him out and he'd gotten himself back on track; whatever had happened, it was behind them.

If nothing had happened, then what was wrong with her? That was their unspoken question. So after high school Naima had gotten the hell away from Alice, Texas by heading for college in San Antonio, mission city of her military base birth, San Francisco of the Rio Grande Valley. San Antonio was where

Naima met Carina, in the process realizing both that she was a lesbian and also the life-or-death necessity of being out about it. Cari was queer as fuck but not out, a cute Chicanita with a pixie haircut, and Naima kind of liked her except that Cari was constantly falling in love with unavailable women, one after another. Older women who wanted to be with someone more comfortably out, women with partners, straight white women: when Naima met Cari she was obsessed with a girl in her dorm, and one winter Saturday between semesters, Naima accompanied Cari as she drove around the city's suburban Northside for hours looking for the girl's parents' house, finally pulling into its driveway to gaze longingly at where she stayed during breaks. Cari transferred schools not long after, to a small private college in the deep piney woods of East Texas, and almost immediately fell in love with a sorority girl named Sherrilyn. Around this time, Naima noticed that Cari's attachments had evolved from obsession to paranoid delusion. She would call Naima back in San Antonio to tell her that she and Sherrilyn had a mystical connection, evident in tiny but unmistakable signs, like a certain combination of numbers appearing on the dry erase board outside a dorm room, or in the clearing of throats. Coughing and throat clearing in particular Carina imagined to signify suppressed desire, the truth of desire in circumstances that made its expression impossible. On the phone Cari would fall into a trance and channel growling voices; in her more lucid moments, she worried these spells and visions were because of the pot.

Whatever the reason, it was weird and getting weirder—but Naima stuck by Cari, wanting to support a friend in distress and being too young to recognize the intensity of her distress as a possible sign of illness. And being too young, Naima in the end abruptly cut off their friendship, after one last road trip that crossed the slippery line between longing and stalking. During the spring break of their senior year, Naima drove out to East Texas with Cari as she searched for Sherrilyn, intending to deliver a handwritten letter 200 pages long. They found the sorority girl just after midnight in a college town nightclub, dancing drunk in a small pen built to contain the foam-covered bodies of writhing dancers as they slipped and slid beneath a bubble machine spewing white foam onto the dance floor below. Naima had reluctantly agreed to come because she thought that if Cari could only deliver her novel of a love letter, it might help lay her tortured desire to rest. But at the very sight of Sherrilyn dancing with others, other *men,* Cari grew pale with anxiety and aborted mission. Though they had just arrived after five hours of driving, Cari decided they had to bolt town, *now.* They got home at daybreak, and afterwards Naima ghosted on Cari—stopped hanging out, stopped taking her calls. It had all gotten just too intense and exhausting.

But here was the thing: Naima also knew, intimately, the violence done to queer folks in the message that the truth of one's desire was inexpressible or unrealizable or wrong. In Cari's madness, she could see plainly before her the vast psychological devastation inflicted by a culture that not only denied queer love and thus selfhood but, more fundamentally, the possibility of *being loved back.* And so even as she cut things off, she wondered—could Cari have been right? Was it possible she and Sherrilyn *did* have a mystical connection? Hadn't they discussed Freud in her Theories of Sexuality class, his idea that coughing *could* mean suppressed desire, that whatever we cannot speak aloud speaks anyway, slantwise? And resolve flooded Naima then, to name herself and her desire, loudly and without shame, and to never back down.

Armed with her education and her pain and her conviction, she came out to her parents. She hardly expected a celebration. But she was floored by the question in their eyes, worse than their casual denial of her brother's abuse some years ago: Did the love in her grow from some place once whole and intact that had since been corrupted—like a hard drive dropped one too many times? Did she love women because she'd been damaged? Not that what had happened was abuse, of course not. Berto was a good boy; she was the one creating problems for the family.

So she cut off ties, making her home in San Antonio. She didn't have the time or energy to cry or convince or explain to assholes why violence was violence. Just no. *No!* It wasn't okay! And from there—her unashamed declaration, her uncompromising refusal—she found her way to La Alianza and to a family thicker than blood. Sooner or later, everyone in exile found their way to Alianza. You couldn't be queer in South Texas—or mujer de color or simply a person of conscience—without at some point entering the orbit of Alianza, wildlife sanctuary for the wretched of the earth. With wings hanging and beaks clipped they dragged their wounds across its threshold, fresh from beatings and rapes and slurs and the casual violence of denial. Alianza's director Victoria had been there from the beginning, and she had taken them all in, her birds, to release them transformed, to light in the chambers and board rooms and powerlines of the city like grackles, making it impossible for dollars or decisions to flow uninterrupted. Like VAMOS, they were for living wages and jobs with dignity and equitable allocation of resources—but they wanted more than that, because they had to. They were the children and grandchildren of VAMOS, loved but not understood. *Nothing about us without us!* they cried out from the places inside them where softness had been beaten and burned out, where they'd had to harden off their tender, growing edge to survive. Alianza was where Naima had found family and work as Mama Vee's right hand woman with clipboard in hand, her dirty work guard dog, warding off attacks from those who preferred their nonexistence. It was where she caught an 18-year-old Chela in her arms when she came stumbling through Alianza's crimson doors. Chela had been basically homeless since she'd left her family's house, working as a barback on the strip and crashing on a workmate's couch, and one night after work she'd spotted a poster for Alianza's queer art show stapled to a utility pole. It was the color of conviction, a scarlet sincerity fashioned from brand or armband, the color of the first cardinal of winter, of blood on snow. Several months later, Chela had moved into Naima's fourplex apartment off the Nuestra Madre strip. They adopted a dog together, a big Husky mix they named Ramona, after the Zapatista comandanta. Naima schooled her politically and got her enrolled in community college classes part-time—Chela's first serious relationship, her first real love.

So there was that. But the second thing Chela could never have predicted was the way her grandfather would die that first year out of high school, struck in his mid-60s with a galloping case of something none of them had heard of before. First his hands and feet had buzzed pins and needles like bees frantic to burst from his skin. Then his limbs had stiffened until he lost his ability to walk, and eventually to move or swallow. Finally his lungs had frozen and he suffocated to death, his still-intact mind trapped somewhere deep inside his immobile body like a miner down a well. The same thing happened to a neighbor down the street and two neighbors one street over. Other neighbors had developed unusual cancers. And that was when they learned about the chemicals that had been dumped decades before on the nearby airbase—dry-cleaning solvents, engine degreasing agents, waste oil—which had migrated into the groundwater beneath their neighborhood, spreading a toxic plume of contaminants several miles wide. The local health department had investigated but denied any causal relationship between the Air Force's sloppy environmental record and the deaths in Chela's neighborhood. There are toxins all around, said the director of the city's health department on the evening news. For instance, the corn used to make tortillas can grow a toxic fungus. Who's to say those toxins didn't accumulate in the body over time?

Toxic tortillas, of course—if Mexicans died under suspicious circumstances, what else could it be? The day of Welito's funeral was the first time she'd been back home since she went splitsville after graduation. Chela had known her grandfather was sick, but she had tuned out how sick or what it was or why. He had been one of the ones who loved her but, who had been sad for her and wanted to pray about it. But he and Welita had also taken care of her before she was old enough to go to school, while her parents were at work on the base. Welito had taken her fishing in the arroyo that crossed the base and ran flush behind their neighborhood, sitting together on the banks and throwing roly polies of soft white bread at the ducks. She'd left home in jeans and sneakers, hair pulled back in a messy ponytail; when she came back for the funeral she wore her long hair shorn in a mohawk and a dark pantsuit, Naima on one arm to fend off nervous glances. When she came back, there was a sign posted on the banks of the creek: no fishing, no swimming, no contact.

Come work with us, her cousins said to her at the backyard barbecue following the funeral service. Los cuates, Victor and Marcos, the twins. Bien serio in black frame glasses and fifteen years older than Chela, she'd never played with them as a kid; they'd never been interested in her. But for as long as she could remember they had worked with their father—that was Papa— at a place he had started twenty years before, a rickety building on the Eastside they called El Centro. What they did there she hadn't known. But Victor and Marcos had pulled her aside that day to show her a report issued by the Agency for Toxic Substances and Disease Registry. Alongside elevated rates of cancer and birth defects in their neighborhood, they'd found things like *trichloroethylene* and *polynuclear aromatic hydrocarbons* and *volatile organic compounds* in water samples taken from wells in their neighborhood—and from the arroyo where she'd fished with Welito. We've been doing a community health survey of the neighborhood, they'd told Chela. We're putting up purple crosses in front of every yard where someone has died of cancer or Lou Gehrig's. We could use the help—we're looking for another full-time organizer, someone we know and trust. Someone who knows the neighborhood.

***

So, Chela says as she drums a riff on the table. That's how I ended up on this panel today. Welcome to the People's Power Summit, people!

Some stirring in seats, some claps and shouts.

Okay, the reason for this Summit is that we have to be able to frame the discussion on transition. If we don't, they will. We have to have our own plan, a people's plan that says what we want and what our solutions are. We can't just be *against* stuff, we have to have a vision of what we're *for*. So after our opening panel we'll break out into smaller groups—

Chela pauses, she turns her head at the sound of the door to the meeting hall creaking slowly open. The room follows her gaze to the sight of a baby-faced man poking his head around the door. Is this the People's Power Summit? he asks with a smile. He is a few years older than Lali, somewhere in his mid-30s, with slick dark hair and pastel dress shirt tucked into jeans, his sleeves rolled to forearms as though he's about to hoist the first shovelful of dirt over his shoulder at a ceremonial groundbreaking.

Speak of the devil, mutters an older Black man in red bandana sitting behind Lali. As the visitor walks in, Chela rises to gesture him to the front of the crowd.

Mayor Mike, says Chela, extending a hand for him to shake. Thanks for coming. We weren't sure if you were gonna make it today. So we're about to go into our breakout sessions, but I know a number of us have questions for you—

The room erupts into a scuffle of whispers. But first! Chela calls out, to reign them in again. But first. I think a lot of us are here because we're concerned about the city's transition efforts, specifically the Seismar deal, so we wanted to have a chance to dialogue before we break out. Mayor?

He speaks easily, but he is careful, cautious, vague. The necessity of building a bridge to new energy economies. The importance of clean technology jobs. The need to balance opportunity with considerations of risk. From the back, a tall Anglo woman with straight grey hair cut in a smartly angled bob asks a question about how the city plans to ensure best practices in mining. At her question, the same grizzled voice from behind Lali snorts with impatience: Guess *you* never had to breathe flaring fumes. That's the kinda mess they were talkin when they grandfathered that refinery on the Southside into staying open for *years* after it shoulda closed, till they had their redevelopment plans. Following best practices, they said—ha!

Then, beside Lali, Paloma rises to her feet, retrieving some laminated placards she had been sitting on and setting her handicam down.

Mayor Mike, she begins. Don't worry, she says as his eyes flash recognition. I won't be singing today. She grins expansively. Not right now, anyway. Oye Mayor, I do appreciate your attendance. And what I want to ask, I ask from my heart to yours. If you can, please hear my question as a person and not a politico.

Did he blink or wince at the term? Lali can't tell.

What I want to know, Paloma says, is how you feel in your heart of hearts about the irony of a transition away from fossil fuels on the back of the biggest mining boom South Texas has seen to date. Even bigger than fracking, they're saying. She pulls dozens of sticky notes from her back pocket and sorts through them, slipping red reading glasses from atop her head to the bridge of her nose as she reads each one aloud.

Here we have, *Waste rock and tailings contain radioactive isotopes, heavy metals, asbestos-like particles, and acids left over from the leaching process, sometimes mercury.* And, *Overtopping of tailing dam. Collapse of tailing dam by seismic event or poor construction or pipe leakage.* Mira, Mayor. She raises one of her placards.

Look at this picture from the Great Basin Desert in Nevada. They had been using a dry lakebed to hold wastewater, and it soaked into the desert floor and into the groundwater. I know in the sealands they're already reporting spills of radioactive wastewater from trucking accidents; the roads aren't equipped for all those trucks. What will happen here, over the most sensitive part of our aquifer? I ask you as one human being talking to another.

First Brown mayor since Henry Cisneros: they say he will be president one day, from the Westside to the White House. His face remains open, neutral in the face of confrontation. Of course he understands their deep concerns; in fact, he shares them. Like them, he too wants a clean and healthy future for his children, and his children's children. And this is clearly the best path forward toward that horizon. And he has every confidence the process will be safely monitored by those whose job it is to regulate mining activity.

Except they don't *have* no regulations yet, says Mr. Red Bandana behind Lali. That node shit's too new.

But the Mayor is confident that in 30 years time, they will have figured out how to address any unintended consequences that may have arisen. Oh, and he also has to go—another meeting beckons; but he is appreciative for the invitation and for the important work they are doing.

You tried, Lali whispers as he slips out the door, rubbing Paloma on the back.

***

At lunch Lali wants cookies only, sweets, because her stomach is still upset and sweet carbohydrates are the least offensive food she can imagine, always have been. She hesitates at the table where organizers have piled donated boxes of Nutter Butters and Oreos, her hand hovering as she glances around to assess whether she will be noticed and judged, and catches the eye of a man she recognizes from the film festival. But he smiles approvingly and, without knowing he is doing it, puts her at ease. Mmm, Imma get some of those too, he says. A man unafraid of his appetites, a man who brims with emotional acuity, an unthinking compassion for the ticks and twitches of mental life. That is how he strikes her.

So later, when he takes a seat beside where she sits alone in the meeting room—everyone else has filed out into the hallway with their plates, standing and eating and talking—she doesn't mind, even though she is concentrating hard on tonguing peanut butter filling from her cookies, not sure how her body will respond to food. Where's the baby, he wants to know. It's what everyone always wanted to know when Nena wasn't with her.

With my brother-in law, she says as they shake hands, feeling the usual reluctance to reference her marriage. It's not that she wants to hide it as much as it feels odd when she says it, as though it were untrue. An indissoluble marble rolling around in the mouth.

Now she remembers who he is; he is the man from the post-film discussion whose words had carried weight when he spoke. She understands why when he introduces himself: he is Joel Champlain, staff writer at the *Volt*. I've been writing a series about the city's stake in the mineral rush, he says. That's why I'm here. How about you?

Oh, she says. Oh—I'm the new Just Transition organizer for El Centro. She steers the beans on her plate in slow circles to make it look like she's eating. I think I am, anyway.

He laughs, but no, it's true: she's still not sure if she's actually been hired.

He looks like a reporter, in a long-sleeved, untucked button-down, grey corduroys, camera bag, sneakers. He wears his hair swept back from his forehead; tufts of grey escape above the ears. His beard is gone and his face is smooth save for a single patch in the valley beneath his lower lip. And the outline of a cigarette pack is visible in one shirt pocket, nestled between pens. Didn't all reporters smoke? Something about the pressure of deadlines. Something about the loneliness of documenting a scene yet never taking part. She observes these details as they sit together without talking, while the folks from El Centro run film footage from a people's caravan they took to somewhere. Lali forcing her way through the cookies with a measured concentration.

***

After breakout sessions they are all supposed to reconvene in the meeting hall to piece their people's transition plan together, but discussion snags and unravels on the thorn of best practices versus no mining at all. It is astounding to watch: Naima rocketing to her feet, backed by Chela and Red Bandana, in a shouting match with the chair and co-chair of the local chapter of Wilderness Defense who remain seated, confounded but equally adamant. No, we totally agree with you, they keep repeating. We don't want any mining at all either! But a hard line is not realistic or strategic. Why not seize the moment to win some actual changes to existing policy? Right now there are no regulations on the books. You realize that, don't you? We have a chance to affect that!

You mean *you* have a chance! Naima jabs a finger in the faces of the two Wilderness Defense women. Our communities are *never* consulted, *never* invited to sit at the table! And you know what? We don't want to sit there either! What we want is a fucking *table flip*, she yells, throwing her hands high to send an imaginary table toppling before her, its plates and glasses and cutlery flying.

Teary-eyed, the chair shakily gathers her things and hurries from the room, co-chair tailing behind. Holy shit, Lali thinks. On the one hand Naima was right: *flip that fucking table*. And on the other—

The only consensus they can come to is to convene again at some future point when they'll be far more ready to figure out what comes next. They'll have to figure out when later; right now they have to be out of the building by 5 on the dot. But by the end of the Summit, Lali's position at El Centro is official. She is to report to Centro's office on Monday at 9, Chela informs her. Her cousin Dulce, who does the books, will help her with all the paperwork.

Oh, and don't forget—we need to do a huuuuuge protest next week! Chela reminds Lali as they pull away from their goodbye hug. Probably Wednesday, since the mineral rights vote will be Thursday, remember? When I see you Monday, I'll pass on the sign-in sheets from today, so you can start getting everyone back together for Wednesday.

Lali's relief at secure employment at last just as quickly turns into a shiver of panic. Get everyone back together on Wednesday? How the fuck was something like that supposed to happen. Like trapping feral cats.

But when she arrives at the office on Monday for her first day, she finds she has been saved by the Seventeen White Men, by all appearances: hunched shoulder to shoulder around Victor's computer screen, Victor and Marcos and Chela and Papa and Dulce stand with mouths hanging open, watching something unfold onscreen. Something has happened, something big. Just days before the city's vote on whether to lease out its mineral rights to Seismar, an anonymous source has leaked information that the company has been withholding knowledge of a serious discrepancy between projected and actual rare earth prices. Supply is more scarce and prices more volatile than Seismar suggested in their initial conversations with the city—who could have predicted it?

On Victor's screen, the CEO of Shitty Power and Light, who is also the chairman of the board of the public-private partnership helming the city's transition plans, stands behind a podium flanked by Mayor Mi'jo who grew up on the Westside but doesn't even speak Spanish, plus all the council members. He is solemn. He is regretful. His lower lip balloons like a bulldog's as his jowls droop down and downer, pulling at the corners of his mouth. Yes, it is true—there appears to be a significant discrepancy between the numbers Seismar made public and the data in the economic feasibility analysis.

And did the Transition Team know about this discrepancy in advance of the vote? the reporters shout from off camera. Did they plan on telling the council before they voted?

Wait, wait, go back! Victor howls, seizing the mouse from Chela's hand and tracking the video back in time ten seconds. Oh *shit*! He explodes, slapping his thighs and rocking forward in his chair. Look at him about to cry, right *there*, when they ask the question! They're all, and did you know—and dude looks like he's gonna cry!

Research Notas 3:
From Colonial History to Anglo Rule

In *The Politics of San Antonio* (1983), Booth and Johnson place contemporary power relations in San Antonio within a historical timeline that stretches back to the city's roots in Spanish colonial rule. They argue: "San Antonio's public policy makers have usually operated within a set of ideological constraints that, with little public consent, maximized governmental support of the local economic elite's interests."[16] They define elites as those who "appear most greatly to influence the most important decisions for the city, and who [are] most influential in setting the *agenda* determining which questions are considered at all and which are not."[17]

After San Antonio's incorporation as a city in 1837 following Texas's independence from Mexico—but before U.S. statehood—its elites were criollos, the descendants of Spanish settlers. The Civil War created wealth for these elites, and this capital created the banks whose founding families—Brackenridge, Maverick, Frost—now name the parks and pavilions of the city. After the Civil War, those who ran the commercial activity in San Antonio were European ethnics: criollo, French, English, German. They became "Anglo," the term for a privileged whiteness whose reference point is always implicitly Mexican, as they intermarried and consolidated their economic

---

[16] John A. Booth and David R. Johnson, "Community, Progress, and Power in San Antonio," in *The Politics of San Antonio*, vii.

[17] Thomas A. Baylis, "Leadership Change in Contemporary San Antonio," in *The Politics of San Antonio*, 96.

power. Between 1880 and 1920, "a new ethnoracial and class order" emerged in which these European ethnics consolidated as "a non-Mexican, 'white' elite [and] began to work together for mutual benefit."[18] A campaign of land dispossession similarly followed. While in 1840 Tejanos owned 85% of town lots, by 1860 this had been reduced to just 7.8%;[19] while in the city's hinterlands Spanish-surnamed owners held less than 20% of ranch lands by 1865.[20] San Antonio's political structure reflected this shift even more rapidly: whereas the first city council in 1837 was entirely Spanish-surnamed (though of course not indio or even mestizo), by 1850 German, French, and English council members had largely replaced Mexicanos[21]—now dispossessed, disenfranchised, and geographically squeezed into the city's Westside "Mexican Quarter".[22]

It was the legacy of Juan Seguín writ large. A Mexicano on the side of Texan independence from Mexico—later mayor of San Antonio and, even so, later run out of the city he had presided over by land-hungry, slavery-supporting, westward-expanding Anglo settlers— Seguín was eventually reviled as a traitor by Anglos and Mexicans both. He'd been a Texas loyalist but in the end he was just too Mexican. He went back to Mexico and they

---

[18] Laura Hernández-Ehrisman, *Inventing the Fiesta City: Heritage and Carnival in San Antonio* (Albuquerque: University of New Mexico Press, 2008), 26.

[19] Raquel R. Márquez, Louis Mendoza, and Steve Blanchard, "Neighborhood Formation on the West Side of San Antonio, Texas," *Latino Studies* 5, no. 3 (2007): 295.

[20] Char Miller, "Where the Buffalo Roamed: Ranching, Agriculture, and the Urban Marketplace," in *On the Border*, 39.

[21] David Montejano. *Anglos and Mexicans in the Making of Texas, 1836-1986* (Austin: University of Texas Press,1987), 40.

[22] Hernández-Ehrisman, 60.

didn't want him there either. Ni de aquí, ni de allá. His statues are ambivalent monuments to racial unease. From Reconstruction until the 1950s, only one Mexicano would occupy a seat on city council. During the Good Government League's takeover in 1951 until the Department of Justice crackdown on San Antonio's local voting process in the mid-70s, Mexicanos would get roughly one seat and Blacks another, but that was it, and they had to tow the line; they had to internalize the master symbols. And there would be no Mexicano mayor until the election of Henry Cisneros in 1981, a century and a half after Juan Seguin's ouster. And there would be no Mexicano mayor after Cisneros until Mayor Mi'jo a generation later.

CHAPTER SEVEN
Algo es Algo

That foggy, misty winter there are no blackouts, but there is the subtle deception of a temperate-enough climate, in which it seems they can forego the protections of heavy clothing. But it is bone-achingly cold at the Centro office, which is heated by ancient gas radiators that leave the building colder inside than out most days. One morning after the turn of the year, blind Joe Ortiz comes in, disappears to the kitchen, then emerges again with a large plastic soda bottle filled with hot water he has heated on the stove to near boiling. For your hands, he says, placing one bottle on Lali's desk and the other on Chela's. He's brought food for them too, two styrofoam cups filled with plain white rice and topped with soy sauce and scrambled egg. To keep the food from spilling on the bus, he has covered each cup with a napkin secured by a stray rubber band. These small innovations, borne of having very little, somehow provide more comfort and satisfaction than having a building that heats itself properly, or breakfast one might actually want to eat in the morning. At her house it has mostly been WIC food—plain corn flakes with milk, grapefruit juice tinged with metal flavor leached from its aluminum container. Some days she would rather eat nothing than have to eat what there is, adequate but not appetizing.

That winter, before she gets the campus interview invitation from the K-State people, there are endless conference calls with the funders during the week; and after work, there is the exhaustion of application tweakings and phone interviews and preparation for phone interviews. But there are fascinating encounters too, shining amid the murk and blur of days, like the free energy inventor who mails a letter to Lali at Centro that floors her completely:

Dear Ms Sánchez O'Connor.

My name is Serafin O. Sifuentes, and I think there is something we need to talk about .

About 2 years ago I tried to get in touch with the city Utility . As you know they are currently wanting to mining for rare metals that is causing all kinds of concerns in S. Texas about water and chemicals etc. I left a message with their CEO that I had invented a Generator that could Convert Atmospheric Pressure Directly into Electricity . In my E-mail I told him also that I had done more than 15 years of research on Unconventional means of Producing energy that is Clean and Cheap to produce and that I had finaly made a Real Discovery and had the Blue-Prints for the Machine , the answer to all our energy Problems .

This machine converts atmospheric pressure (which as you know is everywhere) Directly into Electricity Without the need of fuels of any kind . It uses a common car battery to kick into Activity , Once it is kicked into action it just recycles the energy over and over again at a much larger voltage . in fact once it is Started you can even disconnect the battery . It can produce Voltage enough to Entirely Power a house and disconnect from the city grid . It can be made on any scale. The Invention would look something like the Tower of the Americas about 12 to 15 feet high and would be Instaled in the back yard of a house . And yes it would also look very pretty and would light-up the back yard . A much larger version the size of a Water Tower would Deliver enough Kilowatts to power an entire Subdivision or neighborhood .

Here we are talking about Cheap , Clean Energy that is 100% safe for the Environment . I Tried several times to get in touch with CPL but they never returned my calls or my E-mail . I have reason to believe the Companies they are contracting with are in cahouts with the City and so they have an Obligation to investigate all possibilities that could help solve the Transition crisis . I understand you are working on this too and feel if we unite our resources and put our heads together we can get they to have a meeting and talk about these Possibilities . I KNOW for a fact my machine does NOT violate any of the laws of physics and I Can prove that in Court ! If they do not Comply we can Sue for Action in Court . BUT I am a Senior Citizen and I do NOT have a car nor do I want one! I also do Not have the energy to do so much running around as I did 15 years ago . I will need your help to have this Machine Patented and give Clean and Cheap energy to the world .

So you must ask yourself .... Are you Really the Fighter for Justice and a Clean Environment everybody says you are ?? As the Just Transition Ambassador for the city I am willing to share the Royalties from this Invention with you and we can both become Filthy Rich and Help the planet at the same time . You can get in touch with me . I live right here in San Antonio, Tex., my Phone is 734-8288 . I been up all night thinking about this so I will be sleeping late but you can call me after 2P.M. Call me and I will answer any questions you may have . I live in the Southside area of the city .

Sincerely Yours,

Serafin O. Sifuentes

PS. My cellphone is 922-9675 but I only have it turned on when I am away from home.

Then there is the woman who visits from time to time, pleading for them to do something about GMOs. Look, she's written a children's book—did they know anyone who might be able to translate it into Spanish, or could they possibly? She will hover by their desks, urgently talking, seemingly on the edge of tears. She's not from San Antonio or even from Texas. She goes by Mary but that isn't her real name, she's had to change that because they know about her work on GMOs and are following it, following her. Chela will listen with boundless patience, murmuring response at appropriate intervals as Mary grips the arm of her chair, eyes wide and unblinking. But Lali feels claustrophobic around people who talk too much, trapped between a desire to accept unconditionally and a desire to escape.

So when GMO Mary appears at El Centro early in the year, brandishing an article she's hoping they can put in their newsletter, Lali's stomach sinks. She's the only one in the office. She'll have to weather it or figure out how to tell Mary gently that she can't talk, she's trying to work. But Mary advances on her before she can figure it out, rushing the empty office already explaining the article, which she didn't write—though maybe it can be reprinted, if they contacted the publisher for permission?—but which is about how love is *5,000 times stronger than fear,* according to a researcher who found that by directing love at cancer cells, you could shrink a bladder tumor in three minutes! It's like that book everyone was talking about, by the Japanese scientist—what was his name? Emoto. *A Message from Water.* Well, Emoto said water had a memory; it could remember the emotional temperature of its environment. If you radiated love, water molecules retained a symmetrical shape, but anger and hate deformed their molecular structure so that they became asymmetrical or broken and jagged, or, or, or—

Mary goes on and on. At first Lali clenches against the rush of her words, feeling cornered, pinned, stuck—but at some point the woman begins to make sense. And Lali feels the tension in her shoulders melting, her chest opening, her hand itching for a pen. She begins to take notes, surreptitiously at first, in tiny script, and then concentratedly, feeling Mary nodding a subtle approval. They have found each other's frequency; they are having an authentic exchange.

So this article, what it was saying was that our emotional capacities were a kind of energy—one frequency in the vast electromagnetic spectrum of the universe, same as what shaped the water, you know? Because we were the energy of light and love! That was what we were. But it was exactly *because* of this energetic potential, *because* we had the power to impact matter on a molecular level, that the corporations could exploit us. Because what profit required was a low-level, chaotic energy field in which nothing cohered. That was the problem with the GMOs. By patenting and privatizing life, the corporations were keeping things from cohering and communing as designed. It was *because* the corporations wanted us to be disorganized. They *wanted* us to fight each other, to have high entropy! Our disunity was their consonance, their harmony, their coherence.

But this article, it gave people hope—that was why she had brought it, for the new year, because what it said was that *intention*, the focusing of one's energy field for good, was *key*. That was the very definition of love! And ceremony provided a vehicle or formula for directing intention so as to transform the material world, to transmute hope into reality. Ceremony was a *funnel* allowing human beings to draw energy from the universe for healing the earth. Right now the lines of the electromagnetic fields had been disrupted by industrial development and our thoughts—it was the same thing the Buddhists said, and every other mystical religious tradition--

Like, did she know Uma Thurman, the actress? Her dad was a Buddhist professor. And he said that even a single thought had incredible resonance. If you could focus *one single thought*, despite everything else—that would be an inconceivable liberation. Even ordinary things like washing your hands, if you could do it with total intention—surely she's heard that idea? No? Well, what she was thinking—if they could get a few groups and do this together, maybe Lali could work on that part—was, what if, with total intention, they held an image of what they most wanted for the earth inside their hearts—because minds alone were not that strong, you needed the body too, that's what was taken out of the holy books back in the 9th century, the deep intertwining of body and mind, thought and feeling. But if they could bring all the movement people together that way, in a ceremony of embodied intention, they could move from visualizing *what could be* to effecting *what already was*—they could move mountains.

It was crazy, but Lali thought it made a certain sense.

***

One Monday in late January, at a staff meeting where they sit around a table mapping plans and strategy for the year, Lali is handed the task of organizing an action for the end of the week. We need to have an action, Papa booms. We haven't had one in a while. Just to keep the city on their toes, verda'? Let em know that we're watching.

The others agree. An action! Never mind that Lali has come to the meeting with her own long-term plans for the year carefully plotted out. First some political education, then some ongoing meetings to organize film screenings and panel discussions. That would bring new people in: less action, more talk. But, oki doki, an action for Friday.

It is a last-minute protest, held outside around 5:30 in the afternoon at the downtown utility headquarters, where the city's Transition Team meets. Everyone knows you can't have actions or meetings or public hearings during the day because then working people can't attend—so after work Lali rushes from Centro to the daycare to scoop up Nena, then flies back downtown to join the action, driving around and around on the narrow, one-way downtown streets before she lands parking. But when she gets there, running breathless with Nena jostling in her arms, the only ones who have shown up with their banners and signs are the Centro familia, plus one television cameraman doing interviews in Spanish. With the sun setting behind the cold glass and red brick of the utility headquarters, the blustery day is quickly turning cold, and Lali struggles to get Nena zipped in her fuzzy purple jacket. No! Nena shakes her head vigorously, wriggling out of jacket sleeves and away from Lali, then plopping down on the sidewalk to wail. Nothing can persuade her. She doesn't want to wear a jacket, and she doesn't want to be held, and she doesn't want to be there. She's been in daycare all day and it's dinner time. But it's Lali's action, given to her by Papa, and if anything goes wrong, it's on her.

Shh, says one of los cuates, not quite irritated but anxious, waving a hand at them. Shh—they're interviewing Chela!

Lali is already bristling with anger when the woman waiting at the bus stop across the street begins to yell at her.

Put that child's jacket on! she calls through cupped hands. It's freezing cold!

She doesn't want to wear it! Lali calls back.

Well, then take her home! Take care of your child first. Forget about whatever it is y'all are doing!

I'm doing this for *all the children,* Lali screams back in frustration, so furious she does not hear herself, whether she makes sense or not. *You* come put it on her if you're so worried, you see how easy it is! She can feel Papa and the family standing behind her with their signs, apprehensive but unmoving. Closing in, closing ranks.

Boarding her bus, the woman across the street shakes her head with a disgust visible even across the street, and Lali feels a sulfurous rage erupting to her surface, hot and foul. *You bitch,* she wants to hiss in the woman's face at her betrayal, in the violent tones only men could deploy, the word spat from her lips like nails raking over tender flesh. Shaking, she grabs Nena from where she sits whimpering on the sidewalk and snaps at Victor over her shoulder without waiting for his response: Sorry, we gotta go.

Lali manages to wait until they are both around the corner before she explodes in a fury of molten tears. Once back in the car, Lali and Nena fold together in the backseat for twenty minutes, the child suckling with black eyes wide, gazing upward at Lali quaking and shuddering above her and patting her mother's breastbone with one free hand. Lali catches the tiny hand, kisses it, lifts it to her warm and swollen face. *Baby baby*, she whispers without thinking.

Later that night, back at home, she deliberates before dialing Victor's number. What does she want from him? She doesn't know. Some kind of insight, what it means and what to do. Her question feels too big, like something stuck tight in her throat or chest. It was her action—but it wasn't part of her plans, she knew it hadn't been strategic, and Nena shouldn't have been there—but they say they're doing intergenerational work—but if they were they would know that right after work is the worst time for working parents, so—she is guilty and needs to apologize. She is angry and wants an apology. She is confused and needs comfort or advice from someone who understands how big and hard it is, how beyond them all, someone who has been there. Victor is the director; surely he has wisdom. But when he answers, her words crumple in on themselves like wads of throwaway paper; she cannot get across what she wants or needs to know, and Victor is lackadaisical. At least our people came out, he says, the Spanish language media. At least that. Algo es algo, he shrugs.

***

The only bright spots that winter are the city council sessions where Lali sits in the plush auditorium seating of the council chambers with Chela and Naima, keeping an ear cocked for news of the city's legal entanglements with Seismar. Sometimes checking email, sometimes listening quietly, sometimes snarking in whispers or taking notes. Something is revealing itself, something is coming into view. Lali has not abandoned the student's habit of traveling everywhere with backpack slung over one shoulder, and in her bag is a spiral notebook where she collects notes and thoughts and even poems—*notas,* she calls them—feeling form emerge from nonform, the shape of an argument rising in relief against the chaos of observation, something that would explain the how and why of it, shining a light on what they need to do.

These moments of clarity appear between long bouts of boredom, though sometimes there are moments of levity too. Once Chela burst into the meeting late and unknowingly seated herself one row up from Butch Keller of Keller and Keller, the most powerful developer lobbyists in town and thus the legal representative of Seismar Explorations, LLC. *That man gets whatever he wants,* Sister Soli had warned Chela long ago. *I should know, I ran against his father for Mayor. You see him involved, you know something's up.* And now there he was behind unsuspecting Chela! Lali had to rip a ribbon of paper from her spiral and dash a quick note, twisting over the back of her seat to pass it back to Chela. *Psst! Did you know Keller from Keller Keller & Keller (KKK) is sitting right behind you?*

Chela had glanced behind her surreptitiously, pretending to look out the window, then dipped her head to write back.

I'll be sure to fart extra hard then. Yeah, it felt good to go to the meetings as gutterpunk as possible: braless and menstruating, dirty stinky Chucks with no socks and flapping soles, legs hairy and armpits fonky as hell.

Then there was the time the representative of a rare earth trade group—the United Rare Earth Association—lobbied the council in support of domestic rare earth production. Lali and Chela and Naima had passed Lali's notebook between them, furiously scribbling acronyms for a citizen's lobby that might oppose UREA: The People's Organization of Ore Opposition (POOO). Citizens Against Corrupt Assholes (CACA). Demonstrating Intense, Agitated Resistance without Existing Alternatives (DIAREA).

And then there was the time they played hangman, on a day when they'd been sitting in the council chambers since nine in the morning, waiting for their agenda item to come up. Apparently, it'd been pushed back since Mayor Mike was running late, in that morning on a redeye from a Spurs game in Mexico City the night before. Items had gotten pushed back, items had gotten jumbled around.

So they waited, and as they waited they played hangman, heads huddled together. FUCK THIS SHIT was Naima's secret phrase, which Chela easily solved before stickman hung. LET'S GET HIGH was Chela's offering. Lali's stumped them: POOPITY WOOPITY FLUSHITY WUSHITY PLOP PLOP...PLOP? Chela had whispered slowly as the puzzle finally revealed itself. What's with you and shit, she said, shaking her head. They'd played on, snickering and snorting like middle school malcriadas, and when the mayor arrived with face flushed he flashed them ojo from his seat at the dais, making them shake even harder with silent laughter, eyes streaming.

Today they have come to the meeting to hear the city attorney update the council on the status of investigations into what Seismar knew about the cost discrepancy and when they knew it. And so they are caught off guard by the 20 or 30 people who file up the chamber aisle to excoriate the city for voting the previous week to sharply increase their electric rates.

A *rate* hike? Last *week*? Naima gasps. Did y'all hear anything about a 15% rate hike they passed last week?

Naw, says Chela.

Nuh-uh, says Lali.

Naima leans forward to fold her arms on the seat in front of her, chin resting on top, as the elder members of VAMOS approach the podium one by one. Damn. That's some serious shit in this weather.

Oye mama—tryna hear what he's saying.

The old man at the podium, flanked by a squadron of viejitas, looks worn and disheveled in a rumpled suit that swims on his slight frame, but his voice is firm and practiced. City Power and Light, he is saying, the utility that is supposed to belong to the city, to the people, had the nerve to approach you behind everyone's back for a rate increase? You trust their CEO on this, after all the sneaking around on the Seismar project last fall? What's more, you borrowed a trick from their playbook and actually gave it to them behind everyone's back. And bills are already rising! Just think back to last winter, last summer—we can't even keep our houses livable when it's cold or hot out! Meanwhile big companies like Seismar and the developers of those Smoke Stack condos are getting tax breaks and fee waivers left and right from the city, while *our* homes fall apart from not having the money to fix them. At the very least, you shoulda waited until you were out of your legal mess. At the bare minimum, you shoulda had CPL release a line item budget showing what they want all that money for. But we are *not asking* for the bare minimum. We're telling you no! No rate hike! No means no! And if we have to, we'll recall it!

Behind him the viejitas cheer; Chela stands and emits a wolf whistle.

Ahhhh, Chela...! mumbles Naima, embarrassed but proud. You wanna get us kicked out of here?

Chela ignores her. We gotta connect with those folks!

Who, Manuel Martinez, that old Brown Beret? Naima clucks her tongue. He's okay, I guess, if you like being elbowed out of the way so he can jump in front of the mic. Everyone knows it's the women in VAMOS who do all the work.

I know, I know, says Chela impatiently. Still—that shit's for real! We gotta support.

So go and ask him to marry you already.

Watch me! Chela retorts, bounding off to the corner of the chambers where VAMOS has gathered to debrief. With the council now broken for lunch, the crowd has dispersed into small standing clusters of conversation.

As they squirm in their seats waiting for Chela to return, Lali gazes out over the council chambers. There is dumb old Henry Pharr—Henry Fart, everyone called him, probably even the council—who speaks to every single agenda item at every single council meeting. There are the sharks in suits with their dreams of converting the power plants of yore into the oxygen bars and doggie daycares of tomorrow, idling around for their pet zoning cases. There is Butch Keller giving a Heil Hitler greeting to the city manager from across the room. There is a slate of reporters from the city paper standing shoulder-to-shoulder at the back, looking bored. Where is Chela now? She's moved away from Manuel Martinez and also stands at the back, talking with that *Volt* reporter. Feeling him out for what he knows, undoubtedly. But a pang of something uneasy, wanted but unwanted, runs through Lali. She wants him to look over, to notice her and wave goodbye. Jesus, why? As they file out of the chamber, Chela jabbering excitedly about her discoveries, Lali thinks about turning to wave. But she doesn't, willing that her retreat be an entreat, an invitation.

Whither the Fart? Council Session Theater Suggests Satire May Now Be the Only Way Out

Posted by Joel Champlain (jchamp@thevolt.com) on January 22

It is the kind of meeting where you can tell what people are going to say even before they open their mouths, just by the way they are dressed.

It is the kind of meeting that reminds this humble reporter of Greek theater. Sometimes comedic, in the spirit of catharsis, so we may laugh to keep from crying—witness council chamber stalwart Henry Pharr bowlegging his way to the podium to read through the agenda, pausing at key moments to throw homemade transparencies onto the projector for the council to puzzle over. With Pharr, you can bet these cryptic maps have something to do with the designs of teh gayz on the project of religious liberty.

"Let's see," he says, licking his stubby fingers and turning the pages of the council agenda with a pointedly peevish flick. "So many scandals, so little time! Where shall we start?"

Ah, but if everything is scandal, what can be the point of critique? I always mean to ask him whenever I bump into Henry—outside the abortion clinic, or one urinal down in the men's room of the council chamber—but he always seems too much in a hurry to address the inquiries of unkempt reporters. So many scandals, so little time.

I hadn't intended to go to the theater that day. It was a weekday, a workday, a Thursday morning, and I had gone to the council meeting to update myself on the status of the city's legal dealings with Seismar. The company has been petitioning the city to lease out its mineral rights at the former Mud Creek quarry, developing a node mining project that would significantly expand its operations in South Texas. In its appeal to the city, Seismar has argued that mining for rare earths is a necessary component of San Antonio's transition plan, one that would put the city in a unique position to become a critical point in a regional supply chain that would provide clean energy to the rest of Texas and beyond.

But from all appearances, Seismar and the Transition Team, steered by City Power and Light CEO Eric Nabors, collaborated to withhold information from the city on the economic feasibility of the project, before a crucial council vote that would bring the company one step closer to locating in San Antonio. Just a few days before that vote, a sneaky someone leaked behind-the-scenes details downplayed in the economic analysis prepared for Seismar by GeoData, the independent contractor hired to prepare the report. According to our mysterious mole, the actual supply of rare earths in the Mud Creek formation is far less abundant than mineral right leases are profitable due to market speculation, meaning the road to transition might not be as cheap and easy as hoped.

After a good many months in which the Seismar deal made the news daily, a post-holiday hush has blanketed the city like a freak climate change snowfall in South Texas. This news blackout began after the city filed a lawsuit against Seismar in an attempt to gracefully bow out of a recklessly signed Memorandum of Understanding with the company. Under the terms of the MOU, the city would have a 25% share in the company and receive a 25% royalty on mining profits in exchange for Seismar's legal access to mineral rights. But when council learned last minute that Seismar and the city's Transition Team knew but failed to disclose its numbers were false, the city sued in an attempt to withdraw its financial stake in the project, and Mayor Mike pledged an independent investigation into who knew what and when, not to mention where and why and how. I went to council chambers last Thursday in the hopes of getting some updates on the status of the suit, only to find the mayor was running late in heading home from a basketball game in Mexico City. Oh well, next time.

Meanwhile, city leaders have dutifully continued to ignore repeated calls from a coalition of organizations for a more complete calculus of feasibility for the Seismar project, one that would take into consideration the long term environmental and health impacts of the South Texas mining boom, which many see as the best prospect for the industrial scaling up of green energy. As District 3 Councilman Ernesto Garza wailed in confusion last week, responding to one passionate Citizen to Be Heard who decried the dangers of moving quickly on Seismar without federal or state environmental regulations in place, "But this *is* for the environment—I don't understand."

All of which is to say: What else is new under the sun?

Yet from this familiar ground of frustration and obfuscation sprang unpredicted developments and unforeseen actors. Even as the Mayor pledges a new era of transparency, it seems that, legal challenges notwithstanding, the city has quietly passed a 15% increase in electric and gas rates, to go into effect this summer. Catching the entire room by surprise, approximately 25 speakers, most of them elderly women, addressed the council with unanimous anger. Interestingly, given rising uncertainties about the Mud Creek project, Council is framing this increase as "an effort to offset anticipated costs of transitioning to renewable energy." Leading the elders at the podium was Manuel Martinez of VAMOS—Viejos Against More of the Same—who has been active since the 1980s in the push for more equitable distribution of public services on the historically neglected Westside.

"After 40 years of this, you'd think I wouldn't be surprised anymore," Martinez observed with a wry smile during the council's lunchtime recess. "Our wallets and our drafty houses have always subsidized their desire for more growth."

What about the obvious need to transition to renewable energy, in light of federal imperatives to cut carbon emissions 75% by 2040? "What transition?" Martinez scoffed. "They might as well be swapping out coal for unicorn farts, because everything else is the same. Same players, same game, same free service extensions and tax abatements for Northside development companies promising green subdivisions and renewable golf courses. The name of the game is growth, and same as always we'll be the ones carrying it. Transition my ass. That's for the environmentalists to fight about." And the environmentalists are happy to oblige, if recent tensions—between a transition now/regulate later approach and an unequivocal opposition to rare earth mining—are any indication.

For their part, the Transition Team feels it has the win-win solution that will address the concerns of the poorer council districts over the impacts of the rate hike *and* distract from the Seismar lawsuit in the process. Eric Nabors, CEO of City Power and Light and Transition Team chair, explained it to me: "We plan to earmark a portion of the proposed rate increase for expanded affordability programs like Keep Your Cool. So far we've been able to distribute 1,000 thermometers to seniors and income-qualified households most at risk of—"

Of dying from heatstroke because they can't afford their electric bills?

"—of heat stress, so they can monitor the temperature of their homes and get to one of the city's cooling stations. With additional funds we could potentially distribute another 5,000."

And what's the chance Council is too savvy for such tactics?

Martinez snorts. "In the history of the city there's never been a rate case the utility didn't win. It's about growth, growth for growth's sake. Doesn't matter what's powering it, doesn't even matter what it is that's growing. Nobody gets elected who doesn't buy into that. It's like they got a vendido test they give 'em before they even let 'em run."

I leave the council chambers that afternoon heavy-hearted with the realization that el teatro concilio is more tragedy than comedy, in the way the ancient Greeks understood that term to suggest a set of inescapable determinisms. Poor city people, bound by forces they can neither understand nor alter, between the rock of a credit rating that will sink if they don't approve a rate hike—jeopardizing their shot at federal transition loans—and the hard place of post-carbon realities.

Could it be that, within a universe so close-ended by thermodynamics, the only possibility for action lies in satire? Witness the three heads huddled together at the back of the council chambers, whooping it up like kids at the back of the bus. Surely they are writing a drinking game.

Anytime someone speaks of #energyfutures—drink!

Anytime anyone reminisces about their Chamber of Commerce years—drink!

Anytime anyone says they'd like to thank their colleagues within CPL—three drinks!

Research Notas 4:
Instructions

(As dictated to me by Doña Maria
Elena, la mera mera
vieja of VAMOS
as she pushes us out the door with
armfuls of pens and petitions,
clipboards and maps:)

1. First Contact

First you make first contact.

This is straightforward—you
show up where people
go to pay light bills
that have gone overdue
or to plead disconnection
notices. You go there because
they'll have rates
on the brain
already.

And you position yourself
along an unavoidable line
of their exit from the building.
Don't bother them as they go in,
they're busy,

and don't bother asking
for official permission.
Security's used to us by now
anyway; when we
first started coming
they tried to shake
their brooms at us
and we told them, look:
the sidewalks belong to everyone
so you can't run us off,
it's a public space
and we belong here,
we're the public. Ja!
They didn't expect viejitas
to know their rights
of public assembly
but we had been trained
by the best.
That's what the organizer
from the Industrial Areas Foundation
up north—Chicago, I think
he was from, Raúl—
told us many years ago
we should say.

Stick to the sidewalks
and the public spaces
with your ironing boards y todo
and you'll be fine,

he said. I guess he knows something!

Cuz our other great idea
was to make something up,
tell them we're promoting that
new program CPL has,
the one with the thermometers
as if we're estúpidas—

of course we are not;
we are actually going
to the root of the thing,
hacia las raíces,
all the way down
to crank the wrench
to stop the thing cold
in its tracks—so mi'jas,

grab them
as they come out of the building!
Don't be afraid
to approach your own people,
to talk unsolicited. I promise
you'll be surprised
by what you find,
what you learn
about what nuestra gente
are going through.

That's the reason you're there,
for gente,
so don't be scared.

2. No Tiene Miedo

Of course
some will say no
or brush you off,
that's inevitable.
Some will be hurrying home
to make dinner or
take a shower
before work, take care
of babies or elderly parents.
Some just plain aren't interested.
That's okay. Don't be scared
of rejection.

And another thing—never
never ask them if they have a minute
or if they want to sign a petition.
It's too easy to say no
and besides
the truth is more interesting
anyway. Say:

you're with a community group,
and you're fighting

the rate hikes council passed
and you don't like the way
they're transitioning,
jacking up the rates
on los pobres
so los ricos can keep
their solar-powered
a/cs on full blast
all summer
so companies like Seismar
can get their fat contracts
and get out.
They don't mean to, the city
but that's the model,
they don't have the
imagination to come up
with anything better.

So what you're doing today is,
you have a short survey,
and what you want to know
is how much they pay average
for lights and gas.
And how much is that
compared to their income.
And did they ever get their lights cut
and did they even know the rates went up.

Don't ask them if they have a minute.
Tell 'em: it'll just take a minute.

You'd be surprised
how many people are
willing to help.
You'd be surprised at how natural
and normal it feels
to ask your neighbor a question.

3. Their Lives Already Connect the Dots

Pos here's the thing:
the survey is a tool.
Sure we want the information,
but really it's to get them
thinking on the right
track, me entiendes?
Cuz when it comes time
to ask if they'll sign
you want them to connect it
to their everyday lives.
The survey is how you do it.

Like when you get to the question
about whether they knew
the rates went up
most will say no:

can you believe that?
And that's
when you ask them
if they want to sign
the petition.
See that? That's how it works.

Now some will want
to take the sheet home.
To think it over, they'll say.
That never works, you'll never
get the thing back. The goal
is to get them right there.
The goal is to refuse
to let them refuse, but
without manipulation. No:
the goal is to *inspire*
a yes, enflame a desire,
para animar,
that's why
they call us
animadoras!
With the survey
you won't need to do no
explaining why. No splainin, ja!
They'll splain it to
themselves,
their own lives will.

4. Of Course the Process Isn't Fair

Pero here is lo mas importante: first
you will need to make sure
they're registered voters.
If they're not registered,
no problem, you sign them up
on the spot. We got you deputized,
remember? That's why.
Second
is they have to sign
with the address they registered
under, not where they currently live.
That's where the city
tries to trip you.
That's where they'll try
to throw out signatures.
Who the hell remembers
where they registered to vote?

We've seen it before, decades back
when we were fighting the unfair
budget allocations
for streets and drainage.
They wanted to give each district
the same amount.
It's only fair, they said—
starve the Westside for decades
then give everyone the same

to fix it? No ma'am.
So we fought it,
but that's how we learned
how sneaky they are. We got
50,000 signatures
which back then was a lot!
50,000 signatures
which they threw out half saying
the people weren't really
registered to vote,
because of the address thing.
And whatever little way
we tried to maneuver
within the system,
the system would find a way
to block us.
If it wasn't throwing out
signatures, it was
we used the wrong form
or we wrote in the wrong color pen.
Whatever they had to do.
Any little gap or crack,
they'd wriggle right in
and gitcha.
That's how we learned
the process isn't fair.
I think a lot of us going in
believed the system would protect us.
That is what we had been taught

to believe.

When we learned it wasn't like that
our little lightbulbs went off,
dingdingding!
We lowered our expectations.
And it was like, okay,
so now we know
we're gonna have to be
sneaky
on top of dignified,
we're gonna have to do
double duty
both outside and in.

It's the same now as then,
more than 40 years later.
Not much has changed except now
it's our own people doing it.
Like I said: no imagination.
Just more of the same,
more of the same—why do you think
we're called VAMOS, anyway!
We're viejas against more of the same!

CHAPTER EIGHT
Paloma la Partera

In her initial phone interview with El Centro, Lali had been careful to mention upfront to Victor that she was on the market for an academic position. Likely nothing would come of it though, she told him. She knew the stats on how many graduates ended up secure and salaried in university positions, and frankly, the odds were against her. The odds were against them all; both university and universe tipped toward precarity. But just in case, she'd wanted to mention it. In the event she did get something, she hadn't wanted it to feel like a betrayal.

And they'd seemed cool with that degree of open-endedness at the time. But when she had to fly out of town for conference interviews—hotel-room tribunals of sniffing, circling wolves— she had reflexively held that knowledge close, sneaking out of town Friday evening and returning by Sunday on the fumes of the workweek hustle, breasts swollen and aching and leaking after the brief separation from Nena. When she had video interviews in the middle of the day, she took a lunch hour and rushed home to throw on her interview clothes, changing back again before she returned to Centro. All in the hope it would lead not to the brass ring, but its next incremental step: the three-day on-campus interview of nonstop meetings and teaching demonstrations and job talks and dinners. And when, unbelievably, she had gotten an on-campus interview, she'd kept the news secret and asked instead for time off to present at a conference. How could she have possibly translated the import of something like a campus interview, the threshold it signified within the arcane ceremonies of the academy?

It was all because of the letter she had gotten, on a cold day mid-January during one of their popular education sessions. For pop ed, they were each supposed to read one chapter from a book—this time it was Galeano's *Las Venas Abiertas de América Latina*—but no one ever did. In this world they were all too busy to read much, even if they enjoyed it, too overwhelmed with the work of survival. But Papa never complained, because it gave him the opportunity to lecture on what they'd neglected to read for themselves. During long oratory jags his voice would rise to a bellow when he got to the conquest, excoriating the intellectual leaps of European Enlightenment for what they really were: the mangled bodies of Africans, the theft of New World land and minerals. What was enlightenment for some was eviction and enslavement for others.

Well, of course it was. Everyone knew that. But in the novela of family business only Papa got to be scholar. So she hid the notas accumulating in her notebook and her trips out of town for interviews, assuming these would only meet with blank indifference or irritation, as disruptions to the action items of turnout and the goal of victory.

But the letter! The letter had arrived in her inbox mid-lecture in the depths of January—a real Publisher's Clearinghouse moment. That day, she had kept her laptop cracked as Papa wound up, idly refreshing her inbox at intervals in case anything of interest popped into view. And then, that afternoon, it had. *Campus Visit,* read the subject line, and her heart had dropped into her stomach as though she rode an elevator lurching upward too quickly. Quickly, discreetly, she'd clicked on the message to devour the rest—*short list, Assistant Professor position, Political Science department, Kansas State, Manhattan, job talk, teaching demonstration.* Manhattan—Kansas? Why did that sound familiar? Not because it shared a name with New York City's most glamorous global borough or the country's infamous atomic program. Had she passed through there before, maybe, on her runaway flight from home in 10th grade? Wasn't that the town where she'd stood at the edge of a cornfield watching birds swirl overhead? Never mind: she'd looked up into the room, head swimming with the news, trying to refocus. Almost there, almost free from the brutality of the market and the embarrassment of having to bum money from strangers to make bus fare, from telemarketing bullpens and a lack of health insurance that, days before, had her calling Hector in his cubicle at work, in a panic over the boil on her ass. What if it was MRSA! What would they do then? It was the kind of ludicrous thing you didn't worry about when you could see the doctor whenever you needed to. When you had enough money, a boil on your ass was just a boil on your ass. But now, through her wiliness and hustle, she was one step closer to security. It was almost as good as last fall's letter announcing their approval for food stamps and $800 in retroactive benefits, news that had brought tears of relief to her eyes—except tenure-track would mean the abolition of food stamps. No more re-verification appointments or power outages or stupefying greenhouse heat if only she comes north, to a flyover town in Kansas. Tenure-track was an airlift as the entire blazing structure collapsed. Just a campus visit left, the highest hurdle of them all.

And if the release didn't go out—but she has left her list of press contacts back at the Centro office. So now, the night before her interview, she sits at Alianza swiping tears away as she attempts to reconstruct the press list from memory, hands shaking over keyboard as she looks up newsrooms and names online and cuts and pastes addresses into the email one by one. It is too long, too slow, and there is so much left to do, and she cannot tell anyone why she is crying or why there is not enough time in the world: it is because I have a job interview tomorrow. Because then they would know she intends to escape, that she came home only to leave again so soon, a flake in the land of the committed, a fake on the front lines of the directly impacted.

What is it corazón, Paloma wants to know, concern wrinkling her brow. She has stepped inside the quiet of the office from the meeting clamor outside to find Lali crying in front of the computer. Approaching from behind, Paloma opens her rebozo like immense silver wings to wrap Lali inside, hugging her from behind, smelling like anise and pumpkin and basil. It's okay, Paloma tries to soothe her, cheek against Lali's. Whatever it is, it will turn out okay. Be gentle. When Lali finally reveals her terrible secret, Paloma is unfazed. An interview! How wonderful, Citlali. You should be proud. And Lali doesn't know how to explain that, no, in fact everything is fucked.

So now she is at home pounding fists against forehead at her desk and insisting that it won't, it can't, she can't; now Hector, Nena wedged on his hip, is gently setting before her two bean and cheese tacos on a plate so that she might eat before bed, before backing away quietly to give her space. He needs her to chill the fuck out, he needs her aim to be steady and her mission to succeed—it is his job interview as well, her bread-winning he has banked on, that they have both banked on. But she can't eat, all she can do is chew gum, furiously, a whole pack in one evening. Now she is curled on the bed with the lights off, face swollen and hot; now she is up and frantic again, speeding down Nogalitos in the dark because it is still snowing in the Midwest and she doesn't have a heavy coat handy, she will need a heavy coat, one that looks the part with the suit she has cobbled together from secondhand jacket and pants. Now she is clawing through the inventory at Ross ten minutes until closing; now she is racing back home to stuff coat inside suitcase with suit and shoes, the shoes purchased under similar duress, an hour snatched from work and Nena that she doesn't have, the tag still attached to the coat—it is 100 dollars, 100 dollars she doesn't have—so that when she comes back from her interview she can return it to the store and get her money back.

It's not only the interview but the interview on top of the press conference tomorrow, right the actual fuck on top. Immediately after the press conference she will drive to the airport and fly to Kansas for a two-day campus interview. If she is delayed even a half hour she will miss her plane and her one shot; and if she fails to deliver at two days of presentations and demonstrations and social breakfasts and social dinners, two days of being on and on top of all detail, she will fail her family. But if the people do not show tomorrow for the press conference—and if the people show but the press does not, it will be her fault. More than the interview, she is scared the press will not show, that she will fail the people who have called on them, the movement people, the organizations, for support in their fight against higher light bills. For the people it is not about lights but about life and death, about whether their lives and deaths matter in the eyes of the city. Yet there is not enough time in the world to do everything that needs doing, everything that everyone is counting on her to do.

It will all be okay, Paloma had whispered with her wings spread wide to wrap Lali tight. It will all be okay. And it is, though Lali sleeps little that night, adrenaline and exhaustion dueling in her veins like a thready second pulse. *This is the hardest thing I have ever had to do,* she whispers to the ceiling last thing before sleep, lying on her back in the dark. But when they arrive at the council chambers the following day to stand on the steps in the mild February drizzle, the cameras are waiting already to capture the words and faces of the people, and it falls into place like magic. I got behind one payment and they shut my lights off, says the viejita as rain spatters the hood of her plastic rain poncho. When I called them, they said, if you want to turn them on again, you're going to have to pay a $150 reconnection fee. Didn't tell me nothing about no affordability programs. Didn't tell me nothing except, if you don't pay.

Then Chela kicks off the chant she had written during one long boring council session—lu-ces, gas, en-er-gía!—and Naima catches it and brings up the rear, leading the people in response: Power for people, not CEOs! See-ee-ohs, spelled out like that. Naima had laughed at the ridiculousness of rhyming *energía* with *CEO*s and argued for *mentiras* instead, lies, but Chela had objected. *Mentiras* rhymed better but it was so obvious. Everyone rhymed stuff with *mentiras.* Besides, CEOs was clever. If you did CEOs then you had a play on the layered meanings of "power"—power as electricity, power as both domination *and* resistance, from above and below—and that was clever, you had to admit.

I guess! Naima had conceded, half joking half pouting.

As the press conference concludes, as the people file into the chamber to hear what council will say about the rate case and Lali readies herself to sprint back to her car so that she makes her flight on time, Paloma catches her by the sleeve of her jacket. Gripping Lali by the elbow, she presses an envelope into her hand.

It's for you, she says.

What is it? says Lali, peering inside. She gasps when she sees the bills.

For you, Paloma repeats.

Paloma, no! It's too much, she says, thinking of the woman with the reconnection fee. She shakes her head. No.

It'll be okay, Paloma says. You'll know what to do with it when the time comes.

It'll be okay, Paloma had said again, knowing something. Lifting her hands and predicting a path unobstructed, a benevolent and synchronous fluidity with nothing out of step. And so it is. In the blue winter snow her coat holds and protects her, its tag tucked neatly out of sight in the sleeve. Sleight of hand. It doesn't matter because she looks the part, and her presentation—on what made social movements around water cohere and succeed, or not—itself flows as though she is breathing, she can feel it. They are listening; they are right there with her. When they ask questions the right words form in her mouth unrehearsed. At coffees and dinners and breakfasts with deans and students and professors she performs normal social interactions and normal eating ritual, and she does not collapse from the manic energy spiraling at the base of her brain until she is safely back in her motel room once more.

CHAPTER NINE
The Champ Versus the Suitsnties

Joel had his straight voice, to be sure—the voice you wanted, clean burning and efficient, when you had to piston through those meeting minutes—but he also had a salty voice he secretly thought of as the Champ, as a favorite uncle had called him when he was small. The Champ was clever. The Champ was witty. The Champ cracked his gum with his arms folded, standing at the back of the room. A wiseguy, but never smarmy in the way of the big shot columnists in the city paper, invariably entitled young men who smirked in their columnist head shots. No, the Champ was more trickster than he was cocky or smarmy. Not pontificating above it all but down there with the people. He got thrown out of meetings with the city people, because they knew who he was and what he was about. He filed open records requests each Friday to see what he could dig up: there was always something, someone sending emails instructing someone else on how to thread the eye of a loophole, or some company burying radioactive tailings out on some ranch somewhere in bumfuck nowhere, where they thought no one would notice or care. And they wouldn't have—except for FOIA Fridays. And then everybody noticed and everybody cared. That was how he won awards for stream of consciousness journo poetry, stuff that just came to him, lines connecting the dots appearing through the fog like neon to a drunk. How did he do it? Where did it come from? the people wanted to know.

From nowhere, from the ambient cosmos, from the mind of the omniscience where all poems and news tips gestated, to his brain to his fingers tappity tapping away. He was a lightning rod; he was a prognosticator. And that's why he was the Champ.

He was the darling of all the old white conservationist ladies who lived uphill from his hand-me-down neighborhood. Once he had received an anonymous postcard, mailed to the office of the *Volt*, with only these words: *I want to make out with your face*. It was those old money dames with their grey bobs and earthtone rayons and electric SUVs, his paper mates had ribbed him. Joel had blushed as Rudy thumbtacked the card to the break room bulletin board, but the Champ had crowed: of course you want to make out with my face, muthafuckaaaaas!

Once on a balmy Saturday in March, walking back to his car from a city-sponsored New Energies fair, where he had picked his way through the poster presentations cubicled into the ballroom of the Smoke Stacks, with their recipes for waterless metal processing and kinder, gentler nuclear stimulation—see, there was the Champ again—he was ambushed. In his good khakis, no less. By some suitsnties. It was a straight-up Texas showdown, a rootin-tootin rustle right there in the shadow of the old Dirty Dawson, its stacks and scrubbers since redeveloped into a delightful live/work/shop space, its ground floor available for conferences and conventions. They had kept the stacks as namesake and as facade for the apartments above. The turbines and generators and condensers on the ground floor had become historical referents, architectural details incorporated for an ironic steampunk posterity. The cooling pond had become a waterfront. And the children of the mobile home park community who no longer lived in the surrounding neigh-borhood, pushed out by the rising property taxes of boutiques and ballrooms, continued to live with mercury in their brains.

He could see the utility CEO, flanked by two councilmen, approaching at high noon in their city people clothes, hands to their hips and wide, hair-receded foreheads shiny. The Champ couldn't wait to hear what they had to say, but Joel fought an unhappy tension around his skull. He had a headache. He wanted to go home and lie down.

Joel Champlain? The CEO stepped forward first.

Yes? It was an odd response, on the face of it. An affirma-tion, a question.

Eric Nabors, from—

City Power and Light, right. Good to finally—

Good to meet you. They spoke at the same time, words bumping into one another.

Jinx, the Champ wanted to say as he took Nabors's extend-ed hand. As they shook he briefly met eyes with one of the councilmen, who stood silently behind Nabors, mopping his forehead. Barrera, wasn't it. District 3? District 1, downtown-ish. A paunchy man in his early 40s. Salt and pepper mustache. Nondescript, as the description went. Nuttin special.

I've been following your coverage of the Seismar project, the CEO began. I'm hoping we can meet to allay some of your concerns. It's true the Transition Team has made some serious missteps with regard to transparency. And like any util-ity we've struggled to balance low cost for our customers with environmental protection. But in this case, we feel extremely optimistic that our plans with Seismar are the strongest and most proactive we've ever had for achieving transition. Mr. Champlain, if I can speak honestly—

Joel looked at Nabors, wincing inwardly as he waited for the kick. Go ahead—shoot, he thought.

In all honesty, we do feel some of your coverage of the project hasn't been very balanced. We'd like the opportunity to present our position, if you would be interested in a longer meeting.

Joel stood thinking about the mobile home children of the old power plant, wondering where they had scattered to, what turns their lives had taken. He thought about Luz waiting for him back in the car with the windows cracked. He had to go. But before he did—

Well, in the spirit of a reciprocal honesty, he hears the Champ begin. Your position is already well represented, in the council chambers, in the city paper, and in your ability to rent a space here at—that *name*—ah, at the *Stacks,* and offer the keynote address. All I'm trying to do is give space to what wouldn't get said otherwise. Or, really, what is spoken but goes unheard. That old equal time rule in journalism doesn't work so well when your voice is already the louder one. Know what I mean?

Joel started walking away, head throbbing. Now he really had to go. He felt like he could crunch about eight Advils and wash them down with a quart of coffee.

Call me, though, he calls over his shoulder. I'm open to hearing more. And—here came the Champ again with a wink—you too, Councilman Barrera.

Where did that come from? Something going on there. Not sure what, but something. Joel made a note for the next FOIA Friday.

***

The next day the Champ woke up feeling fine. More than fine! Headache gone. Flexing his fingers before the keyboard like a concert pianist, he dug down, down, down into the delicious tale of his ambush, cracking his gum with glee.

Research Notas 5:
The Rise and Fall of King Henry from the Block

Henry Cisneros: where do I start?

His mayoral tenure was roughly contemporaneous with my childhood, so I didn't realize at the time what a big deal Cisneros was. It's like with little Nena: as she grows up she will only know a world in which Obama has been president, in which someone like Obama has been possible. But what I remember Cisneros for, primarily, embarrassingly, was not his historical significance as much as how hot everyone thought he was, including me: young, trim, handsome, bronze skin and crisp white shirt. In an article infamously titled "Tex-Sex-Mex: Dirty Mexican Men, Aztec Gods, Good Ole Boys, and New Texas Women," Chicanx studies scholar Jose Limón comments on this same iconography, referencing a Texas Monthly article from 1988:

On the magazine's cover we find Cisneros, dressed in what appears to be a very expensive and sophisticated bedtime lounging outfit—totally white, to contrast with his dark complexion—reclining, barefoot, on equally totally white and silken bedding. ... During this period the media regularly refers to his Indian countenance and a woman in a San Antonio styling salon is overheard referring to him as 'an Aztec god,' all of which adds a new dimension to the Latin lover image.[23]

Come on, for real? And yet that's how he lives in my mind, too.

---

[23] José E. Limón, *American Encounters: Greater Mexico, The United States, and the Erotics of Culture* (Boston: Beacon Press, 1998), 142-3.

Henry Cisneros was young, gifted and Brown. Admiring his hotness was admittedly also yucky; Henry Cisneros looked like my dad when my dad was equally trim and young and handsome. He was born the same year my dad was born, part of the postwar generation my dad came from—solidly working class but upwardly mobile, Catholic school upbringing, still understanding Spanish but not needing to speak it outside the home either. Assimilationist I guess, but not only that. Something historically fresh and glistening. The possibility of puncturing an underclass status. "Henry I," Hernández-Ehisman calls him.[24] You have to understand that in San Antonio—unlike other places where "Mexican" is synonymous with "immigrant"—it's not generational status that has impoverished us and made Cisneros's election something new, something improbable. A lot of us have been here since—well, we're just from here. We may have moved around within the upper reaches of Limón's "Greater Mexico," but you know the saying about the border crossing us. In San Antonio it's not immigrant status but entrenched racialization, color lines—Brown and white, over Black and white—which made the election of Henry Cisneros a big deal. It's colonial history, it's Anglo rule, it's rule by a white minority.

So Henry Cisneros felt like making it. Henry Cisneros felt like finally arriving. He felt like a disruption of what had previously prevailed. To some of us, anyway. Because of course Henry Cisneros was only possible because he had the backing of the same Anglo business lobby that has always run the city. The good ol' boy Texans you think of when you think of Texans,

---

[24] *Inventing the Fiesta City,* 159.

not the Mexico-Texans of Américo Paredes, the Mexico-Texans down at the HEB on S. Zarzamora. There is a video you can find online, a tribute to Cisneros's lifetime of accomplishments. In it, a banker and the owner of a certain sports team—former Chamber of Commerce heavyweights who now appear jarringly frail, their faces washed and eyes red-rimmed—take turns praising Cisneros's legacy. It is subtle, but what you can hear in this praise is that they once found him quite threatening to their political and economic interests. Once radically threatening but now iconic, like MLK sanitized on a commemorative stamp. But what the video doesn't explain, what is so subtle as to be unspoken—what you could only understand from outside study of San Antonio's political history—is that Cisneros's election would not have been possible, would not have been even thinkable, without the influence of these men and others like them over San Antonio's electoral process. Political scientist Rodolfo Rosales has called it the "illusion of inclusion." From the 1950s to the 1970s, a local machine of wealthy, mostly Anglo businessmen known as the Good Government League organized to select the candidates who would run for city council, ensuring the continuity of a pro-business agenda as the natural order of things, as neutral and nonpartisan "good government." They were always polite enough to select token Mexicano and Black candidates to run, in eventually illegal, at-large elections that made it effectively impossible for the majority-minority residents of the South, East, and Westsides to enter the political process, either as candidates or as voters.

Before he was elected mayor by popular vote, Cisneros was one of those GGL council selections. He may have appeared within the frame as a visible difference, but it was these other men, whose whiteness and wealth remained largely out of sight, who constructed the frame and thus its contents in particular ways. Cisneros may have looked different, but his political ideology eventually—not at first, necessarily, but eventually—repackaged the trickle down economic theories preferred by the Chamber of Commerce. Cisneros made those theories *sexy*, standing in front of the big new convention center talking about economic development as the horizon of all urban land use decisions. The theory he sprinkled with his political Cholula was that if you attracted big companies to your city, if you courted private investment in huge stadiums and malls and theme parks, it would increase the tax base and bring in jobs and everyone would benefit. The theory went, and still does: a rising tide lifts all boats. And if you could attract private investment, you could improve the city's credit standing among investors, and you could compete globally for further investment even more effectively. When Henry Cisneros said that, he said it with earnest feeling, from the heart. It wasn't about growth just because he was in with the Chamber. For him it really was about community, it was about what he wanted for people like our parents and grandparents, for those who had been left behind. Henry wasn't cynical, he knew what was up. But while he may have given it a far nobler face, it was still the standard playbook, luring private investment northward, away from the people and into the pockets of contractors and companies. Because it never trickles down quite the way they say it does.

***

I know I'm supposed to stop there, with my hands on my hips wagging a finger in your face. But then I remember Henry's wife Mary Alice is the daughter of my grandfather's cousin, or something like that. I remember that a friend's sister is married to Henry's brother, that Henry's brother has shown me great kindness, that Henry's brother jokes about there being only seven families in San Antonio. You know what they say: throw a rock in San Anto, hit your prima's primo. And if they don't say it yet, they do now.

So I hold back, because being hard on Henry feels too much like being mad at your middle-class Brown dad who loves you and only wants the best for you, mad he's not the revolutionary subject you want him to be. It's like that thing about, *Oh, so the moment we become political subjects, you're going to deconstruct the subject?* The way I wiggle out of my own discomfort is to say that it's not really about Henry from the block, Henry from the Westside, Henry who married my grandpa's cousin's daughter. It's that Cisneros materialized a particular discourse. Right? It's not about him, it's about the kind of political arrival sanctioned by those who had ruled and would continue to rule. It's about neocolonial patterns of uneven development manifesting geographically, in the physical shape of the city. It's about a particular postcolonial moment in which Brown and Black men, for the first time—but only men at that point; and, really, only attractive straight men—could act like rich white men. Now, of course, anyone can get elected and act like rich white straight men.

Cisneros is just a discourse—right?

But the other thing Henry Cisneros is known for, of course, is his affair with Linda Medlar, a former fundraiser and big-haired Anglo Texas woman who towards the end of Henry's fourth mayoral term became his mistress. Later, during Cisneros's confirmation process for secretary of HUD, Henry found himself under investigation by the FBI for underreporting the amount of the out-of-pocket payments he'd made to Medlar after they split, compensation for her ruined job prospects and reputation, the evidence recorded in secret by Medlar during their many phone conversations. Many have divined in the story of Henry and Linda a number of motifs: Cisneros the typical politico who can't keep it in his pantalones, Cisneros the race traitor, Cisneros the dashed hope of Aztlan, but more often Cisneros the tragic hero, Cisneros the victim of a Clinton-era surveillance apparatus more obsessed with sexual purity than public corruption. Limón reads Henry and Linda as a New Texas spin on an old Latin Lover theme—Henry as object of the liberated Anglo woman's desire—but it is *Henry's* desire that compels our attention. *Henry's* desire that seemingly floods and overspills its narrow channel of political determinations.

And what about Mary Alice's desire within the political triangulation of her husband's very public affair? What did Mary Alice want, what did *she* long for? Maybe not even Henry by her side. Maybe a world free of men like Henry, with his side chicks and vendido politics. Limón's silence on this question seems to suggest she had none; however, this silence also points out larger erasures of Chicana desire and agency in public life, too often cast as a struggle between Brown men and white men or (per Límon) Brown men and white women.

Would it be gross, then, would it be a similar betrayal to say that there was something interesting and tender there, too, in Henry's desire—a public revelation of the power of longing, the power of forces bigger than power, a force that could be neither refused nor made to fit? A testimony to the unincorporable residuum of mystery. It wasn't about sex, it was about desire as the quanta of the universe, a wave and a particle both, Henry's impossible desire. He'd had to answer what called to him and in him, despite whatever ruin would follow in its wake. Not that it ruined him. If anything, he became even more legendary. But the point remains: Henry had to honor what moved through him, whatever the cost to his marriage and political future. Because it was true. There was something there that compelled surrender. That's how I read it, anyway.

This despite a system set up to sanction and sanctify the desires of men, the sole right of men to desire. Right?

FOIA Friday!

Posted by Joel Champlain (jchamp@thevolt.com) on March 25

In the spirit of contemporary turnings away from the staid journalistic convention of articles and toward what we here at the *Volt* affectionately refer to as "listicles"—still media content, but *lighter, jauntier, snappier!*—I offer the week's top three hits for you to remix. I provide the dots, you the interpretive connections. More energy efficient that way. More column inches for the boner pill ads bringing you this week's brain dump. Catch a whiff, San Antonio:

1. Rate Hike Recap

Or should that be "root canal recap"? As councilman Roy Barrera commented at a monthly breakfast with his District 1 constituents, the utility rate hike council recently passed can be likened to the pleasantries of oral surgery. "Nobody likes a root canal," he thoughtfully observed. "They hurt like hell. But sometimes they're necessary." Awash on a gentle wave of appreciative chuckles, the Councilman broke for informal chat over breakfast tacos on such new district initiatives as Saturday Spayathon and CPL's new Keep Your Cool program, which aims to prevent heat-related illnesses in elders through—wait for it—increased access to thermometers.

Meanwhile, VAMOS (Viejos Against More of the Same) has announced it will be squaring off against the city, organizing a petition drive to recall the council's rate hike decision and put it instead to a public vote. It's a steep undertaking, requiring 10% of the registered electorate, or approximately 150,000 signatures. If successful, it would be the first time utility rates were decided by popular election. Los Viejos and their supporters have already begun mobilizing a squadron of door knockers and positioning themselves at the entrance of libraries and senior centers; look for them standing outside your local post office or bus stop, pushing a clipboard in your face.

2. Node activity and updates on lawsuit against Seismar
With all the hoopla around rate hikes and root canals, let's not forget there's a boom going on! Or a lawsuit over the terms of that boom. To get the lowdown on both, I g-chatted with Eric Nabors, CEO of City Power and Light, at his generous urging last week when we encountered each other at the city's New Energy Fair. Our conversation went something this:

JC: what up nabors...it's joel champlain from the volt
EN: holla!!!
was hoping you'd massage me
haha! i mean MESaGE...stupid autospell
didn't know if you'd be intersted after the way we ambushed you last week at the energy fair
JC: ambushed? no way, that was just friendly tête-à-tête re very serious matter of whether/to what extent constructs of journalistic objectivity serve interests of the powerful
srsly tho i could tell I hurt your feelings...like maybe i gave TOO too much thought to complicated politics of a Transition fueled by intensive mining of nonrenewables. I know it's far less complex than I made it out to be

EN: naw it's okay

i'm just glad we're talking now. I was so worried u were made at

me

*mad

JC: so what's up

you seem kinda down or something

EN: i have all these confusing feelings abt the seismar deal

it's hard to talk about

JC: hey that's what bruhs are for

EN: okay so it's like

there's a part of me that knows it was fucked up to lie

about the numbers

JC: well you can't beat yourself up about it

goes with the territory

EN: right? but on the other hand...

there's a part of me that's like fuck it

everyone knows booms eventually bust!

JC: exactly...why not get in while you can and take   advantage

EN: yeah exactly!

i just feel our ability to transition to post carbon depends on it

i mean if we want to do it in a way where we're still making lots

of money

some of that shit trickles down anyway

and there's jobs for awhile

till the bottom falls out

but still

JC: no reason it can't be fucked up and not fucked up at the same

time

hey btw, how's the lawsuit going against seismar?

haven't heard much since the paper went apeshit on you

the city paper i mean

i would never do that of course

EN: hehe, that's funny, i was *just* about to tell you

like RIGHT right now

we actually settled with seismar the other day

we'll stay in the contract with them

but our royalties increase from 25 to 30%!

and our ownership share decreases from 25% to just 5%!

and we got a bunch of money too

i mean, we found funding for a new affordability program

we're going to buy thermometers for the poor people

so that they can tell if their houses are getting too hot

JC: yeah, i know how confusing that can be for poor people

awesome news tho dude...congrats!

funny, i didn't hear anything about it

EN: oh you know how modest and bashful the city is

JC: hey i just happened to have my calendar open, looks like yall

settled right before city voted in your rate increase

EN: brb, gotta poop!

JC: lol...good luck with that

EN: ok, back! Ahhh...better

JC: i'll just ignore that

EN: j/k, what were you saying?

JC: oh just that i guess the settlement probably doesn't have anything to do with the rate increase...i mean, it's probably just a coincidence that they settled right before they voted to raise rates on people

it's not like the city needs to make up for those lost mining royalties to keep their credit rating, which proves to to the feds they're a solid bet for one of those loan guarantees for clean tech projects...which the mining totally is...not that the city wants one of those, of course...

EN: hmm

JC: i mean i guess it prob isn't the case that the city settled instead of just backing out of their contract with seismar, so that they could leave a window open...

you know, so that they could increase ownership share again if the feds did select the seismar project...

and i KNOW it's not the case that they're using the promise of affordability programs...aka money from the settlement for thermometers...to buy the support of the poorer council districts for the rate increase...cuz they would NEVER do that

EN: your so funny

JC: lol i know

EN: for reals tho, those are some good ideas

And lest you wonder as to the verisimilitude of this account, may I remind *Volt* readers that sometimes the constructions of fiction are far more clarifying than the dissimulations of realpolitik.

As they say on gchat: ;)

3. FOIA Friday!

Seeing as it's Muckrake Monday, I thought I'd share some of the spoils of these past few months' open records requests. Just a taste, though. The main course is still simmering, in the form of an investigative report the city's legal team will soon release on its exploration into the details of the Seismar scandal.

Until then, I've been able to review some of the same memos and emails undoubtedly informing this pending report, and find most interesting what appears to be a love letter anonymously forwarded from a burner email account to <u>someone-else-whose-name-has-been-redacted-out@sanantonio.gov</u>, who then put it on e-blast to the mayor, city manager, city attorney and all ten council districts, cc'ing CPL CEO Eric Nabors along the way—all a couple of days before the Seismar thing went kablooey. Unfortunately for the public interest, the sender erased all user names associated with their account, though we can see they received the original message last July and forwarded it on in early October. However, the domain names clearly establish that someone within the city has been quite literally in bed with someone associated in some official capacity with Seismar. Someone in the know about poetry, not to mention geological data on projected node supplies:

you were asking about writing. i was showing you the lithographic description of the mineral formation and we were talking about writing, to what degree specialized language is necessary. i suppose it isn't, ultimately, though i suppose too that the more important thing than accessibility is knowing what kind of language to use when.

but let me tell you something else. did you know i started out as an english major? before i went into the sciences, i wrote poetry in high school and was even editor of the school literary magazine. i loved words, loved literature, loved rhetoric. i loved reading a text for what it didn't say or couldn't, for what was beyond the author's intention. i remember my amazement when i learned a text could say something other than what it made plain, that it was code to interpret. that you could mine the text for meanings imperceptible at the surface. i guess that's also why, during a required college geography course i thought i would hate, i became bewitched by the language of geology. a passage from a textbook on the rare earths i kept from graduate school, a description of a mineralized zone in canada:

"The property is predominantly comprised of these syenites, carbonatites, massive magnetites, fault-alteration breccias, and syenite breccias. REE-bearing minerals within the Clay-Howells deposit are complex, but primarily consist of a cerium-lanthanum-calcium (Ce-La-Ca) silicate and monazite" (Sage 1988).

i liked it because it was strange—bizarre and beautiful. i wanted to learn that language for myself, how to read and write it. my writer friends thought i was abandoning art for science. but because i was a poet first, i could see that the specialized language others dismiss as "jargon" is also a poetry—precise but oblique, like an oracle speaking truth while evading the eyes of the reader. flume, flux, porphyry, metallurgy, lithography, assay. a technical language is by necessity also a poetic language.

so we were talking about the names of rocks, about writing, but it's the other part of the report i was telling you about that i wanted to send, the economic analysis. i've attached it here. have you heard before of the distinction between field economics and street economics? field economics means the day-to-day reality of extracting an actually existing reserve. street economics (as in "wall street") is about the relationship between a publicly traded company like seismar and the investment capital required to get a resource out of the ground.

street economics is about potential *value. this distinction became very clear a few years back with unconventionals, when shale gas was the hottest shit around. it was supposed to be energy independence—or the bridge fuel to carbon-free, depending on your political stripe. in the case of shale gas, startups gobbled up acres and acres of mineral rights on the cheap, drilled a little so they could call a field a solid investment, then sold off the leases to investors for tasty fees. for their part, investors jumped in to buy leases on land assumed to have high production capacity, pumping billions into drilling. all this demand pushed natural gas prices artificially high; and, taking these inflated prices as reality, production companies made drilling decisions accordingly. that's street economics.*

all of this is only possible in the early years of a boom, because you don't have data on the field economics—how much is there, how much is recoverable, and what it costs to get it out—until later. but once field economics catches up to street economics, actual supply inevitably trumps speculative demand. investors pull out, prices drop, companies pull out and sell off their assets, writing off business losses on their taxes. banks collect huge fees on mergers and acquisitions, workers are laid off, communities are left holding the bag. this is not anything particularly revelatory—it's textbook. it's happened before, again and again.

so what's happening now, again, is that the field numbers from the sealands mines are starting to come in, and gelder doesn't like it. he actually asked me to downplay emerging production data from the sealands so that prices for rare earths at mud creek continue to reflect inflated estimates from speculation. even if i don't, though, what we're seeing at mud creek is that there's just not as much supply as they thought, it's not as concentrated as they thought, and it's going to cost way more to get it out than they anticipated. there's no way around the conclusion that the cost estimate seismar is proposing is based far more on street economics—buying and selling mineral rights leases—than field economics. the land is the play, not what's in it. has anyone on council been briefed on this yet, or the mayor? i gave nabors and the CPL transition team our analysis a couple weeks ago.

anyway, enough of that. what i wanted to tell you—after you left the other evening, i walked through the brush feeling your hand still touching the side of my face as we said goodbye. i walked, pushing low-hanging mesquite out of the way, watching yellow lightning punch at the smoky bottom of thunderheads on the horizon, not threatening rain as much as giving display to the receding heat of the afternoon. the ghost of your hand on my face. it reminded me of the first time you came to tour the site and meet with the company reps. we were both walking from the field back to the trailer, and when we arrived, we reached for the door at the same time—or i reached and then shrunk back, out of courtesy, just as you reached up a second too slow. or you reached first and then i did. in any case, the same rules at the same time produced a miscalculation, a collision in time and social space, canceling out the norms and permissions that would ordinarily constrain our movements. a rippling matrix of mores, glistening like morning spiderweb, ripped when your hand brushed against mine. or was it mine against yours. an accident, in any case. a detail i might otherwise forget, if you were any other person. but because it was you it felt purposeful or at least momentous, in the way my hand continued to tingle, with a burning sensation where our skin chanced to brush, and leaving me wondering after you as you walked back to your car and drove away. wondering: why should i still feel your hand on mine when you were no one in particular to me. were you? i watched you drive until your car disappeared, then went inside.

as then, my cheek burns where it remembers your hand resting there.

***

Well. Just *why* the local governmental recipient of such intimate information then forwarded it to their colleagues—deleting user names but leaving domain names apparent—is unclear, although certainly tantalizing. So too is the question of how many of these titillating details will actually filter up to the official report.

Till next FOIA Friday!

CHAPTER TEN
Toribio Pays His Biles de Luz

He could have been any one of them, part of a cohort that was part of a wave that had already begun to gather momentum like a piling thunderhead and register statistically, in the shape of predictable patterns. Significance, form and meaning, from the emptiness of random collision. Once the start-ups came sniffing around with their thumpers and boomers, the men followed the trail hungrily, sucking up the crumbs like anteaters. These would be followed by the cardboard hotels and apartments, as hastily and flimsily assembled as cutouts from a model kit. Once the money dried up, they'd stand empty and useless and blow away, but there was money now and that was all that mattered. Forever and ever and ever, since they had breached the ancient prohibition and begun to claw into her mountains and mesas and marshlands to get at the wealth she gathered there. Ever since then it had happened the way it was happening now.

He could have been any one of them, but Toribio in particular lived with his brother and sister-in-law and the sister-in-law's mother and the two kids, six and eight, in one of the new cookie cutter three-story complexes on the Southside where the city quickly unraveled into brushland. It was as close as they could get to the mines without having to live in a camp or an RV park. Well, that might have been all right really. Some of the little towns there had luxury camps with staffed laundromats and convenience stores and even on-site mess halls with cereal dispensers and 24/7 coffee. But a place like that was clearly out of the question. A place like that was for gabacho workers—he put los prietos who'd lost their Spanish, "Hispanics," they called themselves, in that category too. But the play had gotten him out of day labor, and that was enough for now.

It was his brother who got him the job. He'd come over first and gotten all his papers in order, and he'd gone to the staffing agency on Military next to the CPL payment center and the EZ Money Loan Store. Toribio had crossed a few months later and didn't have papers yet, but that was before they made the hiring process difficult. Drug test, background check, driver's license, insurance, work visa. But in the beginning they'd take anyone—meth heads, ex-felons, sin papeles, no le hace. Then there had been accidents in the sealands, mostly drivers popping speed to stay awake, and now you had to show you were clean and legal and no felonies before they'd even interview you. But since crossing without papers was a misdemeanor—well.

Now they all share a two-bedroom apartment where the rent was $600. That was okay because split two-way it was only $300 each for his brother and sister-in-law, who worked at the Dairy Queen on South Presa, and they let him stay there mostly rent-free. Just pay the lights and the water, they were nice enough to say, at least until he paid off the rest of what he owed the now out-of-business mobile home park for the lease-to-own traila he'd bought with all the savings he'd brought over, only to have to abandon it. His brother had been smart to move into an apartment straight away. To save money, Toribio had moved into a park that was sold not a few months later to some big developers who wanted to cash in on rising land values. It was because of those apartments they'd built upriver, out of an old power plant. Why anyone would want to pay thousands per month to live in an old coal plant he didn't know. Some of the residents who had lived there for a long time talked about pollution from the plant, the rumors about mercury and birth defects in the kids, but the plant was already shuttered by the time he moved in. He'd liked it there in the park. It was quiet, it was right on the river.

The developers wanted them out of there for exactly those reasons, so they could use the land for condos and coffee shops and Crossfits. Just wipe it clean like a chalkboard and start again. Some of the residents had gone to the city people and wept and begged for their homes—some of them had lived there four decades, had raised children and grandchildren there—but the city people's hearts were unmoved as they explained that for too long the Southside had been neglected, and that the investment would increase the tax base so the schools would be better, the schools their kids would no longer be able to attend. He would say pinche gabachos that only cared about money, but it was Mexicanos like them who had pushed it through! Gabachos Mexicanos. As it turned out, as it always turned out, it was too little too late. The developers had already applied for their permits when he moved into the park, though the manager's office was considerate enough not to worry him about it when he signed the papers on a used traila. And one month later, they all got a flyer en inglés taped to their mailboxes saying the park was being sold and they would all have to leave.

The contract he'd signed with the park said he had to stay until the traila was paid off, and he guessed he could've fought to get out of it, some of them had, but he had no papers. And in the meantime they were putting down surveyor's stakes and cutting the trees and dismantling abandoned trailas around them and he split. No trace. Like there would be no trace of the park. The city people had gone around knocking on doors with a list of other parks where they could move and information on their homelessness services center, but again it was papers, you needed papers to qualify for any of that, and he'd be crazy to move into another parque besides.

Luckily his brother had the apartment farther south, as far south as you could go without leaving town. It was near the refinery on the river, the one they were renovating for yet more luxury apartments. His brother's apartment building was also new; the beige polyester carpeting was clean, and the walls smelled like fresh paint. The kids stayed in one room and Francisco and Vika in another, while the mother-in-law had the couch. Toribio slept in the tiny dining area off the kitchen on a bedroll, which he stashed in the corner of the room each morning. It was okay.

Toribio and his brother rise before the sun each morning and don't get back till late. One week on and three days off and another week on. He's had to wait until his days off to get to the payment center on Military, to pay the light bill he's let go overdue. He'd gotten behind as he waited for his first paycheck, and then the second had been eaten by an overdue payment to the mobile home company. And by then the utility people had started sending letters about how they would shut their lights off, even though the mother-in-law had asthma and needed the a/c to breathe when it started getting hot—which already in April it was. He had tried calling the utility people to ask for more time, but the agents only told him he needed to pay; if he didn't they would shut everything off and there would be a reconnection fee to turn it back on. It's better if he comes to the payment center where he can get on an installment plan, they say in Spanish, without a note of concern.

When he exits the center, more promissory paperwork in hand, she's standing on the sidewalk bordering the parking lot, clipboard clasped to chest. She approaches him with clipboard extended as he heads for Vika's truck. He doesn't want to get involved; he raises one hand and waves, smiling, in a gesture of gentle refusal. No, gracias. But she asks, Prefiere Español? Hesitant but earnest. He slows, he lets her hand him the clipboard. Una petición, she says. Contra los...los rate hikes. Sabes que City Power and Light—la...compañía de luz de la ciudad, creo que es como se dice—que CPL acaba de aumentar tus biles? He looks at the papers on the clipboard, reading, then raises his eyes to her expectant face. She is well-intentioned, he can see that, but she's nervous because her Spanish is so bad. Workable, an ear for accent, as though she had grown up around it. But not native and not fluent. She didn't look Mexicana. But he could tell she wasn't pura gabacha either, there was something else. Light brown eyes and medium brown hair, plain straight hair blunt-cut to her chin, but set against deep golden skin. A yellow girl, brownness averaged across all features. He could tell because she looked like his nephews: Vika had grown up here and the father of her kids was gabacho, a shitkicker from her country high school with the big buckle and boots and truck and everything. In one of the boys, brownness gathered in hair and eyes, leaving the skin milky. The other had Indian features but clear green eyes and reddish hair. At their South Texas school there were kids with names like Juan Garfield and Billy Bob Cuahtémoc Rosenbaum. Kids whose hands and arms bronzed brown in the summer, whose legs and feet remained winter white where they went covered, pale as the belly of a fish. But what did a Mexican look like, anyway? To be Mexican was by definition to be mixed—what was a little more?

She's still waiting for his answer, but then she thinks of something.

Estás registrada para votar? Tiene que ser—ah, tiene que *estar* registrada—*registrado*—para firmar.

Pos no señora. No tengo papeles, he almost says, but that would be ill-advised. Quién sabe what that petición was about anyway. So he shrugs it off smiling, turning to go.

But as he's walking back to the truck she shouts out to him in her gabacha Spanish. When he turns back, she's waving one hand in the air and with her other using the clipboard to shield her eyes from the sun, already intense at 11 A.M.

Alto al rate hikes! she calls.

He laughs and waves back. Alto a los rate hikes!

But it really wasn't funny.

***

It's up to las viejas where Lali and Chela and Naima will be collecting signatures each Thursday afternoon. Sometimes they send them to libraries or the tax assessment office, sometimes senior centers to make presentations. Sometimes they contemplate one of the large maps that paper the walls and hand them a smaller neighborhood map and corresponding list of addresses: here, you take this side of the street and you take that side. The weather is still cool enough for door knocking, at least in the morning. On their clipboard is the rap they've developed with las viejas, English on one side and Spanish the other:

hello my name is

i'm with VAMOS

we're here w petition about the rate hikes

did you know the city voted to raise light bills 15% this summer?

did it behind our backs—like w the mining company

we want a recall, that's why this petition

we need signatures, 150,000 registered voters by july

are you registered to vote?

if yes great

if no that's okay, we can register you

so will you sign?

The maps cover the faux wood paneling in VAMOS's little borrowed office, down the hall from the parish kitchen smelling of a thousand spaghetti fundraisers. There are maps of the city, its radial highways and freeway loops casting a spiderweb over the land like a spell, holding it in thrall. Maps that paint-by-number the city's council districts. Precinct maps that illuminate who voted in the previous election, and how. Watershed maps tracing the lacework of creeks as they feed into the river. Lali traces her finger over Mud Creek, where they want the mining site north of the outermost loop, but that map is not from this campaign, says one of the viejas when she catches Lali studying it. Trying to make it fit, trying to sift a single shape from the infinity of sand. That one is from another fight back in the day, explains Doña Alicia, a water project they had wanted on the far Southside that would have doubled their water bills. Two times they had slain it and two times it rose from the dead, but in the end they had won, for once.

There is a census map that magnifies the West, the South, the Eastsides of the city, where las viejas color in those neighborhoods where signatures have been collected already; and every Thursday when Lali and Chela meet Naima at the VAMOS office to pick up petitions—*Mira*, Doña Maria Elena will shout to the room, *las chiquitas are here!*—more and more of the map has been markered in. Lali and Chela are not supposed to be there, they are supposed to be out flyering for the May Day marcha. At the planning meetings Lali has tried to voice the urgency of the petition drive and the need to hold a second People's Power Summit to finish conversations left hanging at the first, but Victor and Marcos are indifferent, then resistant. After May Day, they say. We got some funding for the organizing, so the marcha's the priority.

Well, could all the energy stuff be rolled into May Day, Lali had inquired. Could we have a table, say, where we're collecting signatures?

Victor had shaken his head, face closed and emotionless. Was he colder since she began to collaborate with La Alianza and VAMOS, or was that paranoia? Wouldn't make sense, he said. May Day is about workers and immigrant rights, not energy.

But the rate increases are going to disproportionately burden—

Yeah, no. It's too much of a stretch.

So their Thursday visits to the VAMOS office are clandestine ones. It's so fucked, Naima fumes over her shoulder as she backs out of the parish parking lot in her little Honda. Chela rides shotgun, Lali in the back. We need to push back on that, she says. Let us know when y'all's May Day meetings are. They're supposed to be *community* meetings, she says, an undercurrent of accusation in her voice. So why is Alianza never invited?

Today they're on their way to one of the CPL payment centers. It's an idea Doña Maria Elena first mentioned to Lali when she'd interviewed the older woman for her notas, but Chela and Naima have never been to one before.

What if they try to run us off? Chela wants to know.

Right, so—Maria Elena had another idea. Remember that free thermometer thing CPL keeps going on and on about?

Chela wrinkles her brow.

Yes you do, remember? Naima takes her eyes from the road to glance over at Chela. The ones they used to buy off council? We'll vote yes on the rate increase if you give us money to buy thermometers for all the poor people?

Ohhhhh. Yeah. I remember now.

Yeah, says Lali. So, Doña had an idea I think will work.

At the payment center they post themselves far enough away to avoid flagging the attention of security, close enough to the entrance it seems natural to catch people as they come out. Never on their way in, when they're anxious, Chela reminds them. On their way out, when they're more relaxed.

Or more pissed off, says Naima.

Their rap is the same as the one they use door to door, but with one crucial addition: Have they heard of the city's new thermometer program? Would they like to sign up to get one? When they get pulled by their ears into an empty conference room for interrogation, they've rehearsed their response.

We're trying to sign people up for free thermometers, says Lali.

It's such an innovative program, and people don't even know about it, Chela adds.

Yeah, says Naima. If people don't enroll in the city's affordability programs, all that funding goes to waste!

But security runs them off anyway. If customers want to apply for those programs they can find brochures at the help desk counter. No soliciting, no filming, no political activity. Scat!

It only makes them stronger, it only brings them closer together. They burst from the payment center laughing, Chela running through the parking lot and leaping over bumpers like a hurdler. Whatever, they'll go to a different center.

***

At the end of the afternoon, Naima drops Lali and Chela back at the parish before she heads back to Alianza. They'll retrieve Lali's car and from there drive back to El Centro together, with no one the wiser.

One hand on the wheel, Naima leans out her driver side window over an elbow, craning up to catch a goodbye kiss from Chela. See you later baby, she says. And then, to Lali: May Day meeting is tonight, right? You said Thursday nights at 6?

It comes over her like a flush of embarrassment, like being caught in a lie. Ohhh shhhhiitt, says Lali slowly as she realizes her mistake, the sound like air escaping from a tire, one hand instinctively floating to her forehead. She forgot.

Oh shit what?

There's no way to reel her exhalation back in. I forgot to tell you, Lali says reluctantly.

Tell me what? Naima's expression shifts from confusion to suspicion.

So, Victor changed the meetings to Saturday morning.

He did? Chela says, surprised.

Yeah, says Lali. Her stomach feels cold. Yeah, this morning he mentioned it. Had he suspected something about how they were spending their Thursday afternoons?

I just forgot, she says again weakly. I'm sorry. It's all true, but spoken out loud it sounds thin and craven, like a botched cover-up.

Wow. For real? Y'all advertise one date to the community and then change it last minute so only Victor and Marcos's homies can come? Why didn't you say something to Victor? You know we do Círculo de Cuentos every Saturday morning! Or is it because y'all don't want us there? Is it because we're scary dykes with hairy armpits? Victoria fucking said not to work with Centro but I kept saying no, the work is too important…

Naima, says Lali. But she remembers how subtle contempt can be, Victor's aloofness or Dulce's over-the-shoulder comment as they all dispersed one afternoon after a demonstration outside the CPL building, the Alianza women hauling their PA equipment across the street. *They only like you if you like girls. Not that I wouldn't go out with a few of them.*

Hands gripping the steering wheel, Naima cuts her off. You need to think about your position there and where you stand. *Both* of you, she says pointedly, glaring up at Chela where she stands beside Lali outside the driver side window.

Naima, says Chela. Her face is scared, unhappy.

Come on Chela. Let's go, Naima says, stretching over the front seat to throw open the passenger side door. Chela hesitates, but after a moment moves to the other side of Naima's hatchback and climbs in, glancing back at Lali once with an unreadable expression. And then Naima drives off, leaving Lali to head back to El Centro alone, alone to struggle with the weight of all she has not intended yet inherited nonetheless.

Back at work she passes through the office as quickly as possible, head lowered to avoid eyes, but Victor and Dulce and Papa are out to lunch and Marcos acknowledges her return with only the barest of greetings. How'd it go, he says absently, without looking up from his computer screen.

Good, she murmurs, making a beeline for her desk at the back of the building, where even out of sight she feels exposed and claustrophobic. Just being inside. She leaves her desk to exit the building out the back and wanders the garden outside, dizzy, wondering what to do, if she should leave for the day without saying anything to anyone. If she should leave and not come back. Just get a restaurant job until they all leave for Kansas. Her phone buzzes from inside her pocket and it's Chela texting: *Girl it's not you, shit is all fucked up right now between me and Naima, sorry if you got caught in the crossfire*: but it only helps a little. Sitting on the bottom step of the fire escape staircase that zigzags its way from their second story offices to the garden below, she watches the sky for a while, thick and grey and unmoving.

Then she responds. *no worries…sorry for troubles :(*

And then, *can you text me the number of that city council nun?*

CHAPTER ELEVEN
Heart of the Analysis

You're in luck, says the Sister when Lali calls. I just happen to be in my office today. Why don't you come by, if you have time this afternoon?

The campus slopes downhill, seeking the river that once cut through it. Following the nun's arcane directions, Lali parks in the lot that abuts the stone grotto, its Marian shrine set within a uterine cavern, then follows the signs that point past the turret of stone encircling the dry springhead and toward a landscape that grows increasingly forested. The April air is late-spring tropical, early chicharras taking turns buzzing lazily overhead. Crossing the red footbridge that spans the riverbed, she approaches an island of profuse greenery—vining, coiling, flowering, fruiting—teased from the surrounding bermuda lawn. There she sees the sister, dressed in shorts and sun hat, bending over mounds of earth. As she enters the garden, the heavy, peppery musk of tomato leaves wafts steaming from the soil like heat mirage, reminding her of California, of the Central Valley.

Sisterfarm, reads the painted sign hanging from an arbor entrance fashioned from simple cedar posts. What is this place? Lali asks.

Removing her work gloves, the sister leads Lali to a bench on the edge of the garden. This is my office, says the nun. When I'm not on the road. She winks. I know I've seen you around, at council and in different meetings. But I don't think we've ever gotten a chance to talk. Glad you had some time today.

Well, I left work early, Lali says shakily.

The question on sister's face relaxes into concern. Did something happen?

Lali wipes her eyes, recounting what happened between her and Naima, her and los cuates, El Centro and La Alianza. The sister shakes her head.

Oh, you've walked into a history not of your own making, mi'ja. Poor Chela and Naima too.

We have? Lali looks up, surprised.

Look. Everyone talks about the nonprofit industrial complex, right? Or the military industrial complex or academic industrial this or that. You know about that, right?

Lali nods, still tearful.

So then, you know already that what they're talking about is how corporate structures and interests shape different facets of public life, and how that gets in the way of what public institutions imagine they're doing. Like the groups that get funded to organize rallies and protests—we talk about the nonprofit industrial complex, right? But here's my theory. I think these organizations actually resist the corporate so much that they push past anything industrial and land themselves amidst feudal alliances and conflicts. The problem with organizations like El Centro and La Alianza is not that they're too corporate, it's that they're too familial! They're full of ancient curses and family plots and tragic trysts and brother against brother, sister against sister. The feud between Papa Victor and Mama Victoria goes back a generation. It's old as dirt. Not that there's no legitimacy to it. Everyone knows about the guys who started El Centro and how they treated women in the movement, much less the first generation of out Brown lesbians in the city—but it has hardened since then into the dynamic of a self-protecting scar. Try to mess with it all and you inherit the curse. It's feudal stuff, family rivalries posing as political formation. All to gain the protection of funders or the social capital that comes with *getting the credit*, sole credit for the work, in the search for perpetuity. Eventually organizations exist to keep existing, more than to do whatever it was they formed to do. There are so many ways that organizations, even the most inspired and aspirational—*especially* those, now that I think about it—come to self-protect against knowledge of their internal dysfunction and petty violence.

Soledad turns her face upward, scanning the clouds. I mean, I should *know*.

You shouldn't feel bad, though. It's nothing you did. I mean, I love Naima—I *love* her. What she does for the community is powerful. Just being who she *is* is powerful. But everyone knows she should know better. I'd say she's had to be too hard, but I don't see how that hardness is particularly useful, or even necessary. I've seen her scream at people in meetings, multiple times. And not the people in power who need to be screamed at, either. People on the same side of an issue. Allies, friends. She may have the right analysis. I think frequently she does. But if you push people away in the process, if you become a jerk—what good does it do, to have the right analysis?

I know she's been through a lot.

Well, sure. Of course. But it's not good for the work we do. It's not the best place to work from. You end up sick that way.

I guess I just think that beneath that hardness, whatever you want to call it, is love. For those who have been hurt. Lali pauses, considers, nods. Yeah.

A tile she saw on Chela's porch once, something she made in a community college art class: *amor es dolor*. Immediately an image had arisen in her mind—Chela firing it, painting it, glazing it thinking of Naima, longing for Naima, crying for Naima.

How could it be otherwise, mi'jita? But we all have to learn to live with our pain so we don't hurt people. *Including* ourselves, especially ourselves. It's not possible to transform the forces that injure us if we act from a place of self-injury. If I've learned anything from this work, it's that you need a base, a spiritual grounding, because it is so difficult to place your body in the space of confronting organized violence. I don't mean a religious tradition, although that's been a useful scaffolding for me. But you do need some practice or discipline big and solid enough to bolster you, to take you in its arms.

She folds her arms together in a gesture of tenderness, rocking.

When we're held like that, unconditionally—that's when our pain becomes endurance, courage. That's what allows us to survive in the face of violence and to do this work year after year, decade after decade. Without it, you use the work to reject your own suffering and multiply violence, like a car spinning itself deeper and deeper into its own muddy ruts. We just won't have the ganas to continue fighting unless we have the simple discipline required to stay with our own suffering, to give up on wriggling and squirming away from it, to lay a loving hand against its cheek instead. Anger and pain may be where we start, but it's not enough to be effective. To be effective, our work has to be inward-focused as much as outward. Gloria Anzaldúa said that. It has to be recursive that way. It's right to be angry, but that energy has to be transformed before it can be used. It has to come from love to be politically useful.

And love—see, this is where I differ from some of the sisters in my order. Though not, I think, from many other respectable madwomen! As far as love goes, there is a long prophetic tradition which says there is less distance than we might imagine between the divine and the erotic, the erotic and the political, the political and the divine. It's the longing for one particular other that opens us to a sense of what it must be to love all otherness, all creation, to the extent that one lives one's life to protect it. And that in turn opens us further—her hands move across her chest as if she is prising apart her rib cage—to a knowledge of where our knowledge ends and the unknowable begins. A knowledge of outlines and limitations, the outer lip of our understanding, swollen with a longing to know that eventually gives way and surrenders to unknowing. The structuring absence that mysteriously generates all presence, all substance.

The sister laughs, seeing Lali's eyes widen. Well, I do know about the erotic. I haven't been a nun *all* my life. You know that, don't you? In fact, I probably know even more about the erotic now than I did before my chastity vows.

***

All of her life Soledad had wanted to marry, had imagined the day whenever she would hear the romantic songs on radio KEDA that would play when her mother cleaned house, the singers drawing out the long, descending vowels at the end of each phrase like a plea. And Soledad would stand before the altar in her white dress each Sunday with her eyes closed, hands clasped, mouth open as she waited for the priest to place a communion wafer on her tongue, dreaming of the day she would be devoted not to Jesus—not *just* to Jesus, she would quickly add in her thoughts—but to one human other who loved her back. She would bow her head, she would genuflect before returning to kneel beside Mama and Papa, Loly and Lourdes, Lupita and little Chuy. She was the oldest of five, the decade bead heading up smaller offerings, all of them named for sacred mysteries or trials or apparitions. The one who stayed at home to help Mama and Papa put all of the younger ones through school. The one who stayed home, working and waiting.

What would he be like, the one who would take her hands, lift her veil, awaken her? She could not imagine it. He was a figure whose identity was the darkness of a shadow, whose outline was the dots and dashes of a quantity yet undetermined. Who would he be? She began to look for him after her graduation from Sacred Heart, in the faces of the young men who passed through the doors of the student library at the city college, where she worked the circulation desk before her evening classes began. She still remembers the yellow smell of the books as she cracked open their back covers, ready to stamp their return-by card. She still remembers the heavy creak of her metal cart as she wheeled it through the stacks, looking for the right hands, the right face, as she reshelved books.

Back then, in the late 1950s and early '60s, a teacher was the most esteemed position a girl could attain if she did not become a wife and mother first, especially if she had attended Catholic school and done well—*especially* if she was Mexicana. From all appearances, marriage had seemed to be an automatic rite of passage, but when it did not prove immediately forthcoming, Soledad had majored in education instead, intending to become a teacher. Everyday she had caught the bus from her parents' casita on the Westside to the downtown satellite campus where she worked during the day and took classes at night.

Instead of a public school teacher she became the director of pastoral education at her old parish. It was a job that felt comfortable and familiar, a job that allowed her to stay at home until her fledgling sisters and brother issued forth to their own jobs and marriages and families. Everyone left, but Soledad remained at home helping Papa and Mama. And in the early 1970s, her job at the church became, finally and unexpectedly, the place where she finally met the man she'd been looking for.

He was an organizer from Chicago, trained under Saul Alinsky himself. A base builder. Older than her by ten years—though by this time she was nearly 33 and no spring chicken herself—with a face that was rough but kind, the ghosts of acne scars scattered across his high indio cheekbones.

Raúl had come to town because National was wanting to start something new in San Antonio, something the city had never seen. For too long their barrios had been starved of the funds they needed for basic services. Someone had sent all the money to fund new growth northward, and as a result the streets had flooded, the garbage had accumulated, the sewage had backed up, when there was finally sewerage—until the 1950s, thousands of Westside households lacked connection to water service, and thousands more relied on outhouses and cesspools for waste disposal. Her own family among them at one point. Everyone knew why, but no one had been able to do anything about it because their people were not the ones making the decisions; their people had been locked out of the process.

In the absence of political representation they would have to fashion something out of what they did have: that was how VAMOS got started. Back then Manuel Martinez was young and dashing—kinetic, hotheaded—but they had called their organization *VAMOS* because even then their membership was predominantly elders, the mamas and abuelas of the church who were the ones who kept an eye on the neighborhood, who looked out for each others' kids. Something National had done successfully in the Midwest was to anchor local campaigns to parishes, building power among those who had been most disenfranchised. They were starting their slow descent from the fury of the '60s, from civil rights and Brown power, but they were not after ideological alignment, not aiming for the world-historical. They wanted to change the little things in their neighborhoods that reminded them of their place. The lack of sidewalks, the busted out street lights, the streets pock-marked with potholes. Better services, more light, pipes that didn't break. Things they could touch and feel. Nowadays, they fought environmental battles to protect the aquifer from development north of the city. Back then they had environmental battles too, but their water struggles were of a different kind. Where Soledad had been raised, water issues were about the flood of 1921 that, yes, turned the downtown business district into a lake nine feet deep—but on the Westside devoured 51 bodies whole as walls of water leapt from creek beds to smash into the shacks and corrales like a freight train. Water issues were about the allocations of life and death that inhered in the budgetary decisions that followed the floodwaters: $3 million for an upstream dam to keep downtown dry, just $6,000 to clear brush from the creeks where so many had drowned. And water issues were about the missing pipes that sent raw sewage overspilling cesspools and washing down dirt alleys when it rained, making Soledad's Westside community at one time the nation's capital for babies dying of diarrhea.

Raúl had come to town from Chicago because San Antonio was strategic, a testing ground, to see if the Westside churches there wanted to unite with other parishes around the city to win the basic services their communities lacked. They wanted to start with Sacred Heart because of its large, already active congregation, and he came to town to meet with her. He came to town without any idea of what it might mean to meet.

Their marriage is now long annulled, but she will never forget the day they met. It was not like her to be late, but she was late that day to the meeting Raúl had scheduled with Deacon Shaunessy, who had asked her to attend and listen in. And when she rushed into the room, hand clamped to her head to keep her hat from flying off, he had looked up from where he sat with the Deacon, and there he finally was.

***

And our meeting did something to me that *changed* me, Soledad says to Lali who is all eyes, all suspended breath. Just by looking up and seeing me there. I felt it *here*. She closes her eyes, wedges one fisted hand tight against her breastbone. What was it? I don't think I'll ever fully understand.

So we began to see each other. He was in town for only a few months, to get the campaign off the ground, and we both knew that. But I knew something was happening. Something monumental had begun. Some great force was throwing a switch; the tracks were beginning to groan and shift. So after he moved back to Chicago, he began to write to me—I didn't expect that—and I wrote back. And we kept on writing. He was the one who introduced me to the intellectuals and mystics of the church, the writings of people like Thomas Merton and Richard Rohr. Catholic theologians who wrote within a tradition of liberation theology, in which the political struggle for justice for the poorest was the highest end of love for both God and humanity. Raúl stayed in Chicago for a couple years. He kept trying to get transferred back to San Antonio, but he had to go wherever National sent him. But his letters were absolutely delicious. They were always long, with descriptions of what he was doing and thinking about.

He would send me extended quotes from the books he was reading and his thoughts about what it meant for the work we did. As our own campaign got underway, I started to think about the work I did in a different way, a new way, a political way. In a way that recognized the political as the spiritual in action. And that was part of an understanding that Raúl and I were joined by a common mission. We were physically apart but we were very much connected, intellectually and emotionally and spiritually. But in our letters we never talked about what was happening between us.

Wait—you didn't talk at all about what you were going to do? Lali wants to know.

Raúl was not the kind of man who talked about it.

So you knew he was the one, but—

But we were in different cities. She shrugs. We kept in touch. What else could we do?

But didn't it drive you crazy, not knowing?

Of course it did. I thought it was going to happen right away, our future together. Then a month went by, then a year, then two. And there I was, still in San Antonio, and there he was in Chicago.

So you never talked about it.

No.

But what did you *do*? Lali can't imagine it, living so gracefully with the intensity and uncertainty of longing.

Well, I just—I went on with things. I met other people, I went out. Always as friends, which is what I would tell them. Now I see I shouldn't have done that, but oh well! She laughs.

But you never lost faith that it would happen?

No. But it didn't happen how I thought it would, either.

***

Even though it didn't happen the way she imagined, she had been changed by knowing him. Like that principle Heisenberg had named—he had looked at her and what he saw became something different beneath his gaze. She became a different person and she became more genuinely herself, a person she hadn't known she was or could be. Someone who spoke in front of others at meetings and facilitated community discussions and knocked on doors to talk to the people about their needs. She became persuasive, strategic, policy-minded, abilities she never suspected she had. She began to think about going to graduate school and getting a Master's in history or public administration, to learn more about how the city ran and why. She began to think about running for office—someone in her parish had mentioned it: pos, por qué no?

Well, why not? But the following winter Raúl had come back to San Antonio on the Greyhound, waving a paper bearing the good news: he had gotten a transfer back to the city! They had immediately married and for a few years were happy, in parallel continuing their organizing work throughout the Westside. Things were changing for their community—the ground was giving way, beneath a DOJ ruling that had dismantled the electoral system that had shut their people out. With the people of the parishes they learned how to occupy city offices if they had to; they held teach-ins on the city budget process and figured out how to push their way into meetings on funding allocation. When the head of the water board said there was no money to fix Westside drainage, Soledad and Raúl took 50 people from the churches to his office and refused to leave until they were heard. And they were heard, and somehow money was found.

But she had a dim awareness, when Raúl came back to town, a tiny, uncertain flicker that had grown brighter and more constant over time, that it was too late for her and Raul to last long. Her readings had expanded beyond Merton and Rohr to the prophetic women thinkers of the church, feminist scholars developing a woman-centered theology: Ada María Isasi-Díaz, Yolanda Tarango. It was erotic love that had shaken her open to radical theologies and to political struggle. And now theology and politics were opening her further, to a love that moved beyond the erotic, to an erotics of all creation, all living. A love incarnated in specific human relations but which far exceeded them, which could not be bound by those relations. A love that pointed a way beyond itself, an unending surfeit overspilling its container again and again. The love Raúl had awakened when he looked her way with an unknowing grace had opened her so wide she ached to serve beyond the bounds of human marriage.

And so, Sister Soli says, I left him. Not without a long process of grieving and letting go. But I felt called by something too powerful not to respond. So we got an annulment and I took my vows.

Crazy, Lali murmurs, shaking her head in admiration. It's a guilty pleasure of hers, the grand gesture, the absolute surrender of collapsing to one's knees, palms held open.

The sister smiles. I suppose it was. Life is full of twists and turns that way. But it's not like it came out of nowhere or all of a sudden. The year before I left, we would talk all the time about whether I should or shouldn't and what it would mean for us, for our individual life paths. It was painful for both of us because we had such respect for each other, such a partnership intellectually and spiritually. And physically as well, romantically—at least for me. But as it turned out, he was called to another path too. So it was a relief for both of us to finally surrender to what we each knew to be true, what we had collaborated to protect against for so long. When we both allowed our desire to be as full as it was, we were able to come to a shared peace with it. And we're still close friends, Raúl and I.

You are?

Oh yes. He actually lives with another man now. They've been together for ten years. I ministered to him often when he was in the process of coming out to himself and to his family. It was, she chuckles, another kind of conversion process.

Huh, says Lali, turning it over in her mind.

***

After her vows, Sister Soledad had first taught at the small college her order had founded on the banks of the river that once surged from its limestone fountainhead. The Sisters of Charity of the Incarnate Word had purchased the land around the springs from Mr. George Washington Brackenridge himself in 1899, having arrived from France 30 years before to care for victims of a terrible cholera outbreak.

Which just goes to show, she says, shaking her head, how long this city has been carelessly polluting its water! I'm pontificating, though...like a pontiff, she grins. Sorry, nun humor! Anyway—

Teaching had been fine for a while. She'd been proud to have a hand in developing the first courses at her college on feminist theology and environmental ethics. But it wasn't long before she felt called once again to incarnate the theory she taught, to realize ideas in action, to widen praxis to the size of the love coursing through her. *Lord, make me an instrument of your peace*—her favorite of the hymnal songs they sang at the opening of the order's general chapter meetings. So when the sisters began a community education program, Soledad volunteered to return to her old Westside parish once a week, where she led classes in liberation theology. But ten years later, the teachings that had once galvanized and inspired had little remaining purchase with the community. The goals were the same—to organize the neighborhoods for better services—but the drive and motives were different. VAMOS was no longer animated by a longing for liberation but for what concessions they could win from the city. They had muscled their way to the table in exchange for a softer and more compromising rhetorical bite, and now more and more of their folks were getting appointed to boards and even elected to council seats. Yet the underlying logic of the city held fast, now protected from sight by an intermediate strata of brown-skinned officials.

And the words of one of her fellow parishioners from a decade earlier came back to her, a whisper in her ear. *Pos, por qué no, señora?*

Well, one reason was that she was a nun—but this was before the Vatican proscribed men and women of the cloth from holding public office. Back then you needed only the blessing of your order and your higher ups, and she had gotten clearance from the archbishop, a generally progressive man. So she left teaching once more for the street ministry of a grassroots campaign and found herself elected to city council in her district, the first Mexicana ever on any city council in the United States, the infamous council nun. She was the lone holdout against a cascade of rezoning cases as the city rolled north, paving over the land with impervious cover like peanut butter spread on toast. For her colleagues these decisions were harmless technicalities. The owner wants to sell, the buyer needs to rezone in order to buy. Why not? How could you stop them? But she could make out the shape of the whole in the details, the city expanding like a sealant where rain soaked into the aquifer—thus too polluted runoff from the multiplying driveways and parking lots and golf courses they were authorizing. The editorial board of the city paper would ridicule her: *Mary Margaret doesn't understand economic development.* They ran editorial cartoons depicting her as a penguin, running around in a barnyard of chickens shouting the sky is falling. But the people knew she was with them, so it didn't matter to her. A nun had no agenda except the love of creation.

And then, she says, after a couple of terms of this, I decided I would run for mayor against Butch Keller, Sr. You heard of him? His sons run his firm now, Keller and Keller. Well, old Butch, Butch Sr., was a lawyer like most of them, a good ol' boy from the days of the Good Government League. He'd served on city council for a term back in the '70s, learned the ropes, then not a day past a year—which back then was the blackout period before you could work as a lobbyist—not a day past, he started a law practice representing some of the biggest development firms in their bids to city council for land. The downtown mall, the sports arena, the convention center, the luxury golf resort now sitting over the aquifer, the two theme parks on the outer loop—he was the one who pushed all those projects through, who got all the necessary rezoning permits. Actually, when he registered as a lobbyist they were in the process of rewriting the ethics rules to say you had to wait two years instead of one, but since he'd filed the paperwork already they grandfathered him in. I called him out on it, when I was on council. He knew where I stood.

So when he announced after all those years that he was returning to the ring to run for mayor, I decided I would challenge him. And we all know how that turned out. Or maybe you don't?

I was little, Lali admits.

Well, by that time the Vatican was in its own process of rewriting canonical law to prohibit priests and nuns from holding office, even with the permission of their superiors—

The sisters saw it coming down the pike and were planning to ask for a leave of absence on Soledad's behalf—when, on the eve of the runoffs, Keller's people started their own fuss about grandfathering. The media squawking caught the attention of Archbishop Garcia, a much less imaginative Catholic than his predecessor, and she was forced to give up her campaign or face defrocking. By that point she had made it to the runoffs against Butch Sr. At the press conference where she announced her withdrawal, she shrugged off media questions about her defeat. The point had never been victory anyway. She didn't believe in victory. Real power, real transformation, lay in accompanying those who suffered and those who struggled against institutionalized suffering, those who would never win. She had never really gotten Jesus until she came to that realization. She'd always been more of a Guadalupana.

After her mayoral campaign, she was finally content to go back to teaching at the college. Liberation now was less the sweep of a grand historical vision than a multiplicity of minuscule acts of care and attention. Her parents aged and fell sick, and one after another she helped ease them from this world to the next. She began developing a program for recovering the land around the headwaters of the ancient springs. She gathered students and volunteers and together they replanted native species, and built informational kiosks on the history and geology of the springs where the city began. It was then that she took over maintenance of the nuns' community garden, converting it from an orderly grid of raised beds to an experiment in permaculture. Eventually, then in her late 70s, she persuaded the order to allow her to begin a traveling ministry, an office in her car, driving all over the arid bed of the once-shallow sea whose rare earths now promised to save them from themselves. Trying to connect the dots once more, trying to make it all add up in a way the people could understand. If they could only understand, surely they would know what to do.

***

Now, beneath the cedar post arbor, Soledad blesses Lali before she leaves, drawing a cross on her forehead. Raised Catholic, Lali now keeps no tradition—but she receives the sister's blessing with eyes closed and head dipped; and in the stroke of fingertips across her brow she feels a sincerity of love and goodwill that touches her.

Is there anything I can do for you, Lali asks.

Head tipped to the side, the sister stands looking at Lali for a moment. There is something. I'm wanting to write an essay about the rate hikes issue. This has all happened before. These young men sitting on council now...I knew many of their parents in the days of the movimiento, when the churches were fighting City Power and Light like they are now. And now they've forgotten. They don't even know there is a history here that risks repeating. They've stood on their parents' shoulders and gotten their JDs from St. Mary's or their MBAs from Harvard, but they don't know the history of their own neighborhoods. All the same as before, and yet different too. Same events, different context and meaning because of transition, because time is running out. So it's important to write it all down and come to an understanding. So that's where—I heard you are a professor?

Not quite yet. Technically, I guess. Yes.

Qué bueno mi'ja. And what is it you study?

Political science. The political science of water. The words of a grad school friend, a physics student, came back to her: *If it has to call itself a science, that means it's not.*

Excellent! Sister exclaims. Would you be interested in collaborating with me?

I *have* been making some notes, Lali says.

Research Notas 6:
Neoliberal Politics in the Tilting-at-Windmills Industry:
A Few Final Postulates

Dig down beneath the surface of the post-colonial political moment we're in—inaugurated by Cisneros but realized most fully in current council scandals over mining and utility rates—and you see that something far more impersonal and hard to dislodge is at root: a grow-or-die logic that beats at the heart of an extractive economy, a manic metabolism whose compulsive expenditure exceeds its inputs, which gnashes and gnaws at its own musculature. A hungry ghost or a Tantalus tortured by a waterline always receding. Those who win will call it "development," the triumphal march forward of cities and societies into the setting sun of progress. But remember what Walter Benjamin said about the angel of history, blown forward even as its face turns back toward the mounting catastrophe left in its wake. Remember those left behind or removed to make way, remember those who do not make it, those overlooked, those who will not win.

So urban geographies unfurl from a center like spiderweb according to the internal rhythms of development, no less orchestrated for their seeming ease and inevitability. Precious public money subsidizes further extraction and accumulation by those who already own, disturbing the land and fouling the waters. Within neocolonial and neoliberal urban geographies it is grow-or-die that governs, the growth machine whose invisible longings manifest the city's visible transformations. We'll build a smart grid powered entirely by renewables, they say, as they contract with wildcatters and mine the pockets of the poor who will bear the cost of raised utility rates. We'll construct a low-impact urban villa out of shuttered coal plants, over the cemeteries of razed mobile home parks. These land use patterns repeat, not redress, the colonial structures of decision making over economies that continue to be extractive. Transition for whom? From what, into what?

Sitting with books and articles, with the series Champlain did for the *Volt*, trying to understand these ironies and internal contradictions—most recently, my curiosity piqued by the Kichwa film at Alianza's Extractivism event, I've been reading a book on Indigenous organizing around oil extraction in the Amazonian region of Ecuador. And I'm struck by how much the dynamics described in that book between corporate, state, and Indigenous actors parallel the dynamics here in San Antonio between private interests, local government and the urban descendants of the original peoples of this continent— Abya Yala, Turtle Island. Here, as in Ecuador, the neoliberal approach promotes conflict within communities, where local elites and some members of impacted Indigenous communities are willing to side with the companies and the state in exchange for crumbs. Sawyer in *Crude Chronicles*: "in a pattern repeated wherever multinational oil capital operates in Ecuador, the local inhabitants of Villano were divided."[25]

But support for extraction interests among some segments of a community does not mean the community is in the position to decide what happens. In other words, community

---

[25] Suzana Sawyer, *Crude Chronicles: Indigenous Politics, Multinational Oil, and Neoliberalism in Ecuador* (Durham: Duke University Press, 2004), 59.

support does not mean corporations aren't calling the shots. In fact, Sawyer suggests that community division is *especially* symptomatic of a neoliberal situation, because of the way private interests come to provide some of the benefits the state once did. Where the state has abdicated its responsibility to ensure social welfare, corporations come to appear benevolent. Communities get bought off, then, because they've been otherwise abandoned and dispossessed. In the case of South Texas, mining companies pour money into the infrastructural vacuum of the sealands. They fix roads—the same roads their trucks are destroying—and build libraries and soccer fields and community centers with internet access where none existed before. They donate to the schools and make possible other needed public services like fire departments and EMS in isolated rural areas.

And just as in Ecuador, opposition to these tactics may be unrelenting, but so too are the corporate maneuvers which ultimately prove more powerful. While indigenous resistance may have disrupted extractive activities for a year, ARCO came back after identifying pro-oil segments of Indigenous communities, which it used to create a front group. Just like Seismar with the mainstream environmental groups. While the company has not paid those groups directly (at least, I don't think), the stamp of legitimacy attending their enthusiastic support for the Mud Creek mine (renewables!) has been a tremendous green light for local governments. More than ever, we—the ones who say, *absolutely not*, the ones who seek to understand complexities and complications—are now the crazy ones, the windmill tilters, the ones who cannot possibly win.

CHAPTER TWELVE

May Day! (In Which Sandra Cisneros
Makes an Appearance as Herself)

Okay: Here is Part I of the greatest May Day story in the world, originally posted to Feisbuk. It took place when Sandra Cisneros was in town visiting her old stomping grounds after leaving Tejas for San Miguel de Allende. She's not really from San Antonio but y'all claim her anyway, probably because of all that pedo she had with the King William Association over the audacity of her purple house. Or was it pink? Her wicked, wicked ways and all! That was the first Chicana lit book you found and checked out from the school library—or, shit, maybe it was actually Lucha Corpi—but in any case making you think maybe, as you wrote poems in gym class all slouched up against the bleachers. Maybe you too, even though everyone thought you were a white girl. Sandra on the back cover in a backless black dress looking at you over her shoulder, with short hair in finger waves like a flapper and big silver earrings. Short hair like you, yeah! Cuz when Mexicans thought you were Anglo and Anglos thought you were I-don't-know-what, what you ended up was strange and shorthaired.

So there's that, and then one time, long ago before La Sandra left Tejas, when Hector was working at the Thai Tea in Austin, he actually waited on her when she strolled into the restaurant one day. Her short hair had grown out into an exclamation of waves like *this*, and she laughed a lot as she dined with her friend. That's what Hector said. And then, you also saw her speak at the anti-war marcha, also in Austin—she read prose-poetry above the heads of the marchers gathered there, connecting the dots between the brown faces of gente aquí and gente allá in the Middle East, standing in a gazebo not unlike the one where the speakers at this marcha will also speak.

But it's not like you would know her in a crowd, know what I mean?

Anyway, on this particular May Day, on the first day of May, el primero de Mayo, you've arrived with your nena to the Plaza del Zacate for the pre-march rally—the very plaza where Emma Tenayuca rabbleroused the pecan shellers, that's why y'all call it la Plaza de Zacate instead of Milam Park and why all the marchas in San Antonio either start or end there—and you're lounging in the zacate in the shade. Nena snoozing in her stroller and you kind of laying on your side propped on one elbow, armpits sweaty and stinky. By the time it hits May Day the last little bit of spring cool in the air has been wrung out and you have to square off with the reality of heat. You just gotta be matter of fact about it. Lean into it, it's easier than trying to get away. So then this woman in a flowy shirt-dress thing and leggings and chanclas approaches to talk to another woman standing nearby, trailing a little dog on a leash wearing a homemade shirt that says "legality is a colonialist fiction." Ja! That's pretty clever and insightful, little dog. Makes you think. No illegal immigration without a prior construction of legality, like how Foucault talked about how there was no homosexuality until there was something called heterosexuality, no concept of visible deviance until there's an unseen norm to construct one. And the flyers talk about how May 1st is about workers, and how immigrants are workers criminalized for seeking work across borders despite the border-hopping liberties of capital. And how immigrants are not really immigrants at all, they are indigenous first with rights to itinerancy like the birds of the air or the fish in the sea. Imagine telling a bird it can't fly where it flies. Indigenous first and workers second, that's what the flyers and signs say. All of the organizations are pushing for the same glorious upswell as those big immigration marchas some years back, but those moments can't be planned or manufactured or predicted, no matter how much funding there is. They just happen, even when there's no money, energy swirling around an invisible fulcrum, and no one really knows why.

So this year—maybe because instead of flyering for the march you've been doing the sorts of things you were actually funded to do as the just transition organizer, like collect signatures for VAMOS—this year, the march is small, mostly the same folks who come to all the marchas. And you're looking around at all the people you know and some you don't too and not really paying attention when, all of a sudden, the woman with the dog begins apologizing to you effusively, clearly mortified. You look over to where she is gesturing and see that her dog has just peed on the wheel of Nena's stroller and shoe!

Oh, I'm so sorry. Oh my God! says the dog woman, crouching to blot at the stroller with wads of Kleenex offered by the second woman.

Oh—it's fine, it's just a little pee. Is he a puppy?

No, just mal educada!

Well, his little shirt is very smart.

After you share a final laugh, the two women walk off together, and you more or less forget about the incident—until you notice later that the woman with the dog is in the gazebo speaking. She's the keynote speaker, actually—except, wasn't someone able to get Sandra Cisneros as the keynote? Which means. IT WAS SANDRA CISNEROS'S DOG WHO PEED ON NENA'S LITTLE SHOE!

Part II of the story is the same old stuff that always happens at the marchas. There are some problems with the sound, then there are some speeches and spoken word. Someone must have connections, because not only is La Sandra there, they've also been able to book Mayor Mi'jo to come and make a statement, since this marcha takes place right after some dumbfuck in the Texas lege introduces another one of those check-your-papers bills. So the mayor is there to say how bad it would be for business in Texas and for tourism in San Antonio if they were to pass something like that here, and everyone kind of stands around confused about whether to clap or not. Kind of half-clapping, half-whispering-to-each-other about what a vendido he is. After speeches they line up and there is some tussling for position before the chant kicker-offer kicks off the chants. El Centro has brought a banner that reads "Trajabadores Unidos!" and La Alianza one reading "Unidas a través de Fronteras." Might as well play tug of war over the same banner—it'd save some canvas and paint at least. Oh, it is so like that, and everyone knows it! Not saying for a second either that we shouldn't do these things. Not saying the stakes aren't high. It's because they're high that we should laugh at this element of ritual or theater or carnival, this sacred ridiculousness. That's all. And cuz it's like...can there be some other t-shirt motif, some other motivating motive, besides a woman in pain yelling while making a fist? Damn.

But Part III of the story is something new. As the people take to the streets, you spot the man from the *Volt* standing on the curb taking phone fotos astride his clunky orange cruiser, green bandana wrapped around his forehead like a sweatband, holding back his hair. You pretend not to notice as you pass pushing Nena; as you pass you turn your face away from the camera, from where he stands in cutoffs and sandals. And it's already hot, but a wave of heat consumes your face as you see yourself seen, as if from outside, as you mumble chants, and you think: where on earth did that come from—that *heat*?

III.
RELATIVITY

High Summer
San Antonio, TX

CHAPTER ONE
Grackles and Penguins

Friday, May 26

On her days off Lali experiments with place, driving around the city with the windows down in search of the ideal writing space, the unmoving air at stop lights wrapping her like a blast of vaporized plastic. The right location had to sell food in case she hadn't packed any. But in case it was the end of the month and she had no money, it had to allow you to bring in your own food. It had to be quiet, without music piped in, though music without words—jazz, electronica—was okay. Even better: no Wi-Fi. Above all it had to have good reception, a direct line to the nebulae where words and ideas swirled in inchoate form.

For a while it was the library where her mother, a 5th grade teacher, had taken her as a child, north of the neighborhood where their house once stood, up the street from where her father went to high school—a seminary, in the old manner where boys left home to prepare together for a life of devotion, at once intensely solitary and intensely communal. Instead of military barracks, Lali's Mexican Catholic grandparents had packed all the boys off to the priesthood for their free educations. The Jesuits sent some of them to the deep South for college, but shipped her father's graduating class north to the Midwest, placing bets on how quickly their South Texas nalgas would freeze in the bitter winters of Chicago. It was there at DePaul that her Brown dad met her white mom—the daughter of a postal worker and a homemaker, the first and only one in her large Irish Catholic family to attend college—whose idea of a good time was to meet up with some girlfriends at the local pub and drink with the sexy-but-safely-celibate-if-not-gay Tejano seminarians, many of whom, like Lali's father, would leave the vocation within the year for the forbidden thrill of marrying women.

The library near the seminary is in an affluent part of town, though even here extravagance and necessity are staggered street by street. On some streets the houses are tiered wedding cakes rising above flagrantly evergreen lawns; on others, once-grand homes have been splintered into a dozen efficiencies, their exteriors a labyrinth of front, side, and rear entrances. Once a palatial home, the library now stands incongruously amid the black heat of its parking lot, and beyond that is the parched brown and dull green of the city's water restrictions, come early this year. Army colors, the colors of a land sucked dry.

As a house the interior must have felt spacious, yet as a public space it is oddly cramped, full of hairpin turns and narrow hallways, its former bedrooms now crammed with rows of shelving. But upstairs is a balcony, reconfigured as a hushed, three-table study room, which Lali loves to frequent. Up there the air is crispy with the smell of paper, and the buzz of the circulation desk and children's room are a distant echo below. Most days she reads and writes alone, but some days the seminarian is there, reminding her how close the library is to her father's old life, the fork he could have chosen but did not. The not-taken path she embodies.

He was there the first day she came to the library, and she knew he was a seminarian because he was all in black, cotton shortsleeve tucked into pressed pants, square of white tucked at his throat. After this first encounter he appeared mostly in plain clothes or all in black but without the collar, and if she had not seen him that first day she might not have known his vocation. But once was all she needed. *Grackles and penguins*, her dad and uncles had joked, their names for the fathers and sisters who taught them.

On the days she shared space with the seminarian, he was always there before her, already deep in concentration, so that when she arrived she had to walk past him. After they came to recognize one another, he would sometimes look up and smile in acknowledgment. He was mid-twenties, Anglo, with hair parted on the side, a solid dark beard, and black-framed glasses. Always he sat hunched before an open laptop, surrounded by books and manuscripts. Working, working. She envied his concentration, the sustained reflection suggesting his immersion in a long tradition of study. A clearing away of all else in life that might distract from contemplation, a clearing away of the body and of women.

Part of her wanted that, to attain what her father had declined—a monastic life, if a secular one. As if in the silence and discipline of academic work, she could become the monk for which her father had not wanted to sacrifice romantic love and partnership. Writing and study were passionate endeavors as well, to be sure, but their purest exercise was solitary: they demanded the deliberate focus of the seminarian, a paring away to the most essential. Even at eleven or twelve she recognized this, spending summers taking careful notes from her 1972 edition of *Introduction to Marine Biology*, desperate to figure out how to save the seabirds and seals she'd seen on the news, ruined by Exxon Valdez. Before she realized that saving the oceans would require her to first understand human politics, she was driven to understand the ocean itself, to parse the mystery of its unity into parts that when pieced back together translated secrets into systems and sentences.

By thirty, though, her life had become irreversibly immanent—her concentration continually fraying against the everyday clutter of relationship, dissolving into the buzz and static of work. And yet to live without those distractions was equally unbearable. So was a life devoted to ideas and words at odds with the necessity of relationship? The secular culture of the university insisted one could do both. Not only study and write for a living but devote one's self to a vocation without forgoing relationship, family, embeddedness in community. But like the priesthood, the university had been built by and for men, whose mental focus was only possible because many others bore responsibility for the labor of embodiment—wives and mothers, housekeepers and janitors, farmworkers, the earth itself. It tricked young women into thinking they could work without looking up, escaping responsibility to attachment. *You can have both*, the university whispered...but it seemed you couldn't. In that way the university had retained its medieval, ecclesiastical roots, its aspirations to a pure will scraped clean of all rootedness, an autonomy or agency without the distractions of attachment. Inevitably a man, a young man, sent away from his family to study. She wanted it; she hated it.

But what was the alternative. A different sort of silence, a silencing amid the tornadic roar of dependencies. And so, once a week for just a few hours, she struggles to the top of the stairs of the library for the incredible privilege of reading and writing in unbroken silence.

***

One drizzly, steamy Friday, she pulls into the driveway of the old library branch to find it dark and empty. They are retrofitting the building to upgrade the HVAC, says the sign on the door; closed for construction.

She drives around aimlessly, not sure where else to go, increasingly anxious in a way familiar from graduate school when she isn't working and thinks she should be. Or from high school, when she would drive around listening to music, chewing gum, sipping shallow drags off cigarettes, drinking from a large travel mug filled with icy, artificially sweetened tea. All the restless little habits you picked up for tamping down an appetite. Gum is the only oral habit left over from those hungry days, and though she'd quit the cigs long before Nena was born—couldn't get a foothold on a proper addiction, inevitably coming down with a respiratory bug every time she started up again—she remembers her nicotine-buzzed drives with something like longing. Now she drives flipping through radio stations, guessing at frequency by the number of dial clicks up or down. Her car, the one Hector had taken over for a time and then returned after his Craigslist find, is an old family hand-me-down, without working air conditioning and only one working speaker in the back. When even that crackled, you could sometimes tap on the volume knob to restore sound, but sometimes not. And sometimes the LCD display on the radio would short, and you had to flip around and listen closely to figure out what station you had found.

On what must be the low end of the dial, she hears a touring Renaissance choir reenacting all-but-obsolete scales and inflections, singing a song from 17th century Scotland that she remembers from elementary school music class, attending the school where her mom taught before they moved north of the city. They had sung it together, a bunch of inland urban Tejanitos whose primary experience with boats was fishing in the cooling ponds off the Dirty Dawson plant or taking Christmastime rides on the Riverwalk barges of Yanaguana Cruises, Inc.:

The water is wide
I cannot cross o'er
and neither have I wings to fly
Oh go and get
a boat for two
to carry o'er my true love and I

Then, on what must be the oldies station, she pauses on another song about the ocean, this one about a hot bartending girl named Brandy from a harbor town who had the great misfortune to fall in love with a sailor who loved her back—but alas, not enough to stay. Like the grackles and penguins of her father's Catholic schooling who were married to the church, this sailor had wedded himself already to the comings and goings of the sea. But this man was no scoundrel, despite his wanderings; he'd been honest with Brandy about who he was.

And so Brandy was left to walk the streets at night, lovelorn, fingering the silver chain of the locket he'd given her in place of his hand.

And then, on what sounds like the pop en español station, she stops on a song she recognizes from Centro's Christmas party—a singer begging his lover not to refuse him, over a propulsive guitar aflitter with synthesized Andean flutes. *Oye mi amor. No me digas que no!* At work it had been little more than background music, party music, light enough to blow away like dandelion fluff. But as the song crackles over one working speaker in the solitude of her car, the urgency or sincerity of its basic plea for *yes* seems suddenly new and profound: what she'd dismissed as simplicity was actually ancient, elemental, capable of traveling the world in search of response, for centuries and centuries, like dandelion fluff, like a folksong from 17th century Scotland, first across meadows and marshes and then, after their enclosure, across cities and oceans and deserts, following the people wherever they went. Pop music was the oldest kind of song of all, from the center of the earth itself, crying not merely for the joining of soul—that would be too easy—but for the convergence of bodies, in the aching mystery of their separateness. *No me digas que no. Y vamos juntando las almas. Y vamos juntando los cuerpos.*

Finally, having drifted her way almost to the outer loop that circles the city, she stops on the immense wet tarmac surrounding a highwayside bookstore—it's the best location she can find for today. She navigates her way inside to the small interior cafe at the back, dazzled by so many new copies of so many books she hasn't read. If she stops to look now she will never get to work, but she cannot stop herself from stopping. From a cardboard display she plucks a slender hardback of verse and opens to a random page:

When I am with you, we stay up all night.
When you're not here, I can't go to sleep.
Praise god for these two insomnias!
And the difference between them.

Lips pursed, she flips to the front of the book to check the author and the title. Oh, Rumi. Poets and lovers and Buddhists couldn't get enough of that guy. Still, the words startle her, the way Rumi does, worming their way into her brain to turn something over she thought she had lain to rest. Troubled, she makes her way to the little in-store cafe where she buys a single cup of plain coffee she doesn't want, because it's one of those places where to sit you were obligated to spend money. They didn't even have ceramic cups, only disposable paper ones. She takes a seat by the window and for a long minute watches the still grey air wanting to rain, unable to. Fuck, it was noon already. At 4 she'll need to start heading back across town through traffic to collect Nena by 5. Three hours she's wasted. All because of the library construction and her radio reflections and the poetry display, and something else. What was it?

Distracted, she watches a small child in a rubber-hooded raincoat trailing his mama as he free-feeds M&Ms from a bag, his little hands moist and rainbow-sticky. That's too many M&Ms for a baby, she thinks. He's too little. The littlest possible person. Reminds her of Nena. She feels herself softening as, with a fuzzy attention, she watches him dutifully trot after his mama, her back to him as she strides to the counter to order.

Reminds her of herself. Her own impatience or casual negligence, trying to read Nena a book one-eyed while with another she revises a paper. Always that tension between them, Nena's focused solicitation and the casual distractedness Lali allows herself, knowing it's not hurtful, exactly. Not a slap or a harsh word. A laziness though, or a flight, maybe, from the intensity of another's need or desire. A benign trickery—anything to buy productivity, mobility, ability to concentrate—looming above a vulnerable tininess. It was that complete trust and openness that she as a parent couldn't help but betray in the smallest gestures, evading the terror of its full weight with so many props. Here, have some candy. Mama's busy. Mama's working.

She feels her heart soften further, into sadness, and turns back to the steamed-up window to watch the almost-rain again, chin in her hand. That wasn't quite it, though. It was something else, some way she used to be. A memory of some mode of seeing shaken loose by the book of poems. In high school she had encountered a fragment of Rilke in English class and written it on her jeans in permanent marker. *Yes, for such is our task: to impress this fragile transient earth so sufferingly, so passionately upon our hearts that its essence shall rise up again, invisible, in us.*

Not that it wasn't valuable to interpret the words of others or document the shifting forms of the world, to craft one's interpretations into argument with the clarity of an electron microscope, exposing bare the shape of forces that pushed and pulled them all, bolstering argument with the arguments of others—she gathers books from her bag and opens her laptop, finally, to begin—but it was that she had lost something in the process. Something vital or essential, something she couldn't live without, had been drained away.

She pulls a manila folder from her bag, filled with archival material, and spreads its contents before her. Underlining, coding, looking for evidence of patterns and repetition. She riffles through a stack of Champlain's articles and feels a rush of appreciation.

He was clever, sure, but it was something else too. A flow or a style or a power. The right argument, articulated properly, could cut through the sedimentation of politics like a surgical laser. But his words had an additional power to move, in a world where it seemed like the only writing left was email and job applications and grant reporting, functional writing about writing. What was the term? Technical communication. He didn't have to write the way he did to do his job. He could have just said what happened—reported. But he knew metaphor, he knew poetics. He knew imagery and music and subtlety. It was a playful facility that made her heart ache, that seized and searched her. Sifting through file cabinets, looking for some part of her that had been shoved away as unnecessary or given up as impossible. Some part that had been skimmed off and strained out via the sieve of academic rigor, until all that was left was the silence of exposition, the hush of social science writing. Less writing than typing, twelve hours at a time scrunched in front of a screen. But there was a science to poetry too, all the more precise in its refusal to refuse the figurative. Something about the way he wrote made her fingers long for a pen, for the scrawl of cursive, for letters. When she left paid organizing to return to academia she should send him a note, thanking him for his words.

Maybe that was what the book of poems had disinterred, like a shovel sunk deep into the richest compost of discards, turning it over. A sudden upswell of longing for what used to be—or what could be again, if only, was that it? She pushes it away but it comes back. It used to be all she wrote were poems and letters. And letters were the reason she had set her hopes high on Hector Galindo, despite their awkward chemistry. As teenagers they'd traded hallway notes on occasion after meeting in the tiny alternative scene of their rural high school, Lali a weirdo who warded off whispers about hospitalization by shaving her head to look the part, and Hector an underground comix nerd with a long black ponytail and homemade shirts he'd stenciled to read *artfag*. He'd been sent home for that one, though to Lali's recollection none of the jocks and preps who addressed him that way were ever punished. At the time Lali nursed a shy crush, but she was a sophomore and Hector a senior, older and cooler and popular in his own way, with scene girls crowded around him.

But during Lali's first strange year at Princeton—only Mexican in the top ten of her graduating class, only kid in their school accepted to an Ivy—Hector had suddenly started writing her, as though he'd concluded something, letter after letter with envelopes bulging. They wrote back and forth that way, long conversations about books and ideas and everyday life. He sent her funny doodles he'd sketched about his life in Austin, where he'd gone after high school only to drop out of UT after a single semester. Coupled with the lure of 6th Street's drink-and-drug-fueled music scene, the structurelessness of college had proved irresistible, and he'd lost his full-ride art scholarship in the process. But he'd cleaned up, he wrote, signing up for classes at community college and getting a server job at a vegetarian Thai place. He wrote about the zines he was reading and a graphic novella he was storyboarding. He wrote about how badass she was for sticking with school, always top of the class despite what she'd gone through in high school, how inspiring her drive and determination, how much he worried about turning into his dad—now a drunk living alone in an RV after his mom finally grabbed his siblings and ran.

Lali wasn't sure she'd gone through so much, compared to Hector. He'd grown up poor, the oldest of six in a trailer of chaos ruled by a devout Jehovah's Witness dad who shouted when he drank. Hector's mom recognized her eldest son's sensitivity and talent but lacked the time or resources to do much about it. Only his abuela, who'd studied painting at a DF art school before moving to Tejas and employing those slender artistic hands as a domestica, had encouraged him. Only she had even noticed, really, when he dropped out of school. But Hector was getting back on track: that was what he wanted Lali to know. And she should come back to Texas and transfer to UT and live with him. They could make zines together, political art zines; she could write and he would draw. They would be like Kim Gordon and Thurston Moore from Sonic Youth! Creative partners, romantic partners.

As though drawing up a contract, they had both determined by mail that it had to be right. On paper it had made so much sense. Once, Hector had sent her a short letter that said, only, on a narrow strip of loose leaf hastily torn from a full sheet: *I want to talk with you more than anyone else in the world.* It had thrilled and ultimately persuaded her. She wanted to be that person; she wanted Hector to be that person for her, his words shining a searchlight down inside her and stirring some untapped capacity for desire waiting there. But lying with Hector on his crooked pull-out couch bed on her first night in Austin, Lali had a dim awareness, then a bright dismay, that it didn't feel like the release or homecoming she thought it would be. Instead they kissed and kissed for what seemed like hours, taking turns lying atop one another in their underwear, first Hector and then Lali. Were they supposed to...? Were they supposed to want to...? If they did, wouldn't they just...? But they didn't, not then, held back by nervousness and lack of experience and something else that wasn't there. It'll come, Lali had thought at the time, it'll come if she just kept kissing and rubbing and being kissed and rubbed—but it didn't, and it didn't.

Nor did their promised collaborations. At first they would try, sitting down together to sketch out an idea, or Lali might approach with a script. Here, what do you think? Let's work on it, don't you wanna? And Hector would start, but whatever he started he seemed unable to finish. He would start, but then anxiety would unravel his focus and he'd devolve into tasks that grew progressively more obsessive and avoidant—tweaking his graphic user interface for hours or playing video games online or cleaning the apartment, making big piles of things to put away and then smaller and smaller piles that took longer and longer to make, sorting through papers, sifting through the minutiae on his drawing desk. Eventually he'd have to give up, leaving the piles where he'd assembled them.

It wasn't his fault. He had grown up without her privilege of family stability and the guidance it made possible. But eventually they'd given up on the promise of creative work, both collaboratively and independently. Now on his days off Hector might sketch out an idea for a comic; he might hang a draft of something on the wall to reflect on and then start to pick up the house or stand in the driveway blabbing with Mr. Sosa for a couple hours. He might fix Nena some noo-noos or na-nas or ta-tos—simple meals for which she was always eager, her needs basic and his love for her equally basic and assured. Sometimes Hector thought his love for Nena was the only simple love he felt, unlike the complications of adult relationship. If it was Sunday he might go over to his brother's for a backyard cookout, where they'd drink beer and throw Frisbee with the dog and play video games, but they wouldn't talk about anything important. If he stayed in and Lali and Nena were out, he might watch some porn, sometimes using Lali's computer; she'd find traces of it later, undoubtedly, working on her dissertation or job applications—she was always working or trying to, even on her own days off. Once he'd almost gotten written up at work for looking at porn during slack time, should have, was supposed to, except his immediate supervisor was such a pothead wastrel he didn't give two shits. *What the fuck, Hector:* Lali thought it was funny, sort of, except he could have lost his job. Except at night in bed when they lay together, they held each other stiff-armed before rolling over into their separate sleep. What had he said once, the last time they broke up, right before they'd learned about Nena? *I think I've clung to you because I don't know what to do with myself. I've followed your ambitions around because it's been easier than figuring out what I want to do.*

And I've let you, and it hasn't been right, and I don't think it will be, Lali had wanted to say, to make it definitive, but she didn't—knowing she still needed to be clung to, wishing she could feel something she didn't but knowing it was safer not to. Knowing she too had used Hector as protection from her own appetites and longings, that they had both used each other to hide from themselves. Instead she'd said: *Don't say that, these are just normal anxieties, part of any long-term relationship. Of course I want to stay together, of course.* And they had stayed together, for nearly ten years now.

So much hope and denial had gone into the thing since the letters—that was the tragedy of it. How hard she'd resisted what her body told her that first night together in Austin.

Now, sitting in the bookstore coffee shop, she writes in the tiniest script at the bottom of one of her photocopied news articles, then scratches it out:

there is no right or wrong togetherness / only what you want and don't

CHAPTER TWO
More Explosions, Please!

Wednesday, June 9

With Luz snoozing at his feet beneath the desk, Joel types:
VAMOS a Luchar

No. Too obscure, but also too simple. There was more going on that week than just the emergency meeting he'd attended between VAMOS and the city, as explosive as that had been. There was also the literal explosion at that Southside refinery that had bled jet fuel into the river.

He tries again: *Like Oil and Water*

But that didn't capture it either. The headline had to wrap the whole package together and tie it with a big brassy bow. The headline had to connect the dots. But how? Fingers poised above his keyboard, he stares into the empty screen like a sheet of music he can't decipher. He stands, he stretches his arms up and to each side, he pops his knuckles. Luz stands and stretches too, forelegs long and rump in the air. She follows as he wanders into the staff kitchen to paw through that day's community comestibles, scattered on the counter by the coffee machine. But no coffee. His doctor said he should stay away, no caffeine and no alcohol either. He'd dropped the meds, but it still seemed sage advice. Cutting out sugar would be good too—he raises a hand unconsciously to pinch at his belly, measuring its thickness—but first he should probably sample a piece of the half-gone sheet cake left over from the paper's anniversary party the previous weekend, which he'd somehow missed. Some of the lettering piped onto the cake was gone, but he could see it once read, around a big lightning bolt: *The Volt—20 Years and Still Striking!*

The calendar editor pops his head inside the kitchen in time to catch Joel with a square of cake raised to his mouth, other hand cupped below to catch falling crumbs.

Hey man. Happy Hump Monday. How you be?

Hump Monday was how the editorial staff joked about their midweek start to the news cycle. Their Wednesdays began with an editorial meeting, where they decided cover art and dished assignments for the coming week. This week, Joel had gotten the explosion and rate hike combo loco, which made sense since it was what he liked to write about anyway. Their stories were then due Monday, though that deadline more realistically stretched until Tuesday. Paper went to bed Tuesday at 6pm and was printed overnight, to be distributed Wednesday morning buttcrack early. Now it was Wednesday, Hump Monday, and high noon to boot. Taco time.

Joel starts at Rudy's sudden entrance, then recovers and finishes his bite. Glad you made it in time, he grins. I had to airlift this cake to safety.

Yeah, you missed it last weekend, huh. You had some big plans?

Joel mumbles, nodding his head through a mouthful of frosting, but it's both feint and truth. When you couldn't explain yourself, best to cultivate an air of mystery. Rudy retreats with a shrug, undoubtedly figuring Joel had his reasons, but the success of Joel's deflection still doesn't answer the question: why *had* he missed the party? It had been on his calendar, and he'd been in town; it wasn't like he'd gone anywhere. He'd intended to go. But there was that explosion, followed by that storm, then Luz—

He goes back to his desk with a second piece of cake, Luz trotting behind.

The refinery explosion, the storm, the spill into the river, the explosion at the VAMOS meeting over the rate hike recall effort. Hands laced behind his head, he swivels in his chair, back and forth and side to side. He checks his messages to see if the guy from the state environmental office has called him back, but he hasn't. What exactly had spilled into the river, and how much? Todd knew him there at TCEQ and usually let him have whatever he was looking for, but lately someone new had been handling the info requests. Might be he'd have to go the FOIA route. It would slow things down, but in the meantime he could write around it. Records for the refinery's annual emissions were public enough that, even if he couldn't get numbers for this particular event, it'd probably be okay. From an investigatory standpoint, of course, it'd be better if he had release data specific to this spill. That kind of thing got you gold stars at press club award time. He plucks pen from shirt collar and taps it against his yellow legal pad for a while, trying to construct the skeleton of a storyline from the loose clutch of facts he's gathered. People thought reporters discovered what was already there, tearing back the veil to reveal something essential. And most reporting was. The best reporting, how-ever—really, it was more construction than revelation. Stories weren't excavated so much as extrapolated, like the shape of an ancient creature divined from a scatter of bones.

Rudy and Johana call out to him from the other end of the office, standing at the top of the staircase that divides the upstairs editorial offices from the advertising people downstairs. A spatial arrangement that revealed a political truth: editorial fulfilled a role that was more elevated and rarified, but advertising was the base, advertising made it possible.

Tacos? they want to know. Johana's from downstairs, new, cute, with her black Betty Page bob and her striped knee socks. They must be seeing each other in some capacity. Joel had taken a couple of the advertising women home after *Volt* parties—one of them had liked him and wanted to see him for real—but there was never anything there for him.

No, you go, says Joel. He waves them off, blessing the union of editorial and advertising with a smile, and returns to the work of tapping pen to pad. The cake will hold him over until he can lay this thing down a little, then he'll run across the street for some tacos. First the skeleton, first the spine of a timeline. He lists what he knows, to see if he can make the pieces hang together, in a single story.

1. The explosion—Friday, June 4th, around 1 P.M.

2. The storm—early Saturday, June 5th, around 1 A.M.

3. The spill—discovered/reported Saturday, June 5th at 9 A.M.

4. The elders—found Sunday, June 6th around 3 P.M.

Somewhere in there was the party he'd missed; some time in there he'd been somewhere else, finding Luz. He continues.

5. VAMOS emergency meeting—Monday, June 7th, 6 P.M.

For good measure, he adds:

6. Today: Wednesday, June 9th.

7. Deadline: Tuesday, June 15!!

Well, to start, there's what he found out from searching the archives of the city paper. Turns out this explosion is not the first time, though possibly it's the last—hopefully, given the refinery's imminent conversion to apartments. Turns out the refinery was already old and cantankerous when they closed it, the only one in town, built inland on the river near the southernmost missions, on the edge of the city where there weren't many neighbors at the time. Still aren't many neighbors. A couple apartment complexes, a street with some older homes, but other than that just the state hospital, a few big box stores, a shuttered army base they were talking about turning into a storage yard for mining equipment. You know what he should do, he should make a video and post it as a blog entry, use Google Maps to create something like an aerial survey of the area, so people can visualize where the refinery is and who lives nearby.

Not that no one was affected—tell that to the tenants across the street or to the turtles downriver, for that matter—but it's a good thing the area isn't more densely populated, because what he's seeing from the archives alongside the Toxic Releases Inventory on the EPA site is a pattern of recurrent eruptions and repeated erasures. Every decade or so a fire, a spill, an explosion, an accident, a citation. Then new investigations, new exposés, new exclamations over a forgotten history of violations, new demands for regulations and closure. Then a new owner would take over, investing a little money to bring things up to code until the next time, until this last time. Wonder how this would affect plans to redevelop carbon infrastructure into residential, he muses.

This time around, it was a gas line the construction crew cut by accident. The state environmental office isn't saying why yet, but one of the guys he talked to the night before, when he walked through the apartment complex across the street, said the line was still live; they had missed it when they were shutting things off.

Honestly, we didn't know what they did over there, the guy said. Making some kind of fuel, I guess. There was this flare burning 24 hours round the clock. Sounded like, what was it—like a jet on a runway taking off. Like the biggest power washer in the world. Whhhhhssssshhhh! Like that. At first the noise bothered me, but then I got used to it, like anything else. Actually, when they took the thing offline a few months ago, that was when I *really* heard it. The silence, you know?

How long did they evacuate you for? Joel wanted to know.

Eh, just that night. I wasn't around when it exploded but I heard about it. Some buddies filled me in since they knew where I lived. They said the flames were as high as a six story building, but I didn't see it. Then I came back from work that evening and the whole area had been evacuated for—oh, a mile, mile-and-a-half I guess. They were real good about putting all of us up for the night at a motel. I went to work from there and when I got back everything was back to normal.

That guy was from Maryland. He'd moved there, to the complex across the street from the refinery, to be closer to the mining south of town. There were lots of node workers there in that complex. Black guys from Louisiana, white guys from North Texas, Mexicanos from New Mexico—shit, Mexicanos from Old México. It was hard to find a place in the little towns of the sealands because once the boom started the rents went sky high. Cheaper to live on the outskirts of the city and drive in, even with the commute. An hour there and an hour back.

After his interviews, Joel had sat in his car in the parking lot of the complex for some time, darkened refinery looming across the street as he scribbled notes into his legal pad. They came out like little poems, which he decorated with sketches of the faces who'd come to the door, pinched and wary, like the first guy,

a tall Black man
head wrapped in doo rag
he'd prefer I go away right now
he tries to get me to git
but when I persist he answers questions
hanging halfway out the door

he's lived in this complex for
a year now, moved here
from nawlins to work
in the nodes,
in refining, flushing
metals from rock
with acids

when I ask what it was like
living across from the refinery
he thinks I'm still asking
about the mines:
I give 'em good reviews, he says,

because of the income.
more people are able
to take care of their families.
ain't gonna be here forever—
long term, I'm sure it's not good.
but short term, a good thing.
okay? he smiles, hoping
i'm satisfied now
which i am

So: there was the explosion, then the storm that in one part of the city swept petroleum into the river's swift and rising waters and in another cut lights off and precarious lives short. Then there was the VAMOS press conference first thing Monday morning at CPL headquarters, decrying the death of even one person because of an unjust transition, deaths that would only mount as utility rates rose alongside temperatures. One guy on the Westside they found half-dead from suffocation, after the blackout cut power supply to his breathing equipment. But another guy on the Eastside did die. They found him sealed inside his unairconditioned apartment, a single room in an unregulated boarding house, his body temperature impossibly high. Health department was saying it was too difficult to draw a causal link between the outage and his death since he was already sick, already old, already poor. *Not one more! Not one more!* the chorus of movement people cried, as Joel ran up late to the crowd gathered outside City Power and Light in time to film Manuel Martinez from VAMOS announcing that the people would soon recall the rate hike; they had nearly collected all the signatures they needed. Above the street by several stories, some utility people in dress shirts and pencil skirts raised the blinds of a window to crowd around it, gazing onto the scene below. It was good stuff.

But at the emergency community meeting later that night at the Westside senior center, he was surprised by the level of tension and unrest in the room after that morning's display of unity, threatening to detonate like a corroded gas line. As it turned out, VAMOS had met alone with CPL after the press conference to discuss the possibility of dropping their petition drive, if the utility promised in turn to divert a bigger chunk of change from the city's settlement with Seismar to affordability programs in the poorer districts.

Vendidos After More of the Same ol Shit, one of the Alianza women within earshot had whispered to another. *Guess they're cool with exploding refineries and toxic mining so long as they can tell how hot it is in their house.*

Told you there's no way the city will allow the rate increase to be overturned, muttered the girl from Centro he'd sat next to at the People's Power Summit, the little serious one with the baby. Flipping through pages in her notebook. *It's gotta pass so that they can preserve their credit rating, if they want those federal loan guarantees for the Seismar mine and the refinery rehab.* At this Joel's ears had pricked up: that'd been his theory as well. *Only way to do that is buy off a segment of the poor folks with concessions. Use them as a wedge to break up the power of a coalition. It's so textbook there's probably an equation for it*, she said, pushing her glasses up the bridge of her nose with an index finger. Too large for her face.

For his part, Manuel Martinez had remained unapologetic. *Our people are dying*, he'd thundered. *Even if we get all those signatures—which we* will*—we already know they're going to do everything in their power to throw them out. They got the money, the lawyers, the legislators lined up to change state law. If they have to make it illegal for the people to petition, they will. So why not have a plan B? Why not use our position to win real protections for our people?*

But by that point the meeting had collapsed, all air escaping from its center as the younger women from Alianza and Centro stomped out, chattering and exclaiming over *sneaky-snake sell-outs* and *secret suitsnties* as the viejitas of VAMOS clucked sadly over the departure of their political nietas. To Joel, any absolute *no* seemed a pragmatic impossibility—but maybe it wasn't about that. Maybe the absolute *no* was about the deep togetherness its articulation made possible. You lost at council, then you went out for tacos. He'd felt a pang of loneliness, watching the movement women chatter and banter on their way out of the meeting. They'd never win, but they had each other. Who did he have in this city, or anywhere?

There was one funny part, though. *Hey,* he overheard the Poli Sci prognosticator from Centro say to her workmate, the excitable puppy in the rainbow suspenders: *Hey. You know what would be funny?*

What?

So, what if we went to VAMOS's next press conference at the CPL building dressed in a suit—I have one, I had to get one for job interviews!—holding a sign that says, MORE EXPLOSIONS, PLEASE!

Ah. He'd been searching for the headline, the pulse of the story, its organizing rhythm, and he'd finally found it. More explosions, please!

CHAPTER THREE
Crude Awakening

Tuesday, June 22

Lali had made a list, and each of them had brought what they needed for their character. For the two high school kids playing the politician and the CEO there was a suit and tie, a fat cigar and Paloma's famous play money, imprinted with Mayor Mike's face. For the monster there were plastic chains, a black cape, a skull-faced deathmask that slid over the head of the gangly, newly-bearded Anglo college student beneath. A Latin American Studies and History double major, Joseph had gone on the solidarity caravan when the immigration bill thing had exploded, and the idea for the mask had been his. He'd been staying in El Centro's back house with the other summer interns—copper-headed Rachel from a college in Ohio started by an Indian guru; and Jim, tall and affable Jim who had come from Louisiana in his unairconditioned van and whiteboy dreads. Los cuates liked him because he was handy, knew how to build and fix things—intern labor meant free labor. He played guitar and gardened without shirt or shoes, knowing where to step, not scared of glass or needles. Later that summer, after Lali leaves the city, his hip will shatter in a spray of bullets that tears through the back house where he'd stayed with the other interns, bullets intended for another house.

But in early summer, interning in a barrio backhouse in San Antonio is still an adventure for out-of-state college students, and one night Joseph had seized on the idea to craft a calavera mask out of an old cow skull that hung from the wall of the house by some portrait wire. It already looked demonic, and when painted it took on the cast of a Kabuki demigod. And with the ingenuity of teenagers they had refashioned the wire so that it might cradle one skull neatly within another. The younger high school interns brought mason jars of chocolate syrup labeled CRUDE and 3 liter bottles of Sprite marked MINING ACIDS, and they had emptied their families' garages of plastic fish and fishing rods, seabirds and hardhats, inhalers and plastic rifles. There were coins and a briefcase and a three ring binder one of the younger kids had prepared for Lali so she could narrate. An incoming freshman just out of middle school, Trina—Li'l T, the others had dubbed her—had studiously avoided interaction with the older kids as they laughed and goofed through rehearsals, taking an entire afternoon at an out-of-the-way table to detail the title page of the play, to be slipped into the transparent plastic pocket at the front of Lali's binder. Her work had paid off. Tag-style lettering announced the title: *The Crude Awakening of San Antonio: A Teatro of Terror!!!* A play Lali wrote based on newspaper articles and policy papers, gathered together before her like a hand of cards as she completed the piece longhand in the Centro office, writing and writing with her head down amid the circling din of conference calls and conversation. Writing as feet moved from office to office, as people leveraged and delegated and strategized and mobilized, making the floorboards creak and groan.

One last rehearsal out back, in the garden, before they piled into cars and truck beds for the steps of the City Power and Light headquarters.

***

The Crude Awakening of San Antonio, Or El Monstruo en Cadenas: A Teatro of Terror
Cast of Characters

The Monsters
Little Monster (Ali Resendez)
Big Monster (Joseph Wynn)

The Feeders
CEO (Marcos Mendez)
Politician (Dulce Escobar)

The Community Members
La Niña (Trina Robinson-Vega)
La Vieja (Naima Montoya)
El Mar (Chuy Bustamante)
La Pescadora (Amanda Villarreal)
La Soldadera (Celeste Palacios)
Refinery Worker (Jim Labatt)
Refinery Neighbor (Rachel Rosenberg)
Ya Gna Wena (Chela Escobar)

Narrator (Citlali Sanchez-O'Connor)

[Teatro opens on scene of cast miming everyday activities: walking around, talking to one another, talking on cell phones, reading books, washing dishes, cooking food, catching fish, etc.]

Narrator [Speaking to cast, but also to larger body of passers by]: Gather round, gente, gather round. I want to tell you a story.

[Cast stops what they're doing, gathers closer, sits in large circle around narrator, story time style.]

Narrator: It is an ordinary story, found in any city. It is a tragic story, though one whose ending has not yet been written. It is the story of a creature called POWER.

[Little Monster stands, approaches Narrator in cute monster suit, dressed perhaps as a friendly dragon.]

Narrator: Well, hello there, Power!
Little Monster: Hola! [Mimes childlike activities: skips, jumps, picks flowers, etc.]
Narrator [Reading from book]: In the beginning, Power was taken from its home in the ground to be a caregiver for the world. We brought it here without malice in mind, with the best of intentions—lit streets and warm beds. We brought it into our lives when it was small and docile, and we welcomed its warmth and convenience.

[Little Monster dances around circle, hugs one of the community members.]

Little Monster [Speaking to cast and audience]: Oh, I love you, everyone! Do you love me?

Narrator: But like a stray puppy or a cub separated from its mother, the more we fed it, the more it depended on us for its meals. And though we knew it was wild, we took it in and made it our pet, and soon a dependent relationship formed. It needed us to eat...

[Little Monster approaches different community members, who give her coins, candy, gum, and trinkets.]

Little Monster [upon receiving]: Thank you!
Narrator: ...And we came to rely on it for comfort. We fed power and power fed us, heating our homes and running our machines and cooking our food.
Little Monster [pouring chocolate syrup from a jar on the ground before Community Members]: There ya go!

[With each deposit, Community Members rise and mime a different kind of work, i.e. cooking, washing, driving.]

Community Members: Thank you!
Narrator: So although it was far from its home in the ground, Power grew up big and strong and eventually outgrew table scraps. It needed a job, and a salary with benefits!

[Businessman stands. He's wearing a suit and tie and holds a briefcase full of paper money. He lures Little Monster with a coin, but she shakes her head no. He extends a bill and she shakes her head again. He offers the contents of the briefcase, and when she lunges for it, he dumps the money all over her as she mimes eating greedily. When she finishes, she hands him jars of chocolate "crude" and bags of rocks marked "coal."]

Little Monster: That was delicious! Here, these are for you.
Narrator [shaking head]: It wasn't long before Power grew to such size and strength it became a BIG MONSTER.

[Little Monster exits by sitting next to other community members. Big Monster stands and takes her place. His body is draped with a black sheet and on his head he wears the demon cow mask, but he also holds a large yellow smiley face in one hand that he can raise to hide his demonic aspect.]

Narrator: Power got so big and scary, in fact, that we had to chain it up.

[Roaring and growling, Big Monster leaps out into the midst of the Community Members, who cower, then rise and throw chains over and around the monster. They take their seats again, but continue to hold onto the chains at either end so they are in effect as bound by the Big Monster as he is by them.]

Narrator: Once enchained, businessmen realized they could get even more work out of their captive. But Power had to be persuaded and bargained with, and they had to pay it much, much more. So they introduced Power to politicians, who worked with businessmen to find the money to keep feeding the monster's voracious appetite.

[CEO and Politician stand and approach Big Monster, who raises the smiley mask to his face. CEO introduces Big Monster to Politician, who wears suit, heels, and a big button that says, "Vote for Me!"]

CEO: Councilwoman, I want you to meet a friend of mine.
Politician [flashing big politician grin]: Hi! Nice to meet you.

[After shaking, she looks at her hand, which she has colored with black marker to represent crude. A look of horror on her face, she flashes her dirty hand to the crowd, and with exaggerated motions wipes it off on her pants before rearranging her best campaign face.]

Politician: I've been hearing such great things about you!
CEO [concerned]: You look hungry. Here you go, bud. [Collects some of the paper money on the ground and feeds it to Big Monster.]
Narrator: But there was a problem: the more Power did for us, the more we needed it. And the the more we needed it, the hungrier it got. And the more we fed it, the stronger it got, and the tighter its chains strained over its form and coiled around us, tight as a many-tentacled leviathan.
Big Monster [removing happy face]: Raaaawwwwwrrrrr! Look at how big and strong I am!

[Rattles chains. The community members cheer and applaud, then suddenly cower, frightened.]

Narrator: Now, most of the time, Power was content to eat and work, work and eat.

[Big Monster raises happy face to cover demonic face.]

Narrator: But other times, there were problems.

[Big Monster lowers happy face to reveal demonic face.]

Narrator: For one, it had terrible gas.
Community Members: Ewwwww! Guácala!
Narrator: The people who lived where it ate and worked breathed the foul air and got sick.
Big Monster [fanning backside with happy face mask]: Sorry guys!
CEO: It's cool, B.M.
Politician: Yeah, it's within acceptable stank limits.

[Big Monster shakes chain connected to La Niña, who stands.]

La Niña [holding inhaler]: My grandma says that when she was little, the highway by our house wasn't there. They built it and split this neighborhood in two. The doctors don't know if that's why I have asthma, but it's been a problem since I was four. They give me this to use [raises inhaler] but sometimes it doesn't help. It's scary when you try to breathe and the air won't go in...it feels like you're drowning!

[With La Niña still standing, Big Monster shakes chain

connected to La Vieja.]

La Vieja [nodding, clutching at her chest]: Yes, like you're drowning. I have congestive heart failure. The doctors say I have to use special equipment to help my cells get the oxygen they need. They say it helps to run the a/c. But ay, dios mío—it seems like it's been getting hotter and hotter, and I have to run the a/c more and more. I'm on a fixed income, though. If I run the a/c too much, my bill is too high to pay all at once. Last time that happened, City Power and Light sent me a notice saying they would shut off my electricity. When I told them I needed it for my equipment, they sent me a form my doctor could fill out, but the form still said CPL could disconnect for nonpayment!

[La Niña and La Vieja sit.]

Narrator: Another problem was that Power was kind of... incontinent.
Community Members: Ewwwwww! Guácala!
Narrator: It leaked everywhere. In the water. On the ground.
Big Monster [embarrassed]: Gee whiz, guys. I'm sorry. [Shakes chain of El Mar and La Pescadora, who stand.]
El Mar [wearing blue sheets splattered with chocolate "crude" and covered with plastic fish]: Remember Deepwater Horizon? A deep internal gash. For five months I hemorrhaged and no one could stop it. Five million barrels, they said. When the slick reached the coast they sprayed me with toxic dispersants to help strain off the crude. Oh, I feel sick. [Lays on ground.]

La Pescadora [still standing]: With all the fish gone, how am I going to support my family?

Big Monster [ashamed, hanging head and kicking at ground]: I'm really sorry, really! It was an accident!

CEO [patting Big Monster's back]: Of course it was. Don't worry about it. It's just a little puddle.

Politician [pumping fist into the air]: Drill, baby, drill!

Narrator: And sometimes, our dependency made *us* into monsters.

[Big Monster shakes chain of La Soldadera, who stands.]

Politician and CEO [grabbing La Soldadera's arm]: *Our* fuel is on *their* land! Go get it! [Thrusts plastic rifle into her hand.]

La Soldadera [bewildered]: All I wanted was money for college. The recruiter told me if I went into the reserves, I'd never be deployed. [Salutes and sits.]

Narrator: Toward the end, Power grew so large and hungry it could no longer be controlled—it burst from its chains, destroying everything in its path. We only thought we controlled it!

[Big Monster throws off chains, roars, runs around chasing people. Community members scatter, screaming. He grabs Refinery Worker first; everyone freezes to hear the worker's testimonio.]

Refinery Worker: I don't know what happened. I was just pulling out from the loading rack when I felt the blast. When you hear a boom like that, you already know what it is! I looked back and saw him on the ground, covered in flames. As we carried him across the street, we heard two more explosions behind us from the loading area.

[Big Monster releases Refinery Worker. Community members unfreeze and scatter again, then Big Monster grabs Refinery Neighbor. Everyone freezes.]

Refinery Neighbor: I was at home when I heard the blast. I ran outside and saw a column of thick, black smoke rising from the nearby refinery! Everyone living within a one mile radius had to be evacuated—they were worried the fuel would ignite and cause an explosion capable of killing thousands of people. There's a hospital right by our apartment complex. That's hundreds of people right there—sick people, newborns, people confined to their beds. What happened to them during the evacuation?

[Big Monster releases Refinery Neighbor. Community members scatter. Big Monster next grabs Ya Gna Wena, and everyone freezes.]

Ya Gna Wena: My name is Ya Gna Wena. You might know me as *Yanaguana*, the river that runs through the heart of the city, where tourists walk and river boats run. But I'm also the soil on the banks, the oak and the pecan, the sun and the shade. I am the name for this entire place, the spirit of this place—*ya gna wena*, place where I rest, in the language of the Esto'k Gna. The papers say they don't know how much fuel from the refinery spilled onto the ground, into the groundwater, into me. They say they were little spills, an accident, it's all been taken care of. 1,200 gallons of solvent. 8,600 gallons of crude oil. 1,000 gallons of jet fuel. 400 gallons of naptha. But it doesn't have to end like this—there is a better way.

Big Monster: Well, what is it? I'm tired of this.

Community Members: Yeah! We're tired of it.

Ya Gna Wena: Our power will come from the sun and the wind. Our power will come from the land and the sky.

Big Monster [sits]: Oh! It feels so good to finally rest.

Little Monster: I want to go home, back into the ground where I'm from. I want my mama.

Ya Gna Wena: Our power will be the sun and the wind and the waves.

Narrator: But how will we do it? That matters as much as what we do.

La Niña [standing]: They say they want a rare earth mine across the street from my school!

La Vieja [standing]: They say *our* bills must increase to pay for *their* return on investment!

Refinery Worker [standing]: They say the acids they use to refine heavy metals are toxic, like the fumes from that blast! [Pours Sprite from 3-liter bottled labeled "mining acids" onto the ground.]

Narrator: So how will we do it?

Ya Gna Wena: Will you listen to me this time?

Narrator: How will the story end?

Ya Gna Wena: Will it circle back to the beginning and repeat?

Narrator: Or will we disrupt repetition to create something new?

Ya Gna Wena: Will you circle back anew to recover the original ways?

Narrator: Will there be a new story, unexpectedly?

Ya Gna Wena: And if so, who will tell it?

***

Okay, so it was ham-fisted. But you didn't always need a fine point pen. Sometimes you needed a hammer. And sometimes you needed the sideways glance of metaphor or even something nonverbal or silent—a movement, a texture, a color. Sometimes argument, sometimes poetry, sometimes mathematics, sometimes sound.

After the first performance they take a few minutes to mill around, euphoric, chatting and hugging, before performing a second time, then a third. And Lali thinks more about the hammer and the pen, watching the play unfold again and again, the performers gathering efficiency and confidence with each repetition. What if there could be a form of witness or documentation that did both—half poem and half science, wired together by the declamatory power of street theater? In one single form, you could have the night vision goggles of theoretical argument affixed to the sexual ecstasy of rock opera, to make brilliant the social ecology of connections they lived everyday without ever fully seeing the whole, their bodies at the crosshairs of color and money and water and weather? What if they took the essay, the one she and Sister Soledad were writing, and turned it into some kind of—*epic teatro*?

By the final performance, both print and television media

have arrived with their notepads and voice recorders and camera crews. The city paper hasn't shown, but they rarely did for stuff like this. But Channel 12 and Univision are a pretty solid turnout on their own, and Champlain could be counted on to make it down from the *Volt*: there he was now with his camera bag on his shoulder, led by a dog on a leash. The camera crews wait for interviews on the periphery of the play, but Joel seats himself easily amid the performers, filming atop one leg propped like a tripod for his camera. Beside him, the dog lies quietly with its muzzle on one outstretched forearm. Paloma also films from the sidelines with her handicam, but purely because she liked to, because video was another component of her performance-art-land-ethic thing. Lali remembers the way she lullabied council at the Citizens to be Ignored revue hour, and makes a note to catch her some time and pitch her epic teatro idea.

Lali is relieved to see so many media people. Media hits were the measure of one's success as an organizer. For the funders, they meant the effective meeting of deliverables; while by the logic of shame that seemed to drive much of the mad scramble of organizing, they meant her hire was not a mistake after all. As the last performance ends and the press conference begins—some in attendance dispersing, some staying for more speechifying, others climbing onto city buses to collect signatures from riders—she and Chela glance at each other, preparing for their bilingual media tag team. Lali will take Channel 12 in English; Chela, Univision in Spanish.

That was how they rolled, effortlessly, knowing what to do without having to discuss it in advance. From either side of the CPL steps, they spell their names for the camera into the reporter's Oprah mic; they recite the talking points they practiced earlier in anticipation of the question the media people always asked first: *Why are you here today?* It had taken Lali a while to unhear that *why* as a request for historical or sociological explanation. Now she knows that when the media people ask *why*, it isn't because they want an explanation of systems or root causes. They want the genius of a haiku, precise in its brevity, profound in its simplicity. *We're here for two reasons. First, we want to voice support for the VAMOS petition effort. We oppose all rate hikes, which function as a regressive tax on the city's most vulnerable residents, those who already pay the highest portion of their income on energy costs. We feel the city would do better to weatherize and solarize older homes, starting with those of the poorest residents. Second, we want to draw a link between the closing era of fossil fuels that produced the recent refinery explosion and the rising dawn of a ransition based on dangerous and dirty mining. We can't mine our way out of climate crisis, and we can't change the fuel stock but not the economic logic of grow-or-die that is the real root of both utility increases and environmental damage.*

But what about the studies showing that mining rare earths would lower the cost of transitioning to renewables? The second question intended to throw novices off track by playing devil's advocate, the reporter so bored he might be playing Candy Crush on his phone or smoking a cigarette out the other side of his mouth as he asked.

You were supposed to circle back to your original talking points no matter what they asked, lest they jack your rambling sociological disquisition back in the editing room, remixing it for shits and giggles. *What's clear from the research is, when you look at the real costs of rare earths over the lifecycle of their extraction, refining, consumption, and disposal, it's a bad deal for both public health and environmental quality.* She had it down tight by now, media strategy, from the courtship ritual of the press release to the smooth delivery of content on point in the format they wanted it, all by deadline.

With the *Volt*, at least, there was more room to fumble and stumble one's way through explanation, because their sympathies—or The Champ's, anyway—were clear. Lali glances over at Champlain as her television interview wraps up. Would he want quotes as well? But he is packing his camera and rising to his feet. She thinks about saying goodbye, but something in her holds back, wanting to be noticed and approached.

She might have left but for the dog, which laps at a puddle of soda left pooling on the sidewalk post-performance—one of the high school interns had shaken a three liter like champagne and sprayed it around the plaza in celebration. She laughs at the sight, approaching to bend and scratch at the dog behind her ears. Una viejita, dull golden hair stiff and coarse as bristle, like her grandma's mangy old Dalmations. Petey 1 and Petey 2: they had been diachronic twins, a second to replace the first.

Joel walks over, hand half-raised in greeting. Luz, he says with affectionate reproach, clucking his tongue.

Did you just get her? Lali asks.

Yeah—found her in the park after that big storm couple weeks back. She's old, though. The vet says by her teeth that she might be twelve or thirteen, or even older.

They share a moment of appreciation, gazing down to watch

her long tongue washing the asphalt.

Good thing it's not the chocolate syrup, says Lali. Chocolate is bad for dogs, right?

I've heard that, says Joel. I've never had a dog before.

Oh yeah? Me neither, actually. A revolving door of cats, though.

They laugh. Yep, says Joel, definitely had my share of that.

Oh cats, says Lali, shaking her head with exaggerated regret.

She stoops again to let the dog sniff at the back of her hand in introduction. So...she's nice, Luz? That's her name, right?

Luz, yeah. Wonderful. She's amazing.

Lali rises to find Joel looking not at Luz but at her. He is shifting his eyes sideways and down, in the quickest of movements scanning upward from feet to face and back down again for emphasis, to make sure she knows it bears meaning, that she has neither mistaken nor misread his gaze. And to make sure she understands what meaning it bears, which reading it prefers. Suddenly she is cast outside herself, seeing her hair pulled back to expose the line of her neck, the liner she has penciled for the performance to the horizon curve of her eyelids, the silver hoops dangling from earlobes. Just as suddenly, the plane plummets 500 feet without warning and she drops back into her body, heart beating violently. A backdraft combusts in her gut with a *whoosh*, and with terrible speed races upward to inflame lungs and throat and face, following the line his eyes have traced up her body.

With an explosive comprehension she feels the full power of the moment, its chaotic pinhead dance, teetering between generative and destructive polarities, something she cannot just put away or shrug off before going home. *Just physical attraction, nothing more*. It is but it isn't, it is bigger than that, something sacred and profane, awesome and awful both, like the face of God beheld in Niagara. It is the precipitous coming apart of everything she has sought to build carefully, straw by straw. Remove the right piece and the entire structure toppled like a game of Jenga, the foundation at last exposed as untenable now and untenable always, from the beginning. *Always-already*, as they were fond of saying as grad students. But this laying to ruin, this absolute negation—she knows, even then, that it is also purification, a wildfire clearing space for something new: a negation of negation, a clearer seeing this time around. Therein lay both the power and terror of desire: it signaled the ending of everything solid but false, the beginning of a truth grown from the secret fertility of apocalypse. She had known right away what was coming, in her body.

Some of the kids are approaching now, still in costume, talking about getting tacos. Lali drove them so probably she will take them. Does he want to come too? She lifts one hand to shield her eyes from the sun as it sets behind his head.

Oh, he ate already. He has to get back to the office, deadline you know. He has to get Luz home. Or something—but as he says this, before he turns to go, he reaches for her raised arm and touches her lightly, fingers brushing her elbow for a moment.

Well, she says. I'll be seeing you, then, Joel.

CHAPTER FOUR

Plans Are Made

Wednesday, June 23

At work the next morning, Lali's heart begins racing when she fires up La Chingona—Chela's name for the monster iMac on her desk—to open her email. But a calmness and clarity moves beneath like a great slow river, certain in its course. Somehow she has been waiting for this, since the day she and Joel sat in silence at the Power Summit the previous autumn, watching documentary footage of the people's caravan to somewhere or other. Sitting in their parallel silences. When were you gonna talk to me already. In her inbox, a single sentence opens an enormous expanse, scrolling beneath the open jump door of the plane as she stands at its lip, waiting her turn to dive.

From: Joel Champlain <j.champ@thevolt.com>
To: Citlali S. O'Connor <citlali@elcentro.org>
Date: Weds, June 23 at 8:53A.M.
Subject: (no subject)

Great seeing you yesterday.
-J

Her hands shake as she readies fingers over keyboard, thinking of what she wants to say. She had been meaning to invite him out for lunch before she split town anyway, that was true. Lunch was neutral territory; lunch made sense. Not too quick a response. Write a draft then wait a few.

From: Citlali S. O'Connor <citlali@elcentro.org>
To: Joel Champlain <j.champ@thevolt.com>
Date: Weds, June 23 at 9:18A.M.
Subject: (no subject)

Likewise! I've actually been meaning to see if you might want to get lunch sometime soon. Don't know if you heard through the short short San Anto grapevine, but I'll be leaving Centro soon and moving to the Midwest to start a Poli Sci teaching position there at one of the state universities. It's a visiting position (2 yrs) but I'm hoping it'll turn into something permanent. I can tell you more whenever I see you next. Maybe next week, after my official last day?

--Lali

He must be at work like her, both of them peering into monitors, because he fires back right away. He meets her and raises.

From: Joel Champlain <j.champlain@thevolt.com>
To: Citlali O'Connor <citlali@elcentro.org>
Date: Weds, June 23 at 9:22A.M.
subject: (no subject)

I'd like that. I'm actually looking at tripping down to the coast this weekend to take some shots of a protest happening Sat. There's a big statewide mining conference going on, and some local groups have planned a 'hands across the sand' demo there on the beach, across from the conference site. You and peanut are welcome to come with, if that's not too much hanging out for your taste. We're supposed to do a "guide to summer" thingy in next week's paper, and a beach protest would give us a chance to pontificate on all the Seismar stuff a bit, as if I needed any excuse ;)

-J

Her heart swells, her head buzzes. She types back a time, an address. And plans are made. It's all rationalizable. It's all for work. He's an environmental reporter; she does environmental things to be reported. It makes sense.

It makes too much sense. Now it has been set in motion, a gathering thunderhead of meaning that has reached criticality, like the drama of florescence captured in stop motion: a queasy hesitation before the plunge into full bloom, the agony of contraction before life pulsed forth in a singular expulsion. The moment of crest and descent. The low, deep groan of a glacier about to give way and fall into the sea, unstoppable in the fullness of its power.

CHAPTER FIVE
Hearing Voices, Again

Friday, June 25

No one knew Joel saw and heard the things he did, or that he fought as hard as he did to make sure no one knew. No one save an ex-girlfriend who had moved with him from Dallas to San Antonio a couple of years after the divorce, which paired with his lay off had sunk him so low so fast he thought he'd never pull out of it. Wished he wouldn't. He'd met Angela in Dallas, when it would have been easy to let the nose of the thing drive itself into the ground so hard its thin aluminum crumpled like paper, like trash. He'd had his eyes closed already, waiting for the impact. He hadn't been in love with her, but how could he have been, in those conditions. To not be in love had been a relief. And Angela had been willing to love enough for the both of them, anyway, trying to make it easier for him to say yes to her. She had loved him right away, same as his ex-wife who claimed she knew she loved him the day she met him. And like his ex-wife, Angela had wanted to take care of him, before she started to ask questions about the future. Angela hadn't gotten tired like his ex-wife did, but Joel knew that if he really let himself be known, he would have worn Angela out eventually in exactly the same way, like a pencil eraser scrubbed too hard for too long. And because he did care for her, as best he could, he never let her get too close. Because he cared for her, he'd had to push her away.

That was the thing that didn't make sense to people who didn't see what he saw and hear what he heard. But that was why, when she did start to ask questions—why and how come and couldn't they and what did he ultimately want—that was why he'd bolted, and moved to San Antonio without her. Again she had followed, hoping it could be different, moving out of his old apartment but right down the street from his new one; and now they maintained a friendship both easy and uneasy. Easy, if they didn't talk about what was unresolved. Uneasy in that not talking did not resolve it either, did not make the questions go away. The unspeakability of these unanswerable questions in fact became the basis for their continued contact. Angela had wanted too much, that was what Joel told himself. She had been too attached when they both knew attachment was the root of all suffering. That's the first thing they learned at the Buddhist temple back in Dallas, the first thing out of the abbot's mouth when he and Angela had walked in the door. No attachment, no suffering. Easy.

But he knew the problem was that she had wanted something at all. She had a core desiring self that *could* want things, which formed reasonable expectations for attaining the things it wanted and made reasonable arrangements to get them. What she wanted was basic: to be loved in return or chosen, to be assured of an ongoing, mutually shared framework of meaning for their uneasy interactions, a containing logic or coherence that kept the terror of intimacy safely corralled. One question—*What are we doing? Where are we going?*—and the whole thing crumbled. The threads linking him to the people of the world were chains of butterfly wings, like the ones in the beautiful mosaics hanging in the Chinese restaurant near his house. Thousands upon thousands, shimmering like a heat mirage and utterly frangible on touch. A holograph and a holocaust of butterflies.

Really, she had wanted what anyone would want, what he himself wanted, or wanted to want, if only he could. What he had feared most about Angela and about his ex-wife before her was that if they got close enough they would confirm what he suspected: that he was absent something healthy people knew as self, that he was an engine without an engineer, a body without an *I* looking out of the eyeholes God had cut into his face. Incapable of acting, unsure of where he was or should be or what he needed to be doing. Just stuck, waiting for a set of instructions—external or internal, it didn't matter. But waiting for something or someone that would flip a switch somewhere inside, supply power to the wires like a coin fed into a slot, make the whole contraption light up and hum. That was the risk of accepting love, of being known: that he might not be capable of its return. That love would reveal there was no *I* to be known, no *I* who could love back or receive love. Nothing there. Already damned, or damnable.

Was he damned or not? It could be neither proven nor disproven, that was the maddening thing. He could spend hours on the couch staring at the patterns of light cast on his living room wall from the trees shifting their branches outside his window, trying to ascertain the exact percentage or ratio, saved to damned. No one in the city but Angela knew he struggled. Especially not anyone associated with the professional snarkers at the *Volt*. But no one at all knew that for Joel the struggle was a religious one. Cosmological. Not mental or medical at all, like they said, like they wanted him to believe. His time with the people at the evangelical church, swaying with hands lifted, was the only time he had felt wired in the right way, felt a sense of agency and place, a belongingness—not only among other people but to the universe itself. Part of the energy that ached to act and which acted.

***

His conversion had begun on a street corner in Austin. True, he'd only halfheartedly endorsed the *no gods no masters* credo of the hardcore scene there. And at the punk house to which he moved after high school graduation—the closest farthest-away place he could think of from Waco, where his family had landed freshman year—he began feeling increasingly compelled to keep a bible for protection, wedged between his mattress and the wall. Even though the two guys who'd spat on him and threatened to stomp his ass back at Waco High School had both been bible beaters. At night, holed up in his attic apartment, he pulled it out of its crack to read in secret, the red words of Jesus leaping out at him, in equal parts comforting and terrifying. A promise of apocalypse fast on the heels of a promised salvation. It was confusing. But it was a confusing time, after the spells began to fall over him like a trance. So maybe the guy on the drag could smell it on him like booze, the cavern of confusion and terror that had yawned open inside him, scrambling for something safe and stable to fill it.

But there was other weird stuff that summer too, lights that spun and shot through the sky and reports of cult activity in the area, guys he knew peripherally from the black metal scene who lured runaways to ceremonies in Zilker Park, where they made them mutilate stray dogs after injecting them with rattlesnake venom. Things that scared Joel and seemed too bizarre to believe—except a friend of his had once invited him to a coven when she stopped by the house to buy pot, and another guy he knew claimed to be something called a hubrid, conceived by a human father and human-alien hybrid mother. And then there was the letter that had arrived at the punk house, addressed to him and his housemates but without return address, promising good luck if he copied and sent it to ten people and bad luck if he did not. And beneath this was a nonsensical jumble of letters written in slanting all caps: *TSILYMNOERAUOY UOYKCARTNACI*. Eventually it had hit on him to try reading it backwards: *I CAN TRACK YOU. YOU ARE ON MY LIST.*

The church people in Austin had offered protection, explaining that chain letters were a form of witchcraft in their effort to magnify the potency of either blessing or curse. It was sinful for the sender to usurp the power of God to determine events and predict the future, and sinful for the recipient to entreat favor from forces of darkness. To be scared by the letter or believe in its power revealed one's lack of faith, but the good news was that one could easily recognize the lies of Satan at work and renounce them.

The church people told him all kinds of things, which is not to say they were not true. At age nineteen they told him he was something called a feeler-healer: a transformer, an alchemist of suffering. He was capable of taking in another's pain, changing it inside his body and returning it as good energy. Like a filtration device or a purifier, the opposite of an industrial machine that consumed good energy and discharged waste. The opposite of entropy. Then there was a practice called *tonglen* that he would learn much later, many years after leaving the church and finding his way to the Buddhist temple he and Angela had attended in Dallas. It was a similar practice. Most meditation practices taught relaxation as respiration—as you sat, you placed attention on taking in pure air and expelling tension and doubt and worry on the out breath. Tonglen was different. In tonglen, you deliberately breathed in the world's suffering and breathed out peace and relief. You became a tree instead of a mammal, the lungs of the world, a carbon feeder instead of a carbon polluter. It was a gift you gave to others. There was a mantra that went with it too, which years later he still recites every morning to tamp down on the low pressure system of bad thoughts that would move in otherwise, obsessively circling like vultures, threatening to keep him in bed all day. You imagined a circle forming, first around your heart and then your person and then concentrically outward to encompass those you loved, those you knew but didn't love, those you feared, then finally to all living beings. *May I be happy. May I be healthy. May I be loved. May I be kind. May they be happy. May they be healthy. May they be loved. May they be kind. May all living beings be happy…*

But that would come later, after he had been forced to wander off from where the church people had left him to wait.

After two years inside, he'd found himself outside of the fold with the promise of their short return, but he sat outside for hours, days, months, years before he realized they were not coming back for him. Or that he was not going back inside. He didn't understand why. He had been young then, still in his early 20s, and he'd had to figure out what to do. He tried a semester of college at UT, before dropping out to follow a musician girlfriend out to LA and Portland and Seattle, drinking and drugging and odd-jobbing their way up the West Coast. When that proved finally unsustainable he had come back to Texas to marry a girl from his church days who still loved him and vowed to protect him. They finished college with liberal arts degrees and moved to the Panhandle, and by chance, by luck alone he found journalism—or journalism found him, in the form of a reporting position at a rural paper—and they bore a single perfect child, a daughter miraculously free of her parents' collective suffering. And when his marriage had folded he took a job in Dallas, where another girlfriend had rescued him before the whole thing crashed to the ground. Dallas was where he found the temple and learned about tonglen, before he left those things too. Another job, another city. Now he was all alone in San Antonio, left to wander with nothing left to try, nothing new under the sun: sometimes he felt the book of Ecclesiastes, from his church people days, was nothing more than an antique account of the sickness that swelled his brain, seizing and letting go, seizing and letting go. Swimming in and out of consensus reality, raising inescapable, unanswerable questions about what was real in the end, and whether his sickness was its distortion or, in fact, its revelation.

Except there is a dream he periodically remembers. Two dreams. The first came to him when he was living in Amarillo, Texas with his ex-wife and daughter, in the high plains of North Texas. Just as the voices came and went from his waking life like clouds, there were times when his nights were rich with visions and insights that came in the form of dreams, and it was in the middle of such a period when he first dreamed of a beautiful community of people where everyone was loving and kind and intimate—a sacred home, a Zion or Aztlan that would mean an end to abandonment and the exile of wandering. *You've come home, you've come home!* the people cried as they hugged him. He had woken with the name of the town in mind: Ardmore, Oklahoma. He searched for it on a map and saw the town was not far from the Red River marking Oklahoma's border with Texas, halfway between godforsaken Waco and Oklahoma City. A town wrested from Chickasaw hands—but even they were exiles, forced out from where they'd come—which had turned to nodes when the carbon party ended, and before that to oil when cotton production destroyed the land, and which before that was a railroad town. A boom and bust frontier village, not much different from many others. Ardmore.

The second dream was more recent; he'd had it in San Antonio shortly after he'd split with Angela and moved to the apartment to be by himself. In it he had been outside—somewhere swampy—when he walked past a great hollowed-out tree stump in which George Carlin crouched, hidden beneath a patch of moss. *Psst, kid!* Carlin had hissed as Joel walked past. When he peeled back the moss, Carlin peered up at him from the darkness, his white face shining and somber, and said: *The most ethical and caring people have all been called weirdos before.* Several days later, Joel learned that Carlin had died the day of the dream. Things like that were always happening to Joel. If he wasn't seeing people levitate in a church, he was dreaming of Ardmore, Oklahoma or communing with the spirit of George Carlin as it passed from the world. Whether things like that happened to other people or whether he was just crazy, it brought some comfort to Joel to remember those dreams.

***

The night before his trip to the beach with Lali, he is dreaming about Ardmore again when a scream from the park jolts him awake. Someone is screaming, a man. Why? Instinctively he bolts upright and throws his feet to the floor, bracing his hands against the edge of the bed, senses straining in the dark as he waits to see what will happen next. But the scream is opaque and open-ended, like the screech of brakes without a crash, like early morning gunshots unshadowed by sirens. The sound of it shreds a hole into the night, a question unsettling the air. Five, ten, fifteen minutes pass as he waits for that hole to close around an answer, but there is only indecipherable silence. And in those moments, in the red wash of his panic, sense memories flood his consciousness like a kaleidoscope in bloom. The weight of hands holding him down—*shhh*. Crying around a hand over his mouth. That hand—had it belonged to the man from their old Philly neighborhood, before their unhappy move to Texas? A neighbor charged with molesting several children before disappearing from memory. Was it the greys that had grandfathered his hubrid friend from Austin? Was it the flicker of a story cast from inside the womb? An ambient immersion in his mother's pain, floating in a febrile fluid a degree too high to be welcoming. She had been pregnant with him when his parents separated for a time. He hadn't learned that until adulthood, from one of his older brothers, who informed him one drunken evening that when he came along, taking them all by surprise—the youngest of three boys, baby of the family by ten years—his mother had been forced to drop out of her graduate program in mathematics, knowing she'd have no support at home from her tenured physics professor husband. For a while she'd resisted and they had split up, before she relented and returned and left her program. Was that it, then? But Joel has no solid memories, nothing definite to point to—just sensations and theories.

Then comes a memory-vision of his neighbor's face directly before him, sloppy drunk and angry, calling Luz ugly in the weeks before he got evicted, before Luz got him evicted. *That your dog? Qué fea.* Sitting on the stoop laughing with bottle in hand. After that he'd started to harass Joel with a subtle malevolence, rattling the living room window with his palm as he walked past, stirring Luz into a frenzy of barking that he would then imitate obnoxiously. *Rawrawrawrawr!* He was the son-in-law of the apartment manager who had told Joel when he moved in that pets were okay. Then the harassment started, and next thing he knew he was getting evicted. It could have been that he couldn't keep Luz crated worth shit. Or was it the neighbor who had done it, turned his fortune with his words? *Que fea.* The neighbor. The neighbor danger.

TSILYMNOERAUOY UOYKCARTNACI. Joel jumps to his feet, pulling on pants and shirt and shoes.

He slips out of the apartment by the back door, not wanting to be seen, and drives to a 24-hour Walmart nearby, where he buys a baseball bat as hard as it is light. He buys a candy bar and a pack of cigarettes too, in case someone should worry why one might want to buy a baseball bat in the middle of the night, but no one seems concerned. Maybe in Vermont or Colorado they would be. But not in Texas, where the mascot for his Waco high school—this would have been around the time of the Branch Davidian conflagration—had been the esteemed representative of a white vigilante police force known for its bloody relations with Mexicans and Indians. At pep rallies they'd form one hand into the shape of a gun and shake it at the sky to the beat of the school song. Yeah, not in Texas.

He is still mentally ticking off which states could actually require registration or perhaps a waiting period for nocturnal bat purchases as he drives back home, hardly noticing when he pulls over to park on the Nuestra Madre strip. The bars are letting out, so there is no point going in. And the itch to drink is overly familiar to him, as is his knowledge of the sickness, physical and mental, that will follow if he scratches it. So instead he paces the street, candy bar in one hand and cigarette in the other, alternating between bites and drags. Will he be taken for a street walker? He laughs aloud, smoking and eating. A mosquito lights on the exposed flesh of his calf and feeds; it bursts when he reaches absently to slap it away, a smear of red staining his leg and fingertips.

Some time later, he is not sure how long, he realizes his lighter is empty and stops at a street corner adjacent to a gay bar, leaning against a wall near the bar's entrance. Waiting for someone to come out so he can ask for a light.

It must be too late. The outside lights are still on but everyone has gone home for the night. Except for those who have no home, who like him are left to wander the streets. He does not have to wait long before someone approaches in a filthy heavy coat, pushing a cart. He is Anglo, but constant exposure to the sun has leathered his skin to a deep red-brown. He's not from here. No, he is from here.

Got a cigarette? he wants to know.

I do, says Joel, grateful for human contact. If you have a light.

Lemme see—I might. The man rummages around in his coat before producing it, a half-sized purple lighter, the kind sold for cents from plastic tubs on convenience store checkout counters. Look at that! You got the cigs, I got the light. It all works out after all.

They smoke without talking for a while before the man squints his eyes and scrutinizes Joel's face. Hey man. Don't I know you? I think I seen you somewhere. You look familiar.

Joel shrugs. Maybe so. I write for the *Volt*. He tips his head back, exhaling into the light. A sequence of perfect rings exits his mouth, the smoke changing color as it floats across the neon rainbow of the bar's marquee. Amazeballs!

If the man appreciates this small accomplishment, he doesn't let on. Eyes fixed on Joel's face, his attention is elsewhere. Wait, he says slowly. Maybe you know me? That must be it. Everyone knows me!

Could be. What's your name?

Cabeza de Vaca! He burbles with raspy laughter, clapping Joel on the back. Kidding! That shipwrecked fool come wandering through here, didn't know his ass from his a-hole no matter how many journals he filled up with notes! Nah, I'm Anthony. You know, like the saint?

He gestures behind him to the neon sign above the bar's entryway, which spells out its name—*St. Peter's*, ha ha, good one—as it cycles colorfully through the spectrum of the rainbow flag.

That's what they call me. That's who I am. Evangelical doctor of the church! Hammer of heretics! Professor of miracles! See, I've been around. Born 1195! So I know a lotta shit about a lotta shit. Unlike ol' Mr. Cowhead, *I* know where the lost things are hidden. Like you needed a lighter, dincha?

Saint Anthony. I've always wanted to meet a saint, Joel murmurs. It seems that he's hearing things again. A constant low mumble, muffled, sometimes worried and sometimes angry, like a television on in the next room, three televisions set to different channels. He listens, trying to figure it out, separate or sort them so that it makes sense. He should be getting back home soon, to snuggle with his bat. He has to get up in the morning and drive to the coast for the protest with the girl from El Centro. The woman. Jesus—she had a kid already, a Ph.D. But she looked like a kid, like fifteen or sixteen. Big tea-colored eyes that ate up her small face behind those tortoiseshell glasses. Dirty black Chucks and raggedy backpack like a teenager. He had to go—but there was one more thing.

Listen—do you know why we are here? Or why I'm here. Why am I here in this city, of all places? What am I supposed to be doing?

Don't even worry about that, man! Look, I started this city, so I know what makes it run. Pretty soon you're gonna know everything too. Here, walk with me a little.

They amble up the sidewalk together, Anthony catching Joel at the elbow when he stumbles.

Tired, Joel mumbles. I'm tired.

I can tell! Anthony clucks, sympathetic. Trouble sleeping, huh? Must be that pack of cigs in your pocket weighing you down! Tell you what. Give me half of what you got and I'll tell you everything I know.

***

In a different part of St. Anthony's city, Lali can't sleep either. She lies awake thinking about the trip to come. She is excited to travel with the newspaper man; she has cobbled together a picnic lunch from the dregs of their kitchen. A peanut butter and honey sandwich, a cheese sandwich with mustard, overripe bananas. When around 1 or 2 am she finally does drift off, she dreams: about someone she loved once, a college professor of hers, a literary theorist. A mystic, a hermeneutic. A diviner of meanings submerged within texts. A finder, a revelator. Once he had told her: *the trick is to be in the world but not of it.* Once she had stood before him in the hall before class on the day after the first election in which she was old enough to vote, stunned by the strength of her disappointment, surprised by her surprise at the defeat of her third party candidate, though surely she must have known he would lose. Surely she must have known nothing would come of her hope in the face of power's centrifugal force. He had been kind, standing there in the hall with her. He had seemed to know what to do. How to occupy an impossible space between hope and despair, the tensile space that made right action possible. *The only hope is no hope,* he'd said once in class. But what did that mean?

She wakes knowing she has been dreaming about Joel. He is the one she has been waiting for: she just knows. He is the one who knows something she's been trying to understand. It will be the last night for some time that she can sleep.

CHAPTER SIX
On the Coast

Saturday, June 26

When he comes to pick her up, swinging his long legs over the makeshift baby gate she and Hector have bungee corded to the top of the stairs, Lali notices that Joel has dried blood running down his calf. Eh...cats, he says when asked, distractedly swiping beneath the cuff of his shorts. Half dressed for work in customary Smiths shirt over obligatory khakis, Hector comes out to meet and greet, to shake hands and say goodbye in one gesture. Good to meet you, see you later, have a good time. He's not concerned; he's used to Lali running around all over with all kinds of people.

Lali is more excited than he or anyone knows. She woke already dragged backwards into a receding tide of excitement, struggling against it. She forces neutrality: they are going to the beach, but she won't wear a swimsuit. As Joel waits, she loads Nena's carseat into the backseat of his car, then Nena herself, then the bag of snacks she has packed. From her blanket in the back, Luz lifts her head to watch with patient eyes. Do you have a tape player? she wants to know, referring to Joel's car. She has cassette tapes, she can bring them. He raises eyebrows. I think that may be a little too modern even for me, he smiles.

And then they are ready. She will be neutral until she knows for sure how it will go. But in the car they begin by trading dreams.

My head has that fuzzy feeling you get, he says, when you don't sleep enough?

Do you need me to drive?

Oh—no, I'm okay. It's just, last night I was having these—nightmares, I guess.

Really? Why? What of?

Just...you know. I don't know. He throws a glance in her direction, flashing a crooked smile. Half abashed and half something she can't make out, his eyes shielded by a pair of women's cheap sunglasses.

I had this dream last night—she should be neutral but she can't wait to tell him!—I had this dream last night that I was part of a synchronized swimming routine. It was part of a campaign. We were performing for Charlie Gonzalez—the congressman, you know? Trying to get him to support a bill.

This surprises him into laughter, clearing away the foggy uncertainty of the previous moment, and they talk. And talk, as Luz and Nena doze in the back. They are supposed to talk about his plans to leave the paper and go back to school but they talk about everything else. A documentary he watched about theoretical physics. Did she know molecules of water could register emotion? A clip she saw once, waiting in the food stamp office, of some conservative senator on *The View*. Did Joel know that this man in his heart did not believe the conservative position on climate change, though as a public figure he felt obligated to represent it? You could see it on his face, the incongruity, when Whoopi Goldberg cornered him. And you could see it as despicable hypocrisy, Lali tells Joel. What did Sartre call it? Bad faith. But in that that incongruity you could also see how the senator's humanity exceeded his structural position of power and also how power worked as structures or positions, no matter who embodied them, no matter their humanity. The world was endlessly fascinating, endlessly intriguing.

When the city has fallen behind them, Joel stops at a gas station for coffee while Lali waits in the car with Luz and Nena. He brings it back, dancing for a few steps like a juggler for her amusement, tossing the coffee from cup to cup to mix in the milk and sugar she has requested. Her breath catches, squeezed from the inside by some strange pang. Something about it. It was a gesture she never could have anticipated. It came purely from him, its unpredicted wit and kindness knocking her off balance, filling her with delight and then something like despair—why?

And that pair of women's sunglasses he wore. She keeps looking at him as he drives, talking, thinking that in a weird way he looks like a younger Jack Nicholson. Something about his teeth, straightened from braces years ago, she can tell, but with one incisor still invitingly askew and discolored where metal once held it in. She has a thing for the way organic life by nature, via imperfection or wildness, evades attempts to enforce a master order. A tenderness for that single, wily tooth that got away. It finds her and grabs her and bends her backwards, searching for hidden possibilities of newness or difference, the outer edge of growth that came seemingly from nowhere. An agency she'd always wanted but feared she could not have.

What was it that beckoned, endlessly, like a Chinese cat waving its arm for good luck at passersby in the window of a tea shop? It must have been the possibility of desire that did not exclude words and books. A life of books that did not exclude desire. A life of hunger—for language, for skin—that was not at the same time also a privation. A denial of denial, a radical yes. The possibility of making whole something that had been given to her already rent, like a dress with a tear down the front that she was expected to wear anyway, making do. No, a rift she had inherited in her body but whose origin was long before her birth, handed down through patrilineage.

So she keeps looking at him as they talk, as he drives. They are headed southeast, toward the Gulf of Mexico, and the rising sun outside his window forms a white-bright corona behind his head, like a halo emanating from his core. Could anyone have seen that, or was it something only she could see? It makes her own skin blur and shift as they talk and talk—sometimes she becomes a sister or daughter, at other times a friend or lover, though neither has spoken a word about the interstellar field of possibilities exploding open before them. Who was she—who was he? What was he to her?

***

My birth certificate, I was looking at it recently. Do you know what the seal for Corpus Christi is—or was then, anyway? A fish jumping out of the water in front of some flaring refinery stacks. Can you believe that?

The beach town where they are headed is where Lali was born and lived for the first few months of her life. She does not remember living there but feels connected nonetheless, mythologically, an affinity for a place she knows is part of a larger narrative arc that has brought her to her present location. A significant contingency on which her life has depended. The beach town where they are headed was also once a refinery town: growing up, her family would take a weekend trip to the coast every summer, as soon as school ended, to swim in the Gulf and eat picnic lunches. You knew you were getting close when you spotted the refinery flares on the outskirts, not far from where the Nueces plaited itself into the San Antonio and Frio and Atascosa, a single trensa de rios down the back of Tejas, a back turned to the bloody scrimmages of nation-making that fought over where, at which river, to sever the head of Texas from its Mexican body. Later the great-grandsons of those same nationmakers had built the now-snuffed flares, strange and beautiful torches above a jungle gym city of pipe-line, and it became regular occurrence to step into blobs of tar as you played near the waves. It was no big deal, just part of going to the beach. But now in the shadow of the transition, that everydayness had a different meaning, superimposed on a backdrop of knowing.

Maybe, she muses, on some unconscious level, maybe her coastal origins explained why she'd been so struck by Exxon Valdez as a child. Back then she hardly understood the politics of extraction, of course. But the sight of oil-drenched cormo-rants and loons on the evening news had stirred something visceral and urgent in her. At ten she hung a homemade wood-en placard outside the door of her bedroom—Dr. Citlali S. O'Connor, Marine Biologist—and spent the summer before middle school outlining chapters in a marine biology textbook she'd found in a free box outside their rural library. The text was far above her head, but she sat patiently reading and taking notes, willing the information to cohere as she struggled to master a knowledge of names and parts and relationships.

So how'd you go from seagulls to political science? Joel wants to know.

Partly it was her high school science classes, her bad luck to be taught by football and soccer coaches who by state or district requirement had to teach something, anything, if they wanted to coach football or track or baseball. Her 10th grade physical science teacher's idea for pedagogical approaches to the unit on astronomy, for instance, was to pop *Apollo 18* into the VCR while he chatted it up with the soccer players in his class. Then there was an incident in that same class, same teacher—

She shares the story of the Mexicana student teacher, washed from the room on a surge of white laughter, the students joined in by the coach.

Fucking Texas, Joel mutters. He'd been muttering it since he moved there as a teenager.

These incidents had turned her off science, but they had also nudged her toward a nascent understanding: that repairing ecological disaster meant going further than understanding the *how* of ocean ecology. It meant asking *why*, going down to the roots, studying the human relationships that treated oceans and rivers, water, as sacrifice zone or waste sink for dumping. What was the same, though, was the urge to explain, to outline and map and diagnose systems, making visible the otherwise invisible logics that turned the internal springs and pinons of the thing. And though her obsession with oily seabirds waned, a ghost of these earlier concerns resurfaced around the time of her flight from the elite cloistered weirdness of Princeton for the familiar fuckery of Texas. As she cleaned out the wreckage of the dorm suite she shared with three other roommates, shoving aluminum cans and scrap paper into black garbage bags, something about the sight of the waste scattered carelessly across their living space had stopped her from throwing the bags into the dumpster. Though she didn't know what else to do with them, she couldn't bring herself to throw them away, either. So she hauled them in the bed of her truck back to Austin, where she knew there was a recycling center that would take them, and returned to Texas a raging environmentalist. In fact, her first job out of college was one of those paid petitioners you saw down on the drag, hired by a big green group who paid her a quarter for each signature she wrangled from passersby eager to escape her press for bag bans or river protection or mandatory smog checks—

Oh. She breaks off, eyes trained as they pass to the entrance of a mining operation, vast piles of slag on the flat horizon. Oh look, she says. That's new.

Joel turns his head to follow her eyes. The refineries are offline, he murmurs, but the mines... He waits for a moment to see if she'll continue her story, but she is quiet.

Then she asks: So. Where were you born? And...when? She knows Joel is older but not by how much. There are parts of him, around his eyes, that look much older. But she can't bring herself to come out and ask; she can't make it sound casual enough in her head. It isn't casual.

Philadelphia, he tells her. And they are not quite ten years apart. Somehow it reassures her to know they are a product of the same decade, both in their 30s. Even if she has just arrived and he is about to leave.

He is distracted, looking for tacos. Lali offers a peanut butter and honey sandwich in a plastic baggie—that's all they had at home for sandwich fillings, that and WIC cheese—but he brushes it off. You know how you get sometimes, he says, when you have a craving for something and your mind just fixates on that?

They exit at the edge of the beach town and drive around for a while, looking for taquerías. All of the buildings look depressed and ramshackle, abandoned by refinery money, sagging beneath too-tall palms. Finally they pull into Las Olas del Golfo, its stucco exterior sky blue, its sign a hand-painted seascape with coral lettering. Wait here with Luz? Joel asks, fixing leash to collar before ducking inside.

In the back Nena sleeps on, and Lali lowers the back windows to create a cross-breeze for her, so that she can exit the car to walk Luz around the empty parking lot. It's late morning now and starting to get hot, but it's a balmy, tropical heat and not the oppressive greenhouse heat of the city. They are farther south, but they are closer to the water.

With Joel out of sight, Luz is unhappy. She tugs Lali toward the filmy glass doors of the taquería, whistling high and pitiful from the back of her throat. Lali sits cross-legged beside her on the sidewalk, massaging the top of her head, bending over her to croon in her ear: It's okay, Luz, it's okay. But Luz is inconsolable until Joel reappears, brown paper bag swinging from his hand.

Back in the car, he dumps the contents of the bag into his lap, tossing her the hot foil of a frijol y queso on flour. When he unwraps his taco to take a bite at one end, tilting head and taco to the side like you were supposed to, hot beans squirt from the other end and splatter his shirt front. He laughs at himself with his mouth full, scrubbing at his shirt front one-handed with a paper napkin. Lali is not hungry, but his enthusiasm intrigues her and she eats to follow his lead, hoping to summon a similar abandon.

They are in the city again, but soon the highway hits the Gulf at the very lip of the continent and cannot any longer carry them forward. It slows to follow the curve of the coast, lined on one side by white sand and the grey-green stretch of ocean beyond it, and on the other by the inland reach of streets and hotels and convention centers. That is where the mining people are meeting to reinvent their post-carbon fortunes, and on the public beach across the street is where the action will take place, where Joel will be taking pictures. Everything— sand, water, glass, sky—is white shiny hot, cloudless hot. And look! There is the hospital where Lali was born, right on the water. She points it out to Joel, this place she cannot actually remember, which she knows from a handed-down story of one summer when they cut her out of her sleeping mother.

And, look—there are the people who have gathered across the street from the Rare Earth Consortium, milling in chanclas with banners and signs. It is noon already but they are on move- ment time, Mexican time, and of course haven't started yet; in arriving late, Joel and Lali are punctual. They double back and parallel park on the curb, from the car unloading Luz and cam- eras and Nena blinking sleep from her eyes. Holding hands, Lali and Nena wander off to let Joel collect his quotes and photos, but also because Nena has never seen the ocean before and won't be persuaded to act in concert with the shape of anyone's collective plans. At half past noon the people descend from street to sand to clasp hands at the waterline, voices raised in protective defiance, but that's not why Nena has come. She breaks from the chain of hands, running toward the waves as they recede, and away as they give chase; she stoops to dig holes in soupy sand that immediately fill in on themselves. She is like Luz or like the Gulf wind itself. Where she tugs, Lali can only follow.

It's not why Lali has come either, truthfully. When the people disperse—some of them trickling across the highway with signs to picket the convention center, some of them chatting on the boardwalk—she and Joel find each other again and, without a word, unload from his car their second, stealth cargo of snacks and blankets and beach toys. Over one shoulder he slings a bed sheet, and over that he totes two slender rods of bamboo, cut from the park across the street from his apartment. Once they are down on the wet sand, he spreads the blankets and fashions rods and sheet into a tent, with a pocketknife ripping slits into the sheet to temper wind resistance. Miraculously, by some expert balance of forces, it holds: a shallow cave to shield them from the sun and wind. There they sit together, not talking, breathing the ocean in through their skin.

After a minute Joel says: You came here every summer?

Yeah. As a kid. I stopped in high school, after 10th grade. My parents kept going with my sister. But I was going through this...this period in my life. I had run away from home. I was—I don't know. But I didn't want to go anymore after that.

She glances at him, gauging how much she can say. His face is patient, open, listening.

Anyway, it's good to come back. She looks around, over the waves. The beach is a lot cleaner than it used to be. No tar balls today. Her eyes follow the circle of gulls turning lazily over the white-gold dunes. Rude birds, brash and audacious—but she loves them, their sense of humor. Little clown tricksters of the Gulf: once a gull straight up grabbed a bologna sandwich out of her father's hands as he sat on their family blanket. How sad it had been, as a child, to see their oil-slicked Northern relatives piled on a white tarp, dead upon dead.

Lali and Nena have swum already, Nena in her little yellow suit and Lali in her clothes, rolling her pant legs to the thigh, but Joel has yet to try the water. Out of the corner of her eye, Lali sees him hesitate for a moment before ducking his head to remove his shirt in one swift motion, as if embarrassed, filling her with a painful tenderness, as if she will cry. His body is different from what she is used to looking at. Hector is lanky and angular and bronze, with a stomach that hardly creases when he sits. Her own is two colors, pale yellow where clothes cover it and golden brown above. Joel is as light as moonlight, not fat but substantive, ample in his belly and torso. But his legs are long and muscular, his arms smooth and strong. Out of the corner of her eye.

She hesitates too, before offering: Do you want sunscreen?

If you don't mind. He rummages in one of his canvas bags for the bottle.

Easy, not too light or too deliberate. Neutral, average, like it doesn't matter. But when she lays her hand against his back he dips his head, absorbing the unavoidable significance of her touch. It burns like fever, how lonely he is.

When she has finished, he turns around to thank her. You too? he asks.

Sure. It's only her shoulders and back that are exposed in her sleeveless shirt; the rest of her is covered. And his hand on her upper back is quick, efficient. Think you're good now, he says, rising. Gonna swim again?

She wants to follow, but instead she says, I'm good. You go.

They swim in shifts that way, Joel and Luz, then Lali and Nena. When saltwater crashes over Nena's head and spills into her eyes, Lali carries her crying back to the half-tent, where she lifts her shirt to nurse the child. Joel and Luz are already there, Joel reclining on his elbows with his head tipped back and eyes closed, throat exposed and glistening. Sitting up, he swirls the remaining coffee in their paper cups—and the peach pit and gum wad she has dropped into hers—then pitches it onto the sand and pours both of them water from a gallon jug. She hasn't asked for water but he wants her to have it. He hands her melon next, with his pocketknife slicing a wedge from a fragrant head unearthed from one of the canvas bags. Lali eats hers one-handed, the other cradling Nena's head at her breast. It is warm from the car, salty from her own lips, salty with Gulf sand and wind.

***

Joel doesn't seem to want to stay long or linger. They sit for a while and then without saying why he starts packing their things. Their time is up, and Lali doesn't ask—besides, it is too hot to stay long, so much hotter than she remembers from her childhood visits. Bundling everything into their arms, they reverse their path from beach to street, ascending from cool wet sand to hot dry sand to the burning wooden steps leading to the white-hot boardwalk and the molten air of Joel's parked car. And as they pull out of their parking spot to make way for someone who is waiting for it, Joel says: Here is where we cross paths, Mr. Path-Crosser man. I am pulling out and you are pulling in and never shall we meet again. But it was important that I leave so you could arrive.

On the beach the sound of the water made them mostly quiet. But in the car once more it's like they can't stop talking, a massive flow of conversation like a seal has been breached. There was the time Joel almost quit, after the editor unjustly fired another staff writer. Oh, me too! says Lali: there were the quiet fights with Victor over the petition drive in the weeks before May Day, when Lali wanted to quit. There were the bitter internal conflicts within El Centro. They fight like a family, she tells him. And they protect their own like a family. Probably cuz they are, she snorts. She judiciously avoids mention of anything about her own home life, but Joel chats freely about his divorce several years before. He'd been living farther up the Gulf coast, working at a daily near New Orleans, when his wife took his daughter and returned to Amarillo, where she was from. Joel stayed on in NOLA, letting her have the good car that was paid off, before heading West again for another newspaper job in Dallas. Closer to his daughter but still a universe apart. Before he left Louisiana he would run on the beaches of

Cancer Alley each morning, run and play guitar. Those were the only things that eased his despair.

What happened after that? Lali wants to know. And after that, and that? And then where did you go? And what about now? What does he do when he's not at the *Volt*?

Joel looks uncomfortable. Nothing much, he says. Mostly try to get through the time between 5P.M. and 9A.M. And between Friday and Monday. For all my bitching about work, weekends are hard for me. I'm...I have these periods where I'm...down, I guess? And periods where I'm climbing the walls. More often it's down. And work fills the time.

Joel purses his lips, hesitant, then looks straight at her and says: So when did you go through that bleak period you mentioned, on the beach...? He is trying for nonchalance, but the question and its tone reveal a gravity or urgency, not unlike her need to know his age. Like her, he's assessing some kind of fitness. That or grasping at answers, instruction.

Her eyes search up, to the left, the direction of memory. Thirteen through nineteen? My teens. I had some kind of break. It was a while ago. I'm mostly okay now.

What was it that—or that you...?

It had been simple: you want someone, they don't want you, you want to die. The idea had taken root somewhere: to have one's love returned unopened was a nullification of self, an erasure.

It was like the space inside me that had been filled by wanting, that I had offered up, turned to a vacuum when my love was declined. I had made my wanting plain and available, and it had gone to waste.

It became trash, it had rotted in her hands standing before the gaze of a boy who was looking elsewhere, anywhere else. And what remained inside was a well of grief at a center that no longer existed, a nothingness or something more intense: a nihilism, a nothingness machine whose only purpose was to multiply itself, to turn everything it touched into more nothingness. A negative desire, voracious like a black hole, eating everything from the inside out.

So I turned on myself, I ate myself alive. I wasn't much more than a kid, so there was no way for me to explain what it was or why it made sense. Why it wasn't sick at all. It was society that was sick. Do you know what I mean?

The whole system was sick, the way a girl grew up to materialize as self only in the illumination of a man's gaze. If who she wanted didn't want her then she was nothing, and her own desire counted for nothing. An entire psychic economy organized around the validity and presence of male desire, the unspeakability of anything other. The feminist theory she learned in school eventually gave her ways to say those things, but she knew them first and fundamentally in her own body. Before she could say them, her body said them for her, elliptically, like a poem. Starving became the displacement of simile, a figure of speech that could pronounce all appetite futile or worthless, something needing excavation like a bad tooth. A toxicity to be choked off at the root. In 10th grade she hitched a ride with a boyfriend she only kind of liked, who promised to get her to Canada—but it wasn't home she wanted to escape as much as it was her own body, the irrepressible limits of its physical and emotional hungers. It was a flight from desire, an escape into nothingness.

I felt I would not survive my desire. I didn't want to survive my desire. Do you know what I mean?

It had gone on for some time. Hospitals, therapists, doctors, pills didn't work because it wasn't about food at all—it was about metaphysics, power, questions of being and nothingness. What existed and what did not. What had a right to exist, and who was entitled to want and receive, the basic dynamics of existence. And that metaphysical quandary had no language except a refusal to eat, a cry of agony rocketing through the universe forever in search of consolation. When medicine failed, she'd been on her own to figure it out. She went from lover to lover, seeking partners whose own certainty gave temporary shelter, though she herself felt nothing in return. She said yes to everything and no to nothing, trying to give others what she wanted for herself. She did not know how to say either yes or no: that at her center could be presence rather than absence, an anchor of power whose actions moved outward into the world as surely as spokes on a trued bicycle wheel.

To get better she'd had to become a doctor of philosophy, a political theorist able to heal her metaphysical sickness—that, or to heal philosophy where it was sick, where it had given her sickness. Even through her crisis she'd done well in school, grades never slipping, even through her hospitalization: she had her parents to thank for that. They were both educators, mother an elementary school teacher, while her father had gone into high school administration after leaving seminary. Steady and stable, they were solid folks from working class families who'd achieved a modest, middle class mobility—quiet people entirely flummoxed by their eldest daughter's intensity. But somehow, where school was concerned, they'd managed to gift Lali with their steadiness and stability.

Joel listens. Though he has been raised with agency as his entitlement, he too has been denied, for different reasons. He understands. So if nothing worked, he wants to know, how did you get better?

It was something she had willed herself, against herself, in spite of herself. The pull toward nothingness was so strong. But physical hunger, the body, was stronger. Really, it was that she was tired of hunger as a force she could not make go away, the weight of the water she had dammed at her back, the huge deficit she had rung up. In the end it was easier to open the floodgates than to bear it. And eventually physical hunger subsided.

But the nihilism persisted and shifted tactics. She was eating again by the time she started graduate school, but she quickly found herself overtaken by a new fear: that her body would shame her by ejecting its contents—especially in public places, on the campus shuttle to class or in classrooms where she sat trapped and sweating. Even if it didn't, surely her fear would become visible and risible to others, marking her as strange. It seemed imperative that she appear normal and competent at all times; no one could know she was terrified. But what was not eaten could not be expelled, so again she did not eat. The feeling of hunger became a touchstone, an inner feeling of rightness that made it safe to be in the world in a public way, to project an appearance of normality in social interactions. In seminars and in front of classrooms, she did all the right things in all the right ways, and publications and fellowships and assistantships followed seemingly without effort. She was the envy of the department, a theoretical whiz in a quantitative program, the one most likely to score a job after graduation. But her body atrophied in the massive output of energy required to perform effortlessness, draining to her head so that it wobbled unsteadily on a neck too frail to support it. Leaving the library late at night hauling canvas bags full of stiff hardback books, she felt as fragile and defenseless as a fledgling in an unguarded nest, grotesquely denuded of feathers. A flightless bird flailing in the grass beneath the tree. It was only a matter of time before carnivores circled or talons closed, silently swooping down from above to pierce her, sweeping her up toward extinction to be selected out of existence, unfit. Hidden behind the hard, cold edges of the campus buildings, they were watching and waiting, and she was all alone in that California college town so far from home. At 25, she wept when the doctors told her that her bones belonged to a woman 40 years her senior. They were the eggshells of eagle chicks poisoned by DDT and grown too thin to support life.

So what did you do? Joel wants to know.

It's less what I did. More that a couple unexpected things happened to me. The first was, I got pregnant with Nena.

She hadn't even known she could get pregnant. She had assumed she couldn't, that years of not eating had damaged her body beyond repair. So she and Hector had never used birth control of any kind. She and Hector in fact were only kind of together when it happened—she had moved out and figured that was finally it. And if it hadn't been for Nena, it probably would have been. But she doesn't say that part.

She had known right away that she loved and wanted Nena. Her brain had moved through the requisite algorithms: pros, cons of keeping, terminating. But Nena was a miracle of her body's elasticity and resilience, its fierce determination, arching toward survival. She was a single, perfect pearl formed from a life of intense internal distress. Nena meant it was possible to get better. Nena meant she was stronger and more powerful than she had even imagined. Nena was the beginning of wanting to fight the pull toward self-erasure, of wanting to protect and care for self so she could protect and care for others.

But, also—there was something else, far less precious, far more banal, which was that she came across a book that accomplished more than years in therapy talking about the symbology of eating and puking. It was a workbook of techniques, dedicated on the front inside cover to *anyone suffering from an incomprehensible fear*. Even remembering the words could make tears well in her eyes, to be finally recognized and understood, and to recognize herself as one of many. Ordinary. Until then, she hadn't known there were others like her, or that there were names for things she had always experienced from the inside as an inarticulable strangeness, an alienation from self she must keep secret at all costs because she could not explain it—neither to herself nor to others.

So with the help of exercises in the book, she relearned how to breathe and hold attention on the breath, how to identify stories and rewrite them. What a liberation it had been, to learn basic states of agency she had seemingly never learned—*I can leave if I need to*—or to realize that the strangeness she took to be ontological truth was simply the mental effect of a suffering that was primarily physical, a sudden rush of adrenaline and cortisol that had become automatic, tripped by some association that had gotten lodged there long ago. She didn't know what had happened originally, if anything.

For me too, Joel murmurs. The memory of hands, of being held down.

Lali glances over, but Joel's face is neutral. So that's what happened, she says slowly, reflecting. I got better. It took a long time, but I learned how to get better.

His eyes shine pride and happiness for her—that she got better, that it is possible—before clouding again. I can't seem to go a couple of weeks without crashing, he says.

And then they are quiet again, not yet on the city's southern edge but about to be, the trip not over but about to be. He cranks the volume on the CD that has been playing softly in the background, something a friend burned for him, so they can listen together. *I want another lover*, the singer complains, *someone other than my mother*. I like that line! Joel says, repeating it. Funny.

But he looks at her when he says it. Asking her without asking her. Is he? She eyes him incredulously, sideways, realizing from somewhere deep inside that her response is: Yes. If you are asking me, then yes.

When he drops them home she doesn't want him to go, a desperation filling her chest and belly like drowning. Helping bring their things inside, Joel follows Lali upstairs to the apartment where she fixes him a glass of ice water, which he drinks sitting in an armchair. Nena poops in her diaper and Lali cleans her, then chases after her with a clean diaper as Nena runs around the apartment, naked from the waist down. When Nena is finally clothed and playing quietly, Lali pulls a book from her shelf for Joel, then a draft of the essay she is writing with Sister Soli. We're almost finished, she tells him. Would you be interested in reading it? It's not done, but maybe you could give some feedback—thoughts on how to finish it?

A next time. There has to be a next time. This can be the way.

Definitely, Joel says. But then he has to go, he takes his leave and as he does she reaches up to embrace him—quickly, before he escapes into the world, standing on the threshold between apartment and porch—and before he breaks away she feels the words form from somewhere inside her and leave her mouth, so sincere as to be puerile: You're really cool, Joel. I like you a lot. And he leans down and kisses her on the cheek, so fast she doesn't have time to anticipate or react, before slipping away into the city.

And then he is gone, and she is like Luz at the glass door of the taquería, she is like Luz for the rest of her life, not knowing what will be.

CHAPTER SEVEN
At the Apartment

Friday, July 2

Today is the day. She tucks away a copy of the essay inside her backpack and dresses deliberately that morning before she leaves the house for the library on her bike, knowing she will see Joel, if their plans are on. Maybe they are not on. He is supposed to let her know when he is free but he hasn't said how or when. There is an element of uncertainty or instability to their dynamic that is part of its compelling force, the static between them: would he or wouldn't he. Would they or wouldn't they.

Her deliberateness is about dressing down, not up. She had done this instinctively when they traveled together to the beach, not wanting to reveal too much skin and thereby her own desire. At the beach she had walked straight into the gulf with all her clothes on, rolling up the bottoms of her cheap cargo pants to fashion makeshift shorts. Her armpits and legs hairy and unbothered with. A similar stubbornness directs her selection that morning, of a sloppy plaid flannel and loose jeans and Chucks. It's not about wanting to look unattractive but, with more subtlety, not wanting to look attractive, wanting to look most plainly like herself, to test his intentions. If his feelings were like hers he would love her anyway, no matter what. He would love her precisely because.

Not only his feelings but his ideas about clothing may be like hers, because when he picks her up from the library at

5—*coming to get you now*, he texts, and it's then she knows he seeks her as she longs to be sought—he is wearing his own ugliness disguise, a long sleeved orange-and-white-striped button-down and big shapeless jeans that make him look thicker than he is. But it doesn't matter. It doesn't matter. When she slides into his car and they lean into each other to hug she smells ocean in his skin, something breezy-light and citrus over the darker, richer tidal ferment of his musk, and she knows, and she knows he knows, that it is right.

They park behind his building, and he takes her around the side to the front entrance so he can check the mail, past the narrowest strip of bare-earth yard between sidewalk and fence, wide enough for one old standing pecan. From its trunk to the fence he has strung a hammock, securing each end with hooks. He points out this innovation beaming a shy pride, and the other details she takes in quietly as he rustles through the gold slot of his letter box: the orange cruiser leaning against his apartment's brick facade, dog carrier affixed ingeniously to its metal rack with bungee cords. The tiny city of potted plants clustered around his front stoop, green with tendrils and feathery fronds and flowering succulents.

She steps inside behind him and is surprised by the pungent smell of cat pee, of unchanged litter in a box. She follows him into the kitchen to help feed the cats from a coffee can stored beneath the sink and sees a spillover of crustifying dishes piled on the counter above. None of it bothers her, none of it matters. Her chest surges like surf for this man who lives alone with his animals and plants, casting verse into the digital spaces of an indifferent city. Do they let you write wherever, she wants to know, interested in his position at the *Volt*, because she can't imagine the life of a reporter. Or do you have to write there?

Write there, mostly, he says.

And is it quiet? she asks, thinking about academic writing, where there is no expectation that you be anywhere at any time to put your ideas to page, no rules about where or when or how you work. Write where it's noisy, write where it's quiet. Write during the day or in the middle of the night. At home or on the bus or wherever, it doesn't matter. There is no workplace; everywhere is work. There aren't even any deadlines save the ones you set yourself. And if you fail, you fail unnoticed. You had to want to do it, internally driven by a long-suffering longing to explain.

It's quiet, he says, in an eyebrows-raised sort of tone that reveals curiosity about why she wants to know—but he doesn't ask. He himself is a quiet person, she observes, though his job is to ask people questions and record their responses. She doesn't know his cat, but she refills a water dish and gently sets it on the floor for her—because it is his cat, his dish, his floor, this quiet man whose quietness is a secret. They slide into the booth benches of a built-in dining nook and sit across from one another for a moment without speaking, before he reaches above the tabletop, above their heads, to show her: if you pull on the hanging lamp, it descends from a retractable wire. If you pull again, in just the right way, it smoothly retreats up its elastic cord like a spider on silken guide wire, like magic. He has her tilt her head and listen for the crackle of the ambulance dispatcher in the apartment above them, which housed a local EMS service. That's why there were ambulances at the curb outside at all times. And the tenant before him, an older lady who had died there, had been schizophrenic; he leads Lali to the bedrooms to show her where the woman had papered the bottoms of the windows with a floral plastic film to prevent anyone from being able to see in. In the bathroom she had adhered stickers to the mirror in a neat border, now faded, of famous Hollywood A-listers: Judy Garland, Marilyn Monroe, Marlene Dietrich. And in the living room the floral couch is stained and fur-covered, but on the side table he has arranged magazines in cascading columns, like overlapping cards in a solitaire game, titles exposed like suits. In his modest living space, Joel has gathered a sustenance of beauty from its small objects, fashioning an order or aesthetic that to Lali seems uniquely his.

In the hallway connecting his bedroom to the room where his daughter stays when she visits, he pauses to detail a collection of photos he has organized there, mostly family. There is a dour military grandfather who abandoned his dad; there is Joel as a child birdwatching with his father. There is his daughter as a baby with puffball hair so blonde it looks white. She watches his face as he narrates more than she takes in the photo images, but each time she returns to his apartment in the weeks to come, before her pending move, she stops in the hallway to wonder over the people on the wall, the confluence of disparate places and bodies and memories siphoning into the singularity of Joel. The memory of his eagerness is what draws her back. On that first afternoon in his apartment he radiates a quiet delight that she is there. He wants to share himself, to show her where he lives and who he is, what he is made of. He has been waiting for someone to come, and now he is glad she is there.

And there are books. In addition to the essay, she has brought books with her so they can read together, but he has walls of them already in the living room, books filling his bedroom closet in place of his clothes, books in the bathroom lining a built-in shelf high above the toilet. When he takes her into the bedroom to retrieve another book from the closet, she spots a guitar cradled in its stand and crosses the room to pick it up without asking, taking a seat in a wooden chair draped with pairs of pants. He sits on the edge of his bed before her and they pass the guitar back and forth, trading songs, some learned and some composed.

Singing is basic to Lali, like swallowing water—her mother sang, and her mother before her, all of them knowing without having to be taught where to cast the voice and where it should catch on the coat pegs of notes—yet she has never been comfortable singing and playing for others. But now, in spite of her discomfort, she finds herself moved by some force bigger than individual decision or even desire; it is like she has woken to find herself playing, fingers moving over strings in chords and phrasings that her body remembers, even if her brain does not. She has not played regularly in years. If she stops to think or anticipate, the whole thing will come crashing down. Still, to play without thinking feels entirely ordinary. But to hear the voice that appears only in the intimacy of solitude, in this space where she is not alone, shocks her.

Joel's own voice is not wide-ranging or perfect, it is raspy around its edges, but it makes much of what it has, warmed by a subtle, teasing vibrato—was it there or was it not? It is a voice that knows itself, what it can and can't do. He plays haltingly at first. He fiddles, he starts and stops. He tries out a song from a CD he wore out from listening to it so much, about a man who wore a black eye from picking fights, who despaired at his reflection in that secretly vain way men have, he says. He plays it because it reminds him of a friend of his, killed by the police many years ago. He sings with his eyes closed, brow drawn, as if it is physically painful to recall the melody.

When it is her turn again, she lights first on one thing, then fumbles around for something else she remembers, something easy to play but nice to hear and sing, something that suits her voice. What comes out is the folk song from the radio, the one they sang in music class so long ago, terrible in its simplicity:

The water is wide
I cannot get o'er
and neither have I wings to fly
Oh go and get
a boat for two
to carry o'er my true love and I

There is a ship
and she sails the sea
She's loaded deep
as deep can be
But not so deep
as in love I am
I know not if
I sink or swim

She chooses it for its simple chord progression, realizing only after she has started that she has unwittingly chosen to sing what is true, that she is singing not only for Joel but also to him, without knowing in advance she would do it. Embarrassed, rattled, she thrusts the guitar away from her when she is finished, as if it is bewitched with uncanny knowing. But he gestures it back into its cradle, tired of playing for now.

They move into the living room to do what they came to his apartment to do, sitting side by side on the floor with the couch at their backs, books and papers spread before them. But they are distracted, the books fall from their laps as they twist their bodies toward one another. They talk about Lali's impending move, whether she is ready.

I think so, Lali says, realizing as she says it how much she doesn't want to leave, that the city—home—drags on her body like an iron trawler, like the pole to a compass magnet. Was there a metallurgy of emotion that worked on them as it did objects in the material world? Or were those things only metaphors.

But what rushes to the surface is: I'm so glad I met you.

Joel smiles, but he is distracted, rising to search for Luz's leash. I've been here four years, in this city, he begins.

He trails off, the leash elusive. They will circle Luz around the little park across the street from his building, then he will drive Lali back to her bike where she left it at the library. As at the beach, he's made a sudden, internal decision to depart that he doesn't share aloud. It's okay, though, since Hector—at home with Nena—doesn't know she is there, and she doesn't want to tell him. There is a way to talk about bodies joining where they're not supposed to, about discrete violations of trust marked in time and space or lapses in judgment, sex that doesn't matter. But she has no words, no explanation, for what it means to sing or sit, for the profound meaning to their interactions that has seemingly preexisted them, only waiting for their bodies to slip into place at the right intersection. It is nothing they have done or decided or could have anticipated and everything that has been done already, that has found them and caught them in its design.

Luz dances at the door as Joel hunts for the leash. He finds it, he clips it to her collar. Four years in this city, he continues, and I feel like I still don't know anyone here. I feel like I don't have any friends. His back is to her as he speaks so that she cannot see his face.

Really? Lali is astounded. She follows Joel outside. But the *Volt*—everyone knows you. Everyone loves you, your column—I mean us, we do. The movement people. For us, your column is this...research service. I can't even tell you how many times you've written things I've needed to know as an organizer but don't have time to investigate myself.

He smiles in appreciation, but his thoughts are somewhere else. I might be moving soon. I might be leaving town.

What? Why? How soon?

Soon soon, a couple weeks. Well, one thing is, I'm getting evicted. He chokes out a laugh, shaking his head.

Evicted? What—?

No dogs allowed, apparently. It's actually timely though. I don't know if you heard—well, I don't know how you would have—but the *Volt* got bought out. The company's been talking for a while about moving to an all-online format, and this might be the time. Print copy doesn't pay anymore. And the business model of the publishing company has been to stay the hell away from investigative reporting and pursue a slicker arts and entertainment format. If they do switch over, the likeliest thing is what they call transition and restructuring, meaning any number of us could be out of a job soon. It always happens when there's a new editor or publisher. You get rid of who you don't like and hire your own people. The question for me is whether I look for another place in town or leave town altogether. There's nothing for me here except the job.

They've stopped at the pond and stand looking at the water that remains. The streak of triple-digit days, come early this year, has burned off almost all of what the flash flood deposited a few weeks prior, exposing a halo of cracked earth encircling a shallow puddle. Lali wants to tell Joel that she is his friend, always—somehow she knows she is, even as she knows she doesn't really know him. She wants to put her hand on his back as she did at the beach, wants to take his hand in hers, but she doesn't. So they stand together in silence at the edge of the pond, until it is time for him to drive her back to her bike.

CHAPTER SEVEN
These Two Insomnias

Monday, July 5

You are supposed to get up and do something else until you get sleepy, she knows this, but it's not like her body is not tired. Her eyes feel fuzzy and salty, and in her veins and head thrum the rattling chains of her own heartbeat, her body an echo chamber filled with the sound of its own operations. She'd read somewhere this was an effect of exhaustion, which triggered surges of cortisol that raised blood pressure. And god knew she was exhausted, utterly dragged-out spent—but maddeningly, not sleepy. Those same chemicals doing something to her brain, cycling it at too high a rev to sleep, pulling blood and heat between her legs to pulse and pulse until she levitates in bed at the thought of sitting beside him in front of his couch straining against magnetic force, at the thought of the brush of his lips against her cheek. But it would hurt to get up, to drag trunk and limbs to sitting or standing. And so she lays, thoughts racing alongside blood. Tomorrow she will feel terrible. But what if there is no sleep at all to tell her when today becomes tomorrow? If she falls asleep now she can still get three or four hours in; that was bad but not too bad. That was functionable. But Hector would be getting ready for work soon. What if she fell asleep and he woke her again?

She stands, dizzy, swaying, catching herself against the door frame of the bathroom, where she leans heavily with head lowered until the floor stops pitching and rolling beneath her feet. She seeks pills in the bathroom that will knock her unconscious. This is the third night she has needed to take something. She swallows one, then another, then shakily returns to bed. To wait.

When it comes, sleep hits her like an avalanche of rocks, like a fast death. There is no gradual loosening of consciousness, no sliding of sense and sensation into altered state, no soft awareness of black ink spreading to engulf her. Just a drop cloth of nothingness, its falling around her, or her descent into it, unremembered.

***

She will try something different that night if she can't sleep. First pills, then something different. Or was it the other way around? Never mind: she rises and slips on her sneakers, then slips herself outside to run panting down her street, hoping to feel as still as the surrounding night, light as the air off the river. Exhausted and shaky from nights of insomnia, her body is a bag of jangling plumber's tools, feet flapping on asphalt inelegantly, breath ragged—but in her mind's eye she is bounding with the grace of an Artemis, running alongside her herd of fleet deer. She is Hermes on winged shoes, springing upwards with one final leap as her feet leave the ground.

She soars over the city before gliding back down to pass familiar places, low and close to the ground. There was the flour mill like a castle with turrets, where everyday for many months a handful of Teamster hanger-onners have picketed the entrance, weathering first the cold and then the heat. That's where you would beepbeep and raise a fist when you drove past, right down there. There was the five point intersection, confusing, where approaching trains slowed to bellow their caution as tracks converged. You got used to it, living beside it, that much was true. There was the scrap recycling yard, where with huge pincers they twisted cars open like beetles so their vital stinging fluids spilled onto the ground below. When they chewed the metal, a cloud of fine orange smoke would drift out from the yard to hang over the unshaded bus stop. There was the river behind, where for years, decades, the city people had committed a slow drip of county and city and federal funds to the task of widening some stretches, narrowing others, so that people could walk and bike alongside the river. Was that why, was it for the people? Or was it for some other, more cynical, unspoken reason? Right there was a temporary diverter wall, which scraped the river to one side so city workers could more easily connect the downtown Riverwalk to sidewalks reaching south of the city. There was the Pedicab bar, named for the human-powered chariots parked out in front. Later, when the condos come and the bar becomes the ghost of a vacant lot, they'll say the Pedicab burned down for profit. They couldn't pay the rising taxes and the bar became a burden, so they burned it for the insurance money. But that night there is a poetry reading inside, open mic.

Inside, a woman reads to an empty bar, trying to summon a lover who will not appear:

what makes me walk
around

constantly feeling
the scrape of lungs
and thorax stuffed
full of wadded up papers:
scratchy glass like
asbestos, uncoughable,
contaminated
with resinous dread like
like chemical burn, this
poison bloom
around my heart

is that

i saw your beautiful soul

its shining blue piercing through
the smoky glass
haze of your aloneness
like a halo thru skullbone

and once seen
i can't unsee it

its presence forever
an absence
burned
into my own
viscera,

its beauty my pain
from now on

And then she is flying fast again over houses and stores, making a note of what still stands and what won't for much longer. Five years, ten years, one year. There are signs, like abstract art, featuring the non-sequitur names of realty companies that own the land or hold it for absentee owners, signs mushrooming in the vacant lots and abandoned pavilions of the city. An old Chinese grocery, a tiny used car lot, a cantina. She makes a note of what won't be there when the redevelopment rolls through, what the nothingness signs foretell, what and who is slated not to be there.

She has brought music for her flight, to propel her on via earbuds. On the radio is a song she has never heard before, evidently written by someone clever, because they have taken the lines from the Rumi poem and turned them into a chorus. *When I am with you, we stay up all night. When you're not here, I can't go to sleep. Praise god for these two insomnias! And the difference, the difference between them.* Every time they get to the chorus it makes her cry. It is that brilliant and uncanny, how the song knows exactly how she feels, the oceanic depths and the diamond height of it. It is too beautiful and too good, too big to fit inside her skin.

That was the thing about this thing, this force, which gathered itself about the fulcrum of a secret, the final part per million too many swirling within a finite bubble. The power of it was terrifying but also incredible, a unity of the awful and the awe-ful, a plane ride through a thunderstorm with the clouds on fire. It was a vast outpouring of energy shooting from the liquid metal core of the earth to the sleeping snake at the base of her spine to explode from the crown of her head, an ecstatic pouring forth which also exhausted her to the point of a terminal collapse. It was the massive voltage of lightning searching for a suitable conductor, finding and seizing and blowing her circuits: all metaphors for it veered electromagnetic, energetic. Wheezing and coughing sparks. Whatever it is, it moves according to its own unknowable logic and she can only be dragged behind, knowing she will leap without a net into the ruin of desire even though it makes no sense, even though it is madness. She's going to do it. *She's going to do it.* There is no question.

It was the purity of her conviction that rattled her, appearing out of nowhere in a brain that had made a business of unearthing multiplicity and manysidedness and polytonality. She could go on and on with the descriptors, a multiplying pile of signification, but the power of the thing lay in how basic it was to simply *know*. To look down on herself from the top of the Tower of the Americas, the tossing, turning, burning form that lays in bed, and as diagnostician examine her own intensity. She has never seen something like it before, a longing so great it became a sickness. Viewed from above and outside, it was grotesque—a specimen floating in a jar in a house of curios, an aborted fetus or half-digested twin stuffed with hair and teeth. It was something you read about happening to others, disasters or deformities; then all of a sudden there you were, in a story. A statistic in the vital record, a case study in a historical monograph.

Diving off the Tower, she circles its rotating observation deck before gliding back over the sleeping city to her street, dangling sneakers grazing the tops of trees as she comes in for a landing. She swoops in through the open window of their bedroom to crash back into the body on the bed, rolling to a stop against the wall, as Hector and Nena sleep on and on and on.

CHAPTER NINE
Waves Upon Waves

Tuesday, July 6

On Lali's last day at El Centro—in a few weeks they will split for Kansas—she leaves work early, as soon as los cuates and Dulce get back from wherever it is they go to lunch together. When she hands the keys over to Marcos, they stand awkwardly trying to summon the proper words of ceremony for the occasion. Marcos finally arrives at, Well, have a good time in Indiana. Lali doesn't bother to correct him. Indiana, Kansas—it's all not-Tejas, right? But she says: It's been important for me to be here. I've learned a lot. Because she has. They do the lowdown slap and fist bump thing that makes Lali flush from the vergüenza of insufficient Mexicanness, and that is it.

She's told them she had to leave early to take care of some things at home for the move, and that is tangentially true. What she has to do is finish this essay of hers so she can get copies to Sister Soli and Paloma in time for the public hearing where the city will certify VAMOS's petition drive—or not. She still has to nail the final piece of it, the conclusion. Time is running out. Because if she can get the analysis right, and if Paloma and Rafa can work their art-magic to get the form right, there is no way they can lose, no way power could be unmoved from its course. Right?

So now she is pedaling hard through downtown streets without a helmet, back sweaty beneath the weight of a backpack full of laptop and books, beneath the full weight of afternoon sun. The blast of the a/c through the electronic entrance doors of the library hits her skin like bliss, closing her eyes with relief. A heat advisory this week, she recalls, noting the flyers the health department has plastered to library doors. She ascends the escalator to the children's section, where ordinarily empty tables in long rows cozy up to a wall of windows that yawn out over the entire downtown. You can see the rooftop of the hospital from here, where the helicopters land. You can see rock doves nesting above drainage gutters.

Today the tables are almost full, the library a designated cooling center for those with nowhere else to stay during the day. Squeezing her way to a corner spot to spread books and laptop before her, she gazes out over the city that feels so much like home just as she is about to leave it, again. It always takes a while to start, but today, this last day, feels harder. Her thoughts drift back to the press conference she'd attended that morning. Another one, thank God organized by someone else. All she had to do was attend and stand in silent support as speakers from VAMOS's various neighborhood associations announced that their petition drive was almost complete; soon they would present 150,000 signatures to the city clerk's office for validation. From her place on the steps she had seen Joel there, snapping pictures in his observer's crouch, one leg flexed at the knee and the other straight out before him. He'd snapped, he'd pivoted his weight to his other leg like a yogi, scuttling sideways like a crab to get the angle right.

She'd thought he might be there but she hadn't been sure. It was the first time she'd seen him since the apartment. All the night before she had lain awake, thoughts buzzing. Would she see him again? What would it be like if she did? Her experience on the coast and at his apartment—had it been real or illusory, shared or solitary? But as the speakers begin speaking, she had studied him studying them through his camera, and tenderness had washed over her in waves and waves. His love for people in their struggle and suffering radiated out from his heart like sunshine; she could feel it, see it—in the stories he told and how he told them, in the images he captured and the video he edited, the sound files and the pages of notes, the post-its and the blog entries. In the labored preservation of an archive was an immense love, and a shyness too. There was an effacement of self, a humility in the crouch of the photographer, a graceful stepping aside to hold the door for others. Offering one's folded hands as a stirrup, one's shoulders as boost, so others could speak for themselves and be heard. But where it hid behind the camera, his own face was full of wonder: she could see that there, from where she stood on the steps of city hall with the others, their bodies and voices the raw material of history, the archived.

They had not interacted at that event, although they met eyes at one point when he lowered his camera for a brief moment. A fissure had opened between their public and private selves, which now collided chaotically in the space-time of history. They hadn't interacted, but they knew. And when, in the library, she turns away finally from window to laptop, from her thoughts to the work before her, she sees he has emailed her, a note passed under the table.

Any chance you'll be at Centro strategy meeting tonight? he wants to know.

Shit—her last day, but she'd forgotten about the meeting that night, an important one. VAMOS would be there to walk through the petition submission process and strategize next steps. They were expecting the city to do everything in its power to pronounce the effort invalid.

I found something of yours, he writes. I think, anyway—in my car. Smiley face.

She had thought to retreat from the campaign for a few days at least, now that her time at El Centro had officially ended. But a powerful current of agitated energy pounds in her blood, like too much caffeine but a hundred times stronger, urging her up and on and unable to stop even as her body longs for rest. She has something for him too, the essay that will be the way forward, the way to win. If she can finish it in time.

So she writes: I might. I'll have to see. Last day at Centro today and I am about ready to collapse from exhaustion.

And from a tension between them that is seemingly without relief. But she can't say that.

I would not blame you in the slightest, he writes, magnanimous, but she knows she will go. Because he will be there.

With email open just in case, she tries again to settle into the essay, but after their brief conversation she can't. It's not even that the logic won't gel—she cannot even open the document, cannot even get started. Her mind scatters in all directions at once like light shot through a prism, away from a center focus. She listens to music on headphones with chest aching, wiping away tears. If the men around her notice, they are hardly concerned—or perhaps they understand what it's like when music is just too good, too bright, too meaningful to bear. She places fingers to keyboard and what comes out instead is a long poem that runs like a river. It comes and comes, writing itself, meeting no obstacle, each word like a photograph, capturing in perfect replication the shape of what lies inside her. It has been years since she has written like this, since long before grad school, language a liquid she has tapped or a frequency she has found. She rides it like surf, waves upon waves: she writes until what wants speaking has exhausted itself. Then she rides home on her bike to wait for the start of the meeting.

Paloma will be there, undoubtedly. And Joel, who has indicated he will be there if she will. Who has said, without saying, I want to see you. Please come. Who has summoned her. She will take the essay as is and give it to Paloma and pitch her epic teatro idea. It's unfinished but she is out of time; it's all she can do for now, and perhaps Paloma will know how it should end. And she will take the poem, and when she talks to Paloma after the meeting, she will ask her what she should do with that too. Paloma will know.

CHAPTER TEN
Paloma La Partera, Part 2

Tuesday, July 6

So that she doesn't have to drag Nena with her to El Centro, Lali waits to leave for the meeting until Hector returns from work—and so she arrives late, heart beating too fast and stomach full of burrs. She creeps in and takes a seat next to Paloma, carefully avoiding looking at Joel where he sits in the corner, scribbling notes. The meeting itself is a blur. They're arguing again over VAMOS's secret meetings with the city people to negotiate more money for utility assistance programs and a place on CPL's Transition Team, in exchange for backing off on the petition drive.

It's the same shit you pulled back in the 80s! Victor explodes, yanking at his goatee, round cheeks flushed beneath his black-framed glasses. The problem isn't simply that we don't have enough money to pay our bills! That's just a symptom! The real problem is that the city has *consistently* promoted a kind of development that impoverishes our communities. Meanwhile we're drinking the runoff from all that development and they're fast tracking permits to allow GD mining within city limits! Just having a little extra each month is gonna do fuckall—perdón, he nods at a couple of viejitas in attendance—about alla *that*.

He slams his palm on the table for emphasis, prompting Naima to roll eyes to ceiling and mutter aloud: *Dang, you'd almost think he was out there collecting signatures or something!*

Then there's the older white guy with the long grey ponytail who talks and talks, who attends every meeting no matter what it's about, always promoting a project no one quite understands, some youth peace leadership thing. Back when Lali was carless she saw him once on the city bus with a guitar slung to his back; once he serenaded Nena with "The House at Pooh Corner," the other riders looking on amused. *Okay, let me do a time check*, they are forced to say every meeting he attends. *Leroy, we're glad you're here, but in the interest of time we need to go back to the agenda. If there's time we can add you to the end, okay?* And then they wouldn't. That was the gentle, passive-aggressive facilitation style Chela preferred. Naima would just cut him off impatiently. Straight white man taking up too much space as usual, even if he did have Traumatic Brain Injury from combat! To his credit, Leroy never seemed to mind. Sat back in his chair blinking patiently at them, till the next meeting.

It's all surreal, shimmering in the heat. It's not why Lali has come. She glances up at Joel where he sits in the corner writing notes in a grubby baseball cap. He's in plaid that day, untucked over frayed khaki pants and his New Balances. She watches him out of the corner of her eye as he lays pen and pad down to listen, kicked back in his chair with legs stretched out and head cocked to ceiling, hands laced behind his head. And oh my God, her mind's eye imagines walking up beside him from behind, bending to kiss him, climbing on top of him in his position of repose in that chair, making love as he craned his head back with eyes closed, beautiful in concentration. She has never actually wanted to make love to anyone before.

Suddenly, as if he can feel the force of her thoughts, Joel rises from his chair and ducks out of the meeting, quickly with his head down. Lali is dismayed. She starts in her chair, wanting to rise and follow after him, but the meeting fusses and frets to its messy inconclusive ending, people in knots afterward, exclaiming and declaiming about each other. Leroy corners her on the way out, talking and talking, until Paloma rescues her. Leroy, she says in a gentle-firm tone practiced from her Pre-K teacher days. I'm very sorry to have to interrupt you. But I need to talk to my friend Citlali now about some important matters.

Leroy excused, Paloma wants to know: Will Citlali come back to her house for their chat? Rafaelito is working on a gallery exhibition—*Panochas y Manochas*, it's called, vaginas and man-ginas—and she has to drop off some materials for him. There will be baskets of penises draped in gauzy fabric, and a man-gina constructed from a busted piñata.

Okay, but—

Out the window Joel has come into view again, standing on the curb with Luz, his back to the building. Lali's hope rises again. He must have left to retrieve Luz from wherever he'd secured her outside during the meeting. He must be waiting for Lali, seeing if she will come out and talk.

Okay, but do you have a few minutes to wait for me here? I'll be right back.

Outside on the curb, Joel is quietly hopeful as Lali runs up to say hi. I found this in the car, he says, reaching into his pocket. I'm guessing it's yours? He holds out his hand in a soft fist to meet her outstretched palm, into which he drops her bracelet, a gift from her abuelo, string of lacquered wooden squares that have faded where she has picked off their religious decals. No deeper symbolism there except that los santos had started to peel off from wearing the bracelet in the shower, and that had bugged her like a hangnail. I wore it, he says shyly.

It touches something inside her that is so soft, so untouched she wants to cry, but she glances back at where Paloma stands in the window, watching, waiting for her.

I gotta go, she says, heart thumping. *Say it, say it casual.* But let me know if you'd like to hang out again sometime before I leave town. Maybe we can get a taco or something.

You know I'm always down for tacos, he kids. But his eyes are serious.

Just text me when you're free.

Once more, as on her porch, she reaches up to encircle his shoulders with her arms, standing on tiptoes, as he brushes his lips across her cheek.

***

Paloma came back to San Anto, she tells Lali in the car, because her mother died. Breast cancer she kept a secret from everyone. She didn't want treatment, and when the family finally found out it was too late. But it was what she wanted, it was how she wanted to go. Paloma had still been in Nuevo México then, in Albuquerque, trying to figure out how to extract herself from Mr. Cruz Crackhead who was never going to change.

Wonderful artist, though, and *magnificent* dancer, Paloma says wistfully. I *loved* dancing with Cruz, love love loved it.

But he wasn't going to magically change into someone who would love her in a way that made sense. In that respect death had been Mama's gift to her. Mama had gotten her out of there. But Mama was also the reason Paloma had to leave San Antonio to begin with: she'd threatened to kill Ricky, Paloma's ex-husband, if he ever came around the house again. She had come at him with a kitchen knife as he hightailed it out of the house, then out of the state and Paloma with him. See, Ricky had missed the baby's birthday that year, because he was out running around with his girlfriend. Of course Paloma knew about it—she wasn't stupid! But *he* wasn't going to change either, none of them were. So why get upset to the point that you considered violent revenge or wore yourself out from crying? She had a job to keep, babies to care for. Mama's mistake had been to think he could change, that she had any power at all over what he did. In him Mama had seen the same cruelty and insanity of the man she herself had married.

Ricky, cruel? Not really, says Paloma. He was far too immature to be cruel. Now, neglectful, irresponsible—Mama did have a point there.

So Mama's death had been a gift of graceful extraction and also of atonement. Please come back now, mi'ja, I'm sorry.

Anyway, here we are! she sings, as they pull up to a wooden house recessed within a front yard grown over into a tropical forest, even amid summer's scorch, in the controlled explosion of a system that has become a self-organizing synergy of furrows and feelers and filaments. Come around to this side, corazón, she murmurs, from the car door stretching an arm to Lali for assistance. Together they move carefully from car to house,

Paloma walking on Lali's arm with a slow importance, a mother turtle scraping seaward. Ancient ferns unfurl like smoke where her walking stick clicks against the stone walkway.

It's limestone, she says to Lali. My father was a stone mason at what is now the Sunken Gardens, back when it was a quarry. You know, where the Sky Ride used to run? There by the zoo at the northern edge of Brackenridge Park, right on the other side of that animal gas chamber they just closed. He mined limestone for cement there. Limestone is good, she says, limestone is healing.

Is it?

It is. That's why they use lithium for bipolar. Lithium formed twenty seconds after the Big Bang, you know. Mania and depression—they're disturbances in the brain's electromagnetic frequency, intensifications of its vibratory energy. Lithium de-intensifies the movement of electrons.

Two of her children are bipolar so she must know something. And in her yard, loquat grows—as kids they called it Chinese Plum—and pomegranate, its orbs of mythic fruit dangling beside frosted glass Christmas ornaments nested within the bushy foliage. There is broad-leafed banana, and mimosa with blossoms bursting like fireworks into a thousand pink pompoms, and magnolia too, with fragrant white flowers that withered and bruised as soon as they were plucked from the tree. There are rambling patches of Turk's cap, its weedy runners crowned by roseate furls. There are silver bushes of sage that bloomed purple after rainfall, but only when you'd forgotten it even rained and it could sneak up and surprise you. And nestled within one of the street-facing sages is a political sign from Mayor Mike's most recent election campaign. Rafa has altered it, so that instead of *Vote Mike Sánchez for a New San Antonio,* it says *Vote Rafa Sancho for a Nude San Antonio,* the Mayor's face painted over with Rafa's signature mustache and red lips. Rafa's last name was Sánchez too—but Rafa Sancho was the artist's name he went by. Rafa Man-on-the-Side, Rafa The-Other-Man.

Isn't that funny, Paloma says on the porch. Rafaelito's still looking for submissions for his exhibition, if you know anyone with penis paintings—or pussy paintings, for that matter. She pushes open the screen door with its posted sign: *Artists at work! Before knocking, please call and leave a message.*

From the outside, the house looks tall enough that it could easily be two stories, but it's one story with high ceilinged rooms as profusely cluttered as its front yard. The a/c is out, but with fans spinning crazily overhead and lighting low, the evening heat feels almost livable. As they pass inside, a tall thin man in a pressed green shirt and dress slacks makes his way toward the door from one of the back rooms, a look of surprise on his face. Paloma intercepts his path. Joseph, meet my friend Citlali, she says. Citlali, this is Joseph, Rafaelito's friend who is staying with us. Mucho gusto, mucho gusto. Joseph bows as they shake.

As he leaves, Paloma watches out the screen door after him. In a low voice, she says, His partner kicked him out. I don't know all the details—Rafa knows, but I haven't wanted to ask—but I think it was messy. He's been sleeping on the couch over here for a few weeks now, looking for work and a new place, supposedly. I've been mother-henning him, but lately I've been thinking I may need to change my strategy.

These boys, when they get their hearts broken! she says, making her way to the kitchen. Can I get you some tea, Citlali? she calls. Paloma is one of the few who loves to use Lali's real name, who savors its pairing with the rasquache patchwork of her last, Sánchez-O'Connor. Good solid güerexican name.

I'm good, Paloma, she calls back. Last thing she needs is caffeine at night. Returning with a cup for herself and a plate of cookies and sliced pear and avocado, Paloma clears space from a dining room table covered with dead flowers and coins and papers and candles. She sets the plate before Lali, who all day has only been able to chew gum, her stomach too jumpy for food.

So what's going on, Paloma says, settling herself beside Lali at the table.

There are a couple of things. One, I have an idea I want to commission from you, if you're interested.

She describes her vision of Epic Teatro to Paloma, who listens and nods, doodling on some nearby scrap paper as she concentrates. I can *see* it, she says when Lali has finished. I'm thinking a long, *long* corrido, with angels and a chorus like a Greek play. Yes, this should definitely be sung.

Can you do it in time? I was thinking two weeks, when Council meets to vote on whether to accept the petition.

I'll see what I can do, okay? I can enlist Rafa's help. She studies Lali's face, sensing her anxiety. Is there something else? There's something else, I can see it.

Lali gulps air. The other thing...yeah. The other thing I needed to talk to you about. I—the thing is. I have strong feelings—

She cuts herself off to begin again, to revise and qualify. It seems too strange to be credible that such new, sudden feelings should be so strong.

I mean, I have feelings...for Joel. As she says it, tears build behind her eyelids.

Oh, Citlali! That's wonderful!

Lali gapes at her. You think so?

All love is a mysterious gift that comes from nowhere, says Paloma. It can be neither asked for nor refused. Are you going to tell him?

I don't know. That's what I wanted to talk with you about. I—wrote this poem. Do you think I should send it?

Let me ask you first. Do you have a physical relationship with this man?

Paloma, no! I mean, my feelings are—they're definitely not platonic—

She describes her mid-meeting fantasy and the older woman claps her hands, rocking back and forth with laughter. Wonderful, wonderful, she repeats.

Lali still cannot understand how it could be anything except crisis, collapse, apocalypse. If there was some way, she says, more to herself than Paloma. But it would never be okay with Hector. It's not like we've never been attracted to other people. We've been together long enough that we're pretty open about that. But I don't think he'd be okay with actually opening up the relationship. And I don't even think that's the issue. She presses hands to eyes, whispering. I think the issue is—I never felt like this with Hector in the beginning. I think this is something different, something I can't ignore or live comfortably beside. Meaning it requires—

She can't finish what it will require, she shifts mid-sentence. You know that book *The Awakening* that you have to read in high school?

Not any high school I ever went to, says Paloma, if I'm remembering the right book. Mi'ja, I went to Catholic school! Maybe in college I did. I'm seeing a woman walking into the ocean at night?

Yeah, that one, that's the ending. She walks into the ocean, because once she's awake she can't stay in her marriage and she can't be with the person she wants. The only option available to her is oblivion. That ocean ending...it never made sense to me before. But Paloma, even if I did tell him—I'm leaving in three weeks, I'm leaving—

She weeps, hands still pressed against her eyes, Paloma handing her napkins.

Hearing them, Rafa sticks his head into the room.

Everything okay? he says. What are y'all talking about? Ha, listen to me all nosy.

Poetry, Rafaelito, says Paloma. Something you don't know anything about. They laugh as Rafa pulls up a chair. Lali tenses at his presence, but Paloma rubs her back to reassure her. Rafael can be trusted in these matters, she says. In fact, he is an expert. So what about this poem? Were you going to read it to us?

Ooh, yes, says Rafa.

I don't think I can read it to you right now, says Lali shakily. But you can read it. I want you to. She retrieves the poem from her backpack, Paloma spreading its pages across the table. Rafa scoots his chair in closer and reads along with her, over her shoulder, lips moving. Lali sees sweat beaded there, above his lipstick. Sweat condenses beneath her breasts, rolls down her torso. She pulls vigorously at her collar to funnel the room's warm air down her shirt front and across her clammy torso.

Oh my God, Citlali. Rafa turns to Lali, finished reading. It's so beautiful and real. You have to send this! You're leaving, what does it matter. Let him know how you feel.

Lali shakes her head vigorously, involuntarily. She can't. She can't. What could it possibly accomplish? But she cannot stop what is happening.

Besides. Even if I never said anything to Hector...I don't want to burden Joel. Make things difficult or complicated for him.

Paloma tilts her head, thoughtful. I don't know Joel well, she says. But from my few interactions with him, he seems complicated enough that I don't think knowing would be a burden. And he doesn't strike me as a person who would run from happiness.

***

Later, once Rafa has retreated from dining room table to the private chambers he has fashioned at the back of her Mama's house, Paloma rises and folds Lali in an embrace.

I'm so happy for you, Citlali. But—

She smiles, then turns her head in the direction of Rafa's studio, and when she turns back her eyes are teary. I do understand the difficulty of your position. Don't think I don't. There's a reason I said yes when Rafael needed a place to stay. Not just because he needed an assistant.

Paloma! Does he know?

Like halfway. He suspects. But, I think, what good could come of my saying anything? For me, anyway. He loves men, *loves* them. And young lesbians sometimes, she adds. She shakes her head. And I'm not any of those things. Not a man, not young, not lesbian—though I guess being a hag makes you queer by proxy these days, doesn't it. But you know what, it's okay. I feel loved by him, in the way he can love me. It's not a terrible thing, even though it's not what I dream about. My kids call me crying. Mama, why can't you love someone appropriate! Their dad was a player, and Cruz was an addict—so now they think I'm an idiot who is doomed never to be loved back. She laughs. But someone appropriate *I* might not love. Loving who you love, owning it no matter the response...in some ways, that's the payoff, don't you think? I mean, what alternative do we have?

An impossible possibility, if only Lali could find it. Some needle's eye passage in a great impasse, through which she might thread the truth of desire without destruction of the mountain, without the necessity of oblivion.

***

It makes sense at Paloma's table, surrounded by candles and flowers and gauzy material hung floor to ceiling. But in bed beside Nena and Hector, Lali cannot imagine any solution, any opening that walks the tightrope balance of a Paloma, teetering with grace between joy and despair. That worked for her, but Lali is certain that to speak can only be to snap that wire, to set fire to the bed in which they all lay sleeping. But to not speak would be to undertake a different kind of violence, a self-immolation to preserve a fiction, a murder of all truth-telling, the only condition of real agency. She knows that.

So she goes over it and over it, unable to sleep. In the following days, Joel will text or email and they will meet again, touching without touching, speaking without speaking. Or they may not. And in the days after that, the movement people will present their 150,000 signatures to the city people for verification. If she can survive the nights to come, she will ride her bike up the street to the city offices to accompany them. Not long after, she and Hector will pack all their stuff into a truck and leave the city behind, swirling with its incomprehensible complexity, for something simpler and cleaner and more comfortable, something she was supposed to want and had thought she wanted.

Until then, she lays up, waiting.

***

When Paloma Villalobos-Trujillo was small, but big enough to have outgrown her tiny grandmother, she once stood back-to-back with Abuela María de Jesus, then whirled around to ask, in scandalized tones, how tall her Abuela was anyway. That was Paloma's way of announcing she had achieved a notable stature.

I am seven feet tall, her grandmother responded, always flippant, always mysterious. And seven feet wide, and seven feet deep.

Now Paloma spreads before her the pages of the essay Lali has given her. It's the middle of the night, y qué? Isn't she retired? She lights a vela with the image of St. Jude, summons the 343 cubic feet of María de Jesus Cervantes, and begins to write.

CHAPTER ELEVEN
Black Hole

From: Citlali O'Connor <cit.lali@gmail.com>
To: Joel Champlain <champlainjoel@gmail.com>
Date: Weds, July 7 at 3:24A.M.
Subject: (no subject)

> It's not that anything is wrong
> that's the thing
> from day to day it doesn't feel
> like there is a hole or a gap
> but it's when I'm in the presence
> of something else
> a presence, more
> than a presence, a force that
> compels outward and beyond
> a motive, a desire, an
> attraction that moves me
> beyond myself from
> day to day
> that something feels
> not right: that I should abjure
> stability for this, mobility—what feels
> like a sucking wound inside me,
> a black hole at the center,
> collapsed magnet threatening

to upend all.

I wouldn't, I couldn't
I know the stakes
but it just makes me wonder
what must be wrong, what
must have gone wrong that
this longing wells up
inside me like tears
threatening to overspill
the shape of the life
I didn't know was there
containing it.
What must have gone
wrong, that I can't withstand
desire so that
I want to run
away from myself in
two directions at once:
into danger,
back into the arms
of a safety that
doesn't quite satisfy

Why does it feel

so wrong to write that out
when I know what I've chosen,
when I wouldn't choose other

wise? Or would I?

(What is it?
I'll tell you:
a chance glance
that set me afire after
near a year of gradual awareness
of your being in the world
of your awareness of me,
an inexplicable embarrassment when
we ran into each other. Once
our eyes met across the room
at a city council meeting
and I felt the thrill
of uneasy attraction.
I told Chela I'd dreamed about you,
fantasized about sending you
anonymous postcard before I moved:
thank you for your writing,
I am moved by your words
so much

culminating in
the end of Teatro
when
I looked up and saw you
seeing me, felt the weight
of your eyes on me,
the quality of appreciation

up and down
of that look. Quick and hot
as fire or flush of blood.
A few nights later
I had a dream
about someone else I loved
once, without speaking it,
impossibly once,
our intersecting paths
already preset to diverge
by the gap of age
and station, like now
but I woke up with you on my mind
like a taste in my mouth
I wanted more of.
As if reading my thoughts
as if on convergence course
you crashed into me next morning,
emailed: *great seeing you.*
We made plans to travel together,
daughter and dog in tow,
a short trip out of town
to document an action
on the beach. The water was
beautiful that day, no sign
of tar or jet fuel
rolling downriver
to the Gulf.
In the car our words

rolled downhill too, I
couldn't stop talking to you,
a massive flow of conversation
like a line had been cut
accidentally.
And behind that flow of words
a wall of silence or loneliness
as when you told me
you don't do much at home after work
that home was about survival
until work the next morning
as when I saw your head drop
on the beach when I applied sunscreen
in the slight bow of your head
the smallest hint
that no one touches you

Now my equilibrium's disrupted—
can't breathe, can't concentrate
want to cry, want to talk to you
want to send you this
want to know what it means
and what I want:
is it just to be able to tell you
how I feel, how it felt?
To defuse the danger by
speaking what you're not
supposed to talk about, what
is supposed to remain unspoken?

Or to hear you confirm it or
not, to know what it means to you?
Whether it's in my head,
fantastic, a transference or projection,
or whether it's real at all, the deep
connection I felt?
To have someone soothe me
by explaining what to do
when it's real but not possible or
what to do when it's illusory
or how to tell, or why
I've made the choices I've made,
why I've always run from my own appetites
terrified by what I want, by the black hole
bottomlessness of what feels good,
what feels too good, then retreated
from that depth
only to chase after it again?

I don't want to be that younger self
who runs out the door distracted
each time, incapable of telling
real from illusion.
Who mistakes illusion for real
hurting everyone in her path.
A Katrina of desire, a Tuvalu
swallowed by rising seas,
an Arctic sheet sheared
unstoppably.

I don't understand why
desire would terrify
or why it would hurt to acknowledge
its limits, to recognize desire
while affirming necessity. Why it feels
wrong to feel, and wrong not to say
what one feels, equally
wrong for saying it aloud,
paper or speech.

I think it's just
that I want to tell you
that I love you
although I don't really know you
that I wish the best for you
that I would try to do what I could
if you needed something
that I'm grateful our paths crossed
that what we shared was
powerful and meaningful for me

that I consider you my friend

CHAPTER TWELVE
Sludge Ponds and Sacred Dances

Highest Summer

Lali and Joel do weird things together, in the weeks of hopeful calm descending after VAMOS submits its tens of thousands of signatures for the city people to certify. Lines and lines of signature, shaky and blocky and flowing, on reams of legal paper nested in cardboard file boxes. There is nothing to do now but wait, Lali pushing the pending move from her mind, pretending it isn't happening. It is a window of time outside of time that has opened up, in which to imagine that something else is possible, some radically new or unpredicted outcome. The morning VAMOS had hauled all those boxes of signatures to the city clerk's office downtown, Joel had swung by on his way out of town to pick up his daughter for the summer, and they had sat together on Lali's porch under a mid-morning sun just low enough to be tolerable. There, he had confirmed receipt of the poem. He had approved its minutes and certified the results. So close to my experience there is virtually nothing I could add, he said. All morning, Chela had texted and texted for Lali to come to the city offices—where was she? She was supposed to be there, she was supposed to speak. But she had not slept all night, not one hour. How could she speak, or do anything else normal or stable? That was the day, when Hector got home from work, that she told him she was sure she could not stay. That day of the submission of signatures, three weeks before their scheduled move.

Now Joel's 11-year-old daughter has arrived for the summer, with hair long and straight and eyes clear as the skies of the Panhandle plains where she stays most of the year with her mother. She is as quiet and watchful as Joel and Lali are buzzy and jumpy, shocking each other each time their hands brush, each time feet bump beneath the table. They are cautious otherwise, scrupulous in avoiding intentional contact. Because of daughters, because they don't know what might happen. So they eat dinner together, Joel and Jodi on one side of Joel's dining nook and Lali and Nena on the other. After, when Lali stands doing the dishes at his sink, Joel retrieves an Ayurvedic nutritional supplement from the fridge to show her, various herbs suspended in a tar-like honey sludge—*Chyawanprash*, he pronounces slowly. He digs out a large spoonful for himself and eats it in a single go, then spoons out a smaller amount for Lali to try, urging it to her lips as she stands at the sink with hands submerged. Lali hesitates, embarrassed, then parts her lips to permit his offer, so full of tenderness and erotic charge. No one has ever fed her before, since childhood at least. In the other room, daughters eat ice cream and bang on Jodi's electric keyboard. For those slender few weeks they comprise a mythical family, the fiction of a family for any onlooker.

They do weird things together: Lali knows a place they can all go, she and Joel and the kids and even Luz. It's outdoorsy, family friendly—the shape of a nature park finagled from the city's former wastewater lagoons, at one time the end of the line for its sewage, the sinkhole into which they had poured its entire watershed. Lali knows about it because a chapter of her dissertation had been about the complex urban politics of wastewater management, evident in battles over what to do with Los Angeles sewage sludge. The actual ecological embeddedness revealed by desires to displace human embodiment from consciousness. No, really. It'll be interesting, c'mon. So they drive, early to beat the day's pending swelter, to the far Southside of the city, to the simmering biologic funk that remains where water once went to die.

It's not nasty anymore, Lali reassures a still apprehensive Jodi as they spill out of the car to sniff cautiously at the air and inspect informational kiosks. They had to clean up the site after the Clean Water Act passed. And they had to do something else with the sewage sludge. They couldn't just dump it like they used to.

Now they treated some of it for use as a fertilizer and landfilled the rest. Took em a while, Joel says. CWA was, when, 1970?

Yeah. Most cities had to be dragged backwards screaming into compliance in the late 80s or 90s, especially in Texas. And San Antonio was kinda late to the sanitation party generally. No sewers till the turn of the 20th century, and really the Westside didn't see them until the 1950s. The signs kind of gloss over that part.

She runs a finger lightly over the kiosk's engraved letters describing the city's commitment to sustainability, its partnership with the bird people who now administer the park. Sewage ponds, she knew, were famous for their ability to attract birds, and consequently the bird people who chased after them in their floppy hats and binoculars.

They circle the ponds once, lazily. Jodi walks briskly ahead by herself, arms crossed, Luz trotting after; Nena lags and has to be persuaded, then pulled, then carried—but *not* by Joel! *Only* Mama! Flies seek their bare arms when they stop momentarily to observe the minor goings on of the ponds. They see the boxy snout of a reptile snuffling above the waterline, slipping below its green surface before they can tell if it is turtle or snake. Probably turtle. They pass a docent on his morning beat, binoculars raised as he gazes out over the ponds, and stop to say hello. Did you see that vermillion flycatcher? he wants to know. He's doing a summer bird count, tally sheet in his hand like a golfing scorecard.

In fact Lali had, a red streak of something flying overhead a moment ago, although she hadn't known the name for what she was seeing.

The docent nods approval, giving her a look that is part satisfaction and part pride. Good eye, he says.

It is a real birding moment. A moment of birding subterfuge, passing for bird people, with their camera bags and backpacks and water bottles bumping against their bodies as they walk.

The birds are sparse that morning because of the summer heat, the docent had said, but they do see egrets gliding overhead in a pair—those Joel knows—then skimming the water with legs thrust backwards, to light with precision in just the right spot on a constructed island, where other egrets gather. As they land, the others jump aside to admit them and then ease back in, absorbing them into the group as a pool absorbs the wrinkle of a wave. They see a knot of fifteen to twenty ducks swimming in whirlpool formation, furiously churning the water—why? Lali wants to know. But Joel doesn't know. And farther down on the banks, they find a scattering of feathers outlining what can only be recent carnage, and beyond that lies a ball of feathers, perfectly spherical and light as air. Amazed, they pick it up to examine more closely, holding it to the sun like a gem; Joel cradles it in the palm of one hand to phone-photograph it with the other. Its colors remind them of tiger's eye and its patterning of leopard print, iridescent brown with black mottling. What is it? Maybe an owl pellet or a savaged chunk of flesh? But there's nothing inside to suggest something so gruesome, no bones or gristle or meat. Nothing in their experience that can lend insight or explanation. Just the intimation of a previous violence and this single precious remainder; just orphaned feathers tightly curled into a ball to guard their mystery.

Weird stuff. Synchronicities and inexplicable resonances, like a tuning fork humming. Their next outing is a Black Hat dance performed by an exiled Tibetan lama who travels the world to spread awareness of the orphanage he heads in India for refugee children. Watching the dance is supposed to remove all negative energy, all barriers to hope, all obstacles and delusions preventing one from seeing things as they are.

Nena is with Hector that night, so Lali has a few hours. She is nervous when Joel arrives with Luz in his bright red car—so indelibly bright her head will forevermore turn at the sight of red on the road, even two states away, in case it is him—quiet nervous, not sure if the thing between them will start up, whatever it is. What if it doesn't? Nervous as they park and walk inside the intake building of the homeless mega-shelter where the lama will perform his dance, in an interdenominational chapel hidden somewhere inside its fortress of services. Joel senses her tension, stopping to hug her before they enter the building. Are you scared? he asks. A little, she admits. Don't be scared, he says, smiling into her with arms wrapped round. It'll be okay. And like that, it starts up between them, the frequency that cannot be named.

Everyone has to enter through a single checkpoint, signing in with their names and addresses, submitting backpacks and the contents of pockets to screening before walking through scanners. Luz can stay with them but only if she's collared and leashed and registered.

Foucauldian, Lali murmurs as they retrieve their personal effects.

Who what? Joel wants to know.

Oh, Foucault. French theorist guy, she tells Joel, too much philosopher for political scientists and too political for philosophers. It had been decades since his death, but the halls of academe still rang with talk of bald gay turtlenecked leather daddy Foucault and his alternate theories of power. Not power as top down, a violent force of prohibition emanating from a visible center, which is how the movement people talked about it. Not power as a king ordering the public punishment of criminals or madmen. Power instead as non-local, distributive, disciplinary. Everywhere and nowhere and immanent, arising from within those governed, by an anxiety to approximate norms and expectations. His famous image for this understanding of power was Bentham's panopticon, a circular prison complex with an all-seeing guard tower at its center in which a guard may or may not be, thereby governing through the mere suggestion of surveillance. But governance also via the timetable, the diagnostic category, the standard deviation. The basic Foucauldian thing—and it really was very smart, which was why everyone still buzzed—was that a new form of governance characterized modern society, one that produced new identities and forms of being as much as it excluded or repressed those who did not fit. He had developed this idea over a series of books looking at the history of different kinds of institutions—madhouses, prisons, clinics.

Like this place, Lali says. The city's solution to its own exiled had been not to run them out of town or kill them, but to include them ever more intensively within the workings of the city, to institutionalize their management ever more effectively in its streamlining and consolidation. To process and measure, via discourses of ruthless aspiration. It was a point lost on those who saw only the humanitarian face of this consolidation. But it was not lost on the intersection panhandlers who were forced to decide between mega-shelter or jail, nor on the Food Not Bombs kids like Chela whose weekly food distribution in the park was now criminal, nor on the street ministers who brought their teachings to the underpasses instead of to the shelter. What Foucault had done was point out that the modern shift from power as punishment to power as discipline only appeared humanitarian, when in fact the application of power had become all the more intensive, extensive, inescapable. It was this insight that upset people about Foucault: the idea of power as a fine mesh lacing of productive determinations was damn *depressing*. The idea that there was no outside to power— that was his argument. And he had died, of AIDS, before he had fully developed an account of disciplinary power's failures or ruptures or refugees, its unpredicted possibilities for resistance and transformation.

They are walking now, across the courtyard at the center of the shelter complex and toward the cafeteria that doubles as chapel. All over the dry yellow grass of the courtyard, people sprawl and sit and lie in a muggy purgatory; that was where those who did not want to commit to the shelter's assistance programs were allowed to camp. And you know, she says, the shelter was a concession for the vagrancy law they passed a few years back, to make sure homeless people didn't spoil the view for downtown tourists. You didn't know that? Council voted to pass the most punitive downtown vagrancy law in decades if the business community would put money toward the shelter.

Still—says Joel—still. Meaning: it is still a place of refuge. And he is not wrong to say so.

In the cafeteria chapel they sit against each other at a long particleboard lunch table, close close with legs pressed together, Joel's fingers resting lightly on the back of Lali's arm, above the elbow. His other hand closes tight around the leash that tethers Luz to his side, lying quietly beneath the table. When Rinpoche enters, his hat is indeed black, but it is also draped in yellow sashing and crowned with a grinning calavera, just as his black robe is embroidered blue and gold with the porcine face of a demon, grimacing with tongue out, bordered by floating skulls. He dances trailing a fistful of rainbow streamers from each hand, circling one direction and then another, sending a waterfall of many colored tassels flying from the bottom of his robe.

What does it mean, Lali wonders. What am I seeing, what am I supposed to be seeing?

Afterward there is time for such questions, but Lali and Joel and Luz bypass the line forming before the lama, instinctively reaching for each other's hand as they walk out into the courtyard among intransigent sprawlers and campers. When he says he has a headache, she retrieves a bottle of pills from the little pocket of her backpack and shakes a few into his waiting hand, cupping it from beneath with one of hers, stroking his fingers closed with her other.

They don't have much time. Children are waiting back home, cared for by ex-partners and parents—Joel's are in town. But before they return, they drive to the stretch of river that runs by her apartment. Joel unleashes Luz, who runs barking ahead after a scatter of grackles. They park and cross the tangle of train tracks, to follow the freshly constructed bike path for a ways, walking alongside the water. At the newly opened bike bridge, they slide down the bank to sit on the concrete wall intersecting the bridge abutment, talking about high school and family. We moved out of the city just before I started middle school, she says. We got bought out, and they demolished our house. My folks took the money and moved north, out of the city. It's suburban now, but back then it was the middle of nowhere. As a kid I remember the car ride felt like it took hours.

And it's weird, but even though she spent as many of her formative years in rural areas as she did in the city, she never felt like she was from those spaces, like she belonged. Always a feeling she had been ripped from the city, that a piece of her had snagged on something and gotten left behind, or that something had snagged on her and followed, sewed up inside her body like a surgical error. As a teenager she would walk around outside at night in the big empty spaces north of the city, feeling as though the houses had their backs turned. By night the trees were black shapes, swaying in the warm wind. She would drive around for hours sometimes, looking and smoking and listening to music. She would skip school to drive around, sometimes with others, sometimes alone. Once, on a long backroad detour home, she found a small roadway bridge traversing the Guadalupe where it ran swift and narrow. She had parked and carefully picked her way down the steep embankment to sit by the water, and when she hiked back up she veered off-path to inspect the underside of the bridge. There she had seen a shocking sight, stumbling backwards before scrambling back up the hill: a paper wasp nest the size of a car looming beneath the concrete tresses of the bridge. Years later the memory seems incredible, unreal, but it seems equally incredible she might have imagined it.

Stuff like that, though. The houses may have been suspicious of her, but there were unexpected pockets of something unalienated and inalienable. They should look for that bridge sometime together. They should see if the nest is there still.

He listens with arms hugging his knees, head down. He can sympathize. A move, they say it's like a death, next to a death in its impact on a person's life. When he was fourteen years old, his father abruptly relocated the family from Philadelphia to Waco, Texas, to take a job as chair of the Physics Department at the Bible Belt college there, in the years before the FBI laid waste to David Koresh and his Branch Davidian compound. It was traumatic for all of them, a move from which none of them had ever fully recovered. His older brothers were least marked by it; they were out of the house already, with families of their own. But his parents were estranged for years after, plunged into separate depressions at opposite ends of the house. And that had been when the episodes began for Joel, when the cycles had gathered force and taken shape. Only recently had he been able to talk to his dad about that time. They had bonded over it, because Joel understood what it was to be so low it seemed better to die.

Talking, walking now, propelled by mosquitoes and time constraints off the bridge abutment and onto the bike path back to the car, not touching not kissing but with the charge between them palpable, wondering what would happen, and when.

And then it does, and it's not what either of them expect. But when he tells her about his father, something makes them slow and turn toward one another; something brings her hand up to rest on the side of his face, tender. His eyes widen, his mouth falls open. She lets her hand lie there a few seconds, against his cheek, both of them standing outside in the falling dusk, moths and mosquitoes swarming the streetlight above, joggers and cyclists and strollers passing them from behind.

A powerful helplessness. A powerful powerlessness. Which is to say: there is a line of force between them, but it is unstable. That night she lies awake, feeling his fingers lightly running along the back of her arm. He lies awake, the weight of her knowing hand, her tenderness, against his face for those few seconds, throbbing with the heat of a brand.

CHAPTER THIRTEEN
Swimming

Monday, July 19

Waiting waiting, she waits for Hector and Nena to leave for the night—they are going to his mom's—and then for Joel to text. When he finally does he says he is still waiting too, for Jodi's friends to pick her up for a sleepover. When he texts again, it's to warn Lali he is under the weight of an immense and crushing depression. He still wants to see her but she should know, in case he seems quiet. *Or can't get off the floor*, he almost writes.

Is there anything I can bring you? she asks.

Arms, lips, brain, guts, he writes back.

***

She doesn't wait for the next text. She has to start moving, heart racing as she tears across the city, hot wind blasting through her open windows. The city is fast encroaching on la canícula, the dog days of summer, a season without tenderness or mercy. Where will she go? Maybe Brackenridge Park by his apartment. There she can wait and walk around, to burn off her panic. No, go for a run. There are tall trees, shade. But on the way he texts that his daughter is gone and he is ready for her to come get him. They are going in search of the bridge she remembers from her high school wanderings, to see if the paper wasp nest is still there—or, if not, whether it is possible it might once have been. They can go swimming in the river too, maybe. She has brought water-soaked towels for the trip that they can use to keep cool, to drape around their shoulders and use to wipe down arms and faces. To make of the hot wind a blessing.

She finds him standing with Luz in full sun, in the short brittle grass of the linear park across the street from his building. He smiles at her but it comes out crooked or smashed, as though it has had to struggle to the surface of his face against something heavy.

I need to go for a run or something, she says as they embrace. I feel like I'm about to explode. She can feel it when their bodies press together, the ricochet of her heart echoed between them like a ping-pong ball caught in a too-tight chamber. Joel feels it too. Oh, you are anxious, he murmurs, cheek nuzzled to the top of her head.

She runs like crazy, like she's been shot from a gun, full tilt in skirt with flat-soled Chucks slapping the gravel. Joel's stride is longer and he keeps pace easily, Luz leading on her leash. After one lap around the little park Lali has to stop, drenched and gasping, but she feels better. Something has evaporated, something has been discharged.

You ready to go? she asks Joel. In a couple of hours it'll be dark, and it's an hour north from the city to the bridge, even if her memory serves her well. Joel nods, moving as carefully as a man whose entire body aches after a beating, like a man with a headache the size of a bowling ball.

***

He had wanted to send her an email last night, when his brain knotted and his thoughts began chewing on themselves. He had started to write it, then deleted it. That was the logic of it. The illogic of it. Recursive, a never-ending loop of second guessings of second guessings, what if, but no what if, but maybe if. Whatever its content, always the same form. It'd be a mistake to follow the content. No solutions thataway.

Have you been sleeping with vampires, to cause you to be attracted to me, he had started to write, *and attempt to deliver this payload of sexual dynamite? And: Why the fuck am I even here, with my WASP stock, and not in some redeveloped power plant condo? And: I'm doomed, though, if I can't believe in even this one small chance between people, desperately grabbing for each other as they hurtle past, propelled by the force of ancient stars long exploded.*

Not a love letter, to be sure. He had written and then deleted it, then started again and given up and tried to sleep. His body ached with an urge to leave his bed and go walking, but Jodi was sleeping down the hall and he had to stay. So he lay awake with eyes clenched, pounding fists to his temples, thinking and unthinking and rethinking, and insomnia made the following day's crash inevitable.

Now she is talking about music on the radio, purporting a profundity to songs that have never seemed interesting to him. Just commercial dreck. Insubstantial. They sang whatever words they were paid to sing, whatever words turned the most profit. Didn't they? He'd been a hardcore punk, first on the streets of Philadelphia and later in Austin. But she wants to make a point, to play a tape for him on a deck marked, strangely, *logic control.* On that little flap where you insert the tape. She is asking, Is that okay? It's fine. She asks what his middle name is and he tells her. She asks what is going on with the city people and Seismar: will the city's investigation be resolved any time soon? They'd opened it but that was the last any of them had heard of it. There is something he knows, pretty sure anyway, but it feels too hard and too complicated to formulate. He'd tried to warn her that depression would make him quiet, but she's perplexed anyway, trying to intervene, to change it. Trying to get over or around or through. Looking for a way. They all did. That boulder, though—it could not be rolled away from the tomb. Don't you know he had tried, tried everything he could think of short of lying on a table with a rubber bite guard in his mouth as they zapped his brain with electric current, but nothing had worked and nothing ever would. Not pills, not booze, not marriage, not religious devotion. God had gone away without explanation and there was no help to be found anywhere in the universe.

She tells him, I like you when you're quiet too. Glancing over at him as she drives north, out of the city, Luz in the back-seat. But there are questions in her eyes, the same questions in Angela's eyes, in his ex-wife's—about the meaning of silence, of absence. Questions, that he can't answer.

They sail past the outermost loop, past the future Mud Creek mining site, and the land begins to change. The chain restaurants and billboards and big boxes thin and then it is houses and houses for a while, cookie cutter homes endlessly stamped in vales scraped clean of knobby oak and juniper, with its strips of cinnamon bark and winter-blue berries. The juniper was a weed anyway, the suburban developers had argued before the city people, who listened thoughtfully with chins propped in hands and concurred. Invasive species. Good riddance. Motion, second, consensus. Vote passes, next item.

The death loop, she says, and he looks over, alarmed. But no, that's what they had called the circle of freeway marking the farthest-out edges of the city, back when the city or county or state of Texas or whoever had first constructed it. Because of the high number of fatal accidents. They had built it too narrow and without a divider, hastily, trying to keep pace with development. Pushing it north, money following money like a dog after its own tail. The city had expanded in concentric rings that way, ripples of highway construction like a pebble thrown into a pond.

But soon even houses lose their grip on the land, leaving only the juniper-covered hills, blasted open where the highway runs to make plain their striations of limestone. She turns off the highway into the rural neighborhoods of her youth, driving him past the small middle school where she landed after her uprooting from the city. Pointing out this and that small thing she remembers. The fossilized bivalves she would find in the caliche outside, small stone hearts left over from an oceanic past. The country store everyone knew sold cigarettes to minors. And now they are driving the weave of backroads crisscrossing the hills, hunting for the right one, the one that will unexpectedly broaden into a river valley before becoming a bridge. She is navigating by intuition, trying to find the sequence of turns that feels right, the combination that will pick the lock.

She's done it: they park in the tall grass growing at the bridge's wide mouth and cross the road that will lead them to the water, leaving Luz in the car with windows cracked—they shouldn't be too long and the sun is going down. Lali takes Joel's hand, but he can hardly feel it. Somewhere up there, through layers of heavy clay, she holds his hand. Leading him down the steep embankment. They pause beneath the bridge to gaze upward, but nothing is there. No nest, no suggestion of a nest, no explanation for what she thinks she may have seen once.

They continue their descent, carefully edging their way down a path many feet have worn, all the way to the bottom. There they sit by the water's edge, removing their shoes and socks and rolling up their pants. Green algae licks the rocks of the river's shallows where they submerge their feet, clouds of small black gnats hovering above. Solitary dragonflies zip chaotically. The Guadalupe slips past clear and swift and unconcerned, far below the narrow bridge.

Did you want to go swimming, she says—but before he can reply she is leaning over him suddenly, with one hand turning his face toward hers and placing her mouth against his, finally, finally, after a hundred thousand years at the bottom of a lightless ocean trench. Somehow she has found him there and sunk a sharp hook deep into the meat and bone of his breast—and now she is reeling him upward against a trillion tons of ocean pressure, upward out of nonexistence, upward into blinding sun and searing air and breath. He bursts violently to the surface, gasping, responding to her lips on his with explosive force: sometimes that was the only thing capable of rousing him from his pall of dissociation, like a nuclear test beneath desert sands to jump-start things again. But the mass and force of every other kiss has also accumulated there, a wall of water crashing over them. It is the first kiss in the world. The only kiss that will ever be. A kiss at the end of history. The newest and the oldest thing.

She stands, extending her hands to help him up, and he rises unsteadily. He braces himself against her for a moment, before grabbing her in a bear hug grasp to kiss her, dangling her feet over the ground. She is as light as a child; her feet sway as he rocks her. He sets her to ground and bends her backwards like a Busby Berkeley dancer, his mouth on hers, his mouth traveling her neck and shoulders. The names of bones outlined there against his teeth—scapula, clavicle—always so beautiful to him. When she cries out, he answers without thinking: *yes*.

All of it involuntary, driven by a thrashing impulse to survive, to shake off the lure of quiescence, the final stillness that wanted him there too. They make their way back up the steep embankment in fits and starts, stumbling through twilight dark. She'll walk ahead a few steps, leading him by the hand, and then he'll pull her back or grab her from behind, mouth on her neck and shoulders, hands sliding down the lip of her pants and over her hips, or up her front beneath her shirt.

Inside the thickness of kissing she is still trying to talk to him, to tell him things and ask him questions. He pauses to peer into her face, searching the dark for her features, not thinking of the words that will appear. Sex has always been a way to stanch the hemorrhage of his internal chatter. But what comes out is true nonetheless. I *like* you, he says, the word guttural at the back of his throat, holding her by her upper arms.

Yes, she says, into his mouth. Mouth against mouth. I've never been with someone like this before.

A helplessness in her voice. What does she mean? Again he looks down into her face, what he can see of it. Really, he thinks? The body was common for him, was drunken encounters or misjudgment. An avoidance of something, a flight from or into.

She's trying to explain. Her hands move in illustration, groping at meaning, moving like bats or nocturnal birds emerging under cover of dusk. No, of course she's been with other people. But not in this way. Not like with him.

Something is happening, something serious. It is different this time. He knows it but doesn't know what to say. So he leans back over her, one hand on her back and the other on her chest. Here or home, he says. It's fully dark now. Anyone who happened to be around would not be able to see anything.

Let's go home, she says, taking his hand to lead him back up the hill to the car, where Luz waits for them, then back again south to his apartment.

***

Do you have a lot of...experience? she had asked at the river, the question escaping the corner of her mouth as they inhaled one another, drinking each other in as though parched, dying. For Lali it had been like tasting water for the first time, like not knowing one needed water all along. She hadn't wanted to disappoint. She hadn't wanted to get it wrong. She is thirty-one years old but desire is new to her. She has only ever tried to take what she did not want because another wanted to give it. She has only ever tried to have for herself what another did not want to give.

All of it is a fresh surprise now, to find herself now in another bed, another bedroom. It's been over ten years since she was with someone new. And Hector was her first real partner, as she was for him. Together they had drawn a dotted line inside which it was safe to learn from one other, okay to fumble and laugh when it was ridiculous. But it had been a conscious negotiation. Their yes had been hesitant, deliberate, cerebral—rehearsal for the raw, real shock of this new bed now, this new body that makes her blink hard at her surroundings, at the framed art on his walls and the quality of the light from his bedside lamp. At the river she couldn't stop herself from talking as they kissed, asking questions, trying to explain herself. Embarrassed, talking to paper over the plain exposure of her desire.

He had been incredulous at her admission. He couldn't believe it was true, that she had never been with anyone else. They had stumbled up the hill like drunks and then they had stood together beneath the bridge spanning the black running river, where she had peered up into his face.

No, I've been physical with lots of people. What I'm saying is, I've never been with someone like *this*. Never like with you. I never liked it. It came from them, not me.

He had paused, an odd, indecipherable expression on his face—but his only response had been to ask, sideways, where she wanted to go, and the ride south had cooled them off. In her car they'd eaten almonds from a bag, raw and chewy, and drank warm water from his metal thermos. Back at the apartment they made as if to do ordinary things, bringing bags inside, putting things away. But when she followed him into the kitchen he had suddenly turned to scoop her up, striding toward the bedroom. She must have been over his shoulder, upside down, because she had been dizzy, gazing at the ground before landing on the bed and looking around, amazed to be there.

On the bed he undresses himself first and then her, reaching over to pull her close. When he kisses her again she pulls away, saying, Wait. I want to look at you. When he removed his clothes she had studiously avoided looking at his body or even at her own, not wanting to make him nervous. She is nervous. Unpracticed, unsure how to initiate or ask. But she wants to acknowledge what they are doing, the gravity and ceremony of it, to assure him of her appreciation. She has searched her heart but found no hesitation there, no grain of discomfort or awkwardness or ambivalence.

He lets her look at him, but finally has to ask. Did she want—?

Yes but wait. She isn't ready. The first time in ten years. The first time ever. Finally she is able to say it: yes. Yes—but I like a languorous pace. He laughs at that, and with infinite care climbs inside her. She is not used to the feel of latex mediating between bodies. She is not used to someone who sings their pleasure aloud, the way her father would praise her mother's cooking as he ate, in each utterance the gratitude of prayer. She is not used to not finishing, her desire too big and overwhelming to finish—a boulder trying to roll through a needle's eye—but when they have stopped they lie together, and he says: To be with the right person is a sacred thing.

They lie vined together, unclothed, and when he clicks off his bedside lamp Luz jumps onto the bed at their feet. Lali's eyes are closed, her breathing is even, but it is all too new for her to sleep. Soon his arms slacken around her, and his breathing slows and deepens and eventually grows ragged. She smiles in the dark, enchanted by the sensuousness of that sound, its rapture in sleep, and amazed by her own enchantment, to be taken by snoring because it is his.

In the dark next to her. In the dark was where he had thrown her backwards, backbending her over his arm to kiss shoulder and neck. And when she cried out from somewhere beyond herself, he had responded: *yes*. The word springing unbidden to his lips, low and quick.

There was something chemical or electric in that word. When uttered, it opened a circuit; when shared, the circuit closed, making their bodies into a channel through which the entire cosmos poured, a pouring into that poured them into everything else. But it wasn't simply about bodies. Bodies were never just bodies. They were something else, a medium for the wellspring of deepest presence, of the sacred yes that flowed from the center of the earth itself, secret heart of all rivers, all life, all pleasure. Rising through lips and limbs, his yes meeting hers in return. A confluence of streams uniting, gathering power in their oceanward course.

***

He has been dreaming again, but he doesn't remember about what. But he wakes in a panic, hands closed around his throat. He looks over at where she lies, sleeping on her belly with hands tucked beneath the long of her thighs, head turned away from him. Perfectly still, perfectly silent.

He has to do something but he can't leave, so he retracts his body, still unclothed, into a child's pose. He is a seed, a single closed eye, knees pinned to chest, arms extended out in the stretch of worship. Legs still folded beneath, he breathes himself up to sitting with back straight, hands clutching at his knees. Breathes like that for a minute or two.

There was this woman he knew back in New Orleans. That was where he had gone for work, briefly, before Dallas which was before San Antonio. The demise of his marriage had been imminent, but his wife and daughter had accompanied him nonetheless, for the last time, then they had left him alone on the beaches of southern Louisiana, outside Cancer Alley. And there had been this woman. How had he met her—but he can't remember. Probably he'd interviewed her for one of his stories; she did sea turtle rescue, living alone on Grand Isle. She was an older woman, thirty years his elder. And once she had come across a large loggerhead that had stranded itself on the beach, far from the water. She'd tried to move it but it had proved too difficult for her. Turtles are heavier than they look. Especially if they are sea turtles, they rely on the buoyancy of salt water to make their own mass bearable. On land their center of gravity becomes a danger.

The woman must not have known this. She had tried to move the turtle, but when it couldn't be done, she feared the turtle would die. But she was a woman conversant in Reiki energy work, a Japanese healing art, a laying on of hands to transfer life energy. And so she decided she would disrobe and lay herself nude atop its ochre plated shell, in an offer of comfort and protection.

Joel remembered the feeling of sickness that came over him as she relayed what happened, realizing that what she'd intended as comfort hastened the turtle's suffocation. It hadn't occurred to her, and he hadn't been able to bring himself to say anything about it.

But now, remembering the Gulf Coast beaches of Louisiana, he stretches his body over her sleeping form, as much to comfort himself as her. Sitting astride her thighs, he straddles her, bending to drape head and chest over her back. Arms tucked tight against where she tucks her own arms beneath her body. She doesn't know. She lies still and unresponsive as death.

***

She wakes in the night in a strange bed, feeling him crawl on top of her, naked, resting his head in the valley of her back. She wakes surprised but says nothing, doesn't stir, the weight of his body on top of hers pressing lungs into mattress, compressing her chest. Somehow it relaxes her, somehow it feels safe, until slowly she sinks back down into sleep.

CHAPTER FOURTEEN
Barrera Talks

Wednesday, July 21

It was the hardest thing to stand there with a neutral face when you felt anything but. Since the thing with Christine, even before she dropped her fatal text, he had taken to walking around City Hall like a ghost wanting to cry all day at the impossibility and futility of it all. She'd told her husband, or he had found out—he would never know which one because she had stopped talking to him, like she said she would—and the whole thing had imploded. After that, there'd been no reason to withhold anything she had told him, the bigger stuff, he guessed you could call it, which he should have been thinking about all along.

im sorry, she had texted. *m and i have decided to try again. its not a good idea for us to contact each other anymore.*

Not even bothering with a phone call or with proper capitalization—like all those long letters she had written him about poetry and mining with the "I"s lowercased. He had texted her back with shaking hands—*please let's talk about this, please call me when you get the chance*—but she hadn't responded. He had lain awake all night waiting, all day waiting, unable to believe that was it, that she wouldn't be responding, but she hadn't.

Then again, it had been hard even when they were together, because of the pall of futility drawn over the both of them, the layers of secrecy required. Husband secrecy, city secrecy, like suffocating under heavy blankets in the middle of summer. Each Friday he would drive to the survey site in the sealands to meet her, where Seismar had her stationed in its little trailer ghost town. For months he had carried her with him through the week like the photo of a dead loved one, through meetings and hearings and Councilman Coffeetimes, dogged by a nervous sickness that was half joy and half dread, like a sweet drink built to toxic accumulations in one's blood. It made the professional neutrality required by his position feel like some kind of insane curse. The day of the press conference on the Seismar project had been the worst. That was when news of the numbers had hit and splattered—first the staffers, then the city manager, and finally the mayor and council members—rippling outward from its anonymous source, the pebble he had tossed from a safe distance until its wake became perceptible, unavoidable, catastrophic. False numbers, all based on speculation. That was what she had whispered to him over email, and as they clung together in that trailer in the dark. He'd left her name out of it, hers and his. Just information, passing from mouth to mouth like a children's game of telephone until it reached the right ears. Passing from her mouth to his, with a tenderness that had devastated him.

At the press conference Mayor Mi'jo had delivered the city's official announcement like a man doing his best to clench back a big shit, his rage seeping through the ordinarily unshakable composure Barrera frequently envied. Yes, it was true they had been poised to vote on the issue based on faulty information from Seismar. Yes, the Transition Team had known too. No, at this time they could not reveal who had tipped them off, only that

Seismar had confirmed the inconsistencies. A fuller investigation was for the lawyers to wrest from everyone's inboxes, sifting like prospectors for waning flakes of gold in a moving stream.

All of it had only barely registered for Barrera, because two weeks before she hadn't called when she said she would. It was the second time, a Wednesday, and she was supposed to call and confirm whether they were on for that weekend or not. If so then she would drive to the sealands, and he would. But she hadn't called, and a few days later he had gotten the text. So on the day of the press conference, he had stood stone still behind the mayor at the podium, hands clasped tightly together before him to stop them from shaking, hoping his despair passed for solemnity. Or whatever performance of regretful gravitas seemed proper to the press, who pitched question after question at their hangdog lineup—all of them standing there in their monkey suits, like balloons pinned to a board at the county fair. Trapped, exposed, waiting to be popped.

To his left he could sense 27-year-old García quavering, owl-eyed. He was District 7, far Northwest side. Ordinarily Barrera envied the young ones, the baby-faced councilmen starting their public careers. Second generation stars of their South- or Westside high school classes, like he had been. Solid students at one of the private Catholic law schools in town—their parents wept with pride at their legal aspirations but hadn't wanted them to go far for school—or sometimes a scholarship to Austin or even an Ivy like the Mayor. Their slicked-back hair, their dreams of mayoral or congressional dignity. Not for themselves but for la comunidad. Until today they had not even imagined the random viciousness of scandal nor its inevitability, the ambiguities of power that made implication and complicity unavoidable. They hadn't known the chaos of love, never mind the dissolution of first marriages under the pressures of public life and the desert of loneliness stretching ever after. They assumed purity was possible, that it was possible to remain unassociated and untainted. But it wasn't: that was the tragedy of it. And you wouldn't want it to be, if untainted meant without attachment. Christine had been the first person who had touched him in a loving way since the divorce, since before his tepid, loveless marriage, since ever maybe. Like he had been waiting his whole life for it, and when it finally arrived it had destroyed him. A white woman geologist from the East Coast contracted by a mercenary mining start up in Backasswardsville, Texas. And now he had become a machine politician—how was that possible, how was that even possible in this day and age? To be a fucking *ward boss*, like a stock character in a preachy socialist novel?

So he had been sick about it from the beginning, sitting straight-faced through constituent or council meetings where if it wasn't professional protesters shaking their fingers it was academics lecturing like they knew something others didn't, some expert knowledge that deserved a special listen, believing if they only made the right argument they could flip some switch and reroute the way things had always run. Sick, standing impassive through press conferences and ceremonial dinners while wanting to wail like a weeping statue, like that miracle tree from a few years back that had made the local news—some viejita had found water seeping out of its trunk like tears, and people had come from all over the city to pin photos of loved ones to its bark. Part of it had been the political heaviness of the thing, the knowledge that he was sitting atop his own collapse, but the question that had really unraveled him was: Would she leave her marriage or wouldn't she? Would she say yes to him or not? When they were together, it was so hard to suspend belief in a future that when she was out of sight, the feeling of her absence undid him. Of course there was a future. There had to be a future. Hadn't there? What was the point of desire if there wasn't a future in it?

But there hadn't been, and at least then he knew. At least then it could pass from his body like a painful stone, leaving only the political question to consider. The ethical question, really, because he could have given a rat's ass about reelection by that point. Should he or shouldn't he. Standing before the void that yawned before him, fingering the question like a stone.

Once more he's flipping it over and over in his hand, walking aimlessly through the park the night he finds the dog. Actually, she'd found him. She had bounded out of the thicket of bamboo by the little toy train tracks, covered with burrs and mud. She had reared up like a wildhorse to place her big paws on his running shorts and he had nearly cried.

But when he knelt to put his arms around her, he heard the jingle of her tags: a flat silver heart, engraved with her name— LUZ—and the number of her unnamed owner. Reluctantly, he had called the number on the tag and was surprised to hear Champlain's name on the voicemail recording. *You've reached Joel Champlain. I'm not able to take your call right now, but please leave a message after the tone and I'll call you back as soon as possible.* That fucking reporter. He had been the worst of the dart throwing balloon-poppers, pitching his questions hard and fast with intent to pin down or trap. He knew something, or was beginning to. Hi, my name is Ray, said Barrera, withholding his last. All would be known soon enough.

It is almost 11pm when Champlain calls back, relieved and friendly and chatty. Funny to hear him as just another person, sitting on the edge of his couch as he kicked off his shoes, cradling phone to ear with his shoulder as he put away dishes drying in the rack. Just as Barrera lies on the bed in the dark, stripped to boxers and socks, his soft middle-aged middle blinking up at the ceiling. Just two people talking on the phone and not the roles their bodies inhabited, the positions incumbent upon them during the day, inscribing their orbits and intersections. They are neighbors, even: as it turns out, the clutch of tidy bungalows where he has lived alone since the divorce is not far from Joel's apartment; they both border the park on different sides. Why don't they meet up right now, Joel urges Barrera, it's no problem at all. But Barrera is exhausted and half-nude to boot. They'll rendezvous first thing tomorrow morning, he promises Joel, in the park where the little train tracks cross the river. And before he takes his nightly pills—statins for blood pressure slightly too high, Prozac for a constant low-grade depression his doctor called *dysthymia*—he peers out his bedroom window to the backyard, where he has tethered the dog for the night. In the yellow cast of the streetlight he can make out the shadowy form of her sleeping shape. He is satisfied, he crawls into bed.

***

What had happened was this: Joel had done about everything he could think of to get the dog to stay, but she didn't want to stay. After that first week in the office, it wasn't feasible to take Luz to work with him everyday, but if he left her alone in his apartment she would go crazy from separation anxiety, or wanting to be out and free, whichever it was. Scratching up his front door and destroying his blinds as she clawed at the windowpanes. Or eating holes into the arms of his couch and ripping out its polyester innards. Or scattering and shredding the bills he'd lain out neatly on top of his coffee table, then puking from the stress onto the litter of paper.

His only choice had been to leash or pen her outside during the day, but Luz had eventually foiled every one of his attempts. She had chewed through leashes and leapt over fences and dug where she could not leap. The times she'd gotten free she never went far, wherever it was she romped during the day; by the time he returned from work she would be there, waiting for him on his back stoop as though nothing had happened.

This time is different. This time she is gone gone. It has been two days and still she is missing, Joel's only clue the two doors he finds unlatched and swinging wide open on Monday night: the door of the pen he'd bought to crate her during the day, and—most improbably, most inscrutably—the back door off the kitchen. Well, he *had* been in a hurry that morning, and he must have not secured the latch on the pen. And the kitchen door, apparently he'd left it unlocked, and she must have thrown her not insubstantial weight against it, somehow, until it sprung open—just enough was all she needed, and then she must have—she must have—

It seems entirely improbable, but it is the best he can figure. In any case, when by the second night she still hasn't returned, Joel makes some crude flyers on his computer and posts them around the neighborhood, feeling a stab of futility in the pit of his stomach with each push pin he presses into the creosote-soft wood of the utility poles. He can't keep her. Not here, anyway. Maybe in a different place, when he moves. Have to start thinking about that soon. Maybe a place with a little fenced yard. Somewhere that felt more permanent, more like home—but where would that be? A house with a yard surrounded by a fence ten feet tall, with no cracks and no slats. With doors impenetrable and latches unforgettable. A house in a different city altogether. Lali would be headed out of state soon. Maybe he could hitch a ride north with her to a different life, erase all traces of his time in fucking Texas. Maybe then.

So Joel is surprised when he hears the call on his voicemail late at night. Usually his body perceives these matters correctly, but he is glad to be wrong in this case. He calls back right away and is surprised anew when the caller answers, a baritone voice on the other end, pleasant and polite despite the late hour. He's a neighbor, too: they make plans to meet in the park the following morning, early, before work, and after Joel hangs up he tumbles right down into sleep.

***

The surprises don't end there. In the early morning sun of the park, still early enough to be tolerable out, Ray Barrera stands alone at the bank of the slow-moving river, sleeves of his white dress shirt rolled to expose forearms crossed tightly over his chest, as if to shield his body from cold. Joel approaches quickly until the man turns around to reveal his face, black Ray-Bans shading his eyes. Then Joel starts and stares, his movement forward snagged on a confusion whose haze eventually clears to recognition. The man standing before the river with his back turned looks like a man dressed for a funeral. That might be surprising enough if it were not also Ray Barrera. Without Luz.

Councilman? says Joel, still feeling a lingering confusion.

Morning, Mr. Champlain. They shake warily, unhappily. How are you, says Barrera, voice flat.

Whether this is familiarity or formality, Joel can't tell. Barrera's dark shades eat up all expression on his face.

Enough of this, Joel thinks with exasperation. You called me last night, he starts.

I did.

But I don't see Luz here. Why did you call me last night and say you had Luz?

I did have her. The corners of Barrera's mouth droop. I almost did—she must have jumped my fence early this morning. She was there when I went to bed last night, after I called you, and then this morning—

Okay, well—

Joel's confusion returns, compounded by frustration. Why hadn't Barrera just called him to cancel? Or sent him a text or something. Jesus. Out of habit, he reaches for his pocket to fumble for a cigarette.

Champlain.

Joel looks up and sees Barrera is crying, in fact openly weeping behind his Ray-Bans, his face wadded in a grimace like a tissue.

This never happens, Joel thinks. Well, they say once it happened with Henry Cisneros, during an interview, when he was having that affair with—what was her name, Linda...? Oh. Oh shit.

Is this off the record, Barrera?

No.

Barrera sits heavily on the banks of the river, legs of his funereal pants rising to reveal a strip of dress sock, a strip of naked flesh. After a moment of uncertainty, Joel pulls his spiral pad from his pocket and lowers himself to the bank, beside Barrera.

CHAPTER FIFTEEN
El Corrido de los 17

Thursday, July 22

listen closely my people
to a story few know
it's the terrible story of how
san anto came to grow

in uneven ways
that caused lots of problems
for those who were poor
and had little power

but the problems we see
in the 21st century
are less chance or coincidence
than the labor of many

sprawl at one end
crumbling sidewalks the other
mining profit for one
heatstroke for another

but increasing rates
and light bills unaffordable

> *amid temperatures rising—*
> *these are not unavoidable*
>
> *they have a history, you see*
> *which goes back to the start*
> *there are those who have gained from it*
> *and those who have not*
>
> *and the ones who did then*
> *are the ones who do now*
> *and the ones who do not*
> *should understand how*
>
> *so listen carefully, mi gente,*
> *and we'll tell you why and when*
> *in a story called "The Ballad*
> *of the 17 White Men..."*

***

It went on like that, all day and into the night and on into the following morning. It truly was an epic teatro, a teatro filibuster Paloma had planned and orchestrated and executed. If, by some legal loophole the city had discovered or engineered, if they were going to scrap the entire petition process anyway, by Tonanztín they should have to sit there and listen to the people first. Make 'em work for the privilege. So Paloma had figured out a way to keep them there all night, starting with the rule in the city charter, their own rule, which said a council couldn't adjourn until every person who signed up to speak on an agenda item had spoken. And starting too with the rule that every person who signed up to speak was entitled to three minutes' time—nine minutes if you signed as a group of three or more. But if there were, say, *480 people* who wanted to speak on an item—or, better, 160 groups—you only had to do the math to realize you might be there all day and all night, presuming 1,440 minutes added up to 24 hours, which it sure looked like it did. And then, each of those 160 groups of three or four or five or more might be assigned stanzas to sing or scenes to perform, so that when taken together their testimonio *might* appear to be one single, seamless, uninterrupted performance, the way separate still images consecutively projected at a high enough speed crossed some perceptual threshold and jumped to life as a moving picture. With Lali and Sister Soli's essay adapted into verse—Paloma had chosen the corrido as her form, the narrative poem-song and pop-ed vehicle that was the Chicanx equivalent of Greek morality theater—all she had to do was divide it into 160 parts of 9 minutes' duration, organize the thousands of petition signers into 160 groups of performers, give each group one part, then ask them all to sign up in order. Easy.

So at 9A.M. the council meeting had begun, called to order with the accustomed prayer—this time led by Father Respeto Guerrero of District 4—and by 9:15 Mayor Mike announced they would begin with consideration of Item 1A: certification of citizen-initiated recall process. Someone from the Hispanic Chamber of Commerce read a canned statement against the recall, then Mayor Mike had summoned the People's Power

Performers to the podium. There was a moment of tense silence as the chorus of viejitas, whispering, gathered their robes about them and raised calavera masks to their faces—Rafa had made them out of paper plates—and then they filed to the front of the chamber to sing their opening prologue, Doña María Elena on guitar and Keta on bajo sexto. As their time ran out, another group stood to continue the performance, then another—until, verse by verse and frame by frame, they told the story from its origins to the present: from the founding of the missions to the Mexican War, the Battle of the Alamo, the Republic of Texas, the Treaty of Guadalupe Hidalgo, the tarring and feathering of Juan Seguín. When at 11p.m. they got to the long, boring period of Anglo rule between post-Civil War reconstruction and Mexican revolution, the chorus of viejitas singing off the name of each member of each city council between 1841 and 1924, the District 3 coucilwoman slid surreptitiously from her mahogany leather swivel chair to stretch out on the floor beneath. Still they went on performing. A post-revolution wave of migrants traveled across porous borders to take up residence on the Westside, settling in housing corrales beset by tuberculosis and high infant mortality and seasonal flooding, including the deadly inundacion de 1921—but in the same moment giving birth to mutual aid societies and striking pecan shellers, a teenaged Emma Tenayuca triumphantly pumping her fist on the steps of City Hall. Then came the Good Government League singing barbershop over beers for an hour or two as they instituted at-large voting, VAMOS and Raza Unida gradually encircling them as they beat out a counter-rhythm on ballot box, crescendoing in pace and volume until the Department of Justice appeared stage left, an avenging angel, to grant single-member districts and slay the GGL. By this time all council members were soundly asleep, heads on folded arms or lying prostrate beneath their chairs. Finally, at ten till 9A.M., a winged Henry Cisneros doll—Rafa had assembled one hastily from pillowcases stuffed with plastic grocery bags—descended from the balconies above the chamber floor, suspended at the end of translucent rigging like a piñata. Pinned to one shoulder was a valentine cut-out of Tenayuca and to the other a souvenir button from Six Flags Fiesta Texas.

There he is! cried the People's Power Performers. He is us! Oh, he is finally here!

But don't forget to look up, the viejitas sang in the final stanza, as one by one, seventeen white men appeared above the balcony banister, each revealing the wire in his hand fastened not only to Henry but to the collar of every sleeping form at the dais, each smiling down onto the scene below.

> *Red McCombs and Tom Frost*
> *and Graham Weston too—*
> *in a way names don't matter*
> *but in some ways, pos—they do*

> *So as our song ends*
> *let's not close the curtain*
> *let's raise it instead*
> *so we can be certain*

> *Let's turn on the house lights*
> *Let's backlight the scene*

let's list them like reindeer
so everyone sees:
on Zachary
on Butt
on Benson
on Greehey
on Lifshutz
on Goldbury
on Cavender
on Holt
on Kaufman and Keller
and Keller and Keller
forever and ever
and on and on

We hope when you vote
you'll remember our song.

***

By 9:30 the next morning a fresh phalanx of city staffers had arrived to wake their sleeping charges in time for their unanimous vote: the rate hike would stand. The City Clerk's office had done its due diligence in validating all signatures, but the state legislature had just convened an emergency session to amend the Texas constitution, barring the public from using the petition process to recall city decisions on utility rates. Meeting adjourned.

A ripple. It was there, a wrinkle on water for a moment, and then it was the ocean again.

La Canícula: Late Summer
San Antonio, TX, and Northward

CHAPTER ONE
Joel and Lali Pack Up

Friday, July 23

Afterward there is nothing to do but face the necessity of packing. It can no longer be avoided. Lali turns to the task grimly, a coroner in green gloves handling the objects of the dead. She throws things in boxes out of order, glassware with books, not caring what breaks. All of it broken already anyway. Always already broken and they had never wanted to see it. It was the same for displacement: in moving a rented apartment, you were shocked to realize that you had never fully lived here to begin with—how lightly you'd actually inhabited the place that felt like home. Hector's mom and brothers arrive to help. Everyone knows what has happened, but no one talks about it. Instead they work around it, all of them grim, all of them steadily boxing the wreckage. Hector will move with them to Kansas after all, so he can stay close to Nena. He will live with them at first, out of necessity, then find his own place. A few days before, he'd appeared in the doorway of the room where Lali lay motionless in bed. He'd been crying.

I can't be separated from Nena. You and me—it's fine, I know it's better this way. But Nena—let me come with you. Please.

Of course, Lali had responded, sitting up. Of course. And they'd both cried then, holding each other, letting each other go.

Now a kind of madness has taken up permanent residence in Lali's body, sharpened by insomnia and panic until it threatens to upend all functionality. During the day she sits on the floor trying to prep for the classes she will teach in the fall—Intro to Poli Sci, a large lecture class, and a special topics course called Theories of Environmental Crisis—with massive force attempting to focus thoughts that scatter chaotically like a spill of light on mirrors. She can't do it: she pushes books from her lap and curls shuddering onto her side. *What the fuck is going on? What the fuck is happening to me?* At night she lays awake unsleeping, feeling she has finally swum too far out and soon will pass a point beyond recovery. She will crash and burn in her new position, unable to teach, unable to work. She will have to be hospitalized again; her child will be taken from her. Incompetent. A danger to self and others. She remembers the words from years before.

But there is a question that has been forming inside her, an unasked question that could change everything. So on her last evening in the city, she visits Joel at his apartment. He is her final possible visit, the last person she wants to see. She has things to give him: a bag of uneaten frozen items from their freezer that she can't take with her. A tender cactus transplant in a painted terra cotta pot for his front stoop garden.

She finds him sitting sprawl-legged in front of the couch, mending her straw hat with a rainbow of twisty ties where the weave has frayed. She had left it in his car when they visited the sludge lagoons together. His front door is open; he looks up and smiles when he sees her standing at the screen door.

She lets herself inside, stepping around a pile of empty boxes. What's all this? she asks.

The paper, he says. We finally got bought out like they've been threatening. A big publisher out of Florida wants to slash the editorial budget and convert the format to all-digital. We got the news on Friday. It's not folding necessarily, but may as well be. Everyone got let go.

Oh my God. I'm sorry.

He shrugs. Well, almost everyone. The other big announcement Friday was the press club awards. My node series won first prize for best investigative piece in the alternative weekly market. Of course, he continues, the Barrera story placed too, for best gossip column.

Really?

He's kidding, kind of. Not really, he says. But guess who escaped the chopping block.

Her stomach aches. If only he'd gotten laid off, he might be willing to—

Well, that's great. Isn't it?

It would be, if that was why they wanted to keep me on. But it's all about the numbers, really. Web analytics. Number of clicks, number of likes and shares. So, apparently, in addition to writing the best news series, I also posted the most blog entries in the past year and got the most clicks. That makes me the best clickbaiter of the bunch.

So...you're staying here in San Antonio? She tries for casual and congratulatory but her heart flops around like a dying fish, its throat hooked on the question she has come to ask.

I guess so. For a while. After that, who knows. Regardless, I gotta move. My 30 days past eviction are about up. He grins, but it's a movement of the mouth only.

Oh. Right. Lali looks around. Something else is going on, something wrong or missing. It flashes on her.

Where's Luz?

Briefly, his face registers anger, then relaxes back into sadness. She got away again, he murmurs. I flyered around, but the city got her, I'm pretty sure. I've been checking the Animal Services website practically every hour, but nothing's turned up. Even if she did show, it costs $200 to get them out, and they only give you 24 hours. Or else—

He doesn't want to finish and doesn't need to. Lali lays her question aside and crosses the room to sit beside him, where weeks before they sat together in front of his couch, trying to read. Trying to keep from turning to one another, from reaching hands up to touch face or lips or hair. This time, he slumps over and rests his head in her lap, eyes closed. She holds perfectly still, laying her hands lightly in his hair, not breathing, not wanting to scatter him into flight.

***

It is like any other night where they don't talk about what it means or what will happen. They eat veggie burgers followed by paletas; they watch old Sponge Bob episodes with Jodi. Nena is already with Lali's parents, where Lali will go when she leaves Joel's apartment—North of the city for her last night in Tejas. The following day she will drive back into town to get the moving truck waiting at the apartment, already loaded. Hector will drive the truck; she and Nena will drive separately, in the car.

And when at last it is time to leave, Lali and Joel stand together in the street outside his building and wrap arms around each other. I know you'll do good work, says Joel. Lali says nothing. She wants to ask but she can't. And they kiss each other on the cheek, as they did that first day after the trip to the beach, as they did standing on the curb in front of El Centro. It was the kiss of unconditional solidarity between women and of Biblical betrayal between men, the kiss of the unspoken and unspeakable, too tall and wide and deep to fit into words. Except, oh except—but they kiss on the cheek. And she gives him the money Paloma had given her months ago, still wrapped in its bank envelope inside her backpack like a secret.

For Luz, she says. In case she turns up in the system.

Thank you, Joel murmurs as they embrace again. Thinking about the question, wondering why she doesn't ask, not knowing what he would say if she did.

***

When Lali drives away, she is supposed to head for her parents' house, but instead she drives back to her street where their empty apartment now waits for its next tenant. Passing the apartment, she parks one last time past the tracks, near their neck of the river. She walks to the bike path, where only weeks before she had stood with her hand cradled against the side of Joel's face. Tears stream from her eyes but she hardly notices.

She walks, visions of her father's river stories from his childhood rising before her, fever bright. He used to fish in this river with his brothers. Did he swim? No, it had been too wild. They were scared of snakes and sharp branches. But there was a raft one of the old men who fished there had tied to a tree, and sometimes the kids would take it downstream. And bring it back when they were done? They must have. He can't remember. The question had seemed to confuse him.

Ya Gna Wena notices her approach, and she watches with her eyes closed, breathing deeply. She remembers the pain of the original people, their emissaries burned and ground into dust by the city people sent to greet them, who took their gifts before throwing the ash of charred bone and hair into her waters. Then she ran wide and swift; they could use her in that way, for flushing the filth they emanated. She had felt pain then, pain for her people, but it was one of the only times. Otherwise she was too big, too long, too wide for their suffering and their struggles to make much of a dent, even now in her constricted state. Lali's grief propagates like infrared, but it is only that: it disperses, it comes and it goes, its waves leave no trace. But she is there, Ya Gna Wena.

Lali sits on the banks, knees folded into her arms, a million questions tripping over each other and tumbling down the basement stairs of her brain. Down into darkness.

Like: Will we know each other in ten years?

And: Do we know each other now?

And: Why desire, if it can't hit its mark or create something lasting?

And: What is it to last? What is it that lasts?

And: What did the universe want? What was *its* desire? That was the question at the very bottom, and the answer came back so strong and sharp it felt like waking suddenly in the night. *It wants only for us to decide what it wants. It means only what we decide it means.* That was the terrible burden and freedom both, the freedom to say—to propose, in the dual meaning of that word. To advance an argument or proffer an idea within an ongoing exchange, to stake a claim without resolution save a desire to continue conversation. But to propose was also to kneel, to apply, head bent, in surrender to the other's absolute freedom. To go or to stay, to say yes or no, to speak or not speak.

We must have met in order to talk. To consider the question together.

But it was a terrible question, like the pleas on the radio. Sweetly sung, but terrible all the same. *Oye, mi amor! No me digas que no.*

Listen, my love—don't tell me no. Please, please say yes. The pop song knew her question was a terrible one, not bad but grave, serious. It was a question that made and broke lives, a question that could not be ignored, so heavy she could not ask it yet. But also so dire she could not avoid asking it, eventually. *And someday I will have to ask it, and risk the possibility you will say no. Or worse, that you will not respond.*

She imagined him before her like a stick figure in a cartoon, forlorn, a thought bubble rising above his head filled with ellipses trailing off, dot dot dot. The question had bubbled up and she bit it off in time, because she knew he had no response. Not that he didn't want to, but he didn't know what to say. He was standing perfectly straight and still, waiting to receive some word or sign that would tell him what was right. And he couldn't move until he heard it. She had found him like that, all alone standing still, and she had left him like that, still listening intently for something else. But the signal he wanted wouldn't come—she could see that. He would have to decide for himself. But he couldn't. But it didn't matter. She could see it wasn't his fault. He was like a dog that chose your lap for its head when you were lonely, on a day when you needed it most—or, more truthfully, like a bird that lit on your arm for a moment, a gift you couldn't keep. A dog at least was internally consistent, predictable. But you couldn't be angry at a bird for flying.

I am comforted thinking it will be right to ask only when I feel the answer must be yes. I am comforted thinking that one day, it will be yes.

Lali doesn't know why, but she lowers herself from the banks into the water. Its embrace is waist deep, warm, and she moonwalks along the bottom with eyes closed, letting the slow current take her. Underneath the bike bridge where she sat with Joel, past the empty lot where half-finished, dome-shaped art studios sit like huts, left to rust after the developers discovered how contaminated the soil was by whatever had been there before. Earlier dreams of a renaissance abandoned. Past the opera house of release gates built to divert the river in times of flooding, so the overflow ran beneath ground and not through the downtown commercial district. Past the closed-down, burnt-out refinery, waiting on a transition increasingly uncertain.

She slips through the water like a tear into a torrent, rolling onto her back to float, following the tunnel of her own despair to its center, until finally she surfaces on the other side. Wriggling out of the river's grasp, she spreadeagles herself on the banks, smelling the water on her skin like musty basement, the faint and unwashable trace of repurposed wastewater, of origins and destinations. She hoists herself onto her elbows, and looking around sees the centuries peel back to reveal a land untransformed by sadness: the river's bed widens, and its banks grow thick with cypress and mesquite and pecan, chattering with unseen nightlife. She senses the murky green-black water clearing and river cane rising to surround her, swaying like seaweed. She hears the quiet snuffle of deer and bison grazing amid stands of little bluestem and zarzamora bramble—and beyond them lie the silent shapes of bear and puma and wolf. She sees immense kingdoms of nopales, their tender paddles heavy with ruby fruit, guarded by noble thorns.

I can't survive this longing…I don't want to survive it. Love courses through her, but it is too strong to be nurturing, ripping her apart with the force of a storm. Ripping her out of the earth by the roots, hurtling her into the dark matter of space where they propel past one another, even as they grasped.

Ya Gna Wena watches with eyes closed, hearing without ears. In the sway of her cane, the sweet pompom blossom of huisache, the rustle of snake and rooting of armadillo, she nods. She knows.

When they are together, they are together—but in no way Lali recognizes, no earthly way capable of words or plans. She longs to be with him in some way she understands. But it is not to be, he is not to be with in that way. He is a contemplative, a holy man, a teacher. Her eye is on him, but his is on the sky. Her arms crane toward him, but his point upward, waiting for the ecstasy of ascent, fingers escaping into tree branches like Daphne into laurel—while she is an earthbound Apollo left to books and theory, left to try to understand what will not be understood. The only lesson can be to learn how to bear her own longing, the space of flight and abandonment, without devastation.

But I don't want to, her heart cries out to the darkness of earth. I don't want to bear it.

But I don't have a choice. There is nothing I can do.

Ya Gna Wena does not speak, does not need to, has never bothered to learn. But the rising image of her presence, teeming with the movement of her indifferent inhabitants, is a kind of mute sympathy. She is there:

I know. I'm sorry. I love you.

CHAPTER TWO
Kansaztlan

Saturday, July 24

The interstate north is the fastest route from Texas to Kansas—a beeline until Wichita before it veers northeast, to Manhattan—but its path feels interminable from the inside, swallowed by a too-huge landscape that slowly flattens to dry and die as they pass through Austin, then Waco, then Dallas, a beaded string of highway towns shimmering in the heat. By the time they cross the Red River into Oklahoma, its waters the color of dried blood, Hector has fallen behind. They have agreed to travel at their own pace, Nena and Lali racing North in their car and Hector lumbering behind in the yellow moving truck.

Lali remembers this sprint north from half a lifetime ago, when she and a high school boyfriend had made for the Canadian border to get away from the misery of their own compulsory pairing, to get away from something gnawing at each of them until they sought comfort in misery, driving north and north and north until they forced back the creeping onset of early Texas summer and it became spring again, miraculously, somewhere around here where the soil was red clay. On their first night they had found some grower's freshly plowed field and ate dinner sitting on the warm hood of the car, food they had hastily packed in plastic grocery bags. A giant yellow apple for her and nothing more. Driving north had been about freedom to starve, freedom to die of despair. Freedom to pursue one's confinements undisturbed. When the sun set they had curled up in the hatch of his car, there in the middle of the field with the stars ablaze overhead. They had made Wichita the following day in time for a mid-morning breakfast—plain black gas station coffee, sweetened with aspartame, and half a blueberry bagel from home, carefully shredded and eaten scrap by scrap, slowly, to make it last—Wichita, where they sold his CDs for $80 in gas money. That was back when a used CD could fetch you a few bucks. Now they were less than worthless: obsolete, a liability to cart from house to house, move to move. Something you could only string together now in desperation as yard art.

By the time they stopped for the night on their second day gone, they had made it to Sioux Falls, South Dakota. Sioux Falls. That was where she had confessed her second thoughts—perhaps they should go home?—and where in response her boyfriend had slammed to a stop in the shoulder of an interstate speeding with cars even at midnight, storming off with driver-side door hanging open. She had thought he would leave her there, on the side of the highway in Sioux Falls. Instead the cops had picked them up as they were crawling some alley on the outskirts of the city just past two, looking for a place to sleep. After running their licenses—somehow they had thought to bring those—the cops had right away identified them as runaways, before depositing them in an unmarked holding center for all manner of refugee youth, where their shoes and the contents of their pockets were confiscated. Lali had sweated out the pocket search, praying they would not discover the diet pills she had stashed away, the only thing that could save her from her own inconsolable appetite. They hadn't—found them, that is. But nor had they saved her. She'd simply had to do it herself, for herself.

But before the rising panic of Nebraska and South Dakota, Kansas had been beautiful in the late afternoon. They had come straight shot up the highway, but in Kansas they'd forked off onto a smaller, slower state road that passed through a number of little towns. Outside one they spied a homemade billboard that warned: *Unmarked nuclear waste trucks travel these roads. Keep our children safe and radiation free!* Wichita had been tattered and overcast but also warm and inviting, like a favorite armchair battered by stains and scratches. With sun shining and wind high and cool, northeastern Kansas had been an expanse of rolling green, not at all the grey flatness she'd been expecting. Outside Manhattan they'd stopped for gas, where she watched a cloud of starlings moving like smoke over a neighboring field planted in runners of new cornstalk. It was the first time she'd ever seen starlings, common birds whose deep black wings were speckled white like galaxies. Somehow she'd thought Kansas would be the absent center of the continent. But it turned out there was something there, something that felt like home. And hadn't Kansas once been part of México? It seemed she'd seen maps. And before that it had belonged to the south wind people, the war people, the people who called themselves simply *our people*—who themselves were blown westward from original lands by European settlers, but who took with them the knowledge that the land belonged only to itself. She supposed it still did.

That was farther north of where they were now, past the Red River as the sun sets out the driver's side window. She could keep going until Oklahoma City or she could stop now. Up ahead are signs for Ardmore—wasn't that the town Joel had dreamed about? But when she stops, there is nothing particularly spectacular about the place, and when she dashes inside an off-highway chain motel to inquire about rates, Nena dozing over her shoulder, the front desk woman informs her that the hotel is full of landmen—no vacancy. Because of the mines going in.

She may be a white woman or a Black woman or a Native woman, but she is a plains woman, she has grown up there where the soil is red. She recognizes Lali with a wary eye. You need a room by yourself? she wants to know.

For me and my daughter.

The baby? How old are you, if you don't mind me asking?

Thirty-one.

The woman laughs. Oh, that's good! But you sure don't look it. Here I was worried you was 16 years old and running away.

The visible outline of an earlier self, a historical truth, glowing like bones in an X-ray.

***

She drives on and on, into the night. Red clay gives way to runners of corn, the car's forward motion animating the rows like long legs sprinting. As Nena sleeps behind in her carseat, Lali's thoughts swirl and dip like birds over a plowed field, forming in waves and waves. What will happen, asks the land, with the petition drive, the council meetings, the teatros, the lawsuits? Lali doesn't know.

Except that these things will keep going, move and counter-move, in the eternal dialectic of power, of struggle. Back and forth, undulating like pendulum, vibrating at the speed of color or light. Easy to see defeat in the spread of the landmen or in the city's effort to disqualify voters calling for decision-making power over electric rates. But only if my move north is an absolute break: the final page of leaving town, leaving home. But if it is a movement to another location within the movement, a movement without end point or final referent, then defeat is as much a fiction as victory. Word is that Alianza will be filing a lawsuit against the city. Word is that VAMOS further removed themselves from a coalition effort once promised a seat on the city's Transition Team. Word is the white environmental groups wiggled out of their own uncomfortable alliance as the issue ballooned from dirty energy to rate hikes to voter disenfranchisement. Word is Naima's heart is broken but she won't take Chela back. I won't be there but these things will continue without me. I will step onto the banks and the stream will rush on, to no end; I will step off a train that speeds on and into the future, into a landscape that moves as slowly as time weathers rock. And the sand and the water will fill in the momentary suck where my body has been, and it will be like I was never there.

It seems an extravagance of fiction—what they call a liberty, a license—to imagine that the push-pull of history's scrawl on the present is most legible in the flash points of last minute revelations, affairs and scandals. There are of course revelations and affairs and scandals. But they explain so little. There is no backroom hand tossing out the shaky-handed signatures of the old and the infirm, the blocky capitals of the dispossessed and unregistered. Seats at the dais are just that, empty spaces holding the bodies of individuals who become subject to their function. Power wells up to fill the space created by the movement of bodies in and out of institutions. It is the seat, not the body it holds: that is what is so hard to see. Where does it come from, the respiratory repetition that over time wears grooves into the machinations of the city? Where does it come from, the temporal accumulation, the path dependency that makes it run the way it has run before? It isn't that we can't tip the game at times. But power is probabilities, the likelihood of one outcome over another or another, a weighted preeminence atop an unstable set up. Less Oz the Great and Terrible than the few parts-per-million too many that nonetheless triggers the violence of heatwaves and floods, revelations and affairs and scandals. Or is that too heavy-handed.

I see how it moves. I feel my own movements overwritten onto the movement of the whole, as it moves me, as I am moved, as I am written, as I write myself. But I will never fully understand. Not power, not a love that grieves at the moment of its fullest conception. Not a desire whose currency powers the universe itself yet fails to hit its mark, every time: this transcription is the closest I can get.

Still, still—I remember walking once, along the hike-and-bike path the city built to trace the 13-mile length of the river as it entered and exited the history of a hemisphere, from the headwater springs of the Ojo del Agua down to Mission Espada. To try and put it back to the way they had found it. I remember the biodegradable green weave they had lain over the bare earth so the new growth would take, and the layer of protective platting over that, chain links of plastic like the six-pack rings used to yoke cans of beer. And I remember the new grass growing up around its moorings, taking them over as hoped. I remember the tree-tall nodding sunflowers and the stands of prickly thistle, purple with hummingbird nectar. The seeds carefully researched and scattered, the straight lines un-straightened again, the meanders restored. I remember watching the heron and the egret to understand the mechanics of their flight and landing. Different from what I had imagined.

I remember walking alone not long ago, along the path in early morning, my heart broken from a joy so full it spilled over into despair. I had walked half the night listening to music, and in the morning I found myself on a section of the path the city had almost completed, on the farthest reach of construction south. At a small traffic circle under construction, I ran into a yellow front loader backing up, and a city worker raised one hand to stop me, with another motioning the loader on. Once it had passed, he pulled aside a tarp of black vinyl that blanketed newly hard cement so I could continue. By that time I had taken my earphones out so I could excuse myself and thank him, both of us unexpectedly grinning at each other. The way you catch the eye of other people strolling and biking, the way you nod and smile.

I remember the many stories of the river and what it cost. How they pushed the people off the banks and then, when they returned with different names, pushed them again from the heart of the city to live and die down in the floodplain. I remember my father's story of how they finally mastered the flooding by paving over the place where he and his brothers once played—only to rip out the paving again, in my lifetime, to restore the river for apartments made out of power plants. Tearing up the little homes like paper in the process, scattering their inhabitants like ashes over the water. I know what it took, the earth they moved and the minerals they mined. I know these things, these unaccounted-for repetitions, these patterns pieced together from study or laid bare before me in the land, a layering of etchings and erasures and writings over, there to be read as one walked. Still, in the open way we nodded and smiled as we passed, still—

C/S

Rooted in San Antonio, Marisol Cortez walks between artistic, activist, and academic worlds as a writer, editor, and community-based scholar. She is author of the novel *Luz at Midnight* (Flower Song Press, 2020) and *I Call on the Earth* (Double Drop Press, 2019), a chapbook of documentary poetry about the displacement of Mission Trails Mobile Home Community. She is Co-editor of *Deceleration*, an online journal of environmental justice thought and praxis. She writes to resist all domination and remember the land. For more information on previous publications and current projects, visit
https://mcortez.net/

Thank You

This book has been a long time in the making, and many people have had a hand in bringing it to fruition. Danette Bermea, Mary McCord, and Peggy Marceaux taught me the foundations of creative and critical writing way back when. Maria A. Berriozabal schooled me in much of the political analysis that informs the story. Valerie Kim-Thuy Larsen was my first voice of encouragement and accountability partner, reading every text file chapter of the very first draft as well as a revised second draft. Tamara Pinzon, Ann Cortez, Greg Harman, Eddie Dupuy, Miguel Garza, and Mobi Warren were attentive beta readers, all with important insights into story and character development. La maestra Carmen Tafolla read a section and gave me loving encouragement and concrete publication advice when I needed it most. Jim Lavilla-Havelin read out loud every morning from a draft of Luz to Lucia Lavilla-Havelin, and both provided the thoughtful suggestions and enthusiastic support that gave me the courage to finally submit the manuscript for publication. Kamala Platt edited the manuscript, with her keen ecological, political, and poetic eye providing deep developmental and editorial critiques. Viktoria Valenzuela introduced me to Flower Song Press, but more importantly was my friend in writing, mamahood, and life. George and Catherine Cisneros taught me the responsibility of performance—making one's art public—and also provided a model for living as a working artist. Stone in the Stream/Roca en el Rio environmental writers collective and Women Who Submit were the community I didn't know I needed to give myself permission to make writing a priority. Several presses passed on the manuscript but sent kind notes that gave me the ganas to keep sending it out. Davíd Zamora Casas gave me permission to use his mindblowing painting for the cover, which I knew as soon as I saw it was the visual incarnation of the story I was writing. Juan Mancias, Tribal Chairman of the Esto'k Gna (Carrizo Comecrudo Tribe of Texas) reviewed a key chapter and shared critical knowledge of tribal history and language. Edward Vidaurre at Flower Song believed in my work and in the power of all our words to change the world. Jo Reyes Boitel gave the manuscript a last, deep editorial read and offered incisive final suggestions that made the manuscript shine.

Finally, thank you to my family—my parents, Ann and Carlos Cortez; my partner Greg Harman; and Asra Garza-Cortez and Wolfi Harman-Cortez, my big and little baby, respectively—who loved and believed in me every step of the way.